Th
c

The Split

©Chandler Ogle 2016

This book is a work of fiction. Names, characters, places, and incidents either are products of the author's imagination or are used fictitiously. Any resemblance to actual persons, living or dead, events, or locales is entirely coincidental. No part of this book may be used, reproduced or transmitted in any form or by any means, electronic or mechanical, including photocopying, recording, or by any information storage or retrieval system, without the written permission of the publisher, except where permitted by law, or in the case of brief quotations embodied in critical articles and reviews.

Dedication

To my Editor, Lp Johnson, and my close friend Alexander Bradley, for believing in my vision and inspiring me to do the same.

CONTENTS

THE LETTERS: **PG.**

~Foreword

*Bought as a curiosity,
by a Mrs. Ethel Danz in Columbus Ohio, 2018

A. Fila   1

*Recovered in Bloc Vault C1

T. Acerz, 2134   27

*District N7 (Former Ohio and NW U.S.)

*Found in excavation, 2102

-T. Acerz   59

*LGPB://mn34/con/terra/GM 8721   77

*Bought from A. Fila's Estate, 2094

-T. Acerz, 2131   83

*LGPB://mn34/con/terra/GM 8721   91

*LGPB://mn34/con/terra/UY 9065   95

*Bought via direct sale, from "Dr. Jimenez": 2075

-A. Fila   111

*LGPB://mn34/con/terra/YT 7623   121

*LGPB://mn34/con/terra/MH 1623   135

*Gift from Caribbean Consulate, 2121

*T. Acerz, 2131   141

* ? Undetermined   153

*LGPB://mn34/con/terra/YS 7175   161

*Bought at Auction In former Vatican City; 2079

-A. Fila   169

*LGPB://mn34/con/terra/UQ 5480   183

*Recovered during Excavation; 2080   213

*LGPB://mn34/con/terra/KN 1093   223

*Recovered in Bloc Vault C1

-T. Acerz, 2131   239

*LGPB://mn34/con/terra/MB 9045   259

*LGPB://mn34/con/terra/AJ 2379	275
*Found in Pentagon Storage	
-T. Acerz, 2031	291
*LGPB://mn34/con/terra/BH 9875	303
*Recovered in Bloc Vault C1	
-T. Acerz, 2131	313
*Smithsonian Archives	
-T. Acerz, 2131	328
*LGPB://mn34/con/terra/WD 4522	339
*Traded by native Tribe, 2078	
-A. Fila	354
*LGPB://mn34/con/terra/UY 5463	363
*Bought from A. Fila's Estate, 2105	
-T. Acerz, 2131	377
*LGPB://mn34/con/terra/OT 6198	383
*Gift from Hungarian Province, 2110	
-T. Acerz, 2131	417
*LGPB://mn34/con/terra/UY 8345	423
Bought from A. Fila's Estate, 2105	
-T. Acerz, 2131	435
*LGPB://mn34/con/terra/XC4481	451
*LGPB://mn34/con/terra/NB 3902	467
*Hyesung, North Korea	477
*Recovered in Bloc Vault C1	
-T. Acerz, 2131	491
*LGPB://mn34/con/terra/DZ 7091	507
*LGPB://mn34/con/terra/QE 3219	515
*Bought from private Collector, 2077	
-A. Fila	523
*Found in abandoned Subway tunnels, 2080	
-A. Fila	535
*LGPB://mn34/con/terra/ZD 4006	545

*Bought in auction, 2082
-A. Fila   555

*Narrative returns to only Burlington   559

*Recovered from Bloc Vault C1
-T. Acerz, 2131   567

*Found in abandoned Subway tunnels
A. Fila, 2080   577

*LGPB://mn34/con/terra/AR 0125   587

*Gift from South American Consulate, 2099
T. Acerz, 2131   595

*Bought in Venice, 2077
- A. Fila   603

*Recovered from Bloc Vault C1
T. Acerz, 2131   609

~EPILOGUE

~Coming Soon

~About The Author

Foreword

Arthur Fila, March 1st, 2094

To those who may find this,

The following pages were first found in Hangzhou, China, in 1052 AD. A young temple initiate, named Ao, said that they appeared to him while was gazing at a pool. He pulled them out of the water and, fascinated that the pages stayed dry and the ink did not run, eagerly took them to the monks of his temple. They studied for decades but, although there were just a few pages, they were unable to make out the strange markings. Thus convinced it was from the heavens, the monks guarded it jealously for centuries, and the papers were treated like a treasure as they passed from empire to empire.

The next sighting was in 1493, by a sailor named Gonzalo Franco. Like Ao, he pulled a small collection of papers from the water, these near his ship. In the cover of night he was able to retrieve them without his crew seeing, and stash them with his belongings. Several years later, he made it back to Spain from what his captain called the "New World". Denied the treasure he was promised, Gonzalo traveled for years, trying to find someone to translate the pages, and finally found someone years later, in London, who said they could help. Gonzalo's account ends there, and I assume he was murdered. The next 400-500 years were a haze, as various powerful groups like the Vatican and the British Crown greedily gathered the pages, keeping their accounts of discovery to themselves.

Many times, the letters were turned over in war, or stolen by thieves led by promises of fortune and wealth when told of these "Pages from Heaven". It is through many dangerous journeys, and no small financial expense that I, Arthur Fila, was able to acquire around 200 of these pages. I have marked them with my own name and dating and, like my predecessors before me, I have also marked in the corner of each entry the Date, location, and means by which I acquired it; or the party before me acquired it.

The date appearing with each entry heading however, is part of the original document, as though the author wished to set the scene for a hapless researcher like myself, who only has portions of the book's entire work.

This is probably wishful thinking however, and it would be more likely that it was just part of the way he recorded the narrative, like a type of journal.

Through careful research, I have deciphered much. The language that had eluded scholars and priests for centuries, had been nothing but postmodern English. I estimate the writer lived between 2000-2050 AD based on the vernacular and colloquialisms of that time.

Humanity has reached a dark place, crumbling from within and facing extinction. I continue to put my faith in these pages to bring us new understanding about our history and future. The few I have told about my search and discoveries laugh at me, calling the stories behind the papers a hoax and my efforts a 'worthless pursuit'.

I fear they may be right, as I have rearranged the papers in nearly every configuration and still the truth eludes me. It's like there are parts left to be written, and I have but a fraction of a greater story. Sometimes it feels as though there might even be two stories woven together.

Perhaps in another time or reality someone has a complete copy, I just hope it provides them the wisdom that I seek. I know nothing of the author or how he landed in his predicaments described, or even how his account resolves, but I will continue my toil.

Arthur Fila, March 1st, 2094.

T H E | S P L I T

I

Bought as a curiosity,
by a Mrs. Ethel Danz in Columbus Ohio, 2018
Purchased by A. Fila, 2077

Central Ohio, 2017

I had always hated my dreams. What was essentially a mental 'shuffle button' for the average person, was the cause of my sleepless nights – and weary days. The bank of daily data my subconscious had access to was enormous, and it somehow knew what things I found most unpleasant.

My dream that day was no different, and no matter how hard I tried to force my eyelids open, they wouldn't budge.

"Private Fischer, get on your feet. Let's move!"

I looked up and was immediately confused. My CO, whose voice I had heard and whom I expected to see, had been replaced by a bushy bearded man in a regal blue uniform. I could feel how tired my body was, as I stood up on shaky legs, asking, the mysterious man. "Who are you?"

"Who am I?" the man repeated with laughter, prompting a group of soldiers from my old unit to join in. "I'm Colonel Mustard, of course! Now, get a move on men! You're expected on the field!"

My squad mates saluted simultaneously, "Yes sir, Colonel!" then left through a door in the wall. I paused to look around the room before following. The building made no sense; the walls leaned on one another and the furniture was upside down. Above, I could see no ceiling, only a blank, dark sky that turned a shade of purple at the top.

I left the room and charged after my unit, and when I caught up to the group, tapped one of my friends on the shoulder to ask, "Grant...w-

THE | SPLIT

where..." I had to hold a finger up as I doubled over to catch my breath. "Where...are we going?"

Grant looked concerned for an instant, before his face changed to a smile and he laughed, "Ah, Private Fischer...you almost had me going there!" He shook his head and turned back around as, to either side of our group, football players and old-timey British policemen ran past us. I fell in line behind him, and tried to remember where I was as I began to see structures in the distance that, oddly, looked to be getting no closer, no matter how far we ran.

What the hell was **happening** ?

Then all of a sudden the scene shifted, and I was just feet away from the buildings I had been looking at. I paused for a minute, trying to get my bearings and process the skip in time I had just experienced. I was standing beside a gray cobblestone wall, that I couldn't see the top of as I arched my neck up, but turning back, I saw my unit continuing without me, so I took off at a sprint to catch up.

As I closed in, I heard the sound of marching boots behind me and nearly jumped in surprise; a second group of my exact unit, were behind me, in identical formation. Looking ahead, I saw that the men I had followed were still where they had been. Curious, I slowed down and let the second group pass me, falling into line behind the second Grant where, with a wide step to the left, I could see the two identical groups; both still running, their movements slightly out of sync.

Then sounds began to ring out ahead, and the first group turned the corner at the end of the building. We turned right to follow, and to my surprise they vanished entirely. Trying not to dwell on one specific, bizarre part of an already bizarre situation, I focused on the scene in front of me, and the repeating noise that echoed through it. We had come to a courtyard of sorts.

THE | SPLIT

The center was grass with a gazebo made of vines, and around its edge were schools and churches, all of different designs and from multiple eras.

My eyes were drawn to the same direction the sound was coming from; between a white painted, Adobe-brick school, and a massive, medieval cathedral with Gargoyles and towering spires.

At first it had sounded like a roar, but now that I was closer, it was like the sound of a guttural engine; fierce and challenging, yet unsettlingly human. My unit continued through the courtyard, between the school and church. I took one last look around the area, looking for my other unit – they were still nowhere to be found – and then passed the church and entered a yard, where a battle raged.

Dozens of soldiers from the U.S. Army were fighting wave after wave of a horde of people wearing giant Porky the Pig suits.

I paused, and couldn't help myself, my breath wound out in one long gust of laughter : the suspense built by my troubled mind had led to a battle against. . . an army of animated pigs!

The last few soldiers in line paused and looked back at me, and Grant stepped forward, looking at me sternly, "What are you laughing about, Private Fischer? We got a battle to fight."

The men unslung the rifles from their backs and went forward; I followed their actions, and tried to stifle my amusement. But just as the smile on my face went away, the terrifying roar happened again. Clutching my rifle tightly, I looked around. The sound seemed like it was right next to me but I saw nothing different. We fell in line with the waiting soldiers and began taking shots at the enemy.

The giant, over-sized suits were easy targets, but also offered an extra layer of protection, allowing the pigs to get up and keep fighting. Still, they wielded swords no longer than two feet, and with the line of rifle-

T H E | S P L I T

fire a pile of bodies had begun forming several dozen feet away. I downed one Porky, and lined up the next one in my sights, double tapping my trigger.

Two holes appeared in the suit right next to the heart; textbook perfect. But my satisfaction was interrupted by the roar once again, and I dropped my rifle in surprise. Then, as I turned around to pick it up, I noticed someone doing the same thing at the other end of the line. Standing again, I saw that the other man did the same, and when I turned to go back to the firing line, he took the exact same step.

I narrowed my eyes to examine the man; they then widened in shock when I realized it was **me.** The other me noticed it too. At the same time, we slung our rifles back on our shoulders, and ran towards one another – slamming against an invisible barrier when we met in the middle.

For the first time, our motions fell out of sync as we both reached up to feel the barrier with different hands. I pounded against the unseen wall, waving and yelling, *"Hello!"* but it didn't give way. He did the same thing a moment later; then a black mass appeared behind him. Its features were obscured with shadow, but I could see that it had horns, and appeared reptilian, though I couldn't make out much more.

"Watch out!" I yelled.

Not hearing my warning, he instead screamed and pointed at me; a moment before the creature's massive hand snatched him. Hearing something myself, I turned around – and a massive, clawed hand swiped me across the face.

I cried out in recoil…

Then the world faded around me.

THE | SPLIT

I was in a brightly lit room, slumped over in a chair, where all I could see and hear was carpet and faint laughter. Uncovering my eyes, I lifted my head from my lap to see a room crowded with faces, most of them looking at me, and looked over to see a pair of girls covering their mouths to stifle their laughter.

The man at the front was glaring at me, and finally broke the silence, "Are you alright?" and I slowly put together where I was; for the second time this week, I had fallen asleep during an AA meeting. Only this time I had awoken yelling in fear. Trying to relieve the tension, I smiled. "Yeah, sorry...long day at the office, that's all."

The group leader seemed placated, and turned to the other side of the room. "Alright. Now, we're going to hear from Sandra. Sandra has told me she doesn't like sharing...so please, everyone be respectful."

"My name is Sandra, and I'm an alcoholic."

"Hi, Sandra!" came from all sides of the room – well, from every side of the room except mine.

I had heard enough of these sad stories to last even the most battle-hardened and unrepentant of alcoholics a lifetime. Having nearly washed out of the military, and failing in every endeavor since, I was used to life's general sense of melancholy. Just in my first two decades of life I had been a failed athlete, soldier, and most recently, lawyer. I'd become the man who never was, every single story an open book soon slammed shut by questionable decisions and squandered opportunity; bad habits or bridges burned – all of my shortcomings self induced, as I seemed to lay traps for myself to stumble upon later.

But this was different. These meetings were a requirement, and it seemed that they somehow got longer each time I went, and I wasn't sure how much longer I could continue. Every meeting I'd alternate between checking my watch, and memorizing every detail of the face

THE | SPLIT

belonging to the judge who'd sent me here. In this particular meeting I had begun to take it a little further. Instead of just remembering his face, I had begun to drift off into thinking of what I would do if I ever caught him alone.

Nothing violent, just thoughts about turning the tables on him, like if I could somehow record all of these meetings and then strap the judge to a chair, and make him listen to all of them... see how long he could last. But it then dawned on me that he may actually *like* these meetings. This particular judge seemed exactly the type to hear all of these relentlessly heartbreaking stories and spin it around in his own head to where he might call these stories inspirational.

Normal people always seemed to do stuff like that, always looking for a little inspiration here, a little hope there.

The sound of crying shook me from my usual thought pattern, and I looked around the room to see this Sandra woman weeping and struggling over her words, while the rest of the group, concern in their eyes, were helping her through her talking. Curious, I decided to actually tune in for this portion of the meeting.

"It had gotten to the point where meth was calling all the shots... I was bouncing around from place to place, just trying to feed my boy... trying to, feed little J-J-John." She broke down into tears again.

It made sense, from the sunken eyes to the chipped and crooked teeth, she had meth written all over her.

"At one of these houses, I met Stitch," she was saying. "Things had really gotten out of hand that night, and when the screaming started to make John anxious, Stitch took him for a walk outside. I actually got to see my little boy smile for the first time in years. And later on, Stitch stood up for me when the guy whose house it was wanted me to either put out or get out... got himself a black eye and a swollen cheek in the process. Then as he was leaving, he asked if me and John wanted to come with him, said he had a little trailer just off Grove. He was my knight and s-s-shining armor, *(crying continues)* a-a-and he got me and John out of there. . . we stayed with him most of the summer. When it was time for John to go to his first day of high school, Stitch surprised both of us by saying he didn't want me wandering no more. He said that maybe I should just move in.

I was s-s-soooo happy. I didn't even say nothing when Stitch wanted to take John out shooting after school, even though he knew I don't like that kinda thing. A week went by. . . and I thought t-t-things were going great, but then one day I came home before Stitch did. . . and I opened the spare bedroom John had been using. I saw him. . . and all the blood everywhere. . . and my heart just dropped. What used to be my son, my baby b-b-boy, was spread all over. . . the top of the bedroom walls. His headless b-b-body was on the floor. . ." *(she sobbed for several seconds before she finally continued)*

"He had gotten one of Stitch's guns and shot himself. H-h-he had never been an unhappy boy, it seemed to kinda come out of nowhere. As long as I live I will never forget the color or his blood, or be unable to see the chunks of brains and bone on the walls when I close my eyes. Or the smell. . . the smell will always be in my brain, no matter what I do. It's so bad I've wanted to cut my nose off before. I'll never get my b-b-baby back and I'll always remember that day even if I live a hundred years. After that, I got clean, and have been for three years. I like to think that I'm doing it for John. . . I want to make him proud in death since I couldn't when he was alive. Thanks for letting me share."

I had an intense moment of empathy during that brief instant, between her voice trailing off and the first smattering of applause, but it still didn't have the pull to get a knee-jerk reaction out of me.

THE | SPLIT

It was so heavy; it always was at these meetings. Some of these people had some of the darkest stories I had ever heard or ever hoped to. This one Sandra had just told was one of the worst, but this particular group seemed to have been set on death and stories of loss. In just my brief few weeks there, I had heard from a woman who had her son butchered in front of her by drug dealers and, an actual murderer who was out on parole and had supposedly reformed.

Sandra had made mistakes, but she didn't deserve anything even close to that, none of these people did. I had even begun to feel sympathy for the murderer when he had told his long story.

As the people consoling Sandra fell quiet, the group leader suddenly turned to me. "Would you like to share...? We would love to hear from you. . . you haven't said a word since you first came in a few weeks ago." This gave me pause. I'd known the day would come where he called on me, though he'd never done so before; in previous meetings he seemed always to be trying to make eye contact. I still wished he had picked someone else.

Truth be told, I had been drinking just an hour before, and could still taste the whiskey on my tongue, the metallic tang of the flask on my lips. Some of the members there would call my even showing up to this meeting disingenuous, but to those people I would say that I was really a victim in this situation. I had made a single mistake, one that had just thoroughly screwed me over, but I wasn't a drunk or an addict. Drinking was something I could take or leave. I only tended to drink in excess after traumatic events, or times of change, and even then it was only every other night or so; almost never during the day.

Things started to become uncomfortable now, as I realized the silence following his question had been longer than I had planned. Annoyed suddenly, I decided I *was* going to share with the group today.

T H E | S P L I T

I wasn't sure how much I should share, or how long I would even talk, but I knew that I didn't feel like I belonged with this group, and I wasn't going to censor myself to hide that.

"Yeah, I'm Burl...it's short for Burlington, my mom named me for her maiden name. My younger brother couldn't say my name, and called me Burl...and it just kind of stuck. And anyway. . . my mom's father's side was German, and they were Nazi sympathizers, and I didn't really want that following me around, so I just go by Burl."

The room let out a weak, collective chuckle. Didn't matter who it was, they always just accepted it and moved on.

"I'm not kidding about that. My great-great-grandfather, Otto, had come to Ellis Island around the turn-of-the-century, with his wife and newborn son. America wasn't kind to immigrants, but Otto settled his family down in a mostly German community in Missouri and throughout the First World War remained close to his family back home in Europe. He encouraged his three children to do the same, and when his eldest had a son of his own, my grandfather, he continued this tradition.

My grandfather, like most boys his age, joined the army when the Second World War began heating up, and was assigned to a communications post. Through coded letters, he passed along important information to his father back home, who in turn forwarded it to German high command. Eventually, he was caught and sentenced to a military prison for treason, leaving my grandmother alone with my mother. This deeply impacted my mother growing up, and she didn't get married until she was well into her late thirties. \

By the time she had me and my brother she was 42 years old but, despite her advanced age, we were miraculously both born without any complications or health problems. Anyway, I have a weird name but a normal story. I'm honestly just here making meetings. I got assigned 100 by a judge, and I've just been slowly sitting my way through them...keeping my head down. Some of you all have been through some really devastating stuff, and I'm glad you all have made so much progress, but I'm not an alcoholic."

"You're a liar, though," a voice came through from the back, followed by small amounts of laughter. My eyes shot to the source; a gruff-bearded man in the back, sitting next to two people who looked the same. They were all wearing black leather cuts, heavily patched with motorcycles and skulls. I smiled at him, but there was no warmth in my eyes, only challenge.

He stared back at me, returning my smile as his friends continued to laugh quietly. Then, as I was looking away, my eyes became fixated on a blonde girl sitting in the row in front of him.

Damn. It always seemed to happen to me at the most inopportune times. I was mesmerized, my neck locked into place, staring directly at her face. She was beyond pretty, or cute, or beautiful; she was *exceptionally* striking, the kind of attraction that could turn the most charming man in history into a stuttering fool. Her bright blonde hair was in loose curls that circled her brow like a crown, below it were two brilliant orbs of pure blue that sparkled mischievously when she moved her head, and on either side of them were a pair of raised cheekbones that subtly sloped down to a dazzling white smile. I could feel her presence when her eyes met mine and she smiled. A bright flash went off in my brain, numbing my thoughts and blurring my vision. Either something in my brain had just blown out, or something beautiful had just happened.

I don't know how many seconds I was staring at her, but a voice told me it was too many. Regaining my composure, I straightened up and

T H E | S P L I T

continued my story. "I made a single mistake, and I just happened to be drunk, so they sent me here. I actually still drink, I've never had a problem with it, and I told the judge the same thing. He told me he understood, but that he had to give me something...said he admired the power and raw emotion that comes from these meetings. So, I got a hundred of them and seventy-five hours of community service. I would've preferred to have all community service, but hey, sometimes life sucks."

The group leader spoke up amid building murmurs; "Okay. . . let's say you're not an alcoholic. . . there must have been some reason you were drinking when you made your mistake. Can you tell us about that?"

"If I do will you let me sit for the rest of my meetings?" I shot back, immediately regretting the edge in my words, but not dropping my gaze.

"Yeah, okay," the group leader said sheepishly.

I took a deep breath, and straightened up before launching into my story: "Well, to make a long and painful story mercifully short. . . like about half of the stories in here, mine starts with a girl." Most of the men in the crowd laughed. "College sweethearts, and all that. Well. . . 'college dropout' sweethearts. . . I guess, technically, I had lost my scholarship. From there I joined the army, but was discharged just before completing Basic, and that's when I met her. Her name was Blythe. She'd seen me on campus before, and had dropped out the semester I did. Then a year and a half later we ran into each other at a bar. We loved each other. . . we fell out of love. . . she found some other guy. He came back to our place to get some of her stuff. . . he mouthed off. I was drunk and put him in the hospital. I got ordered by the judge to pay his bills, and come here."

THE | SPLIT

I began to sit down, and then remembered the proper protocol for sharing, and stood back up, "Oh yeah, thank you for forcing me to share. Very therapeutic."

The group leader chimed in immediately, obviously not satisfied with what I had shared. "Everyone's got a story. We all have pain, we all have darkness. Can you open up just a little bit more for the group?"

I could feel the red in my face as I barked out a retort I knew I would regret; "Look man, I didn't have a kid who blew his own head off. . . that's my story, you got what you asked for." The room went silent, until Sandra loudly burst into tears, clearly shaken by my words. Those nearest reached out to comfort her, and joined the rest of the room in shooting angry glances my way.

"Well. . . I think we can wrap this meeting up early," the group leader chimed in. "What do you all think?

I took that as my queue to leave, and wordlessly got up to head out of the back door. At the end of the hall I went through another door to get outside, pausing near the handicap ramp to light up a cigarette as soon as I stepped out.

Before I even had it fully lit, the door slammed open and from behind me I heard the traditional ending to the meeting; "Keep coming back, because it works if you work it!" echo faintly but clearly through the hall, as the blonde I had seen while sharing walked out and started towards me.

I didn't know her name, but I felt like I knew her better than anyone else in those meetings. Now that she was closer, I could see that she was medium height, with a slender, short build, and a nose piercing I hadn't noticed earlier. She slowed her pace, and I realized she was coming up to me, so I straightened up and switched my cigarette to the other hand, away from her.

T H E | S P L I T

"You know. . . " her voice was clear and confident, ". . . you're actually a really good speaker, right? I think we were all on your side, until you made poor Sandra cry. . . for the fourth time this meeting."

I laughed, blowing my smoke just above her head, which formed a small wreath above her and slowly descended into her face. She blinked a few times, but other than that didn't seem to react at all – until she pulled something small and shiny out of her pocket that I soon recognized as a bejeweled vaporizer. She stood there for a second, taking a long pull from the device, and then blowing the resulting cloud directly into my face.

I smiled; she took it as a sign to keep talking. "Regulars here have been talking about you. . . 'That tall guy, in the tie.', 'What's his story?', 'What's he like?'. . . are you trying to keep an air of mystery about you, or is it actual shyness?"

"Would you believe it if I told you it was legitimate disinterest?"

She laughed at this. "Well, it doesn't matter anymore. . . now, they know you're kind of a dick."

"I'm actually a lot more than a dick," I quipped. "I have arms, legs...and even a mouth that always lands me in trouble."

She laughed again. "You could be cute, if you tried harder." The girl paused for a moment and looked at my hand, where I was holding my key fob between two fingers. "You drive a Chrysler?"

Here it comes, I thought. "Yeah. . . " I said slowly. "It's that beat up 200, over there."

She followed where I was pointing and looked at my car, obviously unimpressed. "Ah," she replied. "Well, I might have to take back what I said about you being cute."

I laughed. "Oh yeah? What do *you* drive?"

THE | SPLIT

"Nothing tonight," she smiled. "But I've been working on my grandpa's '63 Impala. It runs alright, but I want to fix a couple of things before I put her back on the road."

"Oh?" I raised an eyebrow. "You're a car girl, then."

"I'm an 'anything with an engine' girl. Tell you what. . . you should come see me at the shop, tomorrow. I can show it to you."

"Shop?"

"Yup," she nodded. "It's where I work. . . Rick's Auto Repair and Body Shop. . . off Maple."

"You're a mechanic then."

"Something like that. Just come by during your lunch break. I'm assuming you have a job and a lunch break?"

"Of course. Usually right after noon."

Suddenly, the door to the building opened and the sounds of conversation poured outside. She turned their way, and then quickly turned back towards me.

"Hey look, I gotta go, I don't really want to talk to those guys in the leather cuts. They're assholes, and. . . I just don't want to deal with it."

"Yeah? You date one of them or something?"

"No, not any of them, they're my ex's friends. He doesn't leave me alone, and neither do they. Club thing, they say. But he doesn't own me, no matter how much he tries." A car suddenly pulled up to the front of the curb. "Ah," she said, slipping her vaporizer back in her purse, "Perfect timing, that's my ride. Will I see you tomorrow?"

"Yeah, I think so."

She smiled as she turned around, calling out over her shoulder, "I better!" while closing the door behind her, smiling at me one last time before the car sped away.

THE | SPLIT

When the building door opened again I turned to see the crowd who had just left the meeting. When they saw me their faces dropped, then picked up the same angry expressions they had worn when I was inside, and pointed glares and angry whispers soon surrounded me as half of the group rushed past. The other half gathered to light up cigarettes and talk. A few of the bigger guys began to glare in my direction periodically, while talking in a small circle.

I knew I probably should be leaving, but I hated the smell of smoke in my car, and the night's cold wind felt amazing on my skin after leaving the hot meeting room. So I smiled back coolly.

There were six of them. A black guy in a brown leather jacket, a bit taller than the rest, and a fat, bearded man in a black leather biker cut started to walk towards me. I ashed my cigarette and looked him up and down, sizing him up. His eyes were yellow. I put him at about 30. I was taller, and probably stronger, than him.

These kind of conflicts were one of my strong points; you didn't get to have the attitude I had without knowing how to handle yourself in a fight. Fitness had been one of the activities I had replaced a social life with, and one of the few things I enjoyed. This wouldn't be the first time I had been outnumbered, either. Some people were good at their work, some people had a hobby they were truly talented at...but me? The thing I was good at was fighting – and I enjoyed it, more than I should have.

It was a bad habit that the Army had taken and refined. During my extended Basic Training, they had shipped combat specialists from multiple branches to come teach us. There was no real art to the method of fighting that they taught. It was efficient, adaptive, and brutal, but lacking the quick strikes and flashy combos of actual martial arts. We were shown how to block strikes and immediately disable our opponent; jabbing people in the eyes, gut punches, or even breaking a bone. They had mapped out mankind's fragile bodies, and turned combat into a simple science. Confident, I began to smile as he walked over and stopped just a few feet away from me.

"You thought your little joke about Sandy was funny, huh?"

"No. . . and it wasn't meant to offend, just wanted the group leader to get off my back." I took another drag from my cigarette, and while exhaling I realized it was about out.

His voice took on a tone of audible anger as he continued, "These people have actually been through things, white boy. . . you come in and do that shit again, I'll knock your goddamn head off."

It was just the wrong button to push. Like a switch, I felt adrenaline start coursing through my body, and my arms and legs loosen in anticipation. A sense of warmth began radiating through my brain and I smiled, breathing out what I decided was my last drag as I replied, "There any bite behind that bark?"

Without warning, the man swung at my head with his right fist. Muscle memory and reflex took over, and I raised my left arm to block it, my hand still holding the cigarette. He recoiled and swung wildly with his other arm, and this one I caught with my elbow.

With both hands knocked down to his sides, I was free to lurch forward, driving my head down in an arc against his face, bringing the top of my skull down into the tip of his nose with an audible crack. Telescoping my left arm out, I grabbed him by the throat, and his cries over his broken nose worsened as I brought my cigarette up right underneath his eye and pressed it down on his cheek, hearing his flesh sizzle.

Shoving him off to the side I looked up to see the other men moving towards me, with the fat biker in front. To their surprise, I charged towards them, and just feet away from the man in front dropped down

T H E | S P L I T

and slammed my knee against his front leg. Already in motion, he was unable to stop himself him in time, and tripped over me.

Moving quickly, I stood back up – two other men were already in front of me – and brought my leg up to plant it in the chest of the man to my right, knocking him several feet back. The other guy jabbed at my face, but I knocked the blow off course with my forearm, countering with my other hand, before jamming my pointer finger into his eye-socket.

The man shrieked in pain and, as the last two men tried to get around him to get to me, I pushed him into them and took two large steps backwards. Eyes a-blur, I rapidly looked at all six men I was fighting. The man I had tripped and the one I had kicked away were stumbling back towards their group, both ready to go again.

Faces twisted in rage, all of them except the first man I had burned now moved towards me in unison. In half an instant, I made a decision. Not wanting to chance a mob beating – or the police being called – I decided to end the fight. Calmly lifting my shirt, I revealed the Kimber1911 tucked into my waistband. I was always glad I had my gun. After being moved to the reserves – meaning no issued firearm – I had gotten a concealed carry license for protection.

The man in front stopped the whole group by throwing his hands up to both sides. It dawned on his friends too, as they all got up to where he stood and saw what I was doing.

"I'm going to leave now. . ." I looked each of them in the eyes, in turn. "But I'll see you guys next meeting. Keep coming back. . . it works if you work it."

"You better never come back here!" the man in front screamed. Laughing, I walked backwards and then side-shuffled off; never fully taking my eyes off the group of guys glaring in my direction.

THE | SPLIT

Taking a deep breath once inside my car, I turned on the ignition and backed out from the parking lot as fast as I could, pulling out onto the main street, feeling the adrenaline start to fade as the air conditioning kicked on and I got some distance from the parking lot.

Just as I was booting up the music from my phone to my car speakers, it suddenly stopped and began to ring. My finger instinctively went to the 'decline call' button, until I saw who was calling. Reluctantly, I slid the icon right to answer.

"Whats up, fag?" the all too familiar voice said. "How was your 'I can't handle my liquor' meeting tonight?"

It was Corbin, my on and off again roommate and only real close friend. Ever since we'd met years ago we'd seemed to mesh perfectly. He was funny, and aggressively gay, with a penchant for apathy that bordered on the nihilistic – there was nothing he couldn't laugh about. I had always enjoyed his company more than anyone else's, and we had a million stories about causing trouble – and just as many tactics for getting out of said trouble. Corbin's mother had said it was the devil that put us in each other's lives.

We had only recently reconnected in the past couple of years, following our different choices of college. He had taken a job all the way across state from our hometown, and it just happened to be near the base where I was inactively stationed. The transition back into each other's lives had been seamless, almost as if we had never stopped being friends at all.

"You don't get to call me a fag."

"Sure I do," he replied simply. "Black people took back the N-word, we gays took back 'fag'. How was the meeting?"

"Terrible, just like always man, but I did actually talk to someone tonight. Cute blonde, I think she came alone. It went just about as well

T H E | S P L I T

as you would expect."

Silence followed for a few seconds until he finally replied, "That could literally mean anything with you. Did you hookup with her in some closet...or did she hit you? Judging from your bitchy tone...it sounds like she smacked you pretty good."

"Neither, actually. . . she just came to chastise me about what I said in the meeting; they almost kicked me out of the group apparently. She did say she wanted to see me tomorrow, though."

He snorted with laughter for a brief moment. "That's good. . . but, you almost got kicked out of the meeting? You asshole, what did you say?"

The next few minutes of my drive I told him about the last few minutes of the meeting, and my comment towards Sandra. He listened attentively, only chiming in with an occasional question, punctuating my sentences with an 'uh-huh', or 'oh, okay'. By the end he was laughing; loud spasms of laughter that rang in my ears even through the car speaker.

"Ah...DOUBLE asshole! That poor woman didn't need to hear that. I'm sure you don't actually feel bad, but you should. . . just a little."

"Oh, and the craziest thing just happened outside the meeting. And. . . by the way, I did feel bad. . . but I have to tell you about this." I told him about the confrontation outside of the meeting, going over every detail as well as I could remember.

"Wow dude, that's insane. Why did you pull the gun out though, dummy? You already got charges, you don't need that."

"There were like six other guys! I'm not going to get beat down by a gang of people if I don't have to."

"Whatever man, that's not really how the law works, but fair enough.

T H E | S P L I T

You coming out to The Green Door tonight? Nick and everyone are showing up now, supposed to be a good crowd."

I briefly considered it as I looked at my car stereo's clock. 10:16.

"No, I think I'm good, man. . . I got to work early. But I might be there tomorrow, for Katie's birthday."

"Aw, you're a dick. I told everyone I was going to try to get you to come, they'll be pissed at me!"

I chuckled audibly. "Why? Those are your friends, man. As long as you're there, it should be fine. . . right?"

"Not true...they're actually warming up to you. . . believe it or not. Some of them have actually said they like you. . . as impossible as that seems. But whatever man, I gotta go. I'm here. I'll talk to you tomorrow I'm sure."

"Alright, later man."

"Hey Burl, wait..." he paused for a few seconds. "Are you doing okay?"

"Of course! What do you mean?"

"We just, haven't talked in a few months. Ever since you got back a few years ago, I've been worried about you. . . everyone has."

"I'm fine man..." I trailed off, searching for the words to make it sound convincing as possible. "Seriously, don't worry about me. I'm getting through this, and monitoring my moods. I'm completely fine. I'll see you tomorrow."

I hung up and sighed. I was a good liar.

The group leader in the meeting had been right, everyone had their pain, some just had it buried deeper than others. But mine had been wired in, made a part of me – chemically – and ever since my discharge I had been experiencing the side effects of a supposedly-harmless serum. All the result of careless decision-making in a moment of weakness, when I'd been approached by an Army recruiter after my first semester of college.

Having thrown away my scholarship by violating its terms, I was disillusioned with the prospect of University. Lost and without purpose, I began applying for jobs, and even filled out a placement test with the military. A week later I had gotten a call from a recruitment office, asking me to come in and discuss the results of my test.

Thinking the outcome to be nothing out of the ordinary, I'd driven down to the office and waited to see the recruiter that had called me. But as soon as I entered his office, I knew something was afoot. The room was too big, the furniture too nice, and even the recruiter looked nothing like what I thought he should have; balding, middle-aged man with doughy, pale skin and an unsettling smile.

His first approach had been one of flattery, he congratulated me on my test results, telling me that my aptitude was off the charts and that I was precisely the type of candidate they were looking for to participate in a special project. He talked about my genetic profile, saying that I had all of the specific traits that the program was searching for. Headstrong, and insecure from my recent failure in school, I bought his little speech; hook, line, and sinker. After just twenty minutes in his office, I was on board. I signed the contract, and five weeks later was deployed to what the recruitment office had told me was Basic Training.

I had expected to arrive at a military base, but instead was shuttled to a remote facility in the Virginian countryside, where I was sent through a strange form of processing. Nearly 12 hours passed while I was being briefed by a group of doctors and military officials in charge of the base. Then I was sworn to secrecy, under the threat of treason, about what I would see during my training, and given several more documents to sign that stated that I understood revealing what went on here would

THE | SPLIT

make me subject to a Military Tribunal – and likely being imprisoned or executed.

In spite of all of this, with the ego-boosting words of the recruiter still fresh in my mind, I signed anyway. Before being released to my shared quarters I was given a series of injections, along with various pills and capsules, all at once. Everyday during my training I was given different medicines and chemicals to take.

They never told me what they were putting inside me, no matter how many times I asked, but even before my forced discharge I had begun to feel the effects of these mystery drugs. Whatever the chemicals were, they were not made to personally benefit me. My mood would swing erratically. The anger and hostility I had begun to feel as a teenager morphed into violent outbursts. My laid-back but ambitious personality changed entirely, and I started to exhibit antisocial behavior, mixed with a general lack of empathy.

I hated to think about it. Focusing on keeping my head clear as I drove down the road, the rest of my drive was uneventful. A Rage Against the Machine song that I liked came on the radio, and I played it loudly until I turned in to my duplex parking lot.

After getting out of the car, before walking inside, I closed my eyes to listen to the now familiar sounds of the neighborhood I had moved into just a few months ago; loud Mexican music drifting down the block, the blended barking of an uncounted number of dogs from every direction, the muffled sounds of my neighbors screaming at each other, audible through the brick walls and carrying faintly into the back alley where we all parked our cars.

The last one was a near-constant. My neighbor, Jim, had been nice to me since the day I moved in. His wife however, was a different story. I paused as I tried to remember her name.

THE | SPLIT

Molly, maybe? Melissa? It was something that began with an 'M'.

I shook my head, giving up; it wasn't worth remembering; she had been a steel-clad bitch since I had moved in – a stark contrast with Jim's desperate but subtle attempts at friendship. And I had only seen her two times – both of which she'd had a look on her face that made her seem as though she was trying to make up her mind between hitting me and crying. Jim, on the other hand, I saw often. A husky man, usually wearing a wife-beater or a shirt with the sleeves cut off. He had greasy brown hair, and a flushed look on his face more often than not. His hands were nearly always dirty, as were his pants; a byproduct of the construction job that he occasionally talked to me about in low, bitter tones.

Lighting up another cigarette, I attempted to discern what they were fighting about this time. while still keeping my distance from their door. I heard the word 'mother' and a few other words, but soon lost interest and spent the rest of my time smoking staring up at the sky, straining my eyes to see if I could see the stars. It was a fruitless endeavor; as usual, the city lights dimmed all but the brightest of them. But it had never kept me from trying to see the un-seeable stars, as had been a habit of mine ever since my dad had explained the night sky to me as a kid.

I extinguished my cigarette in the little pail with sand in it that functioned as my ashtray (Jim's wife had passive-aggressively given it to me one day when she decided she was through with the butts blowing over onto their side of the porch area) and fumbled with the lock on my back door for a second before opening it, immediately closing and locking it behind me – the duplex had never quite felt like home. Sure, it had my furniture, and all of my posters and paintings on the wall, but something had always felt off.

THE | SPLIT

Sinking into the couch as soon as I made it to my living room from the entry hallway, I reached for the remote on top of the collapsible TV dinner tray that stood off to the side, and immediately heard laughter. As the picture sharpened, and I saw it was a stand up comic, I reached to the other side of the couch to open up the mini fridge. Highball glass, four whiskey stones, and a bottle of mid-range scotch. I took a deep breath as I poured the spirit into the glass.

Everything I said at the meeting was really an act, I chastised myself. I probably did have a problem with drinking – not in the amount I drank, but in how I depended on it in times of loneliness and vulnerability.

But three drinks later, I began to feel it. Just faintly, but definitely there; that faint buzz around the edges of my brain, quieting my thoughts. The next half hour I spent on the couch, leaning onto my favorite pillow and switching around the channels.

This was the time of my day I had begun to enjoy the most. The effects of the scotch washed over my sluggish and tired brain, removing all edge from my thoughts, and I felt like my old self again; before the drugs from the project, before Blythe left me, before my charges. My dark thoughts faded away, and my inebriated brain let go of all but the present.

When my eyes began to swell and start to flicker between open and nearly closed, I got up and made a sandwich – ham and Swiss with a dab of mayonnaise – and walked to my bedroom across the hall. The bed was unmade, as usual – dark colored comforter and gray sheets in a tangled mess at the foot – but I climbed in lazily, cursing the tall bedframe, and pulled the cover around me. After plugging my phone in, I mashed the buttons on my alarm clock and then lay there in the dark, thinking of my life and mistakes.

This time though, the highlight reel of regret that usually played was interrupted at intervals by thoughts of that blonde from the meeting.

T H E | S P L I T

II

> No record of previous location
> Recovered in Bloc Vault C1
> T. Acerz, 2134

Central Ohio; 2017

I awoke to the shrill ringing of my alarm clock and out of habit, knowing my love for hitting the button and rolling over to go back to sleep, pivoted to hit the floor with both feet before standing slowly. I glanced over at the clock, even though I knew what it said; 6:31; then slowly walked into the kitchen and turned on the coffee maker, black mug already there underneath.

Hearing the faint whirring as the machine gurgled and started to brew, I walked back to my room and turned at the door to go to my closet to grab my Nike shoes and shorts, then sat down on the bed to put them on before bouncing up up onto the balls of my feet, feeling my calf muscles flex. It was time to do the only part of my day I particularly enjoyed.

Back in the kitchen, I grabbed my coffee mug, blowing on the steaming beverage to cool it down as I headed into my living room to turn on the TV and, resisting the urge to sit down on the couch and wrap the blanket around myself, flipped through until I found a news channel.

I alternated between small sips and continuing to blow on the mug as I watched. The bright screen was divided into boxes of talking heads and various texts, some moving some not. Slowly, my brain adjusted to the change in pace, and I split my attention between watching, listening to the anchor and his guest, and reading the ticker at the bottom of the screen.

THE | SPLIT

But suddenly, the news anchor said something that caught my attention. Looking up, I saw the boxes fade away as the camera changed to a single shot of the man behind the desk.

". . . we are now receiving confirmation about what happened this morning on a Georgia highway. Maddox Hill. . . a controversial figure in the growing field of consumer genetics. . . was one of several people found at the scene of a multiple car collision on Interstate 285. According to reports from the scene, Hill has been transported to a nearby hospital. His current condition is unknown."

Calling Maddox Hill a 'controversial figure' was an understatement. I had been aware of who he was since he first came into the public eye, several years before. An outspoken theist, conservative, and Trump supporter, Maddox was a boogeyman in the world of Academia. But his accomplishments had given him a soapbox, and he used it to continually defy expectations. At the age of 27, he and his research team had done what pharmaceutical companies had tried to do for decades; cured Alzheimer's. Hill had been born to a poor family from a rough area in Atlanta known as 'The Bluff', but as a child he'd spent his time studying, and against all odds graduated at the top of his class; eventually getting his Doctorate in Genetics and Genomics.

As a black man, Maddox had a heart for black youth, and during his public appearances would talk about problems and solutions for the inner city. But his speeches were often construed as unrealistic, or bigoted. Most recently, he had done a series of TED talks on the idea of 'Genetic Responsibility in Parenthood', and had spoken of how, through his research, he had shown that Carriers of the genes responsible for intellectual disabilities, like autism, would often be passed down and lie dormant in future generations. 'Continuing to propagate the problem', he'd called it.

T H E | S P L I T

In a press conference shortly after, Maddox was asked about what he had meant in his comments, about these dormant genes, and while arguing with the reporter had revealed that he thought people carrying these specific genes had an 'obligation to not reproduce'. This of course caused a firestorm. Maddox Hill was denounced as a eugenicist by many of his peers, and his ideas had become a hotbed of Controversy.

"Well Tom," a man on the other side of the desk replied, "I know that we have spent a good amount of time on this network talking about Hill and his research. We wish him a speedy recovery, and of course keep his family in our thoughts and prayers."

I finished the rest of my coffee, turned off the TV, and set my mug on the counter by the sink. Mentally clearing my mind, I switched gears from politically and scientifically engaged and, out in the garage now, opened the garage door slightly to peek out of the bottom, making sure both of the neighbors' cars were gone before I closed it again. Plugging my phone into the stereo, I began my daily workout routine to a combination of early 2K's hip hop and punk music.

I had done the same thing every day for years now; curls, pull-ups, leg presses, jump-rope, and crunches. Afterward, I would let off the rest of my steam by hitting the black punching-bag that had been in the corner of the garage of every place I'd ever lived in.

I had always been happy with the way I looked – I was tall and muscular, prompting people to think twice before they talked shit or started something – but I still pursued it tirelessly, fitness being just another symptom of my narcissism towards other people. It was one more way I could be better than others, a powerful feeling. One that I had grown accustomed to and had made part of my identity.

I got done at 8; a short work out by my standards, they were typically longer. This had been one of my more 'bare minimum' efforts, (a kind that had come too often since moving into this house) meant more to preserve than to improve. And now, heading to the bathroom, I took a detour to the kitchen to heat up the stove – turning the burner knob to '6' – then threw my clothes in the hamper and got in the shower.

Cold water sprayed onto me as soon as I turned it on, and I enjoyed it before it slowly started to warm, closing my eyes and thinking about nothing, pleasantly clear-headed with the tail end of the endorphin rush I had just built up. I had perfected the shower; two and a half minutes exactly, all soap and shampoo dispersed properly in one fluid motion. Getting yelled at about water usage by a penny-pinching father will do that.

I dried off, wrapped a towel around my waist, and walked back into the kitchen – frustrated to realize that I had turned on the stove with an empty skillet on the burner. Picking it up by the handle, I inspected the bottom for burns, but saw no more than the usual, so I set it back down and opened the fridge to pull out my regular breakfast; eggs, bacon, sausage, and toast – or rather, bread and butter. Muscle memory took over as I cooked the entire meal in less than 20 minutes, and 5 minutes after that it was gone. I put the plate in the sink and went back to my room to get dressed.

My closet was divided into work and bar clothes; I moved over to the "work" side of it. Lately, I had been kind of flying under the radar in terms of style, so I decided to step it up, and selected my black suit with dull purple pinstripes, and a matching tie that had brighter purple woven throughout the design. It took about 10 minutes to put it on, slip on my shoes and mousse my hair. Done, I tied my tie and, locking the door behind me, walked out of the house for the quick drive to work – it was one of the main reasons I had chosen that duplex when faced with the dilemma of moving, months back.

THE | SPLIT

Pulling into the parking lot at 8:45, I reached into my suit pocket, my fingers closing around the 'Mad Men'-style, silver cigarette case I used at work – when I'd first started, I'd figured that if I was to have a bad habit on work grounds, I would at least do it with some class – and lit one of the cigarettes with my silver and gold inlaid Zippo, then got out of the car and locked it behind me. As I neared the curb close to the entrance, I saw Sloan lighting up a cigarette of his own.

"Mr. Sloan, how are we today?" I saw him briefly recoil at the opening of my sentence, still unused to me calling him 'Mister' Sloan. It was a recent change, made at the behest of the other Partners, who insisted my informal way of talking to him 'undermined office hierarchy', and wasn't becoming of an employee talking to his employer.

"Living the dream, kid. . . you look chipper. . . early night?"

"Yeah, actually. Went to a meeting, and then went to sleep. Trying to get all these done and put it behind me."

"Good for you, son," he said, smiling. We finished smoking and walked together towards the building, both putting our cigarette butts in the concrete ashtray by the door as we talked about the NBA, something he was obsessed with. I watched a fair bit myself, but hadn't seen any games last night, though I didn't admit that to him. I could still follow the conversation since I'd checked the scores on my phone earlier, so our talk continued as we came upon a small group of people and waited with them for the elevator to take us up to the fifth floor.

Sloan had done a lot for me, and I would always be grateful. We had been close ever since he had hired me, several years before, when I was at a dark time. Back then, Corbin and I were at the same bars nearly every night, always getting into trouble. I had unknowingly 'known' who Sloan was for years, having seen him many times in the background of bars throughout town, but in between our years of pool hustling, bar fights both inside the bar and in the alley behind, and hitting on anything above a 6, Sloan must have blended into the background.

He had first approached me at a place called 'Henry's'. After several changes in ownership, and two years or so of not doing well, I couldn't say what it was called now, but it was a good spot, a fun place that constantly changed with the trends.

On one of those nights, I'd made some serious headway with a redhead, after having to compete in a battle of wits with a quick-talking businessman to win her attention. Sloan had come up to me as she – having finally agreed to go to my place for a drink – went to the bathroom.

He told me he had been watching me, and that he couldn't help but admire my charm and skill for talking to people, regardless of who they were. Then he said that his firm was hiring; a position he thought I would be perfect for.

He got up as the redhead was walking back to the table, leaving his card behind for me. That job offer was probably how I sealed the deal that night; we Googled the information on the card, in the Uber on the way to my house, and she was impressed.

I had called him my 'wing-man' ever since, and he had continued to earn his nickname, on multiple occasions.

Walking in the office, I found work already waiting on me. Tabitha, the executive secretary, called my name from across the office as soon as she saw me, and said that Mr. Hartford and Mr. Donner had asked for me to come to the conference room as soon as I made it in. Hartford and Donner were the other partners in the firm. They were more stern and businesslike than Sloan, but they were good lawyers, able to handle and delegate the massive influx of cases we received. They had never liked me the way Sloan had, and sometimes seemed to openly resent me, but luckily they respected my work and understood the necessity of my job in their operation.

As I walked into the room I saw most of the legal team, already scribbling onto legal pads and typing into laptops, talking about the various work they had ahead of them for the day. When Hartford and Donner saw me they greeted me near the door, papers in their hands.

"Just in time. Mr. Whitman has been calling about an update. . . repeatedly. He plans to come in today with his team. Here are the updates on his case." Hartford handed me the papers from both he and Donner, continuing, "There hasn't been much headway yet, so I'll need you to milk this. He'll be here in about an hour, see if you can take him out for a while. We'll have more to tell him after lunch - try and bring him back around then."

I nodded in agreement, "Yes sir, Mr. Hartford. Mr. Donner. . . has there been any update on the Vega claim? Would you like me to follow up with him today?"

"No, not yet, but I'll let you know before the end of the day, check your email." Donner's voice sounded tired, I thought as he was walking back over to the head of the table with Hartford following him.

I headed out of the door and across to my small office along the wall. The next 45 minutes I spent carefully reviewing the papers I had been given, and becoming increasingly frustrated with what was on them. "Not much headway yet." had been an exaggeration. There had been hardly any change to the case, at all – at least not enough of an update for me to explain to Mr. Whitman without his legal adviser speaking up, and me having to get into a conversation about the specifics of a small section of law I knew next to nothing about.

It was at times like this that I wished I had finished my schooling. I had attended Northwestern, not far from my childhood home, with the hopes of getting a degree in Pre-Law; where I could then transition into their Law School. I was still young, and the college experience for me had been nothing like others described however, the classroom environment didn't seem to suit me.

I found myself not even listening to my professors; their opinion of the knowledge already found in my textbooks didn't interest me, and my grades had quickly plummeted. My arrogance towards my classmates, whom I perceived as simple and boring, kept me from making friends. But, after the university and the army, all of the friends I'd grown up with had moved on.

All except for Corbin. He had stuck with me through thick and thin; and I had rewarded his loyalty with moodiness and isolation. It wasn't until I had met Blythe that I finally patched up our relationship, and it was with their encouragement that I began to branch out and find a degree of passion for this job.

I had settled into the law office, always telling myself I would finish my degree in my free time and join the team, but so far I had just stuck to the same role they had given me the on day I was hired. My job was fairly simple, and played into the office dynamic perfectly.

Hartford, Donner, and Sloan had put their own spin on the big law firm approach. As one of the bigger firms in the city, with a large group of lawyers on staff, HDS had been able to take on some of the bigger cases that smaller firms just simply didn't have the manpower to pursue— typically those requiring a large amount of legal legwork and hearings. We offered our services at price-per-hour, per case, and at a much lower cost than our competitors, making us extremely popular with our customers.

But there was a catch.

T H E | S P L I T

To make up for the low prices, the speed at which cases were handled was relatively slow; we took more time than most of our clients preferred. Still, the slow pace allowed for the firm to pay extra attention to detail, and build cases more thoroughly, usually with an outcome resulting in winning more suits. That was where I came in; I served as the 'buffer', between the partners and the clients.

My official title was 'Executive Associate', and as vague a title as it was, it was all-encompassing. The typical duties on some of the bigger and more drawn-out cases involved finding a way to inform the clients of the updates in their cases, keeping them aware of the progress being made, and making them happy; through a combination of charm and bullshit. I spent my days making sure the clients were occupied, on the company dime, going everywhere from racquetball courts to strip clubs.

Today's meeting with Mr. Whitman was no different. I continued to mentally prepare as I walked from my office to the reception area to meet him, 15 minutes early, just in case he showed up beforehand. Having the partners or the legal team caught unprepared would be a serious slip up, and keeping that from happening was my entire job.

I smiled at the receptionist as I sat in one of the leather waiting chairs. She didn't return my smile, instead narrowing her face at the computer screen with renewed focus, obviously ignoring me.

'Still bitter.' I thought with a smile.

It wasn't her fault, nor was it really mine. I didn't often hookup with girls at the office, but through the years I had made at least a half dozen successful passes; Christie being the last of them, months ago.

I was almost disappointed at how little it took, almost no variation from the formula. I had even warned her that she was making a stupid decision. To no avail; after work, and following a night at the bar, she had still come over.

T H E | S P L I T

I paused in looking at my papers to look at her; still staring intently at the screen. She was cute, pretty even, with a soft face and an even softer voice. I began to feel bad for a moment, but then I strengthened my resolve. She had been looking for something serious, and I knew someone would come along soon to give it to her. But I wasn't going to be that person. I was a piece of my former self, and she deserved someone's all.

Mr. Whitman showed up several minutes early like I had suspected. I stood up to shake his hand and greet him, and my spirits brightened when I saw that the only people with him were his son and one of his executives.

"Mr. Whitman, good morning. . . I'm sure we would both like to make the boring part brief today?"

Shaking my hand, he laughed and nodded, a gesture the other two mimicked. It prompted me to continue, "Well then, just make your way to my office for a moment, and we'll be on our way." They walked past me, and before turning to follow them I leaned over to the receptionist, "Oh...Christie, two glasses of ice. . . *and, call my phone in 11 minutes, exactly.*"

She nodded, and I turned to walk to my office, quickening my pace to catch up to the group. After Mr. Whitman, his son, and I were seated, I looked up at the third man, the executive, Jacobs, to apologize for the lack of third chair in my tiny and cramped office. They all laughed at this, it made me smile; it was running joke we'd had since these meetings had first started a few months ago.

"Well gentlemen, let's get down to the nuts and bolts on this one...so we can get out of here and go do what we're all actually wanting to do this morning. I'm sure legal has already passed along what we sent last evening. We're seeking a settlement, and we really think the plaintiffs are going to go for it. We have Yost and his team in the courtroom this morning, and they're very optimistic, but we won't know anything until about lunch."

"Well, if that's all there is to be said, let's get the hell out of here until there's more." Mr. Whitman said, standing up.

As we all walked out of my office and towards the lobby I saw Christie just picking up the phone, I assumed to call me, and leaned in as I passed by her desk. "It's okay, we actually got out of there earlier than I expected." She looked up for just a second and rolled her eyes as I walked past her.

Mr. Whitman and his entourage got in the vehicle they came in, a black Escalade, still idling under the awning, and I walked past them to climb into the front seat of the company car the firm had so graciously allowed me to use, while I was trying to replace the 200 I hated, sitting there for a minute to allow the tension to ease from my body.

I really liked this car. I had been in love with the Lincoln Town Car basically my whole life; since first riding in my Grandfather's as a little kid. They were butter, the smoothest thing I'd ever driven or was driven in – and I had driven sports cars, even hundred thousand dollar luxury cars. This model was no exception. It was a late-model, and the interior was almost an illusion, seeming impossibly spacious despite how it appeared from the outside.

The moment I was out of the driveway and onto the road I had a wave of nostalgia, thinking of that first ride with my grandfather all those years ago. But, forcing myself to tear away from the memories, I clipped my phone into the mount on the windshield, and then typed the location into my maps to start the navigation.

We were going to a gun range today, as with every time I went out with Mr. Whitman. It was great for me, as it allowed me to bond with the client in a familiar setting. And shooting was well within my wheelhouse; I could get in some much needed range time, something I hadn't had much of lately, due to my DUI.

The drive went quickly as I flew down the highway listening to an outlaw country station on the satellite radio. It seemed fitting for my soon-to-be company, and activity. As I drove through to the gate with the Escalade behind me, they immediately raised it when they saw the card I was flashing out of my window – I had done it a thousand times, figuratively. We followed the gravel road to our covered pavilion and range, talking as we were unloading our gear. Mr. Whitman's companions set up at some of the shorter targets, at about the ten and twenty-five marks, and took turns shooting with pistols first – a .357 revolver and a 9mm Glock, respectively.

They were both practiced shots, but it was really no contest; Whitman's son was always a good shooter, he and I had quickly formed a friendly rivalry. We shot for several hours in the mostly empty range, making small talk about the Buckeyes and Cavaliers.

At that point though, Mr. Whitman motioned me to the counter on the side of the range-house, where he had rolled over a cooler and a wooden case. He opened both and I saw that he was pouring drinks; from a quick glance at the bottle it looked like Scotch, and it looked expensive. I knew what was coming next, the talk about the future; it always came and it always made me laugh.

"So son," he said, trailing off to take a sip of his scotch, "You thought anymore about my offer?"

I smiled. This had started two appointments ago, when he had casually asked if I was still working on passing the Bar, and I told him no, I wasn't working on it. And, although I had thought about his offer – it was generous – he hadn't been the first one to make it.

T H E | S P L I T

    I oftentimes told myself that I would work on taking the test soon, and even that my experience at the firm was somehow building me up to just go do it once and for all, but I never really seemed to get around to it. And recent charges had put a damper on my efforts entirely, even forcing me to drop out of a course that Sloan had strongly encouraged me to take.

    This felt slightly different, though. Something about the position he described to me. . . or maybe it was Whitman, himself. . . made me actually move forward on it, if only just a little bit, so I had gone to the school and met with my legal professor to ask him his opinion.

    "I actually have, quite a bit. . . I met with my professor and told him about it. He showed me a class that will help me study. . . he thinks I'm ready. I haven't told anyone at the firm yet. . . and, this may be a slower process that you anticipated."

    He was beaming. "That's okay! My own legal team did tell me it may be a matter of months. This is good! Let's drink!"

    He was also pouring another Scotch, so I quickly swallowed the rest of mine in two gulps and put my glass on the counter for him to fill, just in time. As we walked back over to the group with glasses in hand, I also had the bottle and he had another two glasses.

    We separated around noon and, shaking each of their hands I told them that there should be new developments back at the office, but instead of going back to work to eat my lunch like I typically did, I made my way towards Rick's Auto and Body Repair; to meet the blonde from the night before. It was about a ten minute drive from the gun range. When I pulled into the parking lot, I turned my car off and had a look around before going in.

    The building was about the average size you would expect for an auto repair shop; four tall garage doors in front, three of them open,

THE | SPLIT

revealing cars on lifts. The words "Rick's Auto" were hung onto the building in red block letters. The place looked busy, mechanics in gray jumpsuits bustled around the garage, various tools in hand, and people shuffled in and out of the glass front office door beside the garage every few seconds. Stepping out of the Chrysler, I made my way towards the nearest open garage door, and as soon as I went inside I saw her, bent over the open hood of a car, her blonde curls in a loose ponytail.

After noticing several of her coworkers staring in my direction, she looked up and saw me, smiling as she pulled a rag from her pocket and set it on the edge of the car's hood.

"Bobby!" she called out, turning to a fat man several cars away, "I'm going on break!" The man muttered that he heard her, and she weaved her way between the lifts over to me. "You came!" she smiled, revealing impossibly white teeth.

"I said I would, didn't I?"

She reached out her hand, but pulled it back to wipe grease on the leg of her pants. "Sorry, sometimes I get so caught up in my work I don't even pay attention to the mess."

"You're fine," I shook her hand warmly.

"I. . . just realized. . . we didn't even catch each other's names last night. I'm Meela."

I laughed and shook her hand again. "I'm Burl. Meela. . . that's an interesting name."

"Well. . ." she began walking towards the entrance to the office, beckoning me to follow, ". . . my real name is Amelia, but my younger sister couldn't say it, and the name sort of stuck."

"Ahh," I replied, moving ahead of her to hold the door to the office open.

T H E | S P L I T

She inclined her head slightly, "Thank you."

The office had wood-paneled walls, decorated with the logos and advertisements of different vendors. The floor was made up of a brick-colored tile, stained with black dots in various places, no doubt the remnants of spilled oil and related liquids. The customers waiting in a row of chairs near the front door seemed to pay us no mind, most of them buried in their phones.

Meela walked past the front counter, greeting each of the receptionists warmly, and led me into a side hallway and through a dinged up white door, back outside and behind the building. Here sat piles of parts, and empty cans of oil tipped over on their sides. A chain link fence surrounded the yard, with strips of barbed wire running along the top.

We stopped in front of a car covered by a light gray tarp. "You ready?" Meela asked me, both hands on the tarp.

"Yeah, let's see this car that's so much better than mine."

She pulled it off, letting it sink to the ground in a crumpled heap, and in an instant I could tell she was right. Her car *was* better than mine, a **lot** better.

The red coat of paint shone brightly in the noontime sun, making the car look almost new. The front was squared, with two contoured lines leading down to the shiny grill, and on the sides of it were the headlights, two right beside each other on either side. The thin-winged logo above stretched the entire length of the hood, and the cab was square-framed as well, with the back slanting down just past the rear seats. And the tires were white wall, completely free from scuffs no matter where I looked. The chrome inside them shone even brighter than the rest of the car, each spoke catching the sun's rays at different points to produce a dazzling effect.

T H E | S P L I T

Meela laughed as I looked the car over in silence, "See? I wasn't lying."

"No. . . you weren't." I said softly, running my hands over the hood gently. "Does it actually run?"

She rolled her eyes. "Do you know what I do for a living? Of course it runs, dummy."

"Well, excuse me. . . " I held up my hands disarmingly. "I didn't know. I don't fix cars for a living."

"Obviously." She looked me up and down, "Nice suit, by the way."

"Thank you," I smiled. "It's one of my favorite ones."

"I guess you weren't lying about actually having a job."

This made me laugh, "No, I was not. But hey. . . I don't have a lot of time before I have to be back at the office. You going to fire her up?"

Meela pulled out a set of keys from her side pocket and unlocked the door, sitting down and starting the ignition. The car roared to life, louder than any car I was used to, and a small plume of black exhaust rose up from the tailpipe, before the engine settled to idle in a low growl.

"It's loud!" I said, raising my voice over the engine as she stepped out of the car.

"Of course it is! Back in 1963, cars were made for performance over safety." Inside again, she killed the engine before stepping back out a few seconds later and closing the door behind her gently.

"So, if it's running fine, why don't you drive it?"

"It's not running the way I'd like," she replied simply, picking the tarp back up off of the ground and covering the back end. "There are still a few things I would like to swap out before taking it on the road."

Grabbing the other end to help her cover the car, I started, "So. . . a girl mechanic. . . " I felt awkward; it wasn't a feeling I was used to.

"What's wrong with that?" she challenged defensively. "Why can't girls be mechanics?"

"I wasn't saying that! I was just saying. . . it's unusual, is all."

"I know," she laughed. "I was just messing with you."

When we had finished we went back into the office through the back door. "Growing up, I was always interested in the way things worked. . . always taking them apart and putting them back together. Eventually my dad got sick of coming home to a house full of parts everywhere, and started showing me how to work on cars. After high school I got involved with the club, and I worked in their garage for a few years. I quit when. . . you know. . . and came to work here."

"Interesting," I said quietly, holding the door to the front parking lot open for her to walk through. "That's the second time you've brought up those bikers. Am I ever going to hear any more about them?"

"Not right now," she smiled, walking with me to the driver's door of my 200. "But I'll make you a deal. . . if you come to the meeting again tonight, we can talk about it more afterward."

"That works," I replied. "I was planning on going anyway."

"You better be," she gave me a quick side-hug. "I got to get back inside, my break is nearly over, but I'll see you tonight."

My journey back across town to my office was more of a crawl than a drive, every intersection was a sea of brake-lights as people made their way to and from their lunch breaks. And usually, I would be a frantic wreck, cursing at my windshield and weaving between lanes. But my brief time with Meela had chilled me out considerably, and after about fifteen minutes in traffic I walked in the front door and past reception.

Back to work.

T H E | S P L I T

By now the partners and the legal team would have finished discussing what went on in court this morning, and soon I would have to break the news to Whitman and his team.

When I made my way to the back of the office, before even entering the glass conference room I could see the partners talking to the head of the legal team that went in this morning. Surprisingly, they chattered excitedly, inaudible as I walked to the door, but I could tell that I was about to receive good news.

"Ah, there you are!" Sloan shouted at me as I walked in the room. Between excited breaths, he explained to me the updates that had occurred that morning, and said that things had gone well for Mr. Whitman's company. It appeared a settlement had been reached.

The gist of the case was pretty run of the mill; 'Big business against the Little guy'. Mr. Whitman was a man responsible for a massive amount of cattle. He owned a giant ranching operation, and represented several of his peers.

But the employees who procured said cattle were known to, occasionally, acquire fresh product through less than scrupulous means; this typically involving a lack of payment or tricky wording in the forms handed out to the men seeking to sell their cattle to Whitman's company.

After about five years of this new business strategy, Whitman had made a number of enemies; all of whom had decided to sue him in a Class-Action suit.

The suit itself was an absolute farce, almost like a trope from an 80's movie where the corporate bad-guy was seen as one of the most devious of villains, because the level of legal counsel the plaintiffs could afford was a measly force compared to the raw manpower of Hartford, Donner, and Sloan.

THE | SPLIT

    This disparity was typical for our business, and one which won us cases by the hundreds, as we were usually hired by the defendant; commonly the wealthier of the two parties. With our army of lawyers and resources we could slow the cases down and force a settlement through brutal attrition, since smaller firms would soon come to realize they simply couldn't afford all of the hours being in court required, and still take other cases as well.

    I listened now as Sloan revealed all the details of the settlement that they had reached, but at the point in the conversation that he began going over the selling points of the settlement that I was supposed to offer to Whitman and his crew, I tuned out. Sloan was rehashing what I had already concluded for myself, earlier, as he'd told me what transpired in court.

    *'Maybe I **would** be a good lawyer,'* I thought to myself, smiling as Sloan wrapped up his proposed pitch for me. The next few minutes were an exercise in patience as I calmly listened and repeated back everything Hartford, and then Donner, explained to me; even though Sloan had already said it all just minutes before.

    But I didn't fault them for the repetition, it was just their style of management; while Sloan tended to be more trusting and let me make mistakes on my own, his two partners preferred to micromanage. Finally, with orders given out and tasks to be done, I moved to my office at a brisk pace, to find Whitman and his crew already seated, waiting on me.

    Our meeting was brief, since Whitman's older son repeatedly referred to an 'upcoming engagement'; nonsense of course – any seasoned onlooker of the group knew such vague talk was code for 'going to one of the (many) strip clubs' on the outskirts of town.

    Whitman was satisfied with the terms of the settlement though, and

THE | SPLIT

told me multiple times to call him with any news of the case being resolved. Promising him I would, I walked them all to the door then returned to my office for what turned out to be a pretty boring afternoon.

I checked Facebook more than a couple times, and sent around a dozen emails to various department heads. Facebook provided an occasional laugh, but the emails were soul draining, mindless prattle about the most mundane specifics – that probably could've been sorted out in less than a minute of meeting face-to-face.

Five o'clock couldn't have come soon enough, and as the clock finally turned, I eagerly gathered up my things to leave. The sun was beginning to set when I made it to the parking lot, this was always one of my favorite things about the winter and fall months; the sunset casting shadows across the cement as it began to fade earlier each day.

I'd always been the kind of person to prefer the dark of night to the cheery tones of day. Not for any practical reason, like work, but purely for aesthetic purposes and the overall feel of the evening. A person who valued deep thought could probably make a poignant metaphor of that, and relate it to my life as a whole; but I am not that person and this is not that kind of story.

After what seemed an eternity, my drive ended and I parked in the alley behind my home. Again I heard fighting coming from my neighbors, but this time much more one sided – with the woman's voice being the much louder of the two.

Ignoring this, I looked down at my watch as I went inside; 5:31. Time enough to relax before I made up my mind about going to the meeting, and/or Katie's birthday party afterward.

As I sat on the couch, after taking off my shoes and unbuttoning my dress shirt, my eyes were drawn around the living room. I paused at the

THE | SPLIT

hole in the drywall; the aftermath of some long forgotten party thrown by the previous tenant. I'd told my landlord I would fix it, and the broken and scratched outlet at the base of the wall near the hallway, for a reduction in rent. When I'd called his office number from the pay phone outside of my CO's house, his voicemail had picked up, and all I'd been able to mumble out was a hurried explanation of my situation, what I'd I hoped for – a six month lease, low rent, and a roof over my head – and a callback number.

If I'd known then the place he had in mind, maybe it wouldn't have been so surprising that he called me back within the hour, asking about my home-repair experience. It was one of the biggest stipulations to my shorter-than-average lease; all of the needed repairs – holes in the walls, scratches, broken pipes, and general atmosphere of suffocating depression – had to be fixed by yours truly.

But, again, the duplex was just miles away from the base, which was an important item on my small list of requirements. He had mumbled something about never again letting a meth addict rent one of his properties, before dropping the keys into my hand.

I looked around; so many small projects, such little motivation. I took a minute to reflect on my laziness, before forcing myself to keep things in perspective. I had done a lot around this place already, and looking again at the repairs I had made gave me a sense of satisfaction. So, feeling good in my measured success, I decided to crack open a beer and play some video games.

But I found myself bored with staring at the screen after playing for a few hours. Something inside me was yearning for adventure – and human interaction. It had been a long and lonely past few weeks, and tonight I felt like doing more than stewing in my poor life choices. Tonight was different. Tonight would be opportunity. Freedom.

THE | SPLIT

Freedom from preconceived choices and notions, freedom from darkness, freedom from routine.

I decided I was going to both the meeting *and* the party afterward. Having time to kill, I went to my kitchen to find something to eat. I wasn't hungry but I knew there might be little chance to eat anything decent later, at the bar.

Standing in the opened fridge doorway as I looked everything over, I paused and frowned – nothing looked good to me. So instead, I opened an upper cabinet to reach for an oatmeal packet. Oatmeal had always been my go-to food when I 'wasn't hungry', and didn't really want anything else. Hot, grainy, and rather tasteless, it met the bare minimum for sustenance; and was better than anything else to slowly and begrudgingly eat.

I finished putting my khakis on during the commercial break of a News program that I was half paying attention while to in my bedroom. The shirt choice was easy; a simple blue, short-sleeved button-up tonight; not too formal but not casual. The perfect choice for a night like this. My watch said 7:30, and while the meeting was only 10 minutes away, I was ready to go. I would take the long way, and listen to music.

The drive was peaceful – well, as peaceful as driving in a big city could be – with minimal traffic and a good consistent pace. The music coming from my phone was a perfect soundtrack; a heady blend of rap and punk. The perfect energy for my, possibly unfounded, optimism about the night's possibilities.

* * * * *

As I got close to the meeting site, my thoughts went back to the blonde for what seemed like the millionth time. There was something different, I didn't know if it was a second wind of positivity, or the apprehension of seeing her again, but I embraced it, letting the images

THE | SPLIT

of her smile carelessly dance around my brain, along with the possibility of potential.

Finally I pulled up, and while walking towards the meeting I saw Meela talking to another girl, but walked past her without making eye contact; from experience I knew that, just like anything great in life, you had to play it cool. Availability could seem unattractive if misdirected. I made it inside the door, but as I walked down the hallway to the meeting room I felt a slight tap on my shoulder.

It was like something out of a cheesy movie. Time seemed to slow as I turned around, then came grinding to a complete halt.

Meela looked perfect, and the moment was every bit as intense as the first time we made eye contact, last meeting. She was wearing a short, dark blue dress, which seemed to match her skin tones and bright blue eyes like she was born to wear it. Her hair was partially up, a masterful blend of messy and done. . . so well-blended in fact that I had a hard time telling if she had actually worked hard on it or not. I'm also sure it was the exact kind of response she had styled it to elicit.

She wore a sly expression, her red lips pursed in an upward crease so as to not let slip a smile by accident, as we stood there. I watched her face, her eyes quickly darting around my face as she looked up at me, doing the same thing I had just done, trying to read me; who I was, my intentions, who I could be.

Though neither of us said a word through this fleeting eternity, we seemed to share our two lifetimes. A beautiful nonverbal exchange of a million subtle stimuli and feelings. It was something of the purest beauty that, due to the cruel nature of the world it took place in, could never be expressed or reproduced.

"Um... hi," she said, giggling softly.

"Hey there," I replied, voice barely above a whisper. From the corner

THE | SPLIT

of my eyes I noticed multiple, swirling forms, all moving past me, which I assumed were people trying to get in to the meeting, but even this day I don't know for sure; they were unimportant. My whole world in that moment was talking to her. A girl I had only just met.

"Rumor has it you got into a bit of a fight last night, after I left."

"Not sure what you're talking about. . . I get into a lot of fights."

She rolled her eyes, and then grabbed my arm, pulling me inside the meeting room, "Come on, let's go sit." We sat in the back and, though avoiding the Bikers from last meeting was her primary purpose for doing this, they sat down near us nonetheless.

When the group came in they paused in the doorway, eyes darting around wildly, then one of them pointed in my direction and the others looked over at me, glaring. There were three of them, two I recognized, and then a third face I didn't. The man I had jabbed in the eye had a deep bruise above his cheek, circling around the inside of his eye socket.

I smiled at them cordially, and turned back around, not even acknowledging their presence again as they sat in the row behind me and Meela. They smelled like sweat, and some smoked-meat I couldn't quite put my finger on; maybe deer, or possum. The scent was pungent, and caught the attention of everyone around them; they all took their turns wrinkling up their noses as they looked back at the bikers, who were annoying and loud, even while people were talking.

Yet I couldn't remember a word they'd said if I was asked.

In fact, I don't think I remembered a single thing at that meeting, other than what was said between me and Meela. We focused exclusively on each other, doing the same cutesy sort of things a pair of middle-schoolers might do; talking in low whispers about each other's lives and, when the meeting volume got low, passing notes. One of these notes had included her phone number.

T H E | S P L I T

As I'd pulled out my phone to type the information in, she'd snatched it out of my hand and began typing for me. When I got it back I looked at what was now her contact; it said, 'Meela', with a bunch of those little yellow smiley faces my friends were always using. I learned a lot about her in what seemed like an incredibly short meeting.

She was an addict through and through, picking up an opiate habit after High School which had spiraled out of control – after moving in with her drug dealing boyfriend. It had turned messy after she filed for a protective order, and he had taken to stalking her around the clock.

From there she had tried her first stint in AA, and like most people there, it didn't take. Eventually she was out on the street, this time with a taste for harder drugs. A taste filled by her boyfriend's motorcycle club, the Den of Carnage; headquartered off of the highway at the edge of the city.

But after six months of dealing, and being a club girl, she was done. She cleaned up, broke up with him, got her own place and started going to AA – where she had stayed with it this time, getting her 2 year chip just a few weeks before I had started coming.

It wasn't entirely one sided; I told her about me; my job, my life after high school, and my current predicament. But my story was dull, it seemed more about unrealized potential and laziness than an actual struggle to overcome like she had done. I stayed away from it for the most part, mainly asking her about herself. A subject she didn't shy away from talking about. The end of the meeting seemed to come out of nowhere, and before I knew it I was on my feet, circled up with the rest of the group to say the closing prayer, one of the longer prayers I had heard since coming there.

But Meela had strategically moved us to the part of the circle nearest the door, and when the prayer ended she grabbed me by the arm and we

THE | SPLIT

bolted out both sets of doors into the cool dark night, using the throng of people behind us as a buffer for our getaway, and left the bikers behind – whom Meela had just confirmed were with her ex boyfriend's MC.

I now turned to her as we continued to speed walk, "Where are we going?"

"It doesn't matter to me, as long as it's away from here."

"You want me to drive?"

She looked up at the night sky, her hands feeling the warm air around us, "It's a nice evening, fancy a stroll instead?"

I smiled, and then nodded, letting her lead the way.

As we flew down the sidewalk, passing the parking lot and a poorly maintained garden that was littered with cigarette butts in just a few strides. At some point I remember looking down and watching how quick her thin legs were moving, taking several steps to every one of mine. I pointed this out to her, and was quickly but playfully punched in the arm, as she squeezed me tighter and tried to quicken her pace. Upon reaching the main street, not too far from the meeting, we took a turn onto a smaller one, then slowed our pace.

She peeked around the corner for a minute, cocking her head to listen for the sound of motorcycles. I had thought this a waste of time, but she told me these three were so bad at taking care of their bikes that it produced a very unique sound, a point I didn't question her on. After she was finally convinced that we weren't being followed, we casually meandered around the streets.

Finally, it was just the two of us; well, just the two of us and whoever happened to be driving or walking by at the time. But in my world it was just me and her. Being outside of the meeting, we could finally talk in our normal voices, a privilege we both abused as we loudly talked about anything and nothing, every few sentences punctuated by laughter.

She was funny, funnier than I had even realized before, as she told me stories from her childhood, and went tit for tat with every flirtatious barb I sent her way. She had so many colorful characters from her life, wacky family members and troubled friends, she made it sound like a movie.

Somehow, this gave rise to my competitive nature, and I began to wonder how I could match her stories; but I simply didn't have as many people close to me as she seemed to. At one point in time I'd had lots of friends, and close relationships with many family members as well. Yet a pattern had begun a few years ago, where I would just hang out with my two close buddies, other friends, and whoever I met out at bars or clubs. And recently I had very nearly stopped even this entirely, having begun to prefer my own company over anyone else's.

That had just reminded me, Katie's birthday party was tonight at the Green Door. I could at least introduce Meela to Corbin.

Me and Corbin went back more than two decades, and he could effortlessly conjure up stories about our checkered past, also being a natural storyteller. It was hard to place exactly what made people want to listen to him, but between his loud, animated voice and intense, rapid eye contact he was excellent at engaging small groups of people. His natural gift of gab had been the beginning of our friendship.

In the fourth grade, we had been paired up by our teacher for a group assignment, to explain several chapters in a book neither one of us had taken the time to read. Just before I stood up to tell the teacher we hadn't read it yet, Corbin had cut me off, telling me to let him take the lead. We both went to the front of the class, and he'd spoken the entire time.

THE | SPLIT

He'd absolutely nailed it.

Despite knowing less than a person who had at least seen the book's cover, he wove together his general impressions of some of our classmate's previous presentations, and turned it into a beautiful speech of emotion and ideas.

He'd clearly had no idea what happened in the book, but the teacher had given us an 'A' all the same. We'd had rocky patches here and there, but from that day we had been friends. He was the perfect person to introduce her to; the only person who had consistently been there throughout my whole life, and could retell it in a way that matched Meela's own energy.

Meela thought this was hilarious, adding that she would love to meet him. We had been walking for a bit now, in between alleyways and down small roads, her arm in mine, making small talk about each others families and growing up. I began to tell her more about Corbin, sharing some of our great stories and how we had become friends.

By the end, she wanted to meet him even more, prompting me to ask the question that I knew would be a difficult sell; even though I wanted her to meet Corbin, I was put in the awkward position of asking a former alcoholic to the bar.

"Well, actually you could meet him, he and some of my other friends aren't too far from here. The only problem is. . . they're at a bar, and I wouldn't want to mess up the good thing you have going back there."

This made her laugh. "You're sweet, but alcohol has never really been a huge problem for me. I started going to AA for much harder stuff, and I've been off that for years."

My heart leapt at her response. "Oh, okay. . . well great, do you want to walk over there then? Hope you won't judge me if I have more than a few drinks." I smiled nervously, waiting for a response. She just smiled

T H E | S P L I T

and assured me it was fine, lowering her hand from my arm to lock her fingers with mine, as we walked towards The Green Door.

After a few seconds of silence, she spoke up; "Corbin sounds great, but I want to know more about *you*. You say there's nothing to tell, but we both know that's not true. Something else sent you to all these meetings, and I have a feeling it wasn't just that girl you broke up with."

I fell silent for a moment, slowly walking forward as I thought of my response. My guard had been up for so long, the idea of even mentioning my checkered past sent chills down my body. What could I tell her that wouldn't send her off and running? Her past had been rough, but she had always pulled through, with remarkable competence.

By contrast, my resume of unfinished duties and broken agreements seemed markedly pathetic.

"I don't think that's a good idea," I replied hesitantly.

She squeezed my arm tightly. "Of course you don't, I know your type. The lone stoic, who shoulders all of his burdens and carries them around until it completely crushes him. I just told you my whole life story, and you tell me about one friend you have. You know. . . it's nice to tell your problems to somebody else, sometimes. It can be a relief, to just be able to vocalize them to another person. What makes Burl, Burl?"

She was right, I hated her for it, but she was right. Besides Corbin, no one knew the 'real' me, and maybe it was time for that to change.

"Well. . . I guess the first thing that put me where I am, happened just after high school. I was a swimmer for my school and not to brag, but I was a damn good one. By the time I graduated, I had accepted a full scholarship to Midwestern. After arriving on campus however, I continued the same habits I'd had from high school. I partied too much. . . ignored school almost completely. I didn't even last half of a semester. My coach confronted me about it, and I lashed out at him. The little speech I gave got me kicked off the team, and they revoked my scholarship."

"Oh Burl, I'm sorry that happened! Everyone makes mistakes, but they don't define you!"

"I wish that was the only mistake I made," I replied sullenly, and for the next few minutes told her about my time at the facility, doing Basic. The topic of my experimental treatment had always made me uneasy, since the threat of treason loomed over my head at all times.

I had learned not to tell anybody about it all. But I told her everything, from the few friends I had made, to my daily routine around the complex. I told her how they had never called me by my name, and instead had drilled into me that I was to go by 'Subject CL-7' while I was on site. I even talked about the fight in the training hall that had gotten me discharged, something I hadn't told even Corbin.

She listened intently, seeming to hold on to my every word, occasionally pausing me to ask questions. Just like Corbin, she was particularly interested in the chemical treatment I had undergone. I told her as much as I could, explaining how it was classified, and how the medics onsite had refused to tell me anything.

"So, even if you don't know the specific chemicals. . . do you know what genes they were trying to draw out?" She tried to ask her question nonchalantly, but her tone betrayed her acute sense of interest.

"Not specifically," I admitted. "But I do remember some of what the recruiter had said, and I've tried to do some research on my own. He mentioned the MAOA gene, and another one. . . called, CADM2, I think. MAOA is known as the 'extreme warrior gene', and is incredibly rare. It's known to produce a rush of chemicals, in times of stress, that focuses a person's mind and removes all forms of empathy, making it easier to 'think as a soldier'. . . or commit acts of violence, impulsively. CADM2 acts as a link between cells in your brain. People with high levels of CADM2 display extraordinarily quick thinking, and are easily able to adapt and solve problems. I don't know what the relation is between the two. . . but I have a hunch.

I imagine their experiments were two-fold; finding a way to make us less susceptible to resisting orders, and finding a way to bridge the two genes. Combining the two, and enhancing their traits, seems to be a way to program more effective killers. . . or hit men. Someone that quick-thinking, who could be impulsively violent, would be the perfect assassin. And the antisocial traits from both would make them ideal for working alone. Can...we...change the subject? I really don't like talking about this."

"Of course!" she answered. I could hear embarrassment in her voice. "I'm sorry, I didn't mean to-"

"It's fine, really," I interrupted, "I don't mind talking about it a little. . . and like you said. . . it did feel nice to tell someone." She looked up at me and smiled, and for the next few minutes we walked in silence. It seemed that she didn't know what to say, but I was enjoying the moment and even with no conversation, I enjoyed her presence. Upon rounding the last corner, I saw the building and was immediately awash in the light and sound coming from within.

It was a typical night, the party had spilled out of the bar and there were a jumbled group of people, ranging from the front door all the way down to the parking lot, covering nearly every step of walkway in between. I felt Meela tense, and her hand tighten around mine as I took the lead through the throng of people, bulling and slipping my way through to the door.

The bouncer barely even saw my face as I crossed the threshold into

THE | SPLIT

the raucous and humid bar, Meela still in tow. He knew me... I would even say he knew me well – I had helped him stop multiple fights over the last few years.

ＴＨＥ | ＳＰＬＩＴ

III

District N7 (Former Ohio and NW U.S.)
Found in excavation, 2102
-T. Acerz

Central Ohio; 2017

Corbin's voice cut through even through the various, deafening commotions characteristic to The Green Door, like a gruff but vaguely effeminate foghorn, and I found my table of people almost immediately.

"Burly Burl!" he shouted, coming up and grabbing me in a fierce bear hug. Though he was a little shorter and looked to be a fair bit heavier than me, Corbin was no pushover. He had wrapped his arms around both of mine, and though I prided myself for my fitness I knew from prior experience I wasn't stronger than him. Underneath his pudgy and unassuming frame was the result of fifteen years as a power-lifter.

He soon loosened his grip to look down at Meela. "And, who is this? You know this guy whose hand you were holding is a total douchenozzle, right?"

This forced a smile and reluctant laugh out of her. "Yes. . . yes, I know. But I think he's getting better," she said with a grin as he shook her hand, looking up at me. "I'm Meela. I assume you're Corbin?"

"Ah, Burl must've told you about me. Don't trust that one. . . he's an infamous trash talker."

This got another laugh out of Meela. Corbin then introduced her to the rest of the table. I knew most of the people there but, as always, there were a few new faces – dates and new friends – among the dozen or so people sitting at the table that Meela slowly met. She talked to every one of them, delighting both the girls and guys alike.

THE | SPLIT

She was a natural, her tact and wit put the group at ease instantly, and after meeting everyone, she immediately dove into the nearest conversation.

Corbin was explaining something to the laughter of those nearby, as our friend Ryan looked over at him with a look of disbelief on his face. "So then. . . what are you saying?"

"I'll just start my explanation over." Corbin took a swig of his drink and set it back on the table. "You're a Christian, right Ryan?"

"Right."

"So you believe in the devil?"

Ryan looked around the table before replying, wondering where Corbin was going with this, "Well yeah, sure."

"Then, you remember the story of Jesus being tempted in the desert. . . by Satan, after fasting for forty days?"

"Of course."

"Well," Corbin paused and took another drink, ". . . what I'M saying is, that if the same conditions were fulfilled. . . do you think the devil would show up for another person?"

"What do you mean? What are you trying to do here?"

"So, say. . . I went out into the desert and fasted for forty days. . . which would probably be good for me, let's face it. . . " he slapped his gut, and the group around him laughed. "But. . . if I were to fast, and be in the right desert at the right time. . . do you think Satan would show up and offer me the same deal?"

Ryan snorted with laughter. "Probably not, but even if he did, what would you do?"

"I'd accept his offer, of course! Power over the whole world in exchange for bowing to the guy once? Kind of a no-brainer."

T H E | S P L I T

The conversation devolved into fits of laughter as Ryan attempted to change Corbin's mind, but soon gave up and let it rest. Then the discussion shifted as the group began to talk about a new show several of them were watching. I suddenly felt a tap on my shoulder, looking up to see Corbin standing over me, motioning with his head towards the bar, where the line was several people deep.

I stood up to follow him; he had read my mind. When I got to the bar I turned back to see Meela talking to Katie and her friends, the whole group laughing. Katie must have caught me staring though, because as soon as she saw me all humor left her face and she subtly motioned to Meela, then motioned to me, shaking her head ever-so-disapprovingly.

I knew what she was upset about. Meela hadn't been the first girl I had brought around this group of people, in fact, I had brought several girls with me to hang out with Corbin and his friends after ending things with Blythe, which had won me a bit of resentment from the female members in our friend group.

They'd liked each of these new girls, and hated to meet a new person they got along with, only to never see them again.

And as if to drive the point home, I looked to my left and saw Macy Simms standing just a few people down from me. Macy was your average barfly, with a good sense of humor and a massive tolerance for liquor. We had hooked up about two months back, just before closing time, and the last time Corbin, Katie, and company saw me that night was when I put Macy in an Uber and stumbled over to their cars to explain how I couldn't make the after-party they had all been excitedly talking about.

Tonight wasn't about Macy, though. I was done being that guy. Turning firmly the other way, I saw that Corbin stood off to the side of the bar, waiting for me and sipping on his drink.

T H E | S P L I T

I made conversation him, and after what seemed like an hour, the bartender came back with two double rum and cokes. I wasn't sharing; I just hated waiting in line, so I always doubled up when I was there.

When I made it back to the table, someone was telling a story about their vacation to Mexico which made no sense to me. Not that it should have, I've just always hated walking up to stories in progress. Meela saw me a few seconds later and, to my surprise, gave up her seat to Corbin and moved to sit on my lap.

But we'd only talked for a second before we were interrupted when Katie came down and sat in the previously empty chair across from me, with a question that seemed innocent enough; although as someone who knew her I could sense her true intent. "So Burl, where did you find this one?"

"AA, actually. . . I decided that I'm going to ease myself into it, instead of all at once," I gestured to my rum and coke. This got a laugh out of Meela, but Katie remained stone-faced.

"Getting girls to relapse, that's kind of a new angle for you, isn't it?" Katie said with a smug, cold smile on her face. The question hung there for a minute of awkward silence, and at first Meela thought she was kidding. But the smile she cracked quickly faded after looking at both of our faces.

"Hey, Meela," a voice came from beside us. "Sorry if I'm interrupting anything, but do you want to go to the bathroom with me?"

It was Claire, coming in to save the day. She had always been one of my favorites in the group, and I felt like I could've kissed her. Meela nodded, with a nervous laugh, before standing up to follow her to the restroom. With her gone, I turned to face Katie.

"What the hell was that? You got to stop blowing up my spot. I really like Meela. She's a nice girl." This made her laugh.

"She IS a nice girl, and I'm just looking out for her. She said she only met you yesterday, and she likes you a lot. Don't make her a one night stand, Burlington."

"I like her. . . a LOT," I repeated slowly. "I haven't felt this way about someone since Blythe. . . hell. . . maybe even ever."

Katie's eyes widened slightly, "You mean that?"

"Of course I do."

"That makes me happy. We all really like her, dude. . . she BETTER come around again."

"She will, I promise."

When Katie nodded and went back down to the other end of the table, I took a sip from my drink and stared at the wall, instead of joining in a debate about something Corbin was in the middle of, his words getting quicker every second. The bar was far from a quiet space, with the sounds of pool balls cracking against each other and a dozen different drunk conversations whirling around the background. But Katie's words had affected me, and I could hear them over everything, tumbling around my brain despite my trying to pick them apart and push them down.

I really *did* like Meela, I could feel it. Somewhere beneath the physical attraction – and sexual compulsion – was a deep sense of connection and longing. She was more than just a girl, more than just a person. It seemed like whenever I saw her or had her in my thoughts, I would see through the body she wore and into who she truly was.

Just the thought of getting to discover more about her was intoxicating, and pulled me in further.

I slammed the rest of my drink and looked up, feeling uncomfortable with myself. Emotional introspection was never one of my strong suits, and often left me distant and numb when in company. Hoping to remedy this, I started for the bar to get another drink, but felt a tap on my shoulder.

"Hi," Meela said, as she lay her head on my shoulder and wrapped her arms around me from behind. "You weren't trying to get up, were you?" She giggled.

I slowly raised up my now-empty glass, "Well, I actually was going to get another drink. . . but you're making that difficult."

She giggled again and slowly slid off of my shoulder, "What. . . you're not even going to ASK to buy a lady a drink?"

I had turned around when her question stopped me dead in my tracks. "Uh. . . "

But she smiled and grabbed my hand. "Oh, come on Burly man. . . " she said playfully, ". . . a few drinks never hurt anyone! Like I said, drinking was never really my issue."

This made me smile. "I'm 'Burly man' now, huh?"

"Yup. . . just came up with it. Whatcha think?"

"Eh. . . I'm sure it'll grow on me." We both laughed.

Things were going smoothly. We made small talk about the crowd while we waited in line, and when we got to the counter I got two more rum and cokes. She ordered the same, but made them doubles, insisting that I had gotten ahead of her and that she needed to 'catch up'.

Walking back to the table we could see that the chairs had been pulled a few feet away and gathered into a large circle. The group was talking about some big casino trip they were trying to make next month.

We sat down in a pair of empty seats, and Meela kept nestling in closer and closer to me as the conversation progressed. When we finished our drinks and I offered to get our next round, she told me she wanted the exact same thing.

The line was a bit longer this time, but after four drinks I was definitely starting to feel the liquor. The rum was beginning to soften my edges and make the whole scene more enjoyable, so the wait didn't bother me as much. This time, I got back to the table to find no one there.

Looking around for a few seconds, I noticed the whole crew outside, playing that game with the bean bags and the slanted board with a hole in it. 'Corn-hole', I think Corbin had called it one time. As I sat all the drinks down on a table, Meela ran up to give me a hug and grab one of hers, announcing to me that I was on her team. We were playing against Claire and this guy Ben, who I had assumed was her date.

It was rough at first, my first few throws went wildly off target while everyone else playing seemed to score bag after bag. And the scoring didn't seem to make sense. But Meela understood it, so I just kept playing. After about fifteen minutes the game seemed to wind down; I had made a few, but Meela was really carrying our team. She was quite the 'Corn-hole' player, though she had just missed her last shot – an important one, she'd told me.

"You're up, Burly man…" she said, resting her hands on her head in a nervous pose, ". . . this is for the win." I took a deep breath and tossed a back-underhand at the wooden target. The throw felt nice leaving my hand; solid release, right amount of force, the bag wasn't spinning. It hit the front of the slope with a soft thud, and with a short slide went straight down the hole. Meela shrieked, grabbing my waist to whirl me around, and an instant later I felt her lips on mine.

She held me there for just a second, then pulled away to beam at me – before pulling me into a hug. My mind felt on fire, every single impulse and thought was overridden with a tingling warmth.

THE | SPLIT

Attempting to tune in to the world around me, I faintly heard Corbin congratulate me on the kiss, and joke to Meela about whether she was still sure about me.

I ignored him, continuing to hold on to her tight. My senses felt fried, running on half-power, yet everything seemed like it was right.

Until I saw him. A man in a leather cut, standing beside the bar, was staring directly at me through the glass window. I tried to focus, and look at his face and clothes more thoroughly, but the edges of my vision still seemed sluggish and unresponsive. As soon as Meela broke the hug, he disappeared back into the crowd.

Was I seeing things? Could a Den of Carnage member have seen her here? Had we been followed? The story of Meela and her run-ins with her ex-boyfriend's gang had admittedly induced a bit of paranoia, so there was of course the possibility that this was just a member of another club, or maybe even just a leather vest enthusiast.

I opted for the last of the three and tried to put any worries aside. Meela had just kissed me, and due to my nearly catatonic response, it might have been the best kiss I'd ever had.

I put my arm around her and joined a conversation already in progress. It was hard to talk, my thoughts felt cluttered as I tried to process the huge amount of emotional data I had just received all at once, but I preferred to listen anyway.

'That was amazing,' I thought to myself. 'But do I really think I'm ready for any of these feelings? What if I just quickly lose interest, and cast her aside. . . like Katie was saying? I can't even trust my instincts, they're always wrong...so I have nothing to go on here.'

My inner monologue raged back and forth behind my stoic smile, but then I felt Meela reach up and put her arm around me. Looking down at her as she looked up at me and smiled, my thoughts quieted.

T H E | S P L I T

"You want to finish these and go get two more? I'll probably be good after that, you got me pretty drunk. . . if that was your intention, job well done."

I laughed, and we walked over to the bar to once again wait in line. Now that she had mentioned it, I did a quick mental step back and realized that I too was quickly approaching drunk. We had been going here for ages, and they had poured my drinks stronger than usual for as long as I could remember. Every drink seemed closer to two, and I had drank seven.

We talked about how drunk we were feeling as we walked back to the table, sipping, and those drinks seemed to disappear in a matter of minutes, as I loudly planned an upcoming trip with Corbin. Both of us laughed as we insulted each other and discussed our ideas. Our interactions were always harsh, and neither of us were afraid to mock each other's deep personal issues. Most people found it comically off-putting, but Meela seemed to think it was the funniest and sweetest thing in the world.

Eventually though, her eyes began to droop, and she suddenly announced to the group that she was leaving, adding that she wanted to see them all soon. I quickly found myself saying something similar, feeling her pull my arm, but as I turned when she began to walk away, I heard Corbin whistle loudly.

It was something he had perfected; one of his many attempts to embarrass and trip me up over the years. But I smiled and followed Meela on through the bar and out of the front door, where she stopped at the curb and turned around to look up at me.

"So. . . I've had a really hard time sleeping alone. . . since Derek."

"The douchebag biker?"

"Uh huh," she nodded. "So. . . I've decided you're going to sleep with me and keep me safe tonight."

"Oh, you did?" I smiled at her.

"Yeah, get an Uber. . . where's your place?" her eyes were half open and her words were starting to slur – like mine had been for the last fifteen minutes. "We need to swing by mine first."

It was five minutes away, I told her as I got a ride on my phone., then lit up a cigarette, as we both sat on a nearby bench to wait for our ride. She told me that she would need to grab things she'd need for work in the morning, so when the blue Sonata pulled up, driven by a thickly accented Middle Eastern driver, Meela gave him directions to her house.

As it turned out, her place was really close by, and while she ran inside I talked to the driver about why he drove and what all he did. I found him fascinating; he had been a doctor at home in Pakistan, but had fled to America following some unspecified religious persecution. When he arrived here, he discovered he was unable to be a doctor, due to American regulations, so he was working as a nurse and driving on the side while trying to get his certification back.

I was wrapped up into the conversation, listening to him talk about his home and how ridiculous the American medical system was, when I saw dark figures at the corner of the street. They slowly moved into the view of the street light where I could see them; three bikers, now standing across the street from Meela's house.

The driver suddenly stopped mid-sentence, realizing my attention was elsewhere, and followed my eyes through the window. "You know deez men?"

"No, but I think they've been following the girl I'm with. . . she used to be involved with them."

T H E | S P L I T

"Bikers are trouble, boss. . . she needs to hurry up."

As if she'd heard him, Meela suddenly burst out of the door, carrying a small bag. Locking her front door she ran over to the car, kissing me on the cheek as soon as she got in. I told her about the bikers on the corner, who had now moved out of view of the street lamp. Her eyes widened, and she then described who they were perfectly, and wasn't shocked in the slightest when I confirmed it.

I began to wonder if her problem was worse than she had previously told me.

Looking back at us suspiciously, the driver quickly took off towards the address I'd given him earlier, when we were talking. We had just made it past a stop sign and were turning back onto the main street when I saw them. Three motorcycle headlights following right behind us.

"Ah shit," our driver mumbled, as I felt his foot tap down on the accelerator. The car burst forward, and we weaved in and out of traffic, with the bikes never too far behind. The navigation on the dash said we were 9 minutes away from my place.

The driver began nervously talking in Urdu, then Meela spoke a few words in the man's native tongue.

"You speak Urdu?" I raised my eyebrows in surprise.

"A little," she nodded.

"What did you say?"

"Is that important right now, Burl?"

"No," I admitted. "Just curious."

She sighed, "I told him that we wouldn't let him get hurt."

But we were a little more than halfway when we heard even more engines than before, and looked back to see three more bikers drive into the formation, just in front of the previous three.

Meela narrowed her eyes, craning her neck to get a better look. "*Dammit*," she swore. "It's Derek!"

I looked at the one in front that she seemed to be staring at. He had the biggest bike, and he was the biggest one in the group. Long brown hair, with no shirt under his cut, and covered in tattoos. He looked, by every metric, exactly like his reputation.

When he got to the front of the group, they began to close the distance quickly, riding with reckless abandon, going between cars, on top of the lane lines, even using the shoulder to pass other drivers, and eventually surrounded the car on both sides. The driver hugged the lines on the middle lane then, as the exit approached on the right, he suddenly sped up and at the last minute cut across two lanes onto the exit, forcing the bikers to slow down and merge behind a slow-moving semi.

Now, I tapped him on the shoulder; "Turn here, on Elm."

"But, this is not your street."

"I know, just do it." He fish-hooked into the neighborhood without slowing down. "Here," I tapped him on the shoulder again. "Pull over, and kill the lights." The car came to a screeching halt, and the driver turned off his lights before parking along the curb. "There you go," I handed him a twenty dollar bill, "Sorry I don't have more. Wait here for a moment, and then leave when you feel safe." He mumbled his agreement as Meela and I stepped out of the car.

"Stay right behind me," I cautioned her in a low tone as I crossed the street. We were going to cut through the alley of my across-the-street neighbors; it was dark, and I had used it before in a similar circumstance.

THE | SPLIT

As I led her off of the driveway and into the alley off the side of the house, I could hear the motorcycles rumbling all throughout the concrete alleyway, the sound reverberating off the concrete making it hard to hear from where. But they weren't far off.

Finally at the end of the alley, I threw a hand up to stop Meela. Just in front of us was a light fixture hanging off the corner of the house. The rumbling from the bikes appeared to be coming from all directions now.

After looking both ways at the road in front of my house, I grabbed her hand and we sprinted through the neighbor's yard and onto the street; headlights hit us as the bikers turned the corner, blinding me and sending a chill down my spine.

Meela screamed, I quickened my pace, bolting towards the house. Looking over my shoulder at the lights, I saw that there was just one; they had split up.

Dammit Burl.

Once inside, I immediately shut the door behind us, bolting both deadlocks, but I could hear honking and hollering from the man outside as the other engines seem to get closer. Meela's breathing quickened as she listened with me, and I threw an arm around her, taking my Kimber out of my waist band to set it on the table by the front door.

As I moved up to look out of the peephole and monitor the situation, she began to stammer out the truth. "I'm s-so sorry I got you into this." Her breathing was rapid and shallow, and tears began to roll down her face, "He's legit crazy. . . you need me to talk to him, to stop all of this. Everything I told you was the truth. . . but I left out some of the craziest stuff. He still has his guys following me. . . he's even had the president of the club harass my parents and sister. He's obsessed with me, and I can't get rid of him. . . and now I've brought him on y-y-you."

The situation seemed to be worsening near the street. All six of the

T H E | S P L I T

bikers were now outside, and Derek was on the phone, yelling about something and gesturing wildly.

"I c-can. . . " Meela spoke up, seeming to slowly regain her composure, "I can fix this, I promise. Let me go out there."

"No, Meela. You've told me what he's like, and we both know what he'll do to you. I'm going to watch outside, and if tries to come in here we call the police. Okay?"

"Okay. . . but what if –" She was interrupted by the ringing of her phone. She looked down, and turned pale. "It's him."

"Do you want me to answer it, Meela? I will."

"No," she shook her head, taking a deep breath before tapping it to answer. Angry-sounding, muffled tones caused her to hold it away from her ear. Derek was screaming into the phone. "Derek..." she closed her eyes and sighed, "Why are you here?"

"He's someone I met at AA. We went out afterward. He's nice, and I like him."

"Who cares what you think about that? Why would I give a shit about anything *you* think about anyone in my life?"

"**You** are the worst part of my life, Derek! Leave me and my date alone."

"You know what? He **is** a date, and I don't care how you feel about that."

"*No* Derek, you need to leave. . . I- I-" She put her hand over the phone and turned to me, "He's not letting me talk."

"Give it to me," I said firmly. She reluctantly put the phone in my hand. I put my ear to the receiver;

"-and Meela, I don't CARE what dates you want to have. You belong to the club, to the family! You know all the things we did for you!"

THE | SPLIT

"Derek," I spoke up, stopping him mid sentence. "This is Burlington."

"Oh, so she puts **you** on the phone now?"

"Derek," I repeated, "I don't know what happened in the past, but you need to leave now."

He let out a snort of laughter, "Is that right?"

"If you don't leave my property, I'll be calling the police."

"The police?!" He laughed even harder. "We both know that they won't be here in time to help you, bitch. Me and my boys can kick your door in and be out of here before you even hear sirens."

"Derek, if you come into my home illegally, I'll have the right to defend myself." Silence followed for several seconds.

"Do what you have to *Burlington*." He hung up the phone, and I handed it back to Meela before going back to look through the peephole.

"They're going to come in, Burl! They'll take me. . . and kill you if you try and stop them."

I took a few deep breaths, before responding in a low voice, "Meela, I need you to dial 9-1-1 and explain the situation." She quickly typed the numbers in on her phone, and within seconds was talking to an Emergency Operator, in a steady but nervous tone. While she told them the story, I walked over to the front coat-closet and opened the door. Inside was my pride and joy, the shotgun I had been building onto since my 19th birthday. I took the hard plastic case off, leaving the two halves on the closet floor, and began to unzip the canvas covering.

My Saiga 12 was the best thing I had, for a military-style weapon, with picatinny rails above and below. I had replaced nearly everything in the original design – to better accommodate my own shooting style; from the lightweight carbon fiber stock, to the red dot sight and raised end fin, was all my own. I had even bought several higher capacity drum

THE | SPLIT

magazines, which were devastating. I could spray 16 rounds in just under 19 seconds with the Saiga's quick semiautomatic fire.

Meela had just finished on the phone, and I looked back at her, "You told me you can shoot, can you use this if I showed you how?"

"Y-y-yes," she stammered. I handed her the pistol, and she adjusted her grip while I showed her how to operate the safety, pulling the slide back to chamber a round.

BOOM! The sound of the door being pounded on echoed through the front entry way; they were going to try and break it down.

I grabbed Meela by the hand and pulled her through the hallway, turning left into the living room and leading her behind my couch. "Stay behind me, and keep your head down. We're going to be fine."

She nodded, lowering herself behind cover, both hands on the grip of my pistol. A second loud crash resounded through the house, mixed with the unmistakable sound of wood splitting. The door wasn't going to make it much longer, and part of me wondered what they were doing to break it down so quickly.

Derek's voice echoed through the hallway – he was screaming so loudly I could make out every word clearly, even from my living room. "I KNOW YOU'RE TRYING TO FUCK MY GIRL! SEND HER OUTSIDE, AND WE'LL LEAVE YOU ALONE. FORGET THE WHOLE THING EVER HAPPENED. SOUND GOOD?"

I took a few steps into the hallway – able to now see that there were large cracks on the door near the top and sides of the frame – and calmly but firmly met his voice. "Derek, you need to leave. Meela doesn't want to see you anymore, the police have been called, and I'm armed."

"WRONG ANSWER, BITCH! I'M GOING TO COME IN THERE, BLOW OFF BOTH OF YOUR KNEECAPS, TAKE HER IN RIGHT FRONT OF YOU

THE | SPLIT

AND THEN LET MY BOYS SMASH YOUR FUCKING FACE IN! POLICE AREN'T GOING TO SAVE YOU!"

The third impact shook the house, cracking the wood along the top of the door completely. In the next few hits he would be inside.

I looked down, taking a few more deep breaths and ignoring Meela's loud breathing behind me, then slid the safety on my shotgun into the off position, clicking the drum into its spot on the receiver. The weight of the situation suddenly hit me.

This was real. This wasn't drunk-talk at a bar, and it wasn't a fight behind the school. My whole life I had picked fights, just playing a soldier. I had attempted to be one, but I wasn't now; my mind raced with the impact of taking a life – and the thought of losing my own. This was combat. It didn't matter how many drills I had run, or how many brawls I had been in, this was a feeling I had never had.

My hands were steady, but beneath the surface my nerves twitched uncomfortably, feeling almost like an itch beneath my skin. My thoughts were no better; while a small part of my mind thought of escape plans, and ideas to keep the bikers at bay, the rest of my head was clouded with fear that surrounded and tainted my thoughts.

I tried to push all this down, and to keep my mind empty.

CRACK!

The door was off and I heard it slam on the floor in the hallway as they thundered in.

"Alright *Burlington*... WHERE ARE YOU?!"

I retreated a few steps in the living room, looking over at Meela to make sure she was behind cover. She had my Kimber out, with her finger around the trigger, and was leaning to the left of me.

"Derek," I called out, hearing their footsteps get closer, "don't come around this corner. It doesn't have to happen like this, you can go home."

I heard the whole crew stop for a second, and then laugh harshly, but I pressed on; "I will repeat...if you come around this corner I will shoot. You are trespassing in my house, and I have the right to fire."

"Heh, FUCK YOUR RIGHTS!"

I took a deep breath, and looked up to see Derek and another man round the corner.

T H E | S P L I T

IV

LGPB://mn34/con/terra/GM, 8721
(Translated)

Central Ohio; 2017

They fired first, the pistol's pop ringing through the whole duplex. My response was fluid; I ducked my head behind the sight and squeezed the trigger. The sound deafened me, leaving me in a confusing world of high pitched ringing and muffled sounds. I didn't think he had hit me, but I had definitely hit both of them; both men were on the floor, covered in blood. I saw Derek roll to the other side of the hallway, holding his stomach. I knew I had hit him, but he had apparently avoided most of the buckshot. A third man staggered into sight, and I fired twice, watching him fall back and slump against the wall, dropping a gun to his side.

The last three men stayed behind the corner. My eyes darted from side to side as I watched the narrow walkway. Two of them weren't getting back up, but there were three more, and I could hear Derek screaming from the other side.

"TRAVIS, KILL 'EM BOTH! I'LL GET YOU MEELA! ARGHHH!"

Then from around the corner, I saw a hand holding a pistol, now firing at me blindly. Soon the others were doing the same. I threw myself to the ground behind the couch, pulling Meela with me.

When I heard a break in the fire, I popped up and aimed at the hand holding a gun. I shot twice, tearing a chunk through the drywall and being rewarded with a sharp scream. When Meela grabbed my arm, pulling me back behind cover, squeezing me tight with her nails, I threw her off of me – causing deep scratches in my arm.

THE | SPLIT

But the pain I could feel wasn't coming from my arm, where I expected. Instead, it was my leg. I looked down to see the side of my pants had been torn open, exposing a long, bloody wound. Deprived of most of my hearing and in the throes of a single-minded adrenaline rush, my pain was in the background, so the sight of my own blood brought forth no fear, only anger. When there was a sudden stop in the hail of bullets coming from the corner and a frantic, muffled conversation was followed by clicking noises, I was filled with a brief clarity of mind and, emboldened by the silence and lack of gunshots, stood up and charged towards the walkway.

Rounding it shoulder first, I went right into the path of three wide-eyed bikers and jerked my shotgun up to near the first one's head. He caught the barrel, wrestling with it against his shoulder, then Derek screamed behind me, and I turned to see him slowly start to raise his gun. Even as the man I had my gun on slowly pushed the barrel down off of his shoulder, shots roared out from the other direction; the other bikers were trying to shoot past him. I lurched backwards, stomping down and trapping Derek's gun against the ground then, remaining in a lowered stance, tore my gun from the other man's hands and brought the stock down from my shoulder to my hip, firing 8 times.

The cloud of pellets carved through the first man and into the two behind him, like they were made of paper, leaving behind a visceral scene of gore and mutilation as blood sprayed out in every direction, covering the walls and floor.

Derek suddenly grabbed my leg and hit me at the joint of my knee with a fist. I pushed back, bringing my knee to a right angle, intending to kick him in the face, but his hand was freed, and he brought his pistol up for the kill shot. I was faster shooting, again – and was immediately splattered with blood from my face to my chest.

T H E | S P L I T

Bringing the shotgun down to one side I wiped at my eyes, through blood-smeared vision seeing what was left of Derek's head gushing out of the top of his neck, and cried out with some mixture of ecstatic celebration and relief. My muscles felt tense, and I could feel the blood everywhere, on my face and in my hair, like it was crawling over my skin. It had also covered most of the corridor walls, and formed in puddles half-an-inch thick around my shoes.

Just then the thought of my girl rushed into my mind. Meela - she was my girl. And in the clarity of this bloody aftermath, I knew there was nothing in eternity I wanted more. Walking over to the couch, I could hear her whimpering and knelt to her.

"Ssh..." I consoled, laying down and wrapping an arm around her. "It's okay baby. No one can hurt us now." But she cried out in pain, and recoiled at my touch. Then I felt the warm, wet spot on her chest and my blood ran cold; she had been hit.

Carefully, I pushed down on her shoulder and waist to roll her onto her back so I could see. A dark red spot was seeping through her shirt, centered around her stomach. I felt the tears coming hot and heavy, as my initial shock turned to desperate sadness. "Oh, Meela. . . baby. . ."

Weakly, she grabbed my chin and pulled me close to her face, saying in a breathy, hushed tone, "Burly Burl," a pained smile was on her face, "You saved me."

"No, I didn't." the tears continued to fall down my face.

She laughed softly, but I heard her breath catch as she strained, and there was blood in her mouth. "You r-risked your life, to save mine. . . and now, they can never hurt me again. I love you, Burlington. . . Oh god! I don't even know your last name!" She laughed, again forcing another pained breath. "We've only known each two days. . . but it doesn't matter. . . none of it matters. I never thought I would feel anything like this again, and even a day with you was worth it. I love you, Burly man and. . . "

She coughed, bringing blood to the surface which shot out of her mouth and hit me in the chin, then took a deep raspy breath, and her eyes stilled.

"*Meela. . .* It's going to be okay, 9-1-1 is on their way. Meela...MEELA!" I screamed her name, gently shaking her head, then put my ear to her heart, and then to her mouth. Nothing. She was gone.

My body felt numbed, as shock gripped me like a paralysis, while my brain seemed to split apart with a dull, throbbing pain in the back of my head. Then something inside of me broke as I forced myself to stare down at her stilled body, this girl who had become my everything, and in just a matter of hours was torn away from me. I realized that I had loved her, too.

I love you, Meela.

It was too much. I needed her back, that was the only thing that mattered, or ever could matter. I slammed my hands down onto the ground, ignoring the sharp pain that shot up my right arm as I did it again and again, bellowing towards the ceiling;

"**It's not fair !** The first time I get someone worth fighting for, and she gets torn away. . . in a DAY!" In my anguish, I cried out to whatever God or spirit could hear me; I needed a miracle, and my sorrow had suspended all disbelief. "I'm a prideful man. . . a wicked man. I don't believe in anything or anyone. I live my life for myself and deny the existence of anything greater. . . but if there **is** something greater. . . please! I ask not for myself, but for Meela. I love her. . . and would die for an eternity just to see her come back. I call out to *anyone. . . any thing. . .* that can hear my words. Bring her back, I'll pay whatever price!"

T H E | S P L I T

The tearing pain in my brain suddenly surged, nearly rendering me unconscious and causing me to scream out as I grabbed my head. Forcing my eyes open, I looked around the room in a daze; swirling red and white lights were surrounding the edges of my sight, and despite my trying to rapidly to blink them away they remained.

Then suddenly I heard a cough. Looking down through my obscured vision, I saw Meela gasp for air – and then her eyes jerked open. I rubbed at my own eyes, unsure that what I was seeing was real. It couldn't be.

But, she was back. . . something had heard me cry out!

Suddenly, the lights intensified and my vision was completely consumed, as something tore through my brain. I felt my consciousness leave my body, and then I got pulled through. . . something else.

T H E | S P L I T

V

Bought from A. Fila's Estate, 2094
-T. Acerz, 2131

Undetermined

Every part of my mind cried out in confusion. I was everywhere and nowhere, a collection of thoughts that had nowhere to go. I couldn't see where I was, or even feel my body and surroundings. My senses had left me. Trying to find some form of comfort with this new feeling, I forced my brain to slow down and tried to re-center my thoughts. It seemed my consciousness, or spirit, had separated from my body. I thought back to Meela, and the strange pulling I had felt in my living room. It had been seconds ago, but it had felt like a lifetime. Maybe it was a lifetime; time seemed a strange concept without a body to perceive it.

I thought back to my talk of a spirit, and what I had called out just an instant before. I had been a skeptic all my life, even confidently bragging to other people about it. I had **known** there was no life after death, or even anything supernatural. It defied all logic, and I thought it to be a crutch for slower and more dependent people. But I was past that now, and began to wonder if I had got it all completely wrong.

Was I dead? I remembered the strange lights, like a fiendish hallucination. There had been no pain, just disorientation. Did something happen to me? Was there another shooter?

Meela. She was alive! Bright energy seemed to rush through the strange space where my thoughts now roamed. I couldn't feel anything, but my mind seemed to crackle with flashes of happy images and positive feelings. I wished I could see her, to hold her, or even just to be around her again.

THE | SPLIT

Then pain entered my world again, as I began to regain feeling, and next my mind seemed to slam to a halt, as I suddenly came back into a body. Still, I was immediately grateful for the familiarity of my senses, and felt a small rush of confidence. Gone was the uncertainty of disembodiment, I was Myself again. Only focusing on what was immediately around me while my relief took hold, I glanced up, astonished to realize I was indoors.

I had come to a cavernous room, with rounded walls on both sides that stretched to the ceiling and the floor below, and I was standing on a long, platformed walkway which divided the tube shaped hallway in half. It continued as far as I could see, joining another section of the room. I looked down at the floor and slid my foot across curiously, not recognizing the material, but surprised to find it was almost friction-less.

"*Come.*"

The singular word rang out from deeper within the structure. I listened for it to repeat, but could hear no reverberation coming from the rounded walls. It then dawned on me that I hadn't *heard* it at all, the voice had appeared within my thoughts. I shuddered at this, but soon found myself walking towards the source. The friction-less path aided my walk greatly, and I moved at a brisk pace, somewhere between walking and jogging.

But as I went, I saw movement out of the corner of my eye. The walls were moving. I stopped and turned my body to look at them; how had I not noticed this? The walls emitted a sickly, green tone, glowing with what looked like images; a strangely moving footage beyond my comprehension, arranged in tiles that covered every inch of the walls' surface, no matter how far down I looked.

THE | SPLIT

Forcing myself to look away and avoid staring, I made my way down the platform and soon reached a crossroads, with four identical hallways going in separate directions. At last, I saw the first signs of life since arriving – though 'life' might be the wrong word; strange, black shapes hung in the air above me – and examined them in a state of trance-like shock.

They were like nothing I could even dream of; their outside was jet black, the top half of the 'body' looked slick, and possibly oily. It gave off a faint sheen, from the light of the glowing green walls. The bottom half was covered with mechanical tentacles, perfectly fused to its body. The tentacles appeared metal, but the gleam coming from the covering seemed foreign and hard to place. I focused on the appendages, and noticed the work they were doing; something to do with the wall, tapping and rotating the tips of its various grippers and probes with a dexterity that defied artifice.

Slowly, I walked underneath and past the strange drones, hearing odd noises. There seemed to be a high pitched beeping coming from the bottom of each shape. The skin of the creatures seemed to morph as I got nearer, shimmering and pulsating around the metal legs in a ripple effect, and as it moved around in waves I heard a faint sound that sounded like the wet crunching of food being chewed. I quickened my pace down the platform and past the bizarre life forms.

"*Come...*" Again the voice rang through my head, seeming to come from the left hallway even as it echoed through my mind. It unnerved me to hear things this way, I had always trusted my senses entirely but, having been robbed of that certainty, I felt incredibly vulnerable.

The new hallway was almost identical to the first, but instead of going straight, it began to bend to the right, obscuring what was beyond, but as I rounded the curve in the platform I saw another crossroads.

T H E | S P L I T

Then I was briefly blinded by bursts of white light. The presence was stronger in my mind now, and I felt my brain strain with the weight. I had begun to lose control; my thoughts swirled with images and sounds, and I felt the raw filter of my mind being torn through by the invader.

Focusing on certain unrelated memories helped the speed of the flickering images to slow, but I had no way to shift my thought pattern. This time the searing pain seemed to radiate from my forehead and back into my brain, and I fell to my knee, but though my vision slowly cleared, a strange touch started to curl around my thoughts. Getting to my feet, I limped towards the next path, holding the sides of my head tightly.

Every impulse in my head straining, but I tried to regain my capacities as I continued to press forward. Now an even brighter flash of light covered my sight, and the presence strengthened; I seemed to feel it wrap even tighter around my mind, watching and analyzing my thoughts and memories. I could now also feel its own, but this mind I felt was no mind at all; thoughts, and nothing more. No instinct, no feeling.

But I did suddenly feel a keen interest, one that I somehow knew wasn't coming from me. It had found something it wanted. The speed of the filter suddenly accelerated, faster than I thought possible. Images and sounds blinked through my head faster than I could comprehend, and the foreign sense of interest again grew, soon settling into what resembled satisfaction.

I had made it to the middle of the crosswalk, and now the familiar pain again shot through the top of my neck. I felt my body jerk to the right to take a clumsy step down the platform; it was moving me.

But I still had some control, and quickly tightened my pace into my regular stride, though I could feel it fighting me, pulling forward at my legs, wanting me to move faster. Its grip over my nervous system now loosened, but the onslaught in my thoughts continued, and my space of mental visualization suddenly expanded to a strange depth as the reel of blinking pictures moved to the background, and a collection of memories leaped to the front of my thoughts, smothering my mind's eye and forcing me inside:

I was 8:

Lying face down on concrete, I felt my nose press against the dusty ground, and a dull weight pinning me down. There was laughter heard all around me. It was Mike, a 12 year old who had been held back several times. He'd had it out for me since I'd made the whole bus laugh at his expense, one afternoon coming home. This hadn't been the first fight, or even the first beating. Mike had me by 5 inches, 50 pounds and 4 years, I had never stood a chance as his fists slammed into my neck and the back of my head. My face slapped against the concrete as he was pounding on me, and my vision blinked red.

Then something inside of me suddenly snapped.

I threw my head up and jerked my shoulders and back with a sudden burst of strength that bucked Mike off to my side, then sprang to my feet, looking around to see a loose ring of kids surrounding us in the back alley behind the cafeteria.

There was a silver garbage can near the wall. As Mike grunted, moving from his stomach to his knees, I walked over towards the trash bin, grabbing it by the handles. Strange feelings and adrenaline ran through my body as I lifted the heavy can to eye level, then smashed it down on Mike, who was now on his knees. It made a loud clang, and I watched him crumple to the ground before dropping the can. I was on him in just two long steps, planting my knees on his shoulders, my shins on his forearms, and leaning on him with all my weight, trapping

THE | SPLIT

his arms. He stared up at me with a look of terror on his face as I started swinging on him wildly.

My hands began to hurt, and my arms tired, but I brought my fists down again and again. After a hit to his nose my hands began to feel warmth as blood trickled out of his swollen nostrils. There were gasps from the children around me. I felt hot tears roll down my cheeks.

"Just leave me alone!" I shrieked, slowing down the speed of my punches.

The screech of a whistle shook me, and I looked up to see a shouting teacher running in my direction.

With a strain, I fought to pull myself out of the vision, but the presence remained consumed with watching my memory, and seemed not to notice my absence. I felt senses of amusement and curiosity, dark and alien to any feeling or experience I had ever felt. And though the memories no longer blocked my mental vision, I could still see them floating close to the front, side by side, and could make out every detail, like watching two of them unfold at the same time.

I was sitting in class.

Conversation shot back and forth all over the room as Mrs. Smith, our philosophy teacher, led a spirited debate about the recent occupation of a Middle Eastern country. The side for peace seemed to drown out all those who disagreed, until I angrily spoke up; "When a leader is doing violent things to his own people, the only way to get rid of him is through violence!" When a flurry of voices shot back at me I felt myself turn red, and began to yell back at them.

Another memory came into sight: *I was climbing, with my cousin. We had made it near the top of a cliff face, near my childhood home, when he suddenly lost his grip. Grabbing my ankle to keep from falling, tugging at my leg with urgency, he shouted, his voice trembling. "Pull* me up, Burl!" *I could feel his arm trembling, too...but I also could feel my grip slipping. I tried to slowly lift the leg he was hanging onto, but couldn't bend my knee much, as he gripped my calf and tried to pull himself up. My hands strained, and I felt them drop to where just my last digits were gripping the rock; the weight was too much. Making a decision, I flung my leg out, kicking to the right and to the left, and felt him let go. His screams echoed down the cliff, until I heard him land with a dull thud.*

My mind went dark as everything seemed to stop at once. Still walking, I paused and cautiously reached out, feeling my thoughts slowly settle back into place. The Presence was still there, but distant, watching me from the edge of my mind. Then in a rush, I felt my control return, and my thoughts seemed to collide together as the newly freed parts of my brain all cried out at once. *'What the hell just happened?' 'Who is this in my head?' 'I need to get out of here!'* which only made my mind a confusing jumble.

I closed my eyes tight, forcing my thoughts to clear, and eventually a train of conscious observations – and a small stream of questions – was left. I felt like myself again. Then my foot jerked forward; I followed the queue and walked, quickening my pace with anticipation.

T H E | S P L I T

VI

LGPB://mn34/con/terra/GM, 8721
(Translated)

Undetermined

The hallway ended in a massive room, forcing me to stop and marvel at its size. The walls were the same, still green and moving, but I could see no ceiling or floor, there was only the platform I was on. Looking down the path, I saw that the walkway appeared to widen, then drift towards the center of the bottomless room.

It was stadium sized, at least, I racked my brain to compare it to some of the bigger ones I had been in, and found the comparison appropriate. The presence lifted from my brain, though I felt it express a twisted sense of amusement as I looked up. Then, I saw it. In the center of the room, in the middle of a large circular platform, it sat; a pale, white figure, seeming almost reptilian in features.

It was probably 40 feet tall, higher than my three-story high school building. The skin appeared to be smooth. Its head was flat and curved, and the sides flared out from the neck to the top of its head; like a cobra. There were no eyes, but I could see a rounded bump of – what looked like – a nose, with a small, open slit slowly moving in rhythm, and although it looked like a face I knew I was most likely wrong; everything I'd ever known was irrelevant now. A pair of massive forearms ran under a strange cover, which looked like black clothing laced with wires coming out of its seat.

I felt its presence brush against my mind, but it didn't enter, instead remaining at the threshold, observing me. Tearing my eyes away from the Being and its seat, I glanced around the room, feeling my body flush

T H E | S P L I T

with anger and confusion.

"What the hell is this place?!" I shouted at it from across the platform. I was surprised to hear no echo, but kept bellowing harshly as I moved towards the center, some of the words catching in my throat. "Who the hell are you. . . why am I here? Why are you in my head?!"

The strange Being continued to study me, its feeling of amusement still clear behind shielded thoughts, then it gestured up. I followed its hooked hand, to see a mass of the black drones I had watched in the hallways, hovering above its head in a ring. A number of them surrounded the creature's arm as it brought it down in front of its face, and a strange, green field of mist was dispersed around them. I could hear noises; mechanical grinding, and words from a harsh and bizarre language; Alien tones that were impossible to decipher.

"Hey asshole," I resumed walking down the platform, "Either answer my questions, or just kill me right here. . . because – "

the Being stopped me mid-sentence, with a bolt of pain as it lodged inside my mind. Twisting and burrowing, it wound its way deeper and wider through my thoughts, wrestling for control of my head, much more roughly than the first time. Blinded by the pain, I collapsed to my knees and released my hold. The presence withdrew, in the same rough fashion, my attention now fully secured.

"The gift has been given, the price will be paid."

Its words were a low rumble, hollow and ancient, but also deep and poisonous. I felt the simple sentence bounce around my mind like an echo, every syllable seeming impossible to forget and refusing to be quieted.

"What gift?" I shouted incredulously, gesturing around the room. "This place. . . is this my gift? Being taken from my home, and the woman I love. . . to come here?"

THE | SPLIT

The Being scratched at his massive chair with a single flick of its pale wrist, illuminating a panel near the arm rest, and the drones he had summoned ascended back into the ring above him. Ignoring this, I continued my tirade, "Are you this gift? Did I come here to get thought-fucked by a giant albino cobra with no face? Oh I'm **so** lucky! What a gift!"

I sensed a form of exasperation as the presence gripped my mind with an angry strength. It was dark, foreign, and terrifying to feel crawling over the outside of my brain. But this time I fought it, concentrating wholly on the black nothingness that clouded the space between my thoughts, then felt a tingling on my neck. But there was no pain, and though I felt it enter my movements, I did not bow or falter, standing defiant as shades of red anger now consumed my own thoughts and vision. This seemed to elicit a sense of humor from the presence.

"Well, if you have no answers, send me back. Or like I said, just kill me. My thoughts and my life are not yours to toy with."

My words were filled with a confidence my body seemed to lack; everything about this situation was a nightmare, but in my emotional exhaustion anger seemed to be at the helm.

"You, will have neither life nor death. The life you cling to has saved you from dying, yet you are a thing of death. . . you have no place among the living."

A gray cloud blinked into existence, surrounding me, obscuring my vision and forcing me to try and focus my eyes through the cloud of. . . I could say, tiny flakes; all moving rapidly.

Something was happening; my skin began to tingle, even as I felt my mind being pulled away from the presence, seemingly in every direction. Then, the tingling I had felt began to sting, and suddenly I felt a sharp tug backwards as my thoughts were once again pulled away,

THE | SPLIT

seeming to swirl through an infinite space, as though my brain called to different parts of a body no longer there.

It was a feeling I was sure I could never get used to but, having had even the brief experience from earlier made it easier to bear, so this time I tried to remain centered, avoid panic, and to recall everything I now knew about where I was.

I didn't have much to go on, but I was fairly certain I wasn't dead. The experiences from the green hallway had been too vivid to be a dream. And, though I had no control over where I was going, or maybe even what would happen to me when I got there, I had my mind – a blessing I was careful to not overlook.

I began to think of Meela, and my mother, and felt a sense of sorrow and fear which was quickly covered by hot flashes of anger at my predicament.

How had I gotten here? Where was I going?

The answer to both questions would soon be apparent; I felt my mind sharply 'brake', and then it again pulled itself into a body, making me recoil in shock. My nerves felt numb and unfamiliar. My face had the itch of a mustache, slightly swaying in a faint wind. My arms felt stunted and heavy and, although my eyes were shut I could hear loud, booming sounds around me.

Opening my eyes, I gasped with horror.

This body wasn't mine.

THE | SPLIT

VII

This is a confusing, conflicting pair of pages, bought from Father Gabriel. I believe the alternate series of events could have historically played a part in "The Moment", and other possible quantum theories and unexplained events. - A. Fila

LGPB://mn34/con/terra/UY, 9065

(Translated)

Unnamed Entry

They fired first, the pistol's pop ringing through the whole duplex. My response was fluid; I ducked my head behind the sight and squeezed the trigger. The sound deafened me, leaving me in a confusing world of high pitched ringing and muffled sounds. I didn't think he had hit me, but I had definitely hit both of them.

"Burl!" The voice came from behind me as I charged towards the wall. Sliding the last few feet to guard the walkway, I turned around in confusion. Meela had vaulted the couch, and was running towards the other side of the wall, my gun at the ready. "There's three on the right!" she pointed behind her. We were now parallel, on both sides of the open door to the walkway of my living room.

She was right; my mind quickly worked to analyze the scene. There was a small group coming towards me, I had to act quickly. "Meela!" I stood up, raising the shotgun to my hip as I stepped through the archway, finger on the trigger. "What the hell are you thinking? Get down!"

"Burl, no! Derek!"

Sound came at me from all directions; Meela's scream to my right, the sound of gunshots behind me, a pistol's pop coming towards me. . . But I was the finale. I pulled the trigger seven times in succession, and

THE | SPLIT

the men in front of me split apart like paper. Their bodies collapsed onto the ground in unison, landing in a pool of blood and soft flesh that was expanding every second with the blood pouring from the three fresh corpses.

My mind still in a state of razor sharp focus, I stepped through the pile of dead men towards the door, to ensure that the last of our enemies had fallen.

"B-Burl. . . " Meela's faint voice came the entryway to the living room.

Satisfied that we were alone, I turned back around to go to her – and nearly jumped in shock. Derek, whom I had assumed dead, was now sitting upright, gun in hand. I raised my gun to my shoulder, and nearly pulled the trigger before I saw the hole appear between his eyes, where the bullet had gone through.

Laughing uneasily, I lowered the shotgun to my side, calling out, "Meela?" as I returned to the living room. "Did. . . you shoot Derek? Holy hell, what a shot! I-" My blood ran cold when I saw her. She was sitting on the floor, her back to the wall, slumped over. The pistol lay between her out-sprawled legs, and blood dripped onto the floor from her upper abdomen. Her breath seemed to come in shallow gasps as she looked up at me, wincing painfully, but she was doing her best to smile.

"Y-yeah," she replied, laughing weakly. "That was quite a shot. . . saved your life, Burly man."

"Meela. . . " I looked around in disbelief, watching as the blood began to stain the carpet below her, "...you're hit."

"Really?" she looked down, feigning surprise, again grimacing in pain as she tried to adjust the way she was sitting. "I hadn't noticed. It hurts, but I think I'll be okay."

"We need to get you an ambulance."

T H E | S P L I T

"No!" she suddenly protested. "Listen. . . " Pointing up, she turned her neck to the side. "Do you hear that?"

I paused to listen for what she was talking about, and soon understood.

It was faint but unmistakable; the sound of motorcycles in the distance, growing closer. "What do we do now?" I looked at her for answers, adrenaline continuing to course through my bloodstream as I considered this second risk to our safety.

"You'll have to take me to the hospital yourself, and quick, they'll be here any minute."

Meela had been right about the severity of her wound; though the bleeding had yet to stop, the entrance and exit from the round were small compared to similar ones I had seen in the past, and within the torn flesh there was no sign of shattered bone. The location of the injury seemed fortunate as well; just above her hip and below her stomach, so the bullet appeared to have missed all of her organs entirely. She grabbed a nearby blanket, and wrapped it tightly around her wound with my help. I took the Kimber from her and tucked it into my waistband then, slinging the shotgun around my shoulder by its strap, picked Meela up as gently as I could.

In the front hall near the front door, I paused to open the closet with my free hand, being careful with her as I retrieved a messenger bag from the back corner and slung it around my opposite shoulder. I was considerably weighed down, and strained with every step out of my front door, but went as quickly as I could march towards my waiting car.

"Burl?" I heard a voice as I opened up my backseat, clumsily laying Meela down flat, then setting the shotgun and bag on the floor below her. Jim was standing behind me, his eyes wide in bewilderment.

THE | SPLIT

"Burl, we heard gunshots and we—"

"Jim," I put a hand up to silence him. "Go inside, lock your doors, and call the police. . . don't open your doors until you hear sirens outside."

He opened his mouth to reply, but thought better of it and nodded before turning around and going back to his side of the duplex.

The motorcycles were getting closer. I paused before getting inside of my car, trying to judge if they had made it into the neighborhood yet, racking my brain to think of a way through that would keep me clear of these new pursuers.

But while pondering it I got inside my Chrysler, firing up the engine and pulling out of the narrow drive in a nearly fluid motion. Weaving my way through the narrow alley, I pulled out my phone and dialed Corbin, reaching into the backseat to take Meela's hand in mine while the ringing sounded repeatedly.

'Come on buddy,' I thought, *'Pick up. . .'*

* * * * *

For the third time that hour, I turned on my car to let down the window, trying to stop listening for the sounds of the motorcycle engines which had remained in the back of my mind since leaving my house. Doing my best to ignore the shooting pain in my right shoulder, I moved my head over by the vents, taking a deep breath of the cool air blowing just above the steering wheel, then closed my eyes as I felt the chill make its way down my face.

It had been Meela's idea to drive all the way to Jeffersonville for treatment. Doing her best to remain conscious during the drive here, between grunts of pain she had told me about the Club's reach of influence. Had we stayed in town, the Den of Carnage with their many members would have found us.

T H E | S P L I T

At first, it hadn't been easy to convince Corbin to take me seriously. He'd sounded belligerently drunk when I called, and had brushed away my frantic phone call for help as some form of elaborate prank. Only after I'd called him twice more, screaming through my phone's receiver, did he realize I wasn't joking.

He'd agreed to leave the bar without telling anyone where he was going, assuring me he was sober enough to drive the forty minutes to the Fayette County Memorial Hospital, and had been there when we arrived. After a quick and heated discussion in the parking lot, he'd agreed to take her inside the emergency room to get her care under a fake name.

While they were inside, I took care of my own injuries inside the car. I had stopped the bleeding earlier with the torn remains of a t-shirt from my floorboard, but the rest of the process was considerably more painful.

To start, I'd had to take my fingers into the wound, to make sure the bullet wasn't inside. Then, pulling out the necessary supplies from the top pouch of the bag I had brought from my closet at home, I'd taken a swig from the bottle of cheap vodka I kept on top, before pouring the rest on the raw and exposed gore. I'd had to wait to move past the pain before drying off the surrounding skin, then opening the package of QuikClot and placing the small towelettes against the wound entrance and exit.

Doing my best to keep an eye on the parking lot for any potential bikers, I'd at last sewed both lacerations shut with the small suture kit from the bag and, that done, had spent the next half hour using Corbin's phone – I'd tossed my own out of my Chrysler's window immediately after making contact with him, and he had given me his to use while he waited with Meela inside.

THE | SPLIT

Just minutes after attempting to log on to the Armed Forces database to see my current status, my worst fears were confirmed; my login wasn't working. A quick search engine query for my specific profile made me realize that all traces of my time in the Army were gone, though all other members of my unit, and my CO himself, were visible on the page. I had been removed completely – and I knew what it meant; 'Subject CL-7' had been officially disavowed.

Any attempt to link me to the project I had taken place in, or even to the military itself, would prove demonstrably false; in their own paperwork and even a court of law. I'd had my experience within a Classified Army experiment, and the Military had decided I would reveal that experiment's existence.

This was bad. Doubtless, they had been notified the moment officers arriving on the scene had run my address and revealed my former service. It wouldn't matter that the Den of Carnage was closer to my house than the police were, or that I would probably be declared innocent, in regular circumstances; I had committed murder, and even with the motive of self-defense, I had fled the scene. So right now I was likely wanted for questioning – and there would be an APB put out on my Chrysler.

As I surveyed the parking lot, I weighed out the options the Army had. The most humanitarian thing to do would be for them to simply take charge of the case from the local police, and bring me back onto active duty. They could also take charge of the case, forge a new set of credentials for my information – and this time, send me to a military prison. It seemed the likelier scenario.

Still, deep down I knew better. Several members of my former unit had been charged with violent offenses, ranging from domestic abuse to murder, and most of them had had their sentences waived by being

THE | SPLIT

called back up to Active duty. My friend Matt had been one of these. We'd met at a coffeehouse near base a few weeks after he had been fully reinstated, and he'd looked terrible; shaking in a way he never had before, eyes dark with heavy bags, and looking like he hadn't slept in days. But he'd warned me about what he called "The Debriefing"; a process he and the others had gone through, saying that two of the others had died. He'd refused to go into detail after that however, and had left only minutes afterward. I hadn't seen him since.

And as bad as that was, there were other possibilities which were worse. Since the chemicals and various Trials during Basic, my mentality had shifted; it had been easier to cast aside emotion, and be more objective when examining things critically – and I could not logically conclude a single, more efficient and convenient way than just killing me outright. The people in charge of my former Army program surely thought the same way

A loud tapping at my window nearly caused me to jump out of my seat. I looked over to see Corbin hunched beside me, motioning for me to roll the window down the whole way.

"Did I scare you?" he eyed me suspiciously as he poked his head inside the car. "Weren't *you* supposed to be guarding **us** ?"

"Seriously man?" I eyed him as I pulled out a cigarette from my pack in the console and lit it. "You're joking around, right now? Meela and I have BOTH been shot."

"I don't care," he smiled and motioned for me to hand him his phone. "I don't care what's happening, I will **always** joke around, and you can't take that from me. Isn't that your First Amendment, Mister Patriot? Big Burly Army-guy protecting the Constitution?"

I glared at him, and blew my smoke in his face. "Can you honestly not be serious for one second?"

T H E | S P L I T

"Speaking of 'being serious'. . . " he blinked the smoke out of his face, then took back his arm as he realized I wasn't handing him his phone. "You really shouldn't be smoking. Cigarettes are SERIOUSLY bad for you. . . as bad for you as that atrocious stitch job you probably did on that shoulder. . . and I'm SERIOUSLY surprised there isn't smoke coming out of your wound right now."

I punched him in the stomach lightly, "Jesus, Mary, and Neil Degrasse Tyson. . . you never know when to shut up."

He smiled, "Can I see my phone now?"

I handed it to him, "Look at this."

He stared down at the screen, confused. "What am I looking at?"

"That's my unit."

"Weird, I don't see you on here."

"Exactly."

I watched as he quickly put it together, "Holy shit, Burl. If that means what I think it means, you shouldn't be online with my phone."

This time, it was my turn to be confused. "Wait, why?"

"I know you threw your phone out, but who was the last person you called before you did that?"

"Shit!" I slapped my head in frustration, feeling like an idiot. My blood pressure began to rise as I realized that they knew where we were.

"Yeah, you're dumb," Corbin laughed. "Luckily for you, you have a best friend who isn't dumb. . . I turned off all location services and connected to the hospital's WiFi through some sketchy third party apps I've been toying with.

I punched at him again, this time harder. "You ass, you don't think I have enough going on in my head right now? Why do you have to scare me like that?"

THE | SPLIT

"I just wanted to remind you that I'm smarter and better than you, that's all." His face broke out into a huge grin, as he then opened my door, playfully returning my punch with one to the arm. "Come on, we need to go inside. They should be about done, nurse said I can go back whenever."

I got out of the car, and he continued to talk as he we started our long walk through the parking lot: "I was joking earlier, about you being a patriot. . . but damn," he gestured at his phone, still on the web page I had shown him. "I'll bet you're not a patriot anymore. I'm being serious when I say this. . . I don't think you can go back now."

"Yeah no shit," I rolled my eyes. "Even if that hadn't happened, we still have the biggest biker gang in the state looking for us. Corbin. . ." I stopped walking. After several seconds, he realized I wasn't behind him and walked back to me. When he came close, I put my hand on his shoulder and looked him in the eye. I had thoroughly measured my situation in the car.

My life as I had known it was over. Meela was the only thing that mattered to me now, and in the course of a single evening, my desire to keep her safe had become my sole purpose. I looked at my best friend, realizing that he was the only person who I could rely on. "Corbin. . ." I repeated, when his eyebrows raised at my silence, "I need to get out of here. Meela needs to get out of here."

"Well, duh. I-"

"No," I interrupted, putting a finger near his lips. "Listen. I've thought it out in every way that I could. We're leaving town tonight, right now. You and I are going to go into that hospital, make sure she's okay, and get her outside and into your car. . . you're going to need to drive us away from here buddy, I'm going to leave my car behind. There are also several things I'm going to need from you."

T H E | S P L I T

"Anything Burl. . . what do you need?"

His smile had disappeared, and I could sense in his eyes that he was now being completely serious with me.

"I need the survival kit from your trunk. . . and I'm going to need your Ruger-"

"Aw, no. . . not Bessie," he started walking forward again, but several seconds later sighed, "Okay fine. What else?"

"I'm going to need your grandpa's van."

This had been the one I had expected Corbin to hesitate on, but to my surprise, he didn't miss a beat; "That should be fine, sure."

Corbin's grandfather had been in a Home for the better part of a decade, but had purchased the van shortly before moving. He'd hardly driven it since. Corbin had it regularly serviced, and per his grandpa's customs and wishes, always kept the key above the mirror and the door unlocked.

Growing up, we'd sometimes visit him together, and had listened to him tell stories about the Korean War and his life as a stand up comic in the sixties. But as time passed, his mental condition began to deteriorate; and unfortunately for him it wasn't Alzheimer's or any of the types of dementia being cured through the work of Dr. Maddox Hill.

"Are you sure? I can pay you for part of it now. I have cash in my bag, and maybe I can pay for the rest of it later?"

"Forget it," Corbin shook his head; we were nearing the entrance. "You're going to need all of your money. I was actually about to suggest we stop by an ATM first. Oh wait. . . " he stopped me just before the front door, ". . . before we go in there I need to tell you the story I'm running with."

"What do you mean?"

T H E | S P L I T

"Well, when we got in there, Meela was in pretty bad shape, and so when they asked her what her name was, she actually said it. Luckily, they only caught her last name 'Vasquez', and I told them her first name was Amanda."

"Good catch," I nodded. "Wait, her last name is Vasquez?"

"That's exactly what I thought!" Corbin exclaimed quietly. "She definitely doesn't look like a 'Vasquez'. Fortunately for us, I used that last name to come up with an angle to get you in there to talk to her."

"Oh, this will be good."

Corbin ignored me, "I told them that I was just a friend, but that her brother is on the way. I hope you don't mind, but I already filled out the details of this brother character for you. His name is Juan, he doesn't speak much English and he hates hospitals. Like it?"

He stared at me in silence for a couple of seconds to gauge my reaction, but then continued anyway, "It doesn't matter if you like it, because that's what I told them."

". . . so you just went straight to the top shelf with this racist caricature, huh?" I happened to be nearly fluent in Spanish, a fact he knew and exploited constantly

"Don't put that on me," his eyes widened above his smile. "Besides, I've had more dates with Mexican guys than a Laredo courthouse. I can't be racist.'"

"*Wow*," I mouthed, as I motioned for him to lead the way inside.

The nurse up front greeted him as "Mr. Queer"; he smiled back at me as she led us through the lobby and back into the hospital itself. Corbin giving himself the name "Mr. Queer", or "Mr. Fagg" to strangers had been a running gag between us since he had first come out. I shook my head as I walked down the linoleum hallway; this had been the most

T H E | S P L I T

intense and frightening ordeal in my entire life, and he hadn't stopped goofing off since he had gotten here.

Still, although my emotions were in a constant state of flux, deep down I appreciated it greatly. I felt if I was left in my head too long, I might have gone crazy. Corbin's style of Gallows humor had kept me from snapping.

The nurse led us through the first wing and down another, then past a large, round reception desk where a wall of clear glass separated off into different rooms. We soon reached a new section of wall, where the rooms weren't visible from the outside, and she stopped us in front of it, turning to Corbin and pointing at me; "This is the brother, I assume?"

Corbin looked at me and nodded, and I cocked my head before patting my chest, *"Hermano? Sí."*

"Well sir," she motioned to Corbin, "I'm going to need you to wait outside. Family only, past this point." Corbin nodded, and stepped back as the nurse opened the door for me, before she also stepped back.

I paused and took a deep breath, preparing myself for whatever would come next, then moved to open the door to Meela's room. It was small. The bed in the center was hooked up to an IV, and several machines I didn't recognize. Meela was resting in the center of it, her torso slightly raised by the curve of the adjustable bed. Her eyes were closed, her curls less perky than they had been, even in the car hours before. She wore a thin blue hospital gown, and I could see a set of wires running down from the neck-opening to one of the machines. But she was beautiful, like an angel with broken wings. She lie there peacefully, her skin glowing slightly beneath the fluorescent lighting.

Then I felt a tap on my shoulder, and nearly jumped in surprise when I turned to see her doctor standing beside me. I had been so focused on Meela I hadn't noticed much else. "Mr. . . . ?"

"Vasquez," I said quickly, building upon my lie.

"Ah, Mr. Vasquez," he looked down at a clipboard. "It's nice that she has family here with such late notice. Before you speak with her, I feel it's prudent for me to update you on her diagnosis."

"*Sí.*"

He spoke slowly, accommodating for my imaginary language barrier, and waiting for me to nod that I understood every few sentences.

"Like I told her friend earlier, the bullet missed all vital organs. It did do some damage to the area around her kidney, but we were able to remove the fragments and stop the internal bleeding. I can say with fair confidence that there shouldn't be any long-term damage. . . but, she needs to take it easy. Her kidney won't be operating at full strength until the area heals. She'll need to stay hydrated and avoid any alcohol, or other such pollutants -"

"But she going to be fine?" I interrupted in my best accented English, nearly slipping up and silently cursing Corbin for this character I was supposed to be playing.

"It looks that way, yes." He was a patient man. "She'll need to take it easy for a few days, but she should be able to mostly recover tonight."

"Thank you, doctor. If you no mind, I speak with her alone?"

"Of course." He turned and left the room, closing the door behind him softly.

I walked over to Meela's bed; my face felt hot, and my breathing was quick – shallow. Her arms were to her sides, palms upward. Slowly, I slid my hand over towards her, taking her hand in mine gently, and ever so faintly felt her fingers curl around mine, bringing a bright smile to my face. Her eyes cracked open, two brilliant blue orbs behind heavy lids, and she smiled, sending chills down my body.

T H E | S P L I T

"You came..." she whispered.

"Well of course," I grinned. "I'm the one who brought you here, remember?"

She let out a weak chuckle, her chest rising only the littlest bit. "Something... happened, Burl."

"Uh, yeah..." I replied. "You got shot." She opened her eyes a little wider, to roll them.

"Something besides that, dummy."

"What happened?"

"It was... as I lost consciousness. The last thing I remember... I was looking up at you, and I had a terrible pain in my side. Then, I was... gone... in a place unlike any I had seen before. Something saved me. Burl. Something I can't even describe... unlike anything in the world. It saved me because of you, Burl, because of something you did. I know it sounds silly, but I can feel it. And... wherever I went, it made me stronger."

"Stronger?"

"Yes, even in this hospital bed I can... feel, more. I can think about more. My body is stronger... than it has ever been. But, that's not all, Burl... you're going to think I'm crazy, but... I died. The time I'm talking about... where I was brought somewhere else... was in your living room. When I came back, the moment seemed to repeat itself. I was behind the couch, once again... but this, time I didn't cower in fear. This time I helped you, I saved you, even. It was like... the first time that I had been shot never even happened. This time, I was shot by a different person, in a different place, in a different spot in your living room."

"That's probably just the drugs, baby," I patted her on the head.

"No!" she blurted, sitting up slightly. "It's something more. I'm telling you Burl, this *happened*. It's almost like. . . time itself went back, and gave me another chance. And this. . . moment. . . it made me into more than I've ever been. It. . . ugh, this is so hard to explain. But, baby. . . when I was in that place, there were whispers everywhere, but I could only hear one word. . . 'run'."

"Run. . . where?"

"It doesn't matter. But we need to run, Burl. The police must know about what happened by now, and Derek's club is a lot bigger than just those few men at your house. They're looking for us too. We're not safe here."

I smiled, glad she had come to the same conclusion that I had. "I think you're right Meela. It was smart, getting out of town. . . but they'll find us eventually. The sooner we get out of here the better. Can you walk?"

She lowered the guard-rail on the side of the bed, and pivoted her body towards me, slowly placing her feet on the ground. After pulling the two sensors off of her chest and laying them on the bed, she pointed, saying; "Grab my clothes from the chair behind you." but as I turned to reach for them, I felt her hand touch my leg. "Wait."

I turned around, "What is it?"

She beckoned me forward with her finger, wrapping her arms around my neck, and pulling me into a kiss. It only lasted for a few seconds before we pulled away, and she smiled at me.

"Alright Burly man, let's get out of here."

T H E | S P L I T

VIII

Bought via direct sale, from "Dr. Jimenez": 2075

-A. Fila

Cuba; 1898

I was lying on my back, and could see nothing but the blue sky and the sparse tops of trees, the leaves being the first thing I could fully make out; sharp green vibrantly contrasting with the calm sky.

But, my ears rang, and I heard the unmistakable whizzing of bullets overhead. When I sat up my legs and lower back cried out in pain, as tensed muscles pulled into place. I seemed to be in a crater of some kind, the brown hole seeming out of place from the rest of the sandy grass field. Trying to lift myself without the use of my aching legs, I planted my hands down to either side of me, noticing the feel of the dirt beneath them, and slowly pulled myself onto a knee.

The sun was low in the sky, giving me little light with which to see. Was it setting, or rising? What time was it? And where was I?

Feeling the warmth of a large wet spot on the tan fabric I was wearing, I realized my arm and chest were bleeding. As I examined further, I saw that the shirt matched the pants in color, and they were covered in straps and buckles. In my peripheral vision, I could see streaks of the same tan moving past me.

They quickened at the sound of another loud boom, then a hand grasped my shoulder, and I felt myself whirled around by a man standing behind me, looking down and smiling. He was a big man, at least in proportion to my new body, and there was laughter in the eyes above the jet black mustache with matching chops that he wore as he

THE | SPLIT

spoke to me, his voice gruff and hearty; "Well are you going to lay down in that hole all day? We got a war to win!" I looked up in confusion, which caused him to laugh. "Who are ya, boy? What unit are you in?"

"Unit. . . " I faltered for words as the stranger grabbed me by the forearm and yanked me to my feet. "I don't know what unit I'm in. . . or, who I am. . . or even where we are."

He shook with laughter, calling out over his shoulder to a lanky man who was running up on our left; "You hear that, Johnson? This one doesn't know who or where he is. . . must've got his bell rung pretty good."

Johnson smiled and slowed his pace, wrapping an arm around my shoulder and urging me forward. "Your head will clear soon, do you remember your name, lad?"

I racked my brain, and was greeted with a sharp pain. Then, my sense of self was pushed aside, and I felt a strange rush of emotions and memories, which I had never felt or lived, pour into my mind.

I was Charles. Images of a man I knew to be 'my' father filled my head-space. I remembered riding into town as a courier, and saw the familiar faces of the city that had surrounded me since boyhood. Then as suddenly, my perspective jumped and I was Burl again.

My thoughts were a panicked mess as I tried to comprehend sharing a mind and body in which I was a stranger, and I clutched my head with a yelp of pain as a tear seemed to rip through the center of my brain, causing a lightheaded sense of disembodiment.

But finally, I felt the two halves of my persona settling, and began to somehow perceive through the view of them both. Both Johnson and the mustached man now showed concern, slowing down to a limp and holding me tightly to keep me from falling.

THE | SPLIT

"I'm... Charles," I muttered weakly, forcing my steps to continue forward when I felt the two men let go.

The bigger man clapped me on the shoulder and roared, "Well, good to have ya Charles. I don't know who you were with, but you're coming with us. It's going to hell out here, Kent's back at camp, with this damned fever, he can't keep a Commander alive. I heard they're down to the fourth-in-command up there."

He slowed his pace to spit on the ground, then continued, "Damn ambush cut our lines to ribbons, and the cannons at the top of the point are pounding us. Heard a crewman back there saying our guns can't match for distance and this is likely to keep on. We're gettin' out of here, going to meet with the volunteers and the third Calvary at the forward camp near the base of the Kettle. Just follow the darkies, up ahead... they're going the same way!"

He gestured towards a large group of soldiers clumped together tightly in front of us, moving quickly through the grass and trees; the only black soldiers I had seen.

'Darkies.' I thought with distaste. It was a hateful sentiment, completely lacking in creativity; a word from a time where people's fear and hatred of anything different was packed into slurs and violence. I then had to halt this train of thought, chastising myself for my sense of moral hindsight.

Still, this had been the last clue I had needed; I knew what and where this place was. The palm trees, the uniforms, the facial hair, and the culture; I easily recalled it from history, and the military books I had read through the years.

Cuba; in the midst of the Spanish-American War. My mind reeled with the revelation. Had I actually gone back in time... or was this some fevered dream? Was this real?

THE | SPLIT

Was my time with that nightmarish creature real? Had I died back in my living room? Or had that not even happened?

Fearful questions gripped me, but I slowly tried to settle my thoughts. Wherever I was, whatever this was I was here, and I needed to focus on what was around me to discover why. So as we quickly marched through an increasingly denser wood, I listened to the mustached man, Henry, and Johnson talk. It was more evidence that my Cuba hunch was right.

They spoke loud and freely, interacting with anyone we passed by in our march, and adding them to the conversation, but I refrained from talking and merely listened intently. No one seemed to mind; Henry was talking enough for three men, droning on and on, laughing incessantly throughout.

"So I told the Captain, if Kent really wanted me in his unit so badly, he could pull his shit-caked britches up, stop vomiting, and leave the tent to tell me. Ole Cap didn't like that one at all. . . he turned his horse around and started yelling about insubordination. So I just joined the nearest group of soldiers who didn't look sick, and started marching. Probably get court marshaled, I reckon. Well. . . if the damned mosquitoes and Mausers don't get me first." He roared with laughter, and the rest of the group joined him.

A squat, pockmarked man to my right spoke up, "Ah, who gives a damn about Kent, or your damn court marshals. I just came from the left flank. . . cannons broke our ranks, sent the whole group scattering. I heard someone shouting Colonel Wikoff was dead, and we were to regroup with his man, Worth, and started to walk that direction. Then the cannon fire started again. . . barely made it out. Took some shrapnel to the arm," he pulled up his sleeve to show a nasty gash setting in a deep crimson patch of dried blood.

THE | SPLIT

"Went to sit under a palm tree for a minute and collect my stuff, and my damn fall had broke apart my kit. And no sooner had I gathered all of the bullets I could see, finally found my canteen, and threw my Krag over my shoulder to march, I see a bloodied man screaming and running towards me, holding his own arm. There was a blood coming from his mouth. . . it was. . . horrible. He started screaming that Liscom was dead, and we were doomed if we continued. I asked him about Worth and he just laughed, coughing blood everywhere. Then he fell to the ground. He gave his last words to me, right there, telling me what happened. . . his voice was just a whisper. . . Worth had been struck by cannon fire, and last anyone saw him, he was beneath his horse, shrieking. I started the other way. . . heard some men saying Lt. Colonel Ewer was in charge now, but who knows if he's still with us."

Silence followed this story for a few uncomfortable seconds. I looked around at the faces of the men walking in a loose circle. The horror of their surroundings seemed to dawn on them for the briefest of seconds, before it was cut short by Henry in a jovial tone:

"Well that's why we're going to Kettle, right boys?!" He looked around wildly at the group, and gradual laughter followed; the tension slowly eased. The men continued to talk as we marched on, speaking about the disease in the camp and the disgusting displays of what I knew to be yellow fever and malaria, undercut with several bawdy stories of nights at homes they longed to return to.

I gradually paid less attention. Looking down at the blood on my uniform, I realized that whatever it was, it hadn't killed me – or even wounded me as far as I could tell. Nothing inside me hurt, and I felt no pain when I pressed down on the spot where the blood had started; it seemed to have stopped. I slipped my hand through my shirt to confirm, then began to pat my uniform, to see what I had been issued.

THE | SPLIT

My chest pockets were filled with bullets, while the ones on my stomach had a canteen and a small, engraved compass. A leather strap hung across my shoulder and to my waist, like a sash, and felt heavy behind me. Turning it around I found the wooden stock of my Krag rifle, already loaded. At my waist hung a large Bowie knife. The metal seemed crude, but unique, and slightly more primitive than any like it that I had ever seen.

Coming to the edge of a small grove of palm trees, I was greeted by my first full blast of the sun's rays since arriving. It was rising, fully visible now with the bottom of the bright yellow circle barely above the horizon. I slowed my pace, grimacing as I covered my eyes, trying to get a full scope of what was ahead.

A mosquito buzzed around me, and before I could turn it landed on my lower arm. With a deft movement I slapped at it, feeling the tiny body crunch beneath my hand – then a memory rushed its way to the front of my mind, blocking my other thoughts out.

Kneeling on the ground, I felt pain in my throat and eyes. A hole had been dug, just in front of me, filled with the unspeakable, and the smell it gave off filled my nose and raised the bile in my stomach. My throat was afire now, my vision blurred with streaks of red, and when I looked down at my hands I saw the skin was thin and yellow, like old paper.

My stomach lurched; I could not hold it in anymore, pain tore through my body as I vomited into the hole for what felt like tenth time today, and it was some time before I was able to get to my feet. Upon doing so, I turned left and was chilled to the core at what I saw; beneath clouds of flies, sat a pile of sallow, yellow bodies, baking in the sun.

I felt sick myself, but somehow resisted the urge to vomit as I had in the memory, and looked down again at my hands instead, reassured to see they were the normal, pale white color they had been earlier, and

THE | SPLIT

not the sickly yellow hands from that memory. Still ignoring the loud group of people around me, as well as the dull pain in my stomach and the scorching heat of the sun, I began to mentally take stock of my situation as I walked on.

This was Cuba. I was in the middle of the Spanish-American war; a war I knew that America had won, having been an avid reader and student of Battle History. It had been short, and was glossed over by most of the books I had found, but I knew more than most would about where I was and what was to come. And fortunately, what I knew best about the whole conflict was the battle which, I assumed, would be waiting for me at Kettle Hill.

Theodore Roosevelt and his Rough-riders had claimed victory on that summit, and he had used his account of the battle to help win his presidential campaign. And, in spite of the shadow of death all around me, I had to admit to a slight curiosity – and excitement – at the prospect of seeing Teddy. Every since I was a boy he had been my favorite president; I recalled fondly talking with my dad about him when I was eight. I had just learned what a president was in class, and had asked my dad who his favorite was. He'd named a few, but the only one that stuck was Teddy. The story of his changing from a sickly and asthmatic boy, to the robust War Hero President, was something I carried around my whole life. It always reminded me to focus on strength in times of weakness.

Soon, I began to hear the clamor of voices ahead as we neared the source of the sound, and saw the dark shadows of a crowd just above a small ridge, with more coming into view. The sun was high enough now to see most of the Camp. There was a scurry of activity; a large number of men and horses. Some drank in small circles, others tended their mounts. Some were carrying sacks and crates through the grounds.

T H E | S P L I T

Upon approaching the perimeter, we were stopped by a tall black man who wore the uniform of a Buffalo Soldier. I knew the Buffalo Soldiers well; they were black-only battalions, renowned for their bravery and survival – despite the cruel intentions of their white commanders. This one, along with a few of his comrades, was standing in the middle of the two heavy wagons which were blocking our path, forming a sort of makeshift entrance to the camp.

"Who do you fight for, soldier?" his voice was deep, and sounded cautious.

"What sort of question is that?" Henry shot back. "We fight for the damned Union! Let us through!"

"I am sorry, Sir. . . but I need to know who you fight for. . . who heads your unit?"

"None of your damn business, Darkie. That's who I fight for. Now get out of my way, before I beat you so bad you swim back to the jungle."

The small group I had come with laughed and jeered this exchange, with more voices in support of Henry coming from behind, as more soldiers herded into the camp. Tensions were mounting, and I heard screams of *"Move nigger!"* coming from all around me.

Henry meanwhile moved through the center of the black soldiers, trying to walk through the wagons. The soldier raised his hand to Henry's chest, to stop his advance, and was met with a closed fist. Henry swung twice, knocking the man to the ground then, standing over him, pulled his knife from his belt. I saw him drop to a knee, bringing the blade up.

"You'll learn your place today boy!"

The darker man's fellow soldiers hung back, terror in their eyes. I sprang forward, bellowing, "Enough!" catching Henry's wrist in his

THE | SPLIT

downswing and twisting him to the ground. Silence followed, and I felt all eyes on me and Henry. "The real enemy is up there! What do we gain from killing each other before the battle even starts?" The yelling hurt my throat again, but I continued, "This day will end in plenty of bloodshed and death, let's not start now!"

Henry rolled to his feet and away from me. I saw him quietly talking to Johnson and some others, but I walked to the soldier, lowering my arm to help him up. He looked at it with distrust, before finally grasping my forearm and letting me pull him to his feet.

"I'm not going to hurt you," I told him as he dusted the grass and dust off of uniform. "I don't know what unit I'm in, or even how I got here. . . took a shell, and my memory went blank. Most of these men behind me are the same way, all scattered survivors from the ambush on Kent's brigade up near San Juan hill. We're just looking to fall in, and get up that damn hill. . . from the looks of it you could use our help."

A few seconds passed as the soldier thought on what I said, before finally motioning us through. I walked through the wagons and immediately hung a left, turning around to allow the rest of the group to go through. I knew to never turn my back on an enemy, and I had just made several. Soon enough, Henry passed me, fury in his eyes.

"Coon lover," he muttered, spitting on my boots.

I received similar insults from other members of the Company, until they had all passed me, but I saw the Buffalo Soldier touch his chest, prompting the other soldiers to do the same. I nodded, and they turned around to man their posts.

T H E | S P L I T

IX

LGPB://mn34/con/terra/YT, 7623
(Translated)

Cuba; 1898

There was yelling, lots of yelling.

Blue and tan uniforms swirled around, moving equipment and readying horses near the base of the hill. Nearby, I could hear the crashing of cannon fire and sounds of battle coming from far off of our left, the number of screams reverberating off the hills indicating that things were going poorly.

I looked up to the Kettle's summit, to see Spanish artillery and infantrymen staring down at our position, waiting for orders to engage. There were few cannons on the ground, even near the front of our lines, and most sat untended.

It seemed like Henry was right, the Spanish had a large artillery advantage here, and we were going to take massive casualties – on both sides of the hill.

As if in response to my fear, I heard the dull rolling sound of wheels, and looked over my shoulder. Behind me, rolling along the grass just a few yards away, was our salvation; two men to either side were pushing the brainchild of a man who had intended to create a Death machine so absurd, that it would prove war to be futile.

Dr. Gatling's 'Gatling Gun' had done anything but.

As I looked over the gun, I saw two more coming from the same direction, flanked by mounted riflemen on either side. If anything could help give us an edge, this was it. I'd seen a Gatling Gun back in my own time, on many occasions. Our city Museum had acquired one from a

THE | SPLIT

private collector, and had it staged in my favorite Exhibit. Many times as a young boy I would gaze upon the gun, glancing between each mannequin soldier placed with it, trying to imagine the sounds and feelings such a terrifying weapon would produce.

My reverie was broken by the sounds of shouting in front of me as, about 50 feet away and near the back of the front line, two men on horseback were arguing. Both had patches covering their uniforms, to indicate their status as Officers. The bigger of the two had his back turned, but from the smaller man's face and tone, I could tell that it was he who was in charge.

"Shafter has yet to give an order, and until he does you and your men have been ordered to hold this position!" the smaller man screamed, doing his best to maintain his air of authority. "We plan to attack by the mid-morning sun!"

The bigger man responded in a louder voice, "We'll all *die* if we stay here! Good God! Look around you man! Shafter isn't *here*. . . he doesn't know what we need, or even what's happening!"

"Are you saying that we should break command?" the smaller man questioned, with an air of cold defiance.

Silence followed this question, as the bigger man, still turned around, measured his response. "No, damn you. I'm saying that instead of listening to a man drinking brandy in his tent five miles away, we take this bloody hill before we lose the whole army! These are good boys, from the best schools and families. . . they don't need to be here, and aren't here because they signed some papers and were ordered to come! We came because we knew the only freedom worth having is that you fight for! We are here to defend God and country. . . and we can't do that when we're about to be BLOWN TO BITS AT THE BOTTOM OF A HILL!"

THE | SPLIT

The smaller man had no response. He sat in his saddle with a deflated look. Then, I felt a shiver of excitement run up my body, it was him! President-freaking-Roosevelt was just a few yards in front of me!

What was I going to say? Not talking to him was out of the question, I had been presented with an opportunity that shouldn't have even been possible. It seemed like fate had somehow been rewritten, and this was its purpose.

Nerves on edge from excitement, I jumped as I suddenly felt a hand on my shoulder; it was the Buffalo Soldier, from the camp entrance earlier but he stared at me in respectful deference, as if waiting for me to talk first.

"Uh. . . hello. . . " The scene felt awkward. Did he have something to say, or was he merely acknowledging my presence through touch?

"I been here. . . couple months, now. I ain't seen nobody stand up for a negro, not the white man, not the Spanish man, not even the damn Cubans."

"It shouldn't take the color of a man's skin to decide how to treat him. You do what's right whether they're black, brown, yellow, or purple."

He laughed at this and shook his head. "You are a funny man with funny ideas, but you must be careful. . . you are far from home, funny man. Come, join us. . . you must eat before the battle starts, you may not get another chance." He laughed darkly at his own joke and started walking towards the edge of camp.

Curious, I followed, and we continued for several minutes along the crude path through the middle of the area. When we had almost out of the camp, he turned and walked to a small cluster of threadbare tents. Around and inside these tents were dozens of Buffalo Soldiers, all dressed identically to the one I'd followed, who now walked into the middle of the group.

T H E | S P L I T

The men sitting around a large fire were deep in conversation, and hardly noticed my new friend breaking their circle as he filled two nearby tin pans from the black cauldron hung above the fire, then walked back over to me carrying a full pan of what looked like stew, with steam rising from the brown liquid as he handed it to me.

Greedily, I nearly cleared the pan in a half dozen spoonfuls, realizing how hungry I was as the food settled in my stomach. "Thank you. . . wait, what do I call you?"

The man smiled, "I am Jensen. Who are you?"

I paused, not sure how to answer his question or even what to say. "I am. . . Charles. . . but, I'm really confused. . . because that's not all of who I am."

"Haha. . . oh? You have another name too?"

Before I could answer, the loud conversation around the fire suddenly died. I looked over to see the men all staring at me, and my breath caught in my throat as I glanced from face to face. All of their expressions were hardened, and I suddenly felt I was in a place I did not belong.

"Who is this, Jensen? Why did you bring him here?" A man by the fire stood up and began walking towards us. He was massive, almost a head and a half taller than me, with arms like onyx tree trunks. Veins crisscrossed the surface, tensing each time he moved beneath a short shirt that barely covered his midriff.

Jensen stepped in front of him as he moved closer, heading straight for me. "This is Charles. He saved my life at my post. . . and I invited him here. You have a problem with that?" Jensen looked like a child next to this giant of a soldier, but he he stared back defiantly and did not show any signs of fear as the bigger man looked down at him.

THE | SPLIT

"Maybe, he saved your life just so he can kill you later. The white man is cruel." The men around the fire agreed with the larger man, whispering among themselves as he stepped back.

I could almost physically feel the tension as they waited for Jensen to respond. He stepped forward, pulling me with him and putting his hand on my shoulder, like he was presenting me to the group.

"This man here, is a funny man. I do not know where he comes from, but he talks and thinks in the strangest ways. He kept a negro guard from being beat by a white man, and when I asked him why, he said that where he comes from, color does not matter!" The crowd gasped in astonishment at Jensen's revelation, but he continued over their side conversations, now even louder: "Any white man that cares about the Buffalo soldier, is a friend in my book. Come, Charles. . . tell us more about you, and this strange place you come from."

The whole group looked at me. I froze in fear. What was I going to say? Could these men handle the truth of who I was? Or where and when I was from? Would they even believe me? Deciding I had nothing to lose, I patiently told them the entire truth. Pausing here and there for their many questions.

"My name isn't Charles, my name is Burlington. It's. . . complicated to explain, but I'm a visitor here. . . from your future."

The crowd erupted, and it took several minutes for the group to settle down. Many of the men were shouting at me, but it was impossible to answer, let alone hear questions, when they were all said at the same time.

When the group finally quieted, one man's voice came out from the back, "If you're from the future, what year are you from?" I saw many heads bobbing up and down in agreement of his curiosity.

"The year two thousand, eighteen." I replied.

T H E | S P L I T

Again the crowd went into an uproar and I heard many shouts calling me 'crazy', and many others telling me to leave, but I kept on trying to talk over them. They only grew louder at this. Eventually Jensen stepped in front of me, raising his hands and yelling out for them to quiet.

The men around him muttered in agreement, and I tried to take advantage of the silence by continuing my story – but even Jensen's intervention only succeeded for a few minutes, and the end to this noisy scene only came when a dark old man with bright white hair stepped out from a nearby tent and shouted in a shaky voice;

"WHAT IS ALL THIS COMMOTION?" The clatter died down in an instant, and the men looked about sheepishly as he insisted, "ALL OF YOU, GET BACK TO YOUR POSTS! We have a battle to fight any minute now. . . do NOT make me report this to the Colonel!"

They all got on their feet and scattered like grass in the wind, hard at work within seconds, moving cargo and tending to horses, the old man watching them with an intent scowl on his face. His eyes widened slightly upon seeing me as he looked around the compound, and he motioned for me and Jensen to come towards him.

We started walking his way, and saw him disappear inside the tent. Lifting the entrance flap up to the side, I stepped inside, Jensen just behind me. The inside of the makeshift room was covered in crates, and primitive looking medical tools. I saw the old man sit down at a nearby table in the corner which was covered with books.

He slowly reach for a pair of spectacles and put them on, with shaking hands, then flattened out a crinkled piece of paper on his table before turning around in his chair to face us. But he said nothing, merely examining both of us thoroughly, his quick and intelligent eyes darting between us.

THE | SPLIT

The wrinkles around his eyes creased as he studied my face, but his own face was an observant mask of curious acceptance, making it difficult to tell what was going on his head. I'm sure this was no accident, and would've guessed that every wrinkle in that face told a story; little physical reminders of a proud and dignified life, lived through decades of hate and terror.

This was prejudice I had only learned of in short paragraphs, during a one hour span of time in school, and something I had been deeply privileged to not have experienced – or have relatives who had experienced it. Thus, I knew nothing I could read in books or hear in a history class could compare to the experiences and memories in this man's head of an entire lifetime of subjugation and horror, at the hands of people who looked just like me.

Finally he spoke, "My bat-man told me what was going on outside. He says the men tell him you speak of a strange world, very far from here. You must be careful of that kind of talk, young man. The Buffalo are very superstitious. Words like yours could be construed as insanity, and you do not want your fellow soldiers believing they serve beside a madman."

"I know what I'm saying is hard to believe, but it's true, really!"

He stood up from his chair and hobbled over to me. His back slightly hunched as he walked, but his footsteps were solid and sure.

He stopped just inches in front of me and looked up at my face, and time seemed to slow as he stared into my eyes. . . seeming to look right through who I wore and deep into my innermost thoughts. "I do believe you, son," he said with a smile. "My daddy used to tell me, 'You can always find the truth in a man's eyes'."

"Your daddy sounds like a wise man," I quipped. He smiled bigger at this.

THE | SPLIT

"He had his moments. But, like most other Negroes, he lacked the education to offer much. Now, I'm not disparaging him or anyone else, but many of the brave young men out there have never had a day of schooling in their lives. just confuses them. I would reckon your talk of the future would be. . . unfathomable, to most of those boys. They can't even fully understand what you mean by 'the future'. . ."

He trailed off for a second, clearly emotional over his last few sentences, "But enough about that. If you're really from a time past ours, how did you get here?"

So for several minutes I told him my story, starting with my night at the bar – though I left out a few details, not wanting to confuse him with things he wouldn't be accustomed to. Like the confrontation in my duplex, which I barely mentioned. The pain was still too fresh, the feelings still too raw. I only told him of a struggle, in great detail, and of how afterward the girl I loved had died. I described to him the words I cried out and the feeling I had before being pulled from my body, going into even greater detail about my time in the strange green hallways, and about the otherworldly Being that had summoned me there.

When I'd finished he walked back over to his chair and sat down, clearly overwhelmed by the scope of my tale. "That has to be. . . the most, incredible thing I have ever heard. If even half of your story occurred the way you said it did, it could change our understanding of the natural world."

When he paused I took advantage of the silence to speak up, "Do you mind if I ask you a question, Doctor. . ." and a sad smile appeared on his face.

"I'm no doctor. When I went to school, there were no licenses like that given to negro students, but you can call me by name, Ezekiel Freeman."

THE | SPLIT

"Nice to meet you, Dr. Freeman," I said, shaking his hand and accentuating the word 'Doctor' firmly, "My name is Burl. . . short for Burlington. . . and, like I told Jensen, in the time I come from we are equal. You're just as much of a doctor to me as any white man. I must ask though. . . because of my knowledge on the racial climate of this time period. . . how did you rise up to your station?"

He grinned slightly for a moment, but his face quickly shifted back to the stoicism he had shown earlier. "ONLY through God's guiding hand did I get to where I am today. I was born a slave, most men my age were, and four when I moved to Kentucky, shipped like cattle in a wagon to serve my new masters, the Johnson family. The first few years I didn't work, just stayed in the hot ole cabin all day, while my mama and brothers worked for Mr. Johnson. My brothers were just field hands. . . b ut, my mama? My mama was the maid for Mrs. Johnson herself."

"Mama was the best woman I have ever known. She risked her life to take books from the Johnson's home, and bring them to me late at night. I only had four books, but by the time I was six I had taught myself to read. Then I was sent to the field to work with my brothers and the other men, but at night I would read. Mama got caught taking another and got beat within an inch of her poor life. But I still had my books. Every one of those four books I read until the covers fell off. I thanked my mama everyday for her precious gift.

Then, I was given my freedom at fourteen, but two years later, my mama passed away. We had been staying in town, not far from the Johnson's old farm, and work was scarce. . . even harder for the negro. So a few weeks after my mama's death, I left my brothers and hid away on a train to get North. Once there I became a servant for a distinguished doctor and teacher. He had a heart for me somehow, and soon took me on as an apprentice. After finishing my studies, I took work where I could find it, and about a decade ago took a job with the army as a medical chief of staff for the negro units."

I had become entranced in his story in such a short time, going from inspired to sadness with just sentences in between. This was an amazing man.

"Your life. . . " I started, ". . . it has to be one of the most remarkable things I have ever heard. You are an amazing man, Doctor Freeman."

"I had nothing to do with it," he cut in.

"All that's in my life. . . all I've done, all I WILL do. . . are blessings from God. He guided my path, every step of the way. Every obstacle, every peak, and every valley, he was there. I just try to give the talent and intelligence he gave me, back to those less fortunate. But. . . I know *my* story. . . tell me about the future. I may not have many years left, so indulge an old man for a minute."

So much went through my head at once. "I don't even know where to begin. This next century. . . from now until the year 2000. . . is one of the greatest times of advancement in all of human history. There are cars, essentially motorized wagons, that we ride around in everywhere. They can go almost 5 or 6 times faster than a horse, and they have paved roads. . . to nearly anyplace you want to go. Food has become plentiful and cheap. There are even places you can go to, in one of these cars, and you can stay in your car while they make you hot food within minutes and hand it out to you through a window.

Technology. . . gah, I don't even know where to begin on this one. . . it's advanced so fast you wouldn't even recognize daily life. In the 21st century, there are glass screens, called televisions, that display noise and pictures, and you can watch anything on these screens from great stories to tales of history, to news about current events. And the

T H E | S P L I T

whole world is connected by a series of wires that form this thing called "the Internet", and on this internet you can talk to anyone. . . anywhere in the world. . . in an instant. I. . . I could talk to you for hours about this, what would you like to know?"

His face was lit up with wonder as I described these miraculous inventions, but when I was through his expression dropped, and I could tell he had something to ask me.

"This future world sounds like something out of a dream, but. . . tell me. . . is there still space for me and my people in this future world of yours? What becomes of the negro a century from now?"

I felt my body temperature rise from the impact and sincerity of his question. I was an idiot, why didn't I think of that to begin with? A man who had seen the things, and lived the life he had, would have little interest for such trivial progress. No matter how primitive or advanced we became as people, at the end of the day, that's all that mattered, people. He looked up at me from his chair, his eyes locked with mine, and as I stared back at him I could see the glimmer of hope in his eyes. To him, I must have been the unexpected answer from God that he had asked for his whole life. After a lifetime of pain and working to improve the lives of his mistreated people, the fruits of his efforts, the future of his kind, was all that mattered to him.

"Things. . . things are rocky at first," I hesitated, trying to find the words, but picking up confidence towards the end. "The next few decades, things are mostly the same, and there is a lot of tension. But there are a lot of people fighting to level the playing field, and out of these efforts the 'Civil Rights' Movement is born. . . and, sometime in the 1960's, the Civil Rights Act gets signed. Discrimination was outlawed, the schools were desegregated and, for the first time we began to see racial harmony. . . in most places. As a few more decades

THE | SPLIT

passed, a lot of the more subtle. . . and not so subtle. . . forms of racism became demonized. A cultural stigma became associated with racist views. In the time I come from, there are dozens of black entertainers, making art for both white and black culture. There are black athletes who play alongside white athletes, and black doctors, black lawyers, black architects. There was even a black president. I voted for him, as did most of the country. . . but there are still a lot of issues in the black community – mostly stemming from the unequal playing field during the years following slavery. But we're working to correct them. . . to level the playing field, and bring about true equality. Young people in the year 2018 are passionate for justice, and to see an end to racism and prejudice."

I stopped when I looked down to see his eyes glistening. A single tear rolled down his cheek and he sniffed noisily. I got chills seeing his raw emotional response, and wasn't quite sure what to say. "I'm sorry, I didn't mean to upset or offend-"

"Offend me?" he interrupted, slowly standing up. "Son, you have done nothing of the sort. These tears I cry, these are tears from a joy I wish I could describe. I-" he stopped to sniff again as another tear rolled down his face, "I. . . cannot thank you enough, for the message of hope you have brought me here today. I have prayed for my people every day. I told God that even if it takes a thousand years, to bring my people the freedom we deserve. God did even better than that, he brought me you. He brought me eyes from the future to tell of his glory and mercy. Tell me, do they still pray where you come from?"

"Some do," I responded awkwardly.

"Well, will you pray here with me, right now? My heart overflows with joy, and I can think of no other person to share it with than the God that gave me everything."

THE | SPLIT

I nodded and bowed my head, watching Jensen do the same before closing my eyes. "My ever merciful Lord, you give us so much. In Isaiah you said, 'Shake thyself from the dust; ARISE, and sit down, O Jerusalem: loose thyself from the bands of thy neck, be free!'. My whole adult life I read those words, wondering when it was time for my people to rise up from the dust. But you have shown me, oh Lord. . . with the words of your messenger you have given me more than I could dream of. My heart sings your praises on such a beautiful day. Not even the bloodiest battle could keep me from praising you, nor will the one we fight today. Keep my hand sturdy as I try to heal these broken souls, oh Lord, and keep my new friend and brother Jensen out of harm's way. May your will be done, amen."

As we all opened our eyes, I saw the doctor beaming at me, his eyes alight with a pure joy I had never seen before. He talked to us for a few minutes longer and then had to go about his duties. I promised I would try and find him after the battle, and we walked out of the tent.

When we stepped outside, Jensen turned to me, "Was all of that. . . what you told the old man, really true?"

"Every word," I said, smiling.

We started to walk towards the center of camp, then we heard a loud commotion and cries of "The Colonel is coming!" rang out around me, and it took me a few seconds to realize who they meant, but I soon discovered that they were speaking of Roosevelt and my heart leapt with excitement; I couldn't think of what I wanted to say to him first. There was so much I wanted to ask him.

T H E | S P L I T

X

LGPB://mn34/con/terra/MH, 1623

(Translated)

Cuba; 1898

Jensen nudged me and pointed to my right. I turned around and saw Roosevelt's horse heading in my direction – but my blood then ran cold as I finally saw his face.

This wasn't right. His uniform and mount were normal but, as I raised my eyes to his face, I saw. . . nothing. There was no bushy mustache, no small circular glasses and brash smile like I had seen as a child; his face had no features, *at all* – just smooth skin, starting from his neck and ending at his forehead. My brain cried out in shock, desperately trying to make sense of what I was seeing. I had just heard him talking, how was this possible? Jensen saw my panic and turned to me, concerned.

"That's Roosevelt? It. . . can't be!" I whispered desperately.

"That," Jensen narrowed his eyes in confusion, "is Colonel Roosevelt, yes."

"*Look* at him, does he have. . . a face?" I motioned with my hand over my own face in an unnecessary demonstration.

He looked at me with confusion in his eyes, before bursting out with laughter, "Of course he does, funny man!"

Shaking his head, he walked away, still laughing. I continued to stare at the Colonel, unable to tear my eyes away from something so strange and terrible, and as he rode towards me I quickly took a few paces back, intending to keep my distance. But it was too late. Roosevelt lifted his fist into the air, barking orders to the whole area.

THE | SPLIT

"Volunteers on me! Mount up! We're going to take this damn hill if it's the last thing we do!"

"Hoo-ah!" came from every corner of the camp as men converged on Roosevelt.

He was getting closer, and I had begun to hear a strange ringing as he neared. Backpedaling once again, I smacked into a man behind me and fell forward. Men were all around me now, waiting to hear from him, but in desperation I was scanning the crowd, looking for a way out of the throng.

Teddy was just a few paces away; the ringing had deafened all other sounds, and a stabbing pain started just above my forehead as he slowed his horse to stop. I dropped to the ground, then the ringing ceased and I felt my thoughts overwritten by an unknown force, much like the strange Presence in the Green Hallway before. Images flashed through my minds at impossible speeds; yet these weren't my memories or thoughts, and they weren't Charles'. Moving shapes, and strange life I had never seen before, littered my subconscious. Most made no sense, but eventually the thread stopped on a picture of Teddy himself, face intact. I felt relief – before I saw his eyes and mouth shut and then reopen, pouring out streams of blood.

I screamed. The darkness subsided and my eyes opened to look upon a clump of grass. Above me I could see men staring down with looks of concern and disgust. There were no voices, the space was silent aside from the sounds of distant battle.

'How much had they seen?' I wondered. Had I screamed out loud?

The faceless figure of Roosevelt dismounted his horse near me and extended his hand. The ringing from before had subsided but the ripping pain from my head continued to throb, and I winced despite my best attempts, holding my head and groaning in my discomfort. The

T H E | S P L I T

Colonel withdrew his hand, calling out to his men, "Is the boy alright? Get him on the wagons and take him back to camp, we can't have the fever breaking out here!"

"He is fine, Sir!" a familiar voice called out; I saw Jensen push through the crowd to stand by my side. "He is groggy from the cannon's blast, but he fights like a lion, and we will need him on top of that hill." Roosevelt nodded, allowing Jensen to help me up and get me out of the crowd.

We walked to the edge of the men and sat down on a fallen tree log. In the background, I could still hear the Colonel barking out orders and leading his troops in a rousing speech. It was nice to be away from the mass of men I had just fallen down in front of. Deep from within, the side of my mind where Charles was, I could feel humiliation at what had just unfolded. It was lost a lot of face, and I could in no way explain to the worried onlookers what I was going through, for fear of sounding insane.

Jensen sat, back turned to me, a few feet down the log. Over his shoulder I could see him sharpening a knife, curved and gleaming from hilt to blade as he ran it down the whetstone. It was a strange knife, and seemed out of place compared to what hung at my and other soldiers' hips nearby.

"Thank you. You didn't have to do that," I said to the soldier's back.

"Do not thank me, funny man. Buffalo always sent to take the white man back to camp, the Buffalo never come back. Bullets like hornets, if you hear them it's too late."

I reflected on his words. If my arrival had been any indication, Jensen was right. The thick brush and slow rolling hills on either side of the path had provided excellent cover for Spanish snipers and the occasional cannon. A small group, unable to walk with the vast lines of

T H E | S P L I T

moving soldiers we had been in earlier, would be an easy target for whatever was out there.

"Well then, what now? We can't sit here forever."

Jensen nodded in agreement, "No, and we can't turn around either, Roosevelt is right, we need to charge."

There was again commotion coming from the front of the camp; all of the volunteers were mounting up and yelling at the riders in the 3rd Calvary to do the same.

Roosevelt had been joined by another commander, and they were yelling at the smaller man from earlier in unison, whatever they said seeming to finally push the right buttons; the man turned his horse around and galloped off in the other direction, towards camp, accompanied by several other officers.

As I watched the cavalry ready their mounts and climb into their saddles, I again felt a tug on my shoulder, and looked up to see Jensen gesturing for me to follow, so I did. We walked left for a ways, almost between the two hills now. The rest of the Buffalo Soldiers were there, most already standing at attention, in perfect line with the cavalry to their right, and Jensen and I quickly readied our rifles. I also pulled out the revolver I had found just moments ago in a chest pocket, opening the chamber and make sure I was fully loaded; five rounds, ready to go. Spinning the cylinder around and popping it back into place, I set the gun itself back in my chest pocket.

Orders were being shouted from our right, nearly impossible to hear over the deafening sounds of the other battle already in progress to our left. Jensen was already standing at the line a few feet in front of me, arm at his side, rifle on shoulder, head turned up looking at the crest of the peak.

Taking a swig from my canteen earned me the disapproving looks of

THE | SPLIT

several nearby soldiers who were all standing at attention, so I stood to his right and did my best to imitate his pose, ignoring them.

"Thank you Jensen," I said, in my best attempt at a reverent tone, "I am honored to fight beside you."

This brought Jensen, and several men in front of me, to laughter. "This here is no honor. . . your brothers reject you. . . . they make you fight with the Negro. They give us no horse, and tell us 'keep up'. Many buffalo will die today. . . you, will die today."

"Wow Jensen, good luck to you too." I replied sarcastically.

The faint hint of a smile came to his lips but he did not reply. He was probably right, I admitted; this battle had been a bloodbath, and Buffalo Soldiers had done most of the fighting – and dying – near the top.

I just hoped to make it.

The Burl and Charles sides of my brain seemed to both be handling the threat of extinction differently. Charles had been a religious man at home, but had lost most of his faith upon joining the service. Yet, in times of great peril or stress, he would recite the Lord's Prayer; and this time was no different. As Burlington, there seemed to be room for this fear of death, yet my curiosity about why I had been sent here had morphed into dark questions of if I would even die. Would I return home if I died? Was this all even real? I reached my thoughts towards the outskirts of my mind, to try and feel the presence of the Being that had sent me here, but couldn't find it – or anything else out of the ordinary. The smells, the sounds, the feeling of this dreaded heat slowly burning my skin, it all felt real.

Somewhere back to my right I heard the clicking of a crank, going faster and faster. The unmistakable popping of gunfire followed, and I whirled around to see the Gatling attachment a few hundred feet away, spraying fire and lead towards the top of the hill. It was mesmerizing; a

THE | SPLIT

cone of fire formed at the end of each series of barrels, the barrels themselves spinning too fast to see, and the man turning the crank behind the gun glistened with sweat. But there seemed to be no response from the top of the hill.

All Mauser fire had ceased, and the few cannons still firing seemed to do at a crawling pace. Still, I knew they weren't sitting idle, and images of men reloading cannons and rifles flashed through my brain – as soon as the Gatling guns paused to reload, we would be hit hard by the freshly resupplied defenders.

T H E | S P L I T

XI

Gift from Caribbean Consulate, 2121
-T. Acerz, 2131

Cuba; 1898

A horn sounded, and I heard yelling and the whinnying of horses. Then off went the cavalry, charging up the hill, kicking up a cloud of dust and grass. A man in front of me with a booming voice ordered the remainder of the men forward, and we took off after the cavalry at a brisk place.

My calves quickly strained under the weight of my gear, and I leaned forward to compensate, realizing I had been wrong about the slope of the hill – which had seemed easy from the ground. Next to me a short, squat man was shaking, breathing heavily as he greedily sucked in air, and was soon on the ground, covering his eyes with his hands, crying out. I moved past him, Jensen hot on my heels. The squat man had not been the only one to fall, we passed several in the next few yards; it was heat exhaustion, something Roosevelt himself had talked about in his account of the battle. I understood their feeling, my body felt chilled even though my skin cried out in burning pain.

Something whirred past my face mid-stride, then a shriek of pain rang out behind me, and I turned to see a soldier on his knees, clutching his stomach, his mouth dribbling blood as he called to his fellow soldiers around him for help. As his cries intensified, I found myself moving even faster just to get away from the haunting scene. Halfway up the hill I heard the sharp whinnying of horses, followed by the coordinated burst from a volley of rifle shots, then men began to fall all around me.

THE | SPLIT

In front of me, there was a gaping hole in the line of Calvary, and just behind it a wriggling pile of horses and men all tied together in grotesque death throes. I adjusted my course and began climbing the slope at more of a slight angle, running straight for the pile, my survival instinct overcoming being repulsed by the horrific gore.

BOOM!

The world fell into silence as I saw a wall of fire and smoke come from the top of the hill. The cannons had fired in perfect unison, leaving little time for reaction.

"*DOWN!*" I heard Jensen's voice, muffled over the dull ringing, and without even thinking I complied, dropping to my stomach in less than a heartbeat.

My hearing returned – for an instant; the air seemed to roar above me - only to be then taken again by the ringing of a series of deafening crashes behind me. I rolled to my stomach and looked around, disoriented. A living portrait of carnage was playing out around me. On the other hill, I could see the stalled charge, now about two thirds of the way up, attempting to dig in around another pile of dead men and horses. Just below them was the twisted metal and wood of a group of Gatling guns, now hopelessly dismembered. A wheel lay intact a few yards away, near the bloodied corpse of one of its crewmen. It also seemed all Gatling fire had ceased on the other hill.

I turned to see, on this side of the hill, two men scurrying around the detachment, boxes in hand, swabbing out the barrels and loading new belts into the receivers. On the far right side, one of the guns shot in short bursts, attempting to provide whatever cover they could while the other guns were being reloaded.

Just below me were the scattered remains of the men that had until moments ago been around me, and in the middle of them sat a group of soldiers, screaming out in pain and desperately clawing out at the men around them; their uniforms, like the ground beneath them, stained a deep crimson. I could make out arms and other more gruesome body parts, strewn out amongst the chaos.

Then from the corner of my eye, to my diagonal left I saw the flash of more rifle fire, this time coming from the top of San Juan. Looking over, I saw Jensen sitting up in a daze, holding his arm – just as a bullet whizzed past my waist. Grabbing him by the back of his uniform I dragged us to cover behind a whimpering horse just a few yards ahead.

The left side of his uniform was soaked with blood, and when I rolled up his sleeve to see, there was a long, jagged cut, with a piece of metal stuck into his forearm. I pulled it out, and tried to rouse him.

"Jensen, can you hear me?" When there was no response, and his eyes only stared blankly ahead, this time I shook him, shouting over the sounds of battle, "CAN YOU HEAR ME?"

When he nodded I sat back, leaning against the now still horse, taking a few precious seconds of rest to catch my breath.

The cacophony of rifle fire and cannon shells had fallen into a rhythm, a terrible percussion which silenced the cries of its victims. On both sides men were moving past us, going up the hill; some fell, slumping over their horse and adding to the pile of bodies. Soon, the Gatling fire returned – only to quickly stop.

Jerking my head up, I saw the first of the horsemen in the distance, nearing the crest of the hill and, leaning down to Jensen and the other men now sharing our cover, I told them, "We have to move, now!"

They nodded, and I led the way, going around to the right side of the pile, then up the hill. Once free of the bodies clumped in the center, I could see men on horses, ascending to the top and then disappearing from view. As they rounded the other side into the defender's trenches,

T H E | S P L I T

I broke into a dead sprint after them, Jensen right behind me.

There was screaming and sounds of steel on steel as I came closer to the summit, the shouts of our men in the trenches ringing out with the shrieks of their horses.

The defenders soon swallowed them up, and were once again aiming down at us from the trench, their shots getting closer with every passing round. Buffalo Soldiers were falling all around us from the continued onslaught of crossfire on San Juan, now just above us. The sun was also unforgiving, my clothes were soaking with sweat, my muscles cried out in pain, and every step up seemed like it could be my last.

And at last the sharp pain came that I had been anticipating, as I heard the whizzing fire pass around me all day. The bullet tore into my arm, just below my bicep, bringing blood gushing from the fresh hole and dripping down my arm. My vision blurred and I staggered, briefly losing my sense of balance, but fought to keep my body from going into shock. With my uninjured arm I managed to roll up my sleeve into a tight wrap to stop the bleeding.

My pace had slowed, but I was nearing the top, and at last I saw the dirt of the trench and redoubled my efforts, legs pounding the grassy slope with a new fervor. Jensen had passed me, rifle held at his waist, and fired towards the top of the hill, his hand moving quickly to his belt as he grabbed another bullet to reload. I was just a few feet behind him and gaining, when I saw him get to the peak and bring the butt of the rifle to his shoulder, aiming down into the trench.

Then suddenly, a gleaming spike protruded from Jensen's chest, dripping crimson as his blood spread to cover the entire back of his uniform, and his grip on the rifle loosened, dropping to the side as he fell to his knees with a dull moan escaping his lips. Then a hand grabbed his shoulder to push him off of the blade, and I screamed his name as his broken body rolled past me in a heap, watching hopelessly as it tumbled end over end; while the Spanish man who had killed him now used the butt of his rifle to bludgeon a Cavalryman bent over the top of the trench, helpless.

I brought my rifle to just below my shoulder, pulling the trigger. The man's head seemed to burst open in a red mist and, throwing myself into the trench, I attempted to pull up the badly beaten Cavalryman from the ground. The scene was pandemonium. The few men in our color of uniform were clustered together, surrounded by Spanish infantry and artillery crews who were armed with sabers and revolvers. Near me, a Buffalo Soldier used his rifle as a staff to block the wild swings of a saber, ducking a swipe as he jabbed, causing me to jump left in order to avoid the end of his blade.

We were outnumbered and surrounded, but fresh men from both sides kept pouring into the trench, yelling wildly and rushing to relieve their beleaguered brothers. Frantically, I reached into my pocket for another bullet but, just as my fingers closed around the cool metal, I saw a man charging towards me, saber held overhead. Again lowering my shoulder, I sprinted towards him, catching him just two strides later in the middle of his chest and sending him sprawling backwards.

I then quickly tried again to load the bullet into my Krag, but my hands were shaking and I dropped the round, losing sight of it under a body, and had to retreat to our side of the trench. Crouching down, I drew out another, this time successfully putting it in the rifle and pulling the sight to my face, scanning the trenches for a target. A Spaniard entering from the opposite side of the trench caught my eye and I fired, watching as it landed square in his chest; he collapsed on top of another soldier, who had just run through one of ours with a saber.

THE | SPLIT

Then to my right came the gleam of another saber, arcing downward just a few inches above my face. I turned my head to the side, pivoting my body in the same fluid motion, and the face of the screaming soldier passed by, carried in the momentum of his swing. Dropping my rifle, I wrapped both arms around him in a tight bear hug.

He thrashed and turned, straining his right arm as he tried to lift his saber. My right leg snaked out and wrapped around behind both of his, as I then pushed his weight over my leg and fell on top of him, reaching for my knife. But I was bowled over by a staggering soldier who had tripped above me and landed to my left, coughing out blood and screaming; and now, I was lying within reach of my opponent.

He lashed out to kick me, bashing me repeatedly, each blow shaking my body as his foot slammed into my stomach. His body was sandwiched between the legs of two soldiers fighting above, using their rifles like fearsome clubs, but his arms were free, so he glanced around desperately for his sword - settling on a nearby rifle and swinging it at me. It hit my chin with a loud crack, and pain exploded through my face, bringing hot tears to my eyes.

When he brought it down this time I shielded my face, and the blow landed on my chest. He swatted at me again and I knew I was in trouble. Gathering my strength, I pulled my flat body up on all fours, feeling my left arm immediately start to buckle beneath the weight and blood begin to pour from the bullet I had taken on the hill. But the man continued to swing at me as I tried to crawl away, with a great heave pushing through the two men trapping him and following me.

Panicked, I swept the ground with my fingers looking for something, anything, that could relieve the assault, and felt the cold smoothness of metal underneath the body of a horse. I pulled it up to my face. It was a cannon ball.

THE | SPLIT

Turning around, holding it by both hands, I lunged at the man, slamming the heavy sphere into the side of his face. The soldier cried out, spitting out blood as he held his face, but when he tried to sit up I threw myself forward again, pinning him on his back. He guarded his face with the gun held vertically, jabbing it forward and narrowly missing my own. With as much force as I could muster, I shoved the cannonball into his chest.

His wind rushed out in a loud gasp, then he covered his face with one hand, flailing at me wildly with the other, rifle now lying in the dirt. I leaned my body back, bringing the ball higher and slamming it down again in the same spot.

A fury seemed to come over me then; I swung the cannonball down again, and again, until I heard a crack and the man screamed out in pain. His arms relaxed and dropped to his shaking sides, but one last time I brought the ball up, again driving it down into the man's sternum.

The bone caved inward and I felt my hands being sliced by jagged bones as they went into his body, then they were wet against the clammy flab of his organs. Recoiling from the feeling, I jerked my hands away quickly. When I looked down, what I saw sickened me, and a sudden rush of vomit left my body, covering the fresh corpse – then, again, the taste left in my mouth stinging my eyes.

Blinking away unbidden tears, I got to my knee weakly. But as I pushed myself upward I was yet again knocked over by an unseen assailant and so, remaining on my stomach, I crawled over to the side of the trench before again heaving myself upright. There were far fewer Spaniards around us than there had been when I had fallen. Calvarymen and Buffalo battled the few men nearby, encircling them and swinging downward with their rifles.

THE | SPLIT

Orders were being screamed, but I did not know what they were. My brain seemed fuzzier than usual, and my vision bounced around, causing me to lose focus. I slapped myself on the side of the head and the stinging pain seemed to settle things a bit, bringing my eyesight more level.

Men passed me, shouting, and I started moving, turning to see a sea of Spanish uniforms further down the trench. Where was my rifle? I patted myself, looking for the familiar strap, trying to remember if it had been knocked from my hands or not. Then, feeling a lump in my chest pocket, I suddenly remembered the revolver and quickly pulled it out, cocking the hammer.

Just a few yards in front of me men were locked in a fierce melee – but to either side of the trench, allowing a mostly open lane through the center as far as I could see. Blue, brown and gray uniforms were moving at a rapid pace, gunshots echoed, and I could see swords gleaming in the bright sun. The fierce brawl looked to go for a half mile or further before curving out of sight.

I picked up a nearby saber and charged through the center lane, between countless brawls, jabbing the sword left and right, head moving back and forth as I ran through man after man, each one locked in a death battle with someone else, each going wide-eyed with shock as my blade went through necks and chests alike.

My arm grew heavy with the motion, but I stabbed again and again, quickening my pace, though I got more selective with my targets. When a man suddenly stepped in front of me, raising his own saber with both hands for a killing blow, in a flash I brought the revolver up to his head and shot, and his eyes rolled into his head as he crumpled. Then out of nowhere, my ears began to ring and my vision flashed with static, worsening with every step I took.

T H E | S P L I T

He was here.

I stopped in place, quickly scanning the crowd of people in front of me. About twenty yards ahead stood the faceless form of Roosevelt, surrounded and being clubbed by rifles and pounded on by fists as he desperately grasped the wrist of a swordsman in front. The saber wobbled slightly as Teddy arched his back to avoid the edge. I broke into a run, dropping my sword and hurdling bodies as I tore towards him.

My mind immediately began to feel the effects of Roosevelt's presence, as I had in camp, and Charles cried out to me, pleading as the series of images and ringing worsened, now filling both sides of my mind and strengthening with every step. My vision grew hazy as I felt my head start to darken, but, forcing my thoughts to still, I strained my eyes wide to see beyond the blur.

The swordsman now had control of the sword and I saw Teddy bring his head down with his arms curled around it in anticipation. I shot, bringing my other hand up and slamming the hammer down again and again with the back of it as I fired at the other three men in quick succession, who all fell to the ground.

But Roosevelt grabbed me, and I felt myself grow limp. Slumping to my knees, my eyes rolled back as the strange images burning through my mind grew brighter. Then felt my vision narrowed, and I felt myself falling backwards. Nearly deafened by the ringing, I could yet hear Teddy screaming at me as he tried to pull me to the safety of the side of the trench. His horrifying blank face glistened in the hot sun. Unable to respond, I simply continued to gaze upward, watching a bead of sweat roll down where his nose should've been, feeling myself slipping away.

Then my body was dropped against the side of the trench as Teddy released me to parry a sudden sword attack with his knife, and the change was instant. I felt my control returning, and my thoughts start to calm.

Glancing over my shoulder, I saw that Roosevelt was on the other side of the trench, punching his attacker with the knife in quick brutal strikes, both hand and blade a blur. The man quickly grew limp and fell, and Roosevelt continued down the side of the trench, leaving me behind. With every step he took, my control grew, and I felt elated as I readied my body to push off from the side and stand.

But suddenly I grew cold.

The middle of my chest was torn with a pulling pressure and, looking down, I saw a foot of blade sticking out of my chest, just below my heart. Blood was coming from my chest and back, dripping down my bare torso beneath my shirt, and filling my mouth. As the bayonet now began to withdraw, a strange instinct took over; I pushed myself back, slamming my body further onto it, ignoring my own cry of pain as I heard the strained grunt of the man behind me.

Moving my arm to my waist as quickly as I could I grabbed my knife and, tearing it from my belt, gripping it as tightly as I was able to, I used my legs to push against the trench, trying to move myself even further along the sword as I felt it slide deeper into my body.

'Just a little further.' When my back hit the hilt I struck. With all of my remaining strength I threw my arms out behind me, wrapping them tightly around my attacker's waist. In desperation, he tried to drop the saber and push away from me, but I plunged my knife into his lower back, still holding him with my free hand as I brought the short blade down repeatedly.

The man stiffened, coughing blood all over the back of my head as he fell on top of me and began to cry out, his muscles twitching from fear as his body shut down.

THE | SPLIT

Now I lie there, bent over the side of the trench, looking down the hill on the other side. This was it, my nightmare was over. . . soon I would be released. My vision was fading, blood dribbled out of my lips, and I knew I wasn't far behind the man I had just killed.

Every part of me that was Charles was breaking down, along with all of the fear, the anger and confusion that radiated from him. Even the sounds of the battle waging behind me sounded distant as my hearing faded. I tried to shut it out, to focus on my pain and the dark thoughts of who I was as Burl. They were hard to ignore, but I tried to empty my mind, and looked down for a final glance at the town of Santiago de Cuba in the background. The town was the most beautiful thing I had ever seen, but my first taste of war had been something I never wanted to experience again. How could men do such terrible thing for places this beautiful? My heart longed to be there, to see the place I, and so many others, had died for.

'In another life. . . ' I told myself, smiling with a strange acceptance as my stomach again cried out in pain, and shock consumed my thoughts, forcing my brain to struggle to preserve my sanity.

Feeling weak, I closed my eyes and emptied my mind for whatever was next.

T H E | S P L I T

?

Undetermined

    The water never got hot enough in truck stop showers. No matter how many times I would turn the faucet as far to the left as it would go, I was always left unsatisfied. I was glad to be done cleaning myself and, sliding the plastic curtain open to grab my towel from the hook, thankfully stepped out of the disappointing experience.

    As I dried myself off, I looked at my surroundings with distaste. The room was poorly lit, because two of the four fixtures above were out. The white tile floor was covered in red and black stains, and the corners of the walls were covered with mold. The other men in the room were also unpleasant to look at; at a truck stop, the only people who typically used the showers were truckers. These three particular truckers were in their sixties, and the only one of them wearing any clothing at all was taking hits from a glass pipe and muttering to himself in the corner.

    I didn't look at any of them as I slipped on my pants and took my things over to the sink. Setting the rest of my clothes on the counter, I looked up at the mirror. What I saw within gave me pause. The man in front of me was a stranger.

    I was leaner than I had been in years. The muscular form I had worked to attain over the last several years had transitioned into a thin but defined frame, so I looked like less of a weightlifter, and more of a model, all glamour-muscles and definition, with no real bulk anywhere on me. My face had hollowed out, my cheekbones looked more prominent than they had ever been because the fat had disappeared.

    We had been on the road for months, and I could see the lack of food in my body, the lack of sleep in my eyes. Once a bright mixture of blue

THE | SPLIT

and green, they now lacked any sort of discernible luster, and seemed to be darkening in their centers. We were surviving, but needed to figure out a way to do more.

Still, I had done what I set out to do, Meela was safe, and no one knew where we were. I'd also picked the right one; Meela was no damsel in distress, she often times seemed even better-equipped for a life on the road than I was. The woman I had gambled everything on, had in turn become my world.

As I slipped on my shirt, a copy of the Wall Street Journal on the counter caught my eye, and the date at the top gave me brief pause; 2019. It always took some getting used to, the beginning of a new year. The cover story today was another installment on the phenomenon being called "The Moment". While a large portion of society dismissed it as a myth more facts were coming out, from government agencies all over the world.

On September 27th, 2018, at 11:22PM; EST, a tiny sliver of Earth's population claimed that they had repeated the same minute of time. The official estimates of people who had experienced this were between one million and three million. Less than one percent of the global population.

When I'd first learned of the event from a radio broadcast, my mind had instantly put two and two together, from what Meela had told me in the hospital that exact night. To my best estimate, 11:22 was the exact time Derek and his gang had broken into my duplex. Meela didn't like to talk about it.

Since we'd begun our time on the road we found little time to sleep – and when we did it was in shifts – but lately Meela had taken to hardly sleeping at all. The dreams she had been having since her time at the hospital had grown more intense and, although she never seemed to remember what had happened within them after waking, they seemed to deeply affect her. But anytime I would listen to them discussing the event on the radio or television, she would shut it off immediately. All of my attempts to lure her into a conversation on the subject had been rebuffed for months until, finally one night she blew up.

But after screaming at me for several minutes, she'd grabbed her forehead, and told me in a whisper that she couldn't talk about it. I hadn't pressured her about it after that, deciding to merely wait until she was comfortable talking about what was going on. In the meantime, I'd try to figure out answers on my own.

When I had slipped on my shoes, I wrapped up the rest of my things in my towel and walked out of the shower room, into the truck stop itself. Looking past the ice machine, I could see the shop was busy, with nearly a dozen customers inside. Meela turned from the counter, her hands full with several bottles and a bag, smiling at me as she turned and walked out of the front door.

Almost ready to join her and get back on the road, I went over to stand in line behind the counter to get a pack of smokes before I left, and nearly collided at the last line of shelves with a man coming the other way.

"Look out, dumbass," he slapped me on the shoulder.

I looked over at him as I took my place in line. He was nearly six feet, with a pot belly peeking out from the bottom of his black shirt. Over it, he wore a Camo-coat that was torn in places. His face was covered in an unkempt dark brown beard, the same color as the hair sticking out beneath his flat billed hat.

I looked slightly down at him, with a smile, as I said, "Apologies bud." and turned away. He muttered something under his breath and headed outside.

T H E | S P L I T

After waiting a few minutes, I bought my pack, and walked out the front. A box underneath the door let out a friendly mechanical chime as I pushed it open. Meela was standing between two guys, out near the fuel pumps; one of them the man in the Camo-coat who had just bumped into me. I listened to them for several seconds, then saw the taller man in a worn leather duster point at a Mustang between two rigs across the parking lot.

She nodded and said something to them before turning around and walking to our van. I followed her, catching up to her near the vehicle's hood a few seconds later. "What did they want?"

She took a sip from one of her cans, and set the other above the driver's side door. "They wanted a girl to travel with. . . showed me they had money – and a pretty big bag of meth."

"Pretty tempting offer," I smiled. "What did you say?"

She rolled her eyes, taking another sip. I noticed it was an Arizona tea, just like the other two cans that I bought. I didn't know why she liked it so much; I could barely stand tea itself, so a ninety nine cent tall-boy can of the stuff did nothing for me. "That asshole actually bumped into me there," I told her over my shoulder as I loaded her cans into the front.

"Oh yeah? What, you didn't beat him up?"

I paused for a moment, repeating what she had just said in my head. The $1,300 I had been able to obtain before having to destroy my debit card was nearly depleted. Even without getting any food, I doubted we would have enough gas to reach the Illinois line. That money could really help, and it wasn't going to be hard to sell meth in rural Indiana.

"How much did it look like?"

"How much did what look like?"

T H E | S P L I T

"The money," I sat down in the driver's seat and looked up at her.

"Probably one grand, maybe two. Why?"

"I know how we're getting past Illinois." Reaching into the glove box, I pulled out my Kimber, and the Ruger that Corbin had given me, as well as the short knife I kept in a canvas sheath. She looked up at me as I handed her the Ruger.

"Bessie? Why?"

I laughed and rolled my eyes, "I really wish you would stop calling it that."

"Why?" she looked me in the eyes innocently. "That's what Corbin told me to call her, I'm not going to betray that."

"Fair enough," I nodded. "Whatever you want to call it, tuck it into your waistband, go back to those men, and tell them you'll take them up on their offer."

"So you want to rob them," she pulled back Bessie's slide to examine the chamber, "Or more accurately, you want me to rob them. Where will you be during all this?"

"Coming around those two trucks," I pointed at the two rigs next to the men's Mustang, "Where I'll circle around to the driver side."

"So I'll be walking up to the passenger side, got it."

She chambered a round, and tucked the gun behind her into her waistband. As she walked away I smiled, watching the way her figure moved with her narrow and graceful strides.

I wasn't sure at first, but I was sure now; Meela was a bad-ass. Despite having no military training, or even any training whatsoever, she thought and carried herself like a warrior. Maybe what she had said in the hospital was true, and something had enhanced her. I didn't really detect any changes in her personality or physically – but then, I

T H E | S P L I T

had only known her for two days before the incident. I gave her a few seconds head start, before making my way around the pair of rigs, doing my best to move silently and keep a low profile. I could hear a conversation start as Meela made it to the car first.

"Hey boys."

"So you decided to ditch that loser, huh? I thought you would. You ready to hit the road?"

Meela laughed. "Not so fast, boys. You said you got money, how much would a girl make on a trip like this?"

"You're worried about THAT? Come on, sweetheart. . . get in. Me and Mitch here will take care of you."

I heard her continue to hesitate, as I finally rounded the second truck. Still crouched, I could see from the side mirror that the driver was still occupied talking to Meela, and slid the knife from its sheath as I crept forward, Kimber in one hand, blade in the other.

". . . And I'm telling YOU that I don't get in the car until we talk numbers."

"Baby, baby, come on. You're killing my buzz here."

I sprinted the last few feet, catching the man in the leather jacket by surprise. He reached for the keys to start the car, but I drew the knife to his throat and pressed him backwards against his seat. The man in the Camo jacket looked over, and I pointed the gun at his face. "Hands up, on the dash," I said quietly, motioning with my gun. "Come on." The bigger man complied, but the man in the Camo hesitated.

Meela pulled out the Ruger and held it against his temple. "Do it."

He looked at her in confusion, hurt in his eyes. "Oh come on, baby. . . you're part of this too?"

T H E | S P L I T

Meela stood up a little straighter, looking around the parking lot to make sure no one was looking in our direction, then leaned back down and smacked him across the face with her gun. The man cried out, but Meela covered his mouth with her hand and got in close, her pistol in the center of his forehead.

"Don't call me 'baby' again, got it?"

He nodded. I continued – after laughing at Meela's ferocity; "Money and drugs, on the dash. SLOWLY." The driver glared at me as he reached inside his jacket pocket.

"You're going to regret this, you know? I'll find you."

He set the roll of money down just above the steering wheel. I slid it into my pocket and jabbed my gun underneath the man's chin, forcing him to look up at me. "I'm counting on it," I stared him dead in the eyes, grinning savagely, "Bring more money next time."

Meela waved the bag of meth at me from across the car, before bending over and putting a hand on the glove compartment. "Hey babe, cover me."

I nodded, and dug the blade deeper into the driver's neck before leaning into the car and pointing the barrel of my pistol at the head of the man wearing the Camo jacket, as she pulled open the compartment, revealing a wad of papers; and three pistols, with extra magazines scattered about.

"Oh shit," she examined each of them individually. "Glad I checked, huh? Hey baby, I'm going to slip these into my purse and head back to the car. You got this handled?"

I nodded, watching as she walked away, cramming everything into her small bag, then called to get the pair's attention, "Now boys. . . I've already got a robbery under my belt today, it would be a shame if I had to commit murder as well. You boys are going to need to sit tight until we leave. Are we understanding each other?" They glared at me, hate in their eyes, but they nodded nonetheless.

"Good, but just to be safe. . . " as I walked away I stabbed each of the driver's side tires, then made my way back to the car, keeping an eye on the two to make sure they didn't move. Reaching down, I patted my pocket and a smile came as I felt the money.

What was our next move?

XII

LGPB://mn34/con/terra/YS, 7175
(Translated)

Southern Indiana; 2019

There were many people on the road who would try to accost a young couple and, of those, many were carrying cash and drugs – like the men we had robbed several months prior. Funding our journey with similar robberies, we had traveled through Ohio and Indiana, sleeping in state parks and campsites. We had wisely invested a good portion of our money in survival supplies; a large tent, and a solar generator. And to keep ourselves sharp, we sparred every night when we stopped for rest. Meela was stronger than she looked, and much quicker than I ever could be. Underestimating her could be deadly – and had rewarded me with several bruises and black eyes.

Lately though, she had been complaining about soreness through her arms and legs, telling me they were 'growing pains', and so at her insistence we'd bought a measuring tape. It turned out she was right. When I'd first met her, she was 5'6. Four days ago she was 5'10. I felt like an idiot for not noticing, but attributed it to my seeing her everyday, and the distraction of surviving on the open road.

I *had* begun to notice her body changing in other ways, though, even during nights of passion lit only by a single lantern. Her torso had lengthened and narrowed, the slight amount of fat she had before had ironed itself out completely; the product of not eating, I assumed. Much like I had noticed on myself. The muscles on her arms and legs had toned as well, even displaying a size they had not had before. When we had to fight together, we were unstoppable.

T H E | S P L I T

She was now a tall girl, 5'10 with long legs that were strong enough to break bone when she kicked. I was 6'4, well trained and practiced, but even compared to mine her skills were exceptional. Meela swore she never fought or trained before the incident, and her strange vision.

She claimed that all of her ability came from her injury, and this supposed "Moment". I still didn't know what to believe, she still didn't wish to talk about it at length, but I certainly enjoyed watching her perform her supposedly new talents.

I turned the corner to see exactly what I expected. Meela was at the bar, surrounded by three greasy looking brutes. They eyed me with amusement as I walked back towards my seat next to her, sick smiles of pleasure on their faces. A smile I returned – and then gave a knowing look to Meela. This whole plan had been hers. These three were bad dudes, guys we had specifically tracked down on our trek across the Midwest. The owner of a bed and breakfast in the center of the state had been beaten and robbed by these men, she'd told us one morning over breakfast, unable to stop her tears.

Meela and I had made instant eye contact, the same thought having occurred to us both, and then assured the kind lady that we would get her money back. From the information she'd provided, they hadn't been difficult to track down. Meela winked in my direction as a man broke off from the three and walked towards me.

He had a shaved head and a stringy goatee, with a lip piercing that bobbed up and down as he moved. He was short but moved confidently, planting his hand in my chest as I got in his path. "Hang on there, bud." He smiled, his piercing protruding slightly, "We were talking about things, when you went to the bathroom, and your lady friend over there is coming with us. You can say goodbye or somethin', but then you gotta go."

T H E | S P L I T

I looked around the room. Outside of a few scattered patrons in the booths beyond, we were entirely alone, just as Meela had planned. On the counter next to me were a set of glasses drying on a towel. To my left was a table, and a set of tall chairs. I smiled. There were so many options.

I gave him a chance to be civil, inclining my head and moving to walk around him. "Let's just see what she's got to say about that."

He caught me as I tried to push past him, "She's not gonna get a say in this, and neither are you. You should've never come in here, and I don't know what the hell you were thinking bringing a girl like that in here. Now, get out!"

I stepped back and grinned at him, "That lip ring looks infected. Maybe you should take it out and think about a better look."

He shouted and swung at me with his left arm. I didn't expect him to lead with the left and clumsily blocked it with my forearm, but his next punch I anticipated, and deflected it with my left hand, letting the blow carry past me, then caught his still moving hand around the wrist with my right, and slammed it onto the bar. When he swung with his other hand I pinned his arm down, turning to duck and catching it with my shoulder, then knocked him back with the arm that was free, forcing him to straighten his pinned arm.

Flattening my palm, I brought it down hard on the locked joint; the bone gave a loud crack, and the man sank to the floor howling in pain. Most hand-to-hand fights I had been in were short, but they were always shorter when your opponent didn't know what they were doing.

Turning back towards the bar, I saw that Meela had slammed a glass into the face one of the men; he stood a few feet away, scratching at his eyes. She grappled on the floor with the other.

THE | SPLIT

She was above him, striking wildly, then he brought a bar stool down on top of her, causing her to flinch. It gave him space to wriggle out, and by the time I had made it next to them, he had climbed on top of her, fist back ready to strike.

I lunged towards him, bringing my fist in close to my body and keeping my arm bent as the force of my movement forward cracked against the side of his face. He fell limp, but he was light as I grabbed him by the shirt collar, lifting him off of Meela and throwing him like a rag-doll against the corner of the bar.

He leaned against the edge, trying to get up, but I cocked my hand back and swung at the side of his head. Even as he slipped against the bar, limp, I didn't stop punching him, until I felt a tap on my shoulder and saw Meela, smiling and urging me to follow her.

I glanced for a moment back at the man I had been punching. Blood was running across the counter-tops, in small little streams, and his purple and red face was hardly recognizable. My stomach turned in shock. How many times had I hit him?

Meela didn't seemed bothered by it, she instead stood eyeing the thing we had come in for. In her hands she had two small wads of cash, a pair of wallets, and a small bag of white powder. I reached into the jacket of the man slumped against the bar and found another wad of money, as well as a wallet in his back pocket. Slipping them into my pocket, I looked up to see her peel a pair of hundreds from the money she had found, and hand them to a wide-eyed bartender.

"For your troubles," she said cheerily, waving it at him when he didn't take it.

"T-thank you," he stammered, hands shaking as he took the money.

Meela turned towards me and pecked me on the cheek, "Are you ready, love?"

T H E | S P L I T

"Yeah, Let's go."

She nodded and bounced her way in front of me, leading us up a set of stairs towards the entrance of the building. I looked over my shoulder to see the three men we had just robbed licking their wounds and trying to pull themselves up and regain their composure. It would be several months before they would be able to move past their injuries and work as a crew again.

"Pssst," a voice came from our right.

I looked over at a booth along the wall, just past a bright-neon-purple jukebox, pumping Crash – by the Dave Matthews Band – through the speakers in the corners of the bar. The man wore warm work clothes, and an off white Henley under forest-green zip-up Coveralls. He had the shifty smile of a salesman beneath a coarse, auburn colored beard, as he met my gaze, and nodded. I stopped in place, though feeling Meela's hand tug at mine.

"Come on baby," she tried to urge me along. I held up a finger, motioned with my head at the man sitting down in the booth; she now looked over at him with me.

Having our attention, he gestured at the men we had left behind at the bar. "There's got to be a better way to get money than mugging a lowlife crew like that. Bright young couple like yourselves? How much did you make from that, anyway?"

I didn't intend to answer, and was about to turn to leave when Meela answered in my stead. "About 2200, what's it to you?" Her stare was intense. "We gonna need to add another guy to that group we just robbed?"

He laughed and held his hands up defenselessly, "Whoa whoa...easy there, Lady Rambo. I was just asking a question. 2200 though, seems like a poor payout for a pair with your. . . talents."

THE | SPLIT

"Cut to the chase." I said brusquely.

There had been many a smooth-talker on our journey, and never once did their words prove to be anything but harmful. My cynical nature countered Meela's optimism nicely, and both had gotten us out of bad situations.

It seemed likely that this guy wanted to rob us, or worse. But after showing him what we were capable of just moments ago, and feeling the weight of my loaded pistol resting comfortably in my front jacket pocket, I determined that we were safe for now.

"Why don't you and your dangerous beauty take a seat, I promise I won't keep you long."

"Why should we?" Meela eyed him suspiciously. She was becoming hardened through our countless interactions with shady characters.

"If I were to try and hurt you I would've done it by now," the man grinned, trying to sound disarming. Reluctantly, we sat down, Meela on the outside as I slid my way inside the booth. The man leaned over, looking at both of us in turn, "$2200 is nothing, especially if you're risking your lives. It's been a long while since I've seen a pair like you come through these doors. What are you, ex-marine?"

"Something like that," I said shortly.

He laughed, "Hey, that's fine. You can keep it as vague as you want to. I'm not interested in your past, I'm interested in your future. The group I work for. . . let's call them, unlicensed pharmaceutical distributors. . . are always looking for outsiders to help them with. . . problems, so to speak."

"What kind of problems?" Meela chimed in.

"Well there are always problems. Problems you can't deal with, like the law and the product, and problems you can deal with, like the

T H E | S P L I T

competition."

"Look," I said eyeing the exit, "we're a busy couple, go ahead and tell us what you need or we're out of here."

"A man of business, I like that." He smiled. "Well I'll just get right down to it. You two can make a future in this line of work. A future with real money. We need a rival eliminated. I don't know if either of you have killed before, but you have the look of those who have."

Meela and I exchanged knowing glances. Though we had been supporting ourselves through acts of violence, a job like this was something we could never return from.

But her hand suddenly slipped into mine underneath the table, and she gave me a slight, smiling nod before turning back to the man across from us.

"Alright. . . " I said skeptically. "What do you want us to do. . . and for how much?"

The man grinned, tilting his head back to take a deep swig of his drink, before slamming the glass back on the table noisily. "Okay! Well-"

T H E | S P L I T

XIII

Bought at Auction In former Vatican City; 2079

-A. Fila

Undetermined

Charles' thoughts began to pull through and out of my head like water through a drain, then I could feel my own thoughts slowly expand and fill my mind, eager to claim the space as their own. The pain had worn on my psyche, so although I could feel the unfamiliar body pull away, I lacked the awareness to really respond. The end was near, my death had released me. Soon, there was nothing but darkness.

Then, a world crashed into my view and I seemed to regain my senses. I was lying on the ground, a cool, smooth surface beneath my face. The pain in my gut had subsided, and I nervously un-clenched my stomach, anticipating its return at any moment.

When none came, I lifted my head up. "No. . . " I muttered in disbelief, pounding my hand on the ground as I looked around me, "No, no, no!" It was the same walkway I had been on, what felt like just hours before; the green walls in the background were still moving and morphing. Had I even left? Was any of this real?

I pulled myself to my feet, still relieved to be without the pain of my wounds. My body felt stronger, and I looked down at my arms to see my own hands, realizing I stood a few inches taller than I had as Charles. My relief grew, then as quickly shifted to anger. Despite the comforts of my familiar form, I felt deeply violated. First I'd had my thoughts taken, and then I had been forced to live the horror in Cuba. This had gone too far.

T H E | S P L I T

My brain boiled with rage, and I let out a guttural growl as I started to run; faster and faster down the walkways. The presence reached out as I rounded a corner, I could sense it at each crossroads, feel it growing stronger, showing me which way to turn, but apparently it chose to simply observe, lurking on the outskirts of my thoughts.

Finally, I made it to the open room in which the Being sat, and sprinted down the platform, past where I had stopped before, still moving full speed. I was almost there; it was just ten feet away. My thoughts flared up with caution as the Being on the chair seemed to sense my intentions, but I would not be toyed with any longer.

Within arm's reach, I flung out my hand to grab a hold of its leg, trying to somehow climb up its body. My hand never made it. An invisible force hit my chest with the impact of a truck, sending me staggering backwards into some sort of wall. Soon it was all around me, and I felt myself being squeezed from every side, then lifted into the air even as I tried to thrash my way free, muscles straining. I was unable to move at all, I was helpless.

Twenty feet off of the ground, I was moved closer to the Being. I felt him invade my mind, casting my thoughts aside as he angrily called out, *"Primitive insolence, always using force to solve your problems!"*

I ignored him, gasping out my words as my body strained against the tight squeezing, "K-kill me or send me b-b-back!"

A strange feeling of exasperation emanated from the presence. "Another one. . . Terrans are always stubborn. Death will not come for you, no matter how desperately you try or how badly you crave it. Your existence, your past, your future. . . your very essence. . . belongs to us now. One life for another, the exchange was fair."

Realization dawned on me. *Meela.* Had this thing heard me as I cried out, pleading for her return?

THE | SPLIT

The Presence opened a memory in my mind, to confirm my suspicion. I watched myself from above, holding her small frame as I yelled up to the heavens in anger. The grip around my body loosened then, and I was slowly lowered to the ground.

Moving to back away from the Being and his chair, I at last put together a reply. "What just happened to me?" I challenged, "Why did I dream about Cuba? Whose thoughts were those?"

"There are no dreams here. Your life has left you; only death works through you now. Many across existence cry out for your gift, for the chance to become death, as you have. I don't know whose thoughts you share, we care not for the vessel."

I was stunned; all previous anger had turned into a resentful curiosity. "What now? Do you send me back to another place and time to continue this pointless bullshit?"

I felt amusement in his response, "Such ego and rebellion, yet another trait you Terrans share. You pride yourself in the knowledge of your species' past, but know nothing of your future. The battle in which you fought was a test, a trivial conflict in a one sided war. I can feel your savagery, your fury, your thirst for a greater challenge. Yet, you are as primitive as any life I have encountered. You see time as inevitable, some unstoppable force carrying you through life, and in your arrogance, you tried to manipulate something you can not even comprehend. Did you really believe telling that old doctor about the future would make a difference? Your time is set. . . how could you hope to change your future or your past while you are standing inside of time, itself? Your Doctor Freeman died in that battle, just as anyone who knew details of the future would. The sequence of your world is final, any attempts to alter it will fail."

T H E | S P L I T

"What?!" I shouted in shocked anger, "You talk about life like it means nothing! That man was a better life form than you can even imagine. All he wanted was a glimmer of hope after a life filled with darkness. He was a man of God, something you also can't imagine. You speak with pride gained from knowledge-"

"I am the closest thing you can even perceive to be God!" the Being boomed furiously. "Conquerors who have subdued entire *galaxies* kneel before me, powerless! There is no such thing as pride in my culture, we do not hold high esteem for past accomplishments while bracing ourselves for an unsure future. To us, there is no past and future. I see my beginning and my victorious end, unfolding together, a confirmation of my dominance. Pride is the primitive response of lesser creatures, all imprisoned by a force they can not control. A force **I** see through. . . and manipulate. . . like you interact with form and matter."

"But. . . " I protested, but was quickly silenced as he gripped my thoughts and continued over my objections.

"ENOUGH! You are called for. . . and we watch with great interest."

Before I could speak again, the room dissipated and once again I felt myself pulled away from my form and hurling through the blackness.

Left in the dark isolation of my own thoughts, I became briefly overwhelmed with grief. I had only known Ezekiel for a span of minutes, but in that short time he had left a bigger impression than people I had known for years. In this dark nightmare, he was the eye of the storm, the briefest flash of life in a sea of death.

My journey was short, or at least it had felt that way. Feeling numb from the loss, I had paid little attention to it. But, when I came to a stop I immediately knew something was amiss; I could see a strange scene around me as I floated, disembodied, near the base of a person's head.

T H E | S P L I T

I had no control of my direction, but I could feel myself attempting to enter the mind of the person in front of me as I was being fought. The syncing of thoughts and the entering of another body with Charles had gone nothing like this. When finally I pulled through, I was met with a pounding spike of pain that went through my consciousness. Distrust and fear clouded my thoughts, that I realized was coming from the mind I had just entered and not my own. Nothing was working as I attempted to exert control over this new body, as I had done before. I couldn't see, or use any of the senses.

Then, even my thoughts were pinned into place, gripped by a stronger resolve than I had ever known, as a voice echoed through the hollow shared space where I was trapped.

"WHO ARE YOU!?"

It was a man, I knew that much. But, unable to answer, I felt the mind's touch as it tore into my memories with ease. His thoughts however were shielded, only leaving with me vague emotional impressions as he watched my life go by in pictures.

'Is this the Presence?' I thought in a flash of panic, before another part of my brain reassured me that whatever this was, he was human; the emotions were easy to understand as he rooted through my mind like he was reading a story.

"WHO IS THE PRESENCE?" The man was angry now, he had heard my thoughts and quickly shifted his focus from my childhood to more recent events.

I watched myself in the strange green hallway, feeling his interest piqued and then be overtaken by disbelief upon seeing the figure on the throne. He played the memory again, his mind reeling as he tried to put an answer to the impossible. Yet his crude handling of my mind was far from the quick shuffling of the Presence, and I longed for him to stop.

T H E | S P L I T

"*Please,*" I pleaded, "*I don't know who you are or even where I am, but you have to trust me. I was sent here without choice and don't know how to leave.*"

The memories stopped, but a cloud of suspicion still filled the space and I could sense the man phrasing his response, "*I'll give you time to explain yourself. . . and this 'presence'. . . but first I need to leave and tell my crew goodbye.*"

A blink later and I had vision. I could feel myself in the corner of his mind, loosely held in place by his divided attention. Though his hold had relaxed, I did not test the boundaries, focusing on clearing my thoughts from panic, and observing the room around me.

The place was a mess. The floor looked soggy, water shone faintly through the damp looking carpet, torn walls were stained various shades of green and brown, and the ceiling looked on the verge of collapse, with signs of obvious water damage. The scenery however was secondary to what had really caught my attention. Digital boxes of text and images covered the man's field of vision. Every time he turned his head even slightly, a small marker would highlight different objects in the background, with a small wall of text describing the item. The boxes moved and flickered as I felt my host manipulating the strange interface with his mind.

Having no control over how we turned his head, I waited patiently for a chance to see more. It was difficult to look past the augmented images, but I managed to do so and better scope out the room. He was with two people; a dark haired youth bent over a strange looking monitor, and a tall blonde woman who was crouching and glancing at something outside out of a large hole in the wall.

As he turned to each of them, the interface locked in on their faces and pulled up their physical information, including height and weight,

THE | SPLIT

all beneath a bold lettered code name. We walked towards the woman and looked out of the same hole, keeping our head low as she did. We were high up, I could tell almost immediately. A gray line ran below the building as far as the eye could see in either direction. There was motion on the line, which I soon recognized to be vehicles – of a type I had never seen before – on what appeared to be a road. The sides of the lanes were lit with glowing neon stripes, and the cars all seemed to be going the same speed, in automated precision.

Soon, we focused on a shorter, concrete building across from us, probably half the height of the one we were in. There was a flurry of activity at the entrance; tiny specks seemed to be moving things into the small door up front. As the eyes focused I realized they were in uniform, strange black suits I had never seen before.

"Any sight?" my voice asked, turning to the blonde lady.

"Not yet, transmission said 0200. You think it's a decoy?" her voice was gruff.

"I'm not sure, keep your eyes on it. I have to go take care of something; I'll see you two in the morning. Stay another hour and then head back." The woman nodded as we turned around, towards a door at the back of the room.

The youth at the table was tapping on what appeared to be a blank slate. Every few seconds he would reach up and tap something in the air in front of him, invisible to both of us. He then looked up, concern on his face, "You okay, boss?"

"I'm fine, Luce, send me a summons if anything comes up."

"You got it," Luce responded, and went back to his work. He touched the side of his tablet, then a piece of machinery, in a corner that I had overlooked, began moving. The device detached and the front half soon expanded into the distorted shape of a humanoid.

THE | SPLIT

'*A robot!*' I thought, amazed. The machine was taller than an average human, and covered in a smooth material with a matte black finish. On different parts of the body were chrome stripes, matching the color of the barrels of several weapons visible on back.

I felt my host laugh as he watched me observe the robot in astonishment. *"First, you're tripped up by my interface. Now you're saying you've never seen a UDA. . . or probably any* **real** *drones. . . before? 'Robots'. . . good God. I've been possessed by a pre-millennial spirit..."*

I didn't reply; his derision had thrown me off guard. I had been cast into a world I knew nothing about, and would need to acquire more knowledge, with or without the help of my host.

As we headed towards the door, I saw something else on a nearby table that caught my attention; a thin piece of fabric, dazzling and shifting with different colors and patterns. When we got closer I could see that it was a strange mask, some sort of living screen, with different faces appearing and reappearing every few seconds. I was instantly curious, but had little time to dwell on it as we walked past and it slipped out of sight. We headed out of the room and down a dilapidated staircase, just outside the door.

The building seemed to be falling apart all over, and parts of the path down seemed to be missing, but the digital projection pointed out where the stairs were structurally compromised, along with a safe route showing as a white, highlighted line. In my thoughts, memories and images that were separate from the interface lit up in front of me, and scenes of my host using this building played out; he owed his life to this building, and spent a lot of time in buildings similar to it.

Our left hand reached into a back pocket and pulled out a thin, slick-feeling sheet. As the man pulled it up into sight, I could see it was one of

T H E | S P L I T

those same masks I had been looking at just seconds earlier. He put it on his face, briefly obstructing our vision, before adjusting it around our eyes and pressing down to secure the membrane-like material. I felt it stick, expecting it to feel uncomfortable, and was surprised when I could barely tell it was there.

"What is that?" I asked.

The man seemed distracted but answered me anyway, *"Not sure what the name is, but it's a pretty nice piece of pre-war tech. Here..."* He stopped and turned towards a scuffed, reflective surface on the wall to our right. The face in it appeared normal until he pressed near his jawline, and our features changed instantly.

This brought nothing but more questions. *'Pre-war tech?' I thought with a sinking feeling. 'Where **am** I?'*

He heard me again. *"That's probably the most sensible question you've thought yet, my primitive friend. I doubt the phrase 'Pre-War' tech means anything special to you. . . all of this is probably new to you, judging by your reactions. . . but, to answer one of your questions, Boston. Now, answer one of mine. . . am I just going to have a head-mate from now on? Am I crazy. . . or, what **is** this?"*

"No no no. . . " I laughed at the man's wit and sense of humor, easily imagining that I would've had a similar response to a man from decades before me suddenly appearing in my head. *"Well, I don't think you're crazy. You saw what was in my head. . . where I've been. . . that, thing?"* I felt a chill even thinking about the green halls.

He paused, and I felt him also think about the Being in the hall, with discomfort. *"Your memories. . . your life and your story. . . it all feels so. . . real. I felt pain, unbelievable pain, like my spirit lifting from my body. This is gotta be real, and not just my NI going on the fritz, right?"*

"NI?" I questioned.

T H E | S P L I T

"*You haven't felt it yet? Reach out, to the center of my brain.*"

Cautiously expanding my thoughts, I reached further and further into this stranger's mind, but had to stop abruptly, feeling my influence end at a solid wall. There was something in his brain; solid, giving off a strange energy in spastic jolts that radiated throughout the space. When I touched it, in a blink I felt my conscious train of thought slip into a bizarre display of figures and numbers. Then I was being jerked backwards and out of the strange wall.

"*What... the hell, was **that**?*" I stammered, thoughts of the wall still consuming my thoughts.

"*NI,*" he laughed. "*Or, 'Neural Interface'. To put it simply, the device in my mind that allows me to see the augmented images and information on the world around me.*"

"*What year is this? Do you all have these?*" I had a million questions.

"*Almost everyone... though sadly these days this one seems to be one of a kind. What year do you think it is? This will be fun.*"

"*Why would I have asked you if I knew?*"

"*Why are people from the past no fun?*"

I could sense he was toying with me.

"*Hold that question, what year are YOU from? I'm going to guess... 1997. Those offices and schools I saw looked ANCIENT.*"

"*Wow, pre-century? 2018. Not big on 2010's history in the future, huh?*"

"*No one seems to be familiar with any American history these days.*"

I felt sadness in his response, like a duty was left unfulfilled. "*Yeah I was going to ask about that. This is Boston?*" I looked up at the sky as we left the building and saw dark clouds above, billowing like smoke. They appeared unnatural and disturbing.

THE | SPLIT

"What happened? Aliens? Russians? Global Warming? What year even is this?"

"It's 2085," he replied simply. "And a lot has happened since 2018, OBVIOUSLY. First, the Hydrocarbon Wars and. . . you know what? I can just show you. The people who designed my interface's system included several programs and files to preserve an American view of history. Ah, here it is."

Our thoughts synced up, and I heard his voice speak over a video image that had been placed in front of me. Through my limited feeling of his body, I could tell that he was continuing to walk, and had the same screen open in the corner of his eye.

"Well. . . let me see here, 2018. . .

The world remained mostly the same for a while before you left. Decades continued at the same pace; terrorist uprisings, internet culture, continued consumption of oil. There were some major innovations; with Web 3.0, IOD – the International Object Database – and the first prototype neural interfaces, mankind's direction changed in 2051. The globe was undergoing a wave of unity. Europe had become a super-state, and Central America had formed something similar. Faced with protests of corruption and increased oil prices, most of Asia united under a single faction.

They grew closer with their economies tied together, and cities in the former countries of India, China, and Russia became cradles of innovation. Within just two years of its formation, the newly formed 'Eastern Bloc' had perfected nuclear fusion and had no need for oil. Life changed within the Bloc overnight, but they kept their new discovery a tightly held secret, refusing to share it with the West. With unlimited power, the entire continent of Asia became the center for business and industry."

THE | SPLIT

"But recession gripped America... I remember my father talking about it. I was only 3 when it hit. For the first time in well over a century, America saw poverty as jobs and business flocked overseas. A few years later we discovered our own process for fusion, but the damage was done. The role of economic superpower had shifted East.

Riots and school closings seemed to happen every day, I remember not going to the first day of Grade 1, when the federal district closed it down that morning. There were large amounts of crime in every city, and the needs of people on social programs began to exceed the government's ability to fulfill them. America needed something to improve its prospects, something to compete.

The remaining NASA budget was fed into a company called Nexon. With newly constructed fusion engines, they constructed a small fleet of ships and a giant refueling station they said was for mining asteroids. The world laughed at us, such a feat was universally deemed as impossible. The Eastern Bloc had begun toying with the idea, but no country or business was ready to take such a risk.

It didn't matter to us, America had one last chance. And every launch was successful... they showed pictures of the platform in orbit on my feed that night. I couldn't take my eyes off it, it was beautiful. It would take 10 days before the ships would return, and hopefully send what they found down to the surface. In just 9 days they were back, loading their hauls into the station, which fed it down to the ground below by an elevator on an orbital tether.

Their findings were incredible, massive, rich deposits of nearly every known mineral littered the asteroid belt. Within just a few months we had made dozens of trips and were able to finance twice as many ships. Over a few years, life in America returned to normal, better even. It was an age of prosperity people from your time would've thought a utopia.

THE | SPLIT

Unemployment wasn't heard of; our economy was revitalized and molded into resource extraction, countries all over the world lined up to buy our cheap metals.

Soon, seeing our return, the Eastern Bloc constructed a fleet of their own. Within weeks they were getting their own minerals, though they struggled to catch the United States in production. And a problem soon arose. Backed by new international law, private and sovereign entities were able to claim territory in space and, with the United States' head-start in the new industry they had secured nearly every large and mineral-rich rock in the belt.

So in just a few years, the Bloc had hollowed out nearly every asteroid they had claim to. Their market collapsed, violent riots happened in the mineral deposit towns in Siberia and Karagandy, and the Bloc desperately tried to buy out contracts from US businesses, anything to keep their ships in production.

But although things were shifting for the worse in Asia, It was a great time to be an American. Ships were starting to replace even the most powerful land vehicle. Every little boy wanted to fly into space and see the Earth from above, a dream suddenly feasible in a way it had never been before. I was in the academy to be a pilot, myself.

I wanted to see the stars. . . or at least the asteroids. . . with Nexon. Never got the hang of it. . . became a soldier instead. Probably a bad thing I did, this world can't stay at peace too long. Seeing our decadent lifestyle, the Eastern Bloc and its member states became agitated. New propaganda was dispensed on their entertainment links and news streams, showing life in America and how we were the cause of their problems.

The citizens became incensed, and a call for action reached a frenzy. At international conferences and meetings, the Bloc's language about

THE | SPLIT

what they saw as our sovereign monopoly on the Belt grew increasingly stern. Warnings turned to threats, threats turned to demands, and we seemed to be on Red Alert nearly every day."

The video ended, and the series of images showing the world and discoveries of the future disappeared, but the man continued talking.

"I had just finished up my reenlistment when I signed on with a new type of unit, in Langley. Inside the administration, I was briefed on the daunting possibility of war with the Bloc. We always spoke of it as hypothetical. . . but we knew it was coming, I think we all did. I was given new training, and equipped with this new generation of NI. We were supposed to be a new type of warrior, 'behind-enemy-lines shock troops', my CO had called it. The experimental implant didn't take for some, I was lucky mine did.

The NIs were beyond anything I had previously seen. We were able to interface with nearly anything, communicate with each other, and command by thought, with complete functionality. My life and perspective changed drastically as I got used to it, and I thought the enhancement was going to change the entire world. After finishing the training, we were sent to New York and separated into different buildings by cells.

We received satellite reports that the Bloc was mobilizing, but had no idea what would happen next, so we watched. . . waiting for the potential onslaught. Nearly every coast city was occupied, tanks and armed soldiers standing on corners. . . while the people continued on with their lives like nothing was happening"

He stopped, and I looked around, taking a second to let my mind adjust to the scenery, as I had been almost unaware of him walking, entranced in his story even after the video feed had ended.

T H E | S P L I T

XIV

LGPB://mn34/con/terra/UQ, 5480
(Translated)

Boston, 2085

My thoughts were busy, weighing the changes the world had been through since my time, as we now moved down a street. Boston was finally starting to look more familiar. I had been there a few times as a kid with my grandfather; it was a vivid city, bright with colorful leaves and team uniforms.

But now cars zoomed by that I had never seen before, sleek shapes without windows. And these vehicles were bigger than the ones I was used to, seeming to not even have tires or wheels of any sort as I glanced at the bottom. A rounded shape, extending to just past a slight wheel well, was covered by a stationary circle. Above the breakneck speed of the road I could ships moving above, sparsely covering the evening sky and dimly lit by the setting sun, shining spotlights below.

"Hey," I broke the silence, *"are you gonna keep going? What do I call you, anyway?"*

"My Code-name is Cyrus, but Luce and Jay started calling me Cy. I answer to that."

"I'm Burl."

"Yes, Burl... I know your name. I saw when you skinned your knee after summer camp and what you did after prom. Every memory you've written is seared into my mind like it was my own. Do you not feel the same?"

T H E | S P L I T

I reached out with my thoughts into his, puzzled. *"No, I hear what you think, and feel what you feel, but your deep thoughts and memories are beyond my reach."*

He seemed equally perplexed. *"Curious. Let's put a pin in this discussion and continue later. I've been awake for 36 hours, trying to find something from what I'm beginning to think was bad Intel. . . I won't want to talk about this when I get home."*

"Why did you stop. . . what aren't you telling me? I have so many questions."

He sighed, and I could feel his thoughts shifting into a place of great loss and sadness. *"I know you do, but these are answers you'll have to figure out yourself because...like most people, especially who served, I don't like to think about the Fall."*

"The Fall?" I inquired. Despite my best intention my level of attention had peaked.

"Yes, the Fall. . . the day we lost America."

Mental silence lingered as he paused, lost in his own train of thought. I respected this quiet and silently began to ponder how America could be lost in a day. In my time, we were revered as the world's greatest military power, and in this future America was leading the way in space! It seemed so unlikely a story, such a foreign concept, for any invader to take our soil.

"Yes, it does seem unlikely," Cy said, responding to my thoughts and pulling out of his own. *"But watch and see for yourself our greatest failure."* The world of the street faded away as our minds synced;

He was looking out of large glass window. Below him a city bustled with life, people crowded the walkways as they made their way through the tall, sleek buildings. It took several seconds for me to realize that this was Manhattan of the future, the already impressive skyline had expanded and grown even taller. As he glanced down the line of steel and glass monoliths, the Empire State Building could be seen in the distance, dwarfed by the buildings around it.

The sides of the structures were also covered in glossy neon ads, scrolling along brick and steel surfaces without a screen behind them, in perfect quality – like the images and text being projected in front of me by his implant.

Then I ceased being Burl; I knew nothing but Cyrus, and the memory, through his eyes.

On a street corner nearby, concrete barriers had been erected. Soldiers stood behind it, just specks from this height, but I could tell they stood completely still. Behind them sat massive vehicles, bristling with weaponry. I had served with vehicles like this in war zones, and it worried me to see Civilians walking around them as if nothing was out of the ordinary, without a care in the world, tapping at icons and looking at displays not visible to anyone else.

"Cyrus!" I turned around to see that it was my commander calling my name.

People in identical uniforms covered the whole room. Some walked while others sat on green rectangular crates, tapping away at blank tablets, engrossed in their work. More primitive monitors, as thin as paper, hung from the walls, massive screens bearing a yellow logo as messages scrolled across the top like a ticker.

"Cyrus!" the commander repeated. "Are you okay, son?"

"Sir, yes sir!" I replied, straightening up and throwing my arm up in salute. He raised his hand dismissively and told me to be at ease. "I'm just a little apprehensive, sir."

THE | SPLIT

"Lot of that going around," he said with a grim smile.

In the background, from some unseen speaker panel was blaring Nysa's 'Inspiration', and the pleasant melody with a quick beat had Cyrus' head slightly bobbing. Everything the girl had made was gold, he had been listening to her for years and liked this song more than he had some of her recent others.

Then the room lit up, and the people walking paused in their tracks, looking at a sudden notification on their interfaces. The men and women sitting down also stopped in disbelief, before continuing to type away at an even faster pace. A graphic flashed in front of my eyes. It had a red border with the words "Stand By" at the top, and a smaller message below.

I read the message with urgency, my eyes darting quickly back and forth as I made my way from line to line:

"UNIDENTIFIED SPACECRAFT BEARING BLOC MARKINGS HAVE ENTERED US BORDERS. ALL COMMUNICATION ATTEMPTS HAVE BEEN IGNORED, THEY CONTINUE COURSE TOWARDS RESOURCE RETRIEVAL PLATFORM 1 AND SENTINEL STATION BRAVO. STAND BY FOR FURTHER INSTRUCTIONS. REMAIN AT YOUR POSTS AND BE VIGILANT, THIS IS NOT A SIMULATION."

The message went away when I finished reading.

"Cap, what you know about this?" I heard someone ask across the room, as the captain finished reading the briefing, worry on his face. He wasn't the only one; people all over the room were around him, all talking at once.

"Everyone quiet!" he boomed. "Do what the alert said! Get back to your posts and ready your gear. I want weapons ready and all of you ready to move out, immediately. CMC get on the cameras, I want security sweeps on the bridges and a report from our bay-side perimeter. UDA ops, I want those assets ready to go in two minutes. Cyrus, Ramirez, go to the armory, I need heavy ordnance and reserve UDA on standby."

The room scurried to follow his orders, nervous chatter filling the space as I saw Ramirez already walking out of the door and hurried after him, catching him in the hallway, then slowing down to match his stride as we turned towards the center of the building.

Ramirez was one of the only friends I'd made in the military. We had met years earlier, during a covert demolitions operation in Kiev where my team had been assigned to blow up a bridge, near the Northern border of town. The Russian Bloc had been advancing steadily through the Ukrainian countryside, and looked to threaten the capital and, against my protests, command had sent along a pair of engineers specializing in demolition.

When I'd first seen Ramirez, I hadn't thought much of him; a tall, skinny, Mexican with a thin wisp of a mustache, he looked no different than hundreds of other recruits I had seen during my time in the service. But when he talked, I knew he was a standout.

Ramirez was a demolitions and chemical **wizard**, who had refused scholarships and lucrative job offers to work with the military. He was confident, outgoing, and knowledgeable. The mission, in fact, might have been a failure had it not been for his intervention; a faulty detonator had been issued with our plastique, and Ramirez had swum down the stream by himself to correct the problem. Since then we had remained close friends. I rarely saw him during travel however, or even back home during leave. It had been the military equivalent of a miracle that we had been assigned to the same program for a new NI prototype. but whatever fun we had catching up was quickly overpowered by the pain and terror brought on by the first round of trials.

THE | SPLIT

Programming a new type of neural implant from the ground up required live test subjects., and most of the men who underwent the process had gone insane. A few had even died. But of the twenty-two percent remaining, we were divided into an unspecified number of small groups and given these current assignments. The men from other units had become suspicious at our lack of official designation, wondering aloud which branch we belonged to and what we were assigned to do, but we had all been sworn to secrecy, and were under threat of court martial if we ever revealed anything about our training or the NI prototype itself.

We made it to the armory door; it was double wide with reinforced steel alloy and a panel to the right. Ramirez put his hand on it, and I watched it light up as the bio-metrics beeped in acceptance. The doors slid open to reveal a room with racks lining walls made of dark and extremely dense metal, and there was a panel of text on a nearby strip of wall listing out the vault's technical and chemical protections against attack. Rifles hung from every rack, with vests and equipment hanging behind. Beneath these were drawers, and my NI listed the contents of each in a nearby box of text. Each cabinet contained an abundance of supplies; additional UDA targeting sensors, nanowire, batteries, ammo, and repair equipment for ARRO rifles.

In one corner there was a small platform where nine UDA units were folded up, in their standard shipping configuration. It was enough for a small army itself, but every soldier in the main room kept their kit near at all times, per orders given from our CO. These were just surplus, and other, heavier equipment.

"Kinda makes you wish you weren't a soldier, huh? Lookin' at a room like this?" Ramirez said playfully. Before joining the Army he, like many people in his rough Midwestern neighborhood, had been in a gang.

T H E | S P L I T

"I don't even know what I'd do with this much equipment. . . " I replied.

"Of course you don't," he laughed. "You don't have any friends, Cy! Thought you knew that."

"Who needs friends when you have a room like this?" I quipped.

He laughed, "Touché!"

Opposite the corner from the reserve UDAs was a stack of heavy plastic crates, smaller ones on top, fitting nearly into the wall. I grabbed some of them and started pushing them to the center of the room while Ramirez pulled the folded dolly from the wall and expanded it into place on the ground. Working together, we stacked the crates onto it, loading them high, to where they just passed the handle on back. But as we were about to leave the room, we heard a strange noise and both stopped to look around.

Then all the images and feed from my interface suddenly flickered – along with the lights. After that, I lost my vision entirely, and felt a throbbing pain coming from my head, as though a giant gash was tearing into the side of my skull. Fever heated my brain, hotter than anything I had felt before. To my left I heard Ramirez also cry out in pain, but he sounded distant, like he was in some other room. My body felt slack, and in a panic I realized I could no longer **feel.** Desperate to know what was happening to me, I mentally reached for my NI, and the whiteness lifted. I saw a cloud of figures and numbers swimming through my thoughts, all raw data from the Neural Interface.

"Cyrus!"

Ramirez's voice echoed faintly through the background of my thoughts, and I as faintly felt his hands shaking me by the shoulders. It was as though my body's sense of touch was just a memory. I tried to follow his loud tone, unsure of where or even who I was, knowing only

T H E | S P L I T

that I needed to escape. Pushing out of the NI, I came back into reality and my vision cleared, though my brain was throbbing.

And, the lights were now completely out. It took several seconds for my eyes to adjust in the darkness, but when I finally could see, Ramirez was standing above me, blood dripping down the side of his face. The skin near his eye had been torn by something; a deep hole was in it's place.

"Jesus, what happened to you?" I asked.

"**Me**?!" He coughed, a drop of blood running down his chin. "Look at yourself!" He pointed to the side of my head.

With trembling fingers I reached up; my hair was wet with blood. I felt around, and soon felt the gash I had been given just moments earlier. But the wound was even deeper than I'd thought, the tips of my fingers pushed past the torn tissue and I could feel fragments of bone just beneath. There was a small skeletal laceration, just below the layers of skin. Hearing sounds from the other side of the room, I turned to see Ramirez lifting a small leather bag from one of the shelves. He set it on the floor, and after digging through its contents for a few seconds pulled a steel Med-Torch out by it's handle, then a tube of something, and now walked over to me.

"Are you ready?"

"Ready for what?" I asked, confused.

"Wait. Listen to that," he pointed out the door.

I strained my ear in the direction he was pointing, and could hear muffled sounds coming through the walls. Each sound had a different tone; I soon realized it to be screaming.

"I don't know what's going on out there. . . " he continued, ". . . but it definitely doesn't sound good."

THE | SPLIT

I nodded in agreement as my mind went wild with horrible possibilities. What was happening? Had we been attacked? Did the building malfunction?

Ramirez, knelt beside me with the tools he had just retrieved. "What are you doing?" I asked defensively.

"Fixing the damn hole in your head!" he answered. "Not sure what's happening to the rest of our unit, but if there's that much screaming I would bet the medics have their hands full. Are you ready for this? It's going to sting a little bit."

"Ready for what? What are you going to do?"

"I'm going to fill that space in your skull, with this," he held up the tube. "It's a bio-activated polymer, that can repair damage to bone tissue. I'm not sure how it'll treat ya during the long run, but for now it's your best bet. Damn bro, with this kinda damage I'm amazed you're even sitting up, let alone talking."

Ramirez put the tube to the side of my head and I heard the substance dispense with a gurgling sound and soon felt the lukewarm touch of the sticky material. He had been right, the stuff was instantly hardening. I could feel a peculiar pulling on both sides of my skull as the polymer settled into my laceration.

"Alright. . ." he said, examining my skull, "It looks like that worked. But that was the easy part, this. . . is gonna hurt."

Before I could respond, he set the flat surface of the Med-Torch against the side of my head. The iron felt cool – but then turned red hot in a matter of seconds and I heard a sizzling sound, smelling the burning as hair near the wound was scorched away. Gritting my teeth from the pain, I reached back and grabbed a nearby shelf as hard as I could; it was over in seconds, but had felt like a lifetime.

THE | SPLIT

I felt the wound, the skin was tender to the touch and felt slick, like the skin of a reptile, but there was no more bleeding, and I was grateful it was over so quickly.

"Aaaaand. . . " he pulled out a small bottle from the kit, and rubbed some of the contents on my wound, "The skin should grow back in a few hours, don't know about the hair, though. . . good luck with that one. Okay, now me. I'll do my OWN skin, thank you very much. I don't want you messing with my face. . . our standards of beauty are NOT proportionate." He handed me the iron.

It was more than an iron, technically. The Med-Torch used a chemical reaction inside the tool to heat the surface instantly, upon activation, and allowed wounds to be cauterized in just seconds. It had been developed for field use during the United States' war with the former country of North Korea.

Treatments in cell regeneration had been commonplace for decades, a process simplified through the use of artificially created stem cells. This hadn't been the first time I had been treated with either of these products, and I doubted it would be my last time, even in that day.

Looking him dead in the eye as I powered the torch up, I smiled at him, "You're an asshole, Ramirez," and pressed the corner of it to his face.

Skin sizzled under the heat, and I felt him twitch from the pain, but seconds later I was finished, and as we rose to our feet at the same time, the laceration on his face was now replaced by shiny and raw pink skin. The side of my own head felt strange with the new polymer patching the hole in my skull, and I was also having trouble accessing my NI for information.

I soon gave up when Ramirez started walking towards the door going back out to the hall, and followed.

T H E | S P L I T

Readying our weapons, we left the cases behind. He moved slowly, holding the side of his face tenderly, "Lights are off out here, too. I think the power's out."

"But... That's impossible." *I replied, dumbfounded. Power* **never** *went out anymore. It was a problem from my dad's day, and even then it had been rare. Ever since the dawn of fusion, energy had no longer been an issue, so the sight of the dark hallway filled me with apprehension.*

"Damn TacLight is out, too," *Ramirez grumbled, holding a small cylinder in his right hand and clicking the switch repeatedly, with no effect.*

Mine was broken too, I realized as I clicked it off and on unsuccessfully. "No luck over here either." "You having problems with your interface?"

"What kind of problems?" *he looked over his shoulder at me,* "Small technical problems, or 'it's not working' kind of problems?"

"Not working."

"Damn," *he pounded the butt of his rifle in frustration, and then laughed,* "I was hoping I wasn't the only one. Today is NOT looking good."

"Reminds you of Novgorod, huh buddy?" *I said, trying to keep the mood playful.*

"Yeah," *he answered.* "Except I'm not having to pry a damn Rottweiler's jaws off my forearm." *He pulled up his sleeve and gestured to a series of scars on his light brown skin. I laughed and agreed, as we carefully made it down the hall in the dark, immediately grateful for the training and experience, tailored specifically for this situation, we both had. After a few feet, an orange glow hummed to life near the ceiling.*

T H E | S P L I T

"Back-up power kicked on," I said, feeling relieved. Ramirez nodded in agreement.

As we rounded the corner and neared the forward operations post where the group had massed, shrieks again began to ring out through the walls, bloodcurdling tones that sounded almost inhuman. We sprinted towards them, our sense of duty outranking the orders from our CO.

When I opened the door, I was confused. My eyes darted back and forth, trying to understand the commotion. Small groups of people were clustered around the middle of the room, while others were slumped against the back wall with spooked looks on their faces, and a man near me was praying, hands crossed over his rosary as he turned his head to the ceiling. I cautiously stepped into the room, knees bent, sensing Ramirez leave my side.

Then I saw Cole. He had been a part of my NI training, and we had known each other for several months. Now he was writhing on the ground, screaming incoherently, surrounded by terrified onlookers. His head seemed misshapen, and a bright orange glow surrounded by sparks was coming out of the top.

Blood surrounded his skull in a thick pool, and a chill gripped my body as I realized what had happened; his NI was overheating and melting inside of his brain. I moved around, pushing people out of the way, only to see the others suffering the same fate, in various stages of this horrific process. Clutching my own head I wondered, 'Why didn't this happened to me? Was it going to, or am I safe?' and worry clouded my thoughts for several seconds before I took a deep breath and pushed it aside. I called out; "Commander!" turning all around the room in my search, and at last spotted him in the corner, gesturing wildly at a bewildered CMC officer.

T H E | S P L I T

Running over to him, nearly knocking over a kneeling woman in my haste. I was able to hear their conversation as I got within earshot:

"They're all out?!" he was screaming, indignantly, "How can they all be out? Did you try the reserve battery?"

"Yes sir, we've tried everything, I've never seen anything like this before." The comms officer looked visually disturbed.

"Audio and micro-nav feed are down too, sir!" A voice from across the room called out.

"Well that's just fucking great. Now, you tell me how the whole damn- Cyrus!" he paused mid-sentence as he saw me; "You're alive!"

"Sir, what happened to the other operatives? What the hell is going on in here?"

"Some sort of power surge, the lights and monitors all went out, then they all started screaming. Looks like their damn NIs exploded inside their heads! Poor bastards, I've never even heard about something like this."

"But sir, what could have caused a power outage? I've never heard of one in my entire life!"

"Problems with the city, an EMP, could be goddamn aliens for all we know! Look Cyrus, I'm glad you're okay, but I'm very busy trying to get word from command, is any of your equipment functioning? I'm going to need eyes on the scene while we're trying to get this sorted out. All of our interface systems are offline, we're running on wired connection only."

I swung my rifle off my back and turned on the targeting system. The ARRO logo lit up the screen. "Yes sir, my weapon is live."

"Good. Tell the engineer to raise the window and get me eyes in the air."

THE | SPLIT

I nodded and turned to obey his instructions, hearing him yelling behind me to the techs, "Go into Systems. . . grab the BCR kit, and find a way to run those wires to the roof, I need to find out what the FUCK is going on. YOU! I don't care if you can run diagnostics through the wire! GO into the vault and get the reserves to get my damn UDAs back online! Ramirez! Take them back there!"

I set up my rifle on the ground near the window and crouched down behind it, then took a look out into the city before putting my eye to the sight. The power seemed to be gone everywhere. The sun was still in the sky, but gone were the flashy billboards and displays, so iconic to New York for a century now. The city looked bare without them.

The people below on the street were moving slowly, some holding up tablets to nearby soldiers in confusion. The soldiers seemed equally perplexed, the lights on their armed vehicles had gone out as well, and they scrambled around, trying to see what the problem was.

"Go inside, you fucking idiots." I thought to myself in frustration. This power loss was no coincidence; I had a sinking feeling in my chest as I contemplated all of the horrific outcomes.

The engineer standing near the window pressed against its side, and it retracted towards the ceiling. I fired, releasing the long, narrow, round that exploded out of my barrel and rocketed towards the horizon.

Now, looking down at my scope, I opened the controls to slow the projectile down as it sailed down the street, then I accelerated and it went higher, headed towards the harbor. Now, I motioned for the nearby engineer to tap the side of my gun with his tablet to pair the feed. ARRO stood for Automated Remote Reconnaissance Ordnance. The platform had been around for a few decades, but had since been refined and expanded on. The rifle would fire an explosive round, equipped with nano thrusters that could be controlled remotely from

THE | SPLIT

the user's rifle, but in addition to being a guided missile, the ARRO was also equipped with sensor micro-modules that measured conditions and sent audio and visual feed back to the user, and whatever network he was tied into.

"You see that?" the commander's voice rang out behind me. The feed from the ARRO was being linked to his visual. "Even the Gordon Building is out. The city is going to need to act fast on this."

An emergency siren suddenly sounded outside, its shrill tone blaring between the buildings.

Below my ARRO, I saw the red and blue lights of a police drone moving above the road; a message was being broadcast from its speakers.

"ALL NEW YORK CITIZENS, PLEASE HEAD INDOORS AND FIND SHELTER IMMEDIATELY. TUNE IN TO THE APPROPRIATE EMERGENCY BROADCASTS AND AWAIT FURTHER INSTRUCTIONS."

My round weaved past one last building before I could see the harbor. I guided it past the shoreline, accelerating to maximum speed. Soon, I could see nothing but the ocean below. The commotion behind me continued, with the commander's voice loudest of all, "Inform overwatch of the strength of our position, and ask about the other outposts. We need to know what we're looking at. Corporal! Start preparing ballistics, open the containers in reserve. If we don't have our regular weapons we'll have to make do. IF YOU'RE NOT DOING ANYTHING, GET OVER AND HELP THE UDA TEAM INSTALL THESE TARGETING MODULES!"

As the ARRO continued further and further past the shore, I began to lose visibility in the mist of the distant ocean spray, and had just put my finger on the scope to detonate the round and fire another, when I saw something come through the gray shroud.

THE | SPLIT

Thousands of airships appeared on the horizon, flying in position around the largest ones. My small drone continued towards them for only an instant before a flash lit up from one of the closest ships and I lost feed.

"COMMANDER!" I called out, "We got Bloc ships to the East!"

I looked over my shoulder to see the whole room standing still. Power had been partially restored, though seemingly only to the building itself, as no one looked to be using NI; all eyes were fixed on the footage my ARRO had taken of the incoming fleet that was being projected onto the wall.

The commander moved first, looking around the room at the dozens of people transfixed on the fear-inspiring image. "Get whatever UDA units are functional out on the street! Every soldier with a mechanical rifle, ready and waiting for my orders! MOVE!"

An ordered chaos followed, most of the soldiers went to retrieve the old-fashioned ballistic rifles, then hurried to their positions on this floor and the one below. The engineers and tech personnel continued to move equipment into the room from the armory that me and Ramirez had been in earlier. Any specialists were at their stations sitting down, making do with wired connections to their tablets and the wall mounted monitors.

The UDAs that had been repaired were unfolded and pushed out into the center of the room, and now all at once moved from their idle positions with a synchronized mechanical whir, before falling out of sync as their individual operators walked them over to the window. The window was raised, and ten Unmanned Drone Assets dropped down fifteen stories to the street below.

Just then, a loud cracking rang out overhead; the first of the Bloc ships were passing over us. The second part of the advanced wave flew lower than the first, dropping large pods on the street below, about 200-300 feet apart.

"Shock troopers! Give me eyes on target!" As the specialists scrambled to follow the commander's orders, I turned my scope towards the harbor, to see more ships heading our way. They were covering their landing; a large portion of them were near the shoreline, dropping off hover-tanks and infantry.

My interface was working now; the edges of the output were low resolution and the system was slow, but I could use it. I tuned my NI into the building's wired network, accessing the camera of one of our UDAs below, and in a square on the lower right portion of my vision saw the unit surveying the dropped pod, its mechanical brothers standing around it, weapons pointed. Then the pod suddenly burst open, its outer shell explosively shedding the top layer, and Drones jumped out.

They were humanoid, but smaller than ours, with wiry frames. Unfolding entirely, they revealed long blades and a small machine gun. Our units opened fire, destroying most of the smaller ones instantly as they lunged forward. But one of the Bloc devices made it past the initial barrage, and threw itself blade forward at our drone that was operating the camera feed. In one deft motion our drone knocked it aside with its gun, and then grabbed it with a free hand to slam it down on the road, breaking its head and shoulder bearing.

The camera looked up as the enemy drone went still, then the pod shed another layer, revealing another wave of drones. These were destroyed too, but we lost several of our own in the process, and some of the Bloc units got away, tearing up the street to engage the soldiers stationed at the roadblocks below. The third time the pod opened, it revealed a pair of large, anti-vehicle drones, which tore through each of

THE | SPLIT

our UDAs with a single shot from their powerful cannons. The feed disappeared, but now the wall of windows fully opened as the men around me opened fire.

"Get our assets in the air!"

I turned around to see the commander yelling at a group of engineers who were opening a stack of crates on the dolly. Several seconds later hundreds of hover-drones, ranging in sizes from a baseball to a small motorcycle, poured through the window. My NI lit up with boxes of new visual feeds, struggling to display them all at once.

Thinking the command, I removed all of the cameras and focused on the road below, where I could see the flash of gunfire being exchanged as men and drone units crowded around a column of hover-tanks moving up the street.

Then the massive burst of a tank shell lit up the block, and the firing from our stations off to the side stopped. The men near the tank pressed forward, doing the same thing at the next road block. Our men were fighting bravely, but were well outmatched without the support of air and hovering drone units, and the dead armor unit behind them.

I gritted my teeth in anger, seeing my fellow soldiers' corpses lying across the road, but the enemy column was moving forward, now almost within range. Muzzle flashes lit up from a nearby building, and more soldiers fell as their comrades hurried to get behind the cover of the tanks. Clouds of enemy drones fell out of the sky, new drones filled the sky. Soon, even bigger flashes could be seen coming from midway up the high-rise, and enemy armor exploded on the ground, bringing half of the procession to a complete halt; the other half quickened their pace down the street.

'That building must be another outpost', I thought with a smile, remembering receiving my deployment and hearing the official talking

THE | SPLIT

about multiple buildings being used as strategic strong points, all around the border of the city. The idea was to stop an advance long enough for our own forces to move into the area. I just hoped it would work. As the men around me continued to exchange fire with the advancing drone force below, I fired at the enemies ahead with my ARRO, choosing my shots carefully.

Each round killed groups of soldiers, but it wasn't enough. The column of armored units making their way into the city seemed unstoppable.

A loud humming suddenly echoed off the buildings, and I pulled my face out of the scope to look for the source of the sound as it rose from below the floor, growing louder and louder, into a roar. Then the hull of a Bloc ship came into view right outside the window, turbines pulling at the air.

Clicks sounded from the wings, as its mini-gun barrels began to spin. I saw a bench to my right and threw my body into a roll to get behind it as a million explosions buffeted my eardrums. My hearing left me, the explosions reduced to muffled pops as I wavered into unconsciousness, but I could feel the force of the wind driving me right, out from behind the bench as, on my left, streaks of white light zipped past, forcing me to shut my eyes.

As quickly as it came, the fire stopped, and I heard the faint hum of the ship's engines going around the building, then trailing off into the distance. I lie there for a few moments, trying to regain my bearings, feeling dizzy and sick with the flashing lines of light still lingering on the edges of my eyesight. Now, as my hearing returned I heard the sounds of misery behind me and slowly turned my head, knowing there could have only been one outcome.

THE | SPLIT

Gray scorch marks marred the walls, small fires were scattered throughout the scene, and I could see that a large chunk of the ceiling had fallen, covering the ground with gray debris. There were still pieces falling, one landing just inches from my face. Blood covered most of the floor, and bodies were everywhere, twisted and in pieces from the bursts of the ship's gun. The carnage continued as far as I could turn my neck, at least 20 feet backwards. I sat up, head still spinning from the exchange.

Was I the only one left?

My words caught in my throat when I tried to call out, but I swallowed nervously, taking a deep breath before managing to shakily call out the sign our commander had taught us, "Blue!" and from deep within the building I heard several voices reply with the agreed upon response: "Eagle!"

Slowly, I pulled myself upright, using the torn remains of the bench I had used for cover. My voice felt stronger as I began to feel the adrenaline course through my bloodstream, "Let's hear some voices, who's here? Where is the commander?"

There was no response. I stood up wearily, being careful to try and stay out of view from the road below. The men left alive were struggling to their feet as well.

I looked around at the decimated remains of our former operations center, and saw that the commander was in the middle of the room, dead, his body as torn to shreds as the containers and equipment around him. Processing this as quickly as I could, I straightened up and walked back into the building where the survivors had circled up around the broken dolly.

"Ramirez!" I smiled as I saw him, unable to help myself. "You made it!"

T H E | S P L I T

"Wouldn't miss it for the world!" he laughed. The other soldiers looked at us, confused by our untimely sense of humor.

"Where is the commander?" a thin man in an engineer's outfit asked.

"Dead," I replied.

Silence lingered for a moment, before the engineer piped up again, "So who's in command?"

As the men looked at around at each other, unsure, I made eye contact with Ramirez and stepped forward. "As the two highest ranking officers here, that would be one of us." I pointed at us both, but Ramirez pushed my hand away.

"That would be YOU. I don't want to run this shit show." I nodded, having known that was coming; Ramirez never had any interest for taking charge in any official capacity.

The sounds of heavy fire rang throughout the background, and then without warning one hit our building, shaking the floors and knocking us all to the ground.

When we all stood back up, I looked at the men in turn, my eyes wide with focus. "I'm in charge until further notice. Anyone got a problem with that?" No one replied. "Great. We need to get out of this building and get word from over-watch. Ramirez. . . get those reserve UDAs running in the armory, the rest of you get to the staircase, ready the rappels." The bulk of the men ran further back into the building, stopping to grab the lines and other required equipment from a footlocker in the hall. I followed Ramirez to the armory, surprised when I arrived at how well it looked next to the falling apart building.

"Your NI start working again too?" Ramirez asked as we entered the vault.

"Yeah, about a few minutes ago."

THE | SPLIT

He nodded, pulling a tablet out of a side pocket and getting to work on the pallet of idle drones. "I'm glad to hear it, could've been as unlucky as all those bastards in there. Count your blessings. Hey, what operational parameters am I setting? I'm assuming you want autopilot squad link active."

"Yes." I looked around the room, grabbing a pair of extra magazines for my ARRO and a pistol from a nearby drawer. "Set the directive to guard mode and make the recipient me." An audio message suddenly played through my interface:

"ALL AVAILABLE UNITS, PULL BACK AND REGROUP AT COORDINATES: 42.6334° N, 71.3162° W. ABANDON ALL PREVIOUSLY STATED ORDERS AND REGROUP HERE."

The message played back, and I shut it off before turning to Ramirez, "You get that?"

"Yup. Let's go, I'll follow." I led us out of the armory, hearing the heavy footsteps of the UDA units behind us. We made our way through the crumbling building, all the way to the emergency staircase exit, before another round hit the building. I braced myself against the guardrail to keep from falling, but the rope was waiting for me, beside my belt attachment.

Together, Ramirez and I linked to the cables and descended to the ground floor. The UDAs followed us, jumping down the whole staircase, two at a time, until we had all made it outside and the men circled up around me.

I told them of the transmission I had gotten from command, giving them the option to follow me. Five of them took me up on it. Ramirez opened a nearby sewer grate he found down the alley, and the seven of us descended with our UDA guard, to find the way out of the falling city.

THE | SPLIT

The stream of memories lifted, and I saw that we were standing in a tightly enclosed elevator, its inside dull and scuffed on the panels, dust littering the edges of the floor. I could feel that Cyrus was distant, wrapped in his own thoughts, thoughts that he shielded from me, so I respected his silence and observed the scene around me, aching with curiosity as the door opened. We were walking through a long hallway with doors on either side every few feet.

The walls in here were even worse than the elevator; crumbling, stained brown drywall covered with scorch marks that were a sharp contrast to the modern luxury of the New York floor I felt I had just been walking around in. Racking my brain, I couldn't remember seeing this rough of a building even in my own time.

We stopped at one of these doors, and he pulled a card out of his hip pocket, inserting it into a slot that was about at waist level. A green light blinked and the small door swung inward. Even ducking our heads, our shoulders touched the sides of the doorway. The space was not much bigger than a walk-in closet. A cot was built into the left wall; at its head was a narrow sink, across from a small series of cabinets.

He set down his backpack near the door and opened one of the cabinets, pulling out a white, unlabeled packet and pouring it into a cup on the edge of the sink, where he filled it with water, and downed it in a single gulp.

The taste was hideous, causing me to release my hold on the body and pull back into my own thoughts out of shock.

Cy felt my disgust. *"Well, what did you want, McDonald's? It's not like you need to eat anyway. . . wait. . . do tumors or un-diagnosed mental illnesses need to eat?"*

"So I'm a mental illness now?" I replied dryly. *"And. . . I was just expecting your life to be. . . less, terrible, I guess."*

THE | SPLIT

This made him smile for a brief second before his face evened out, *"What part of that memory I showed you made you think things weren't going to be terrible? Furthermore, I decided you were a mental illness when I remembered it was 2085, and believing in spirits would be silly."*

"Ha, whatever you say boss. Anyway... I don't know... all of it? You kind of left me hanging by a string at the end."

He sighed, rinsing the cup out and placing it back on the sink before climbing onto the small bed. *"I'm tired, and as you probably understand now, not big on reminiscing. Can't you look for yourself?"*

"While you sleep?" This puzzled and excited me; I had never gone through Charles' memories the way I wanted to go through Cyrus' now.

"Well, unless you needed to sleep too? What... do I need to pull out a guest bed?"

I ignored his taunts, feeling his focus lax. His eyes closed even as I pushed my way through the senses and raw data, struggling to find the train-of-thought he had left off on. But his mind was immense, scenes blinked to life all around me.

Then I heard Cy's voice coming from far off: *"Here, this is where it starts. Don't wake me up. Goodnight, talking mental illness... and/or tumor!"*

The memory engulfed me, and once again I was Cyrus.

Gunshots echoed in loud bursts off of the concrete hallways, the smell of raw sewage beneath my boots burned through my nostrils, and savage shouts in strange tongues were coming from behind and to my left. Why wasn't my NI translating?

I turned my head all around me counting, there were five of us left; three men and two UDA. Ramirez was gone. We'd snuck up on a small patrol when first entering the sewer, but were ambushed by their unseen comrades further down the way.

Outnumbered, I'd turned my scavenged TacLight off and ordered the men to push through in the darkness, following my footsteps and using the cover of our UDA units that could see in the dark. I'd told Ramirez to send two of the units moving forward with us, and thought we had all made it through, but it wasn't the first time I had been wrong today.

Shortly after contact with the Bloc patrol at the first junction, we had gotten into an argument. Ramirez insisted that he knew the way, and had tried to convince me to ditch the group and come with him, alone. I'd refused, and in turn attempted to persuade him to stay with us, telling him there was greater strength in numbers. My words fell on deaf ears, and our words became heated. Ramirez was a pragmatist at heart, and in his cynical mind this war with the Bloc was over for America as soon as it began.

He'd taken off alone. I had no doubt he would head home for Midwest, but there was no telling what he would do when he got there.

We crouched together, grouped up in a short thru-way. The only thing that could be heard was our breath, loud noisy gulps of air I wished were quieter. But, we were exhausted, and we were surrounded, and by the number of voices around us I doubted we could find a way out.

Raising my fist to tell the squad to stay in place, I crept around the corner, holding my pistol at the ready; the way was clear. I tapped the wall and motioned for them to follow. We made it to the next junction without discovery, but the lights were growing on the wall and the chattering of enemy soldiers was getting louder. Would they hear the sounds of our UDAs idling in place?

Where was the outlet to the river?

THE | SPLIT

We had been going due west the entire time, knowing we would be bound to hit it soon. Several times, as we laid in cover, I tried to access the sewer maps with my NI, but the device wouldn't boot. On the surface my interface had been gradually returning but down here I got nothing; static clouded my ocular readout.

Then I heard the sound of boots. I stiffened, in desperation reaching for the implant. Light lit up my right eye as the square flashed with graphics and quickly booted up. Within seconds I'd located the map in our unit's files with our corresponding location. Our exit was just feet away, across this last crossroads.

At the last possible moment, as I saw the search light fade and go down another tunnel, I motioned my men forward and we zipped across the path. There, I could see the light of the evening sky cut through, but two Bloc patrolmen were just in front of the gate, and they started to turn at the sound of our footsteps. My training took over – detection would get us killed, and firing would get us discovered.

I lunged forward with my Bowie knife, lodging it deep in the first man's throat, then threw his body off to the side even as the second one put both hands on his waist to reach for his gun and radio. I got to him first, putting both hands around his neck and pinning him against the bars of the gate.

In desperation, he swung at my arms with his own, trying to call out, his face now turning blue. I twisted his neck sharply to the right, hearing his bones crack. His legs dropped to the floor and his expression grew blank.

I dropped him behind me and retrieved my knife out of the other man, then swung the gate open, watching my men as they all dropped the short ways to the riverside. Closing it behind me I did the same, and while I pulled myself to my feet after landing the last few men of our

T H E | S P L I T

unit gathered around, looking at me, clearly wondering how we were going to make it out of the city. Soldiers would be getting executed. We needed some civilian clothes, and a ride out.

Investigating the source of a muffled thud coming from behind me, I turned to see a pile of bodies stacking, as corpses were being thrown off of the bridge above. There was half of my answer.

"There are our clothes," I thought grimly taking off my gun strap and starting to strip down.

I continued to move through the memories, jumping immediately into the next one, in the order Cyrus had set them up.

The rumbling of the truck shook the back as we proceeded down the bumpy road. Groans of pain rang out, and I looked down to see Mitch gritting his teeth and clutching his stomach with blood-soaked hands. He was the last of my men; a new recruit on loan from a local unit, and the only one left from those who had chosen to stay with me when we reached the street from the riverside, instead of returning to his family.

Sarah was tending to his wounds. She was a big blonde woman with square shoulders and a gruff demeanor. We had found her and Jay wandering through Central Park, still in uniform, shifting through bodies for clothes.

"Can you keep it down back there? This is stressful enough."

"Shut the hell up, Luce!" Mitch said, coughing and sitting up out of anger.

"I'm sorry! I'm just saying!"

I smiled to myself. We'd found Luce (short for Luciano) just after Jay and Sarah. Me and Jay had been arguing over whether or not he should bring his AR, and Luce came up to us in the dark alley, asking about the supposed regrouping in Boston, and how we had acquired a working

UDA. After a short discussion, he revealed he was military himself, and told us about his uncle's truck, which we'd taken off after. Just under 24 hours had passed since our first contact with the Bloc, and it seemed I had spent most of it in this traffic.

We were stopped now; I could hear horns ringing out behind us. "What do they want me to **do**?!" Luce screamed, "Drive into the person in front of me? I WOULD GO IF I COULD!"

"Luce, calm down," I looked over at him sharply. "Focus on the road."

Gunshots suddenly rang out, followed by shouting and the wails of a woman screaming. Luce turned his neck to look over his left shoulder and out the window. "Oh Jeez, they're killing the Nexon people man! Just lining them up and shooting them!"

"Luce..."

"We gotta do something! We have guns we gotta help those people!"

"Luce, shut your damn mouth, and drive. A lot of people have died and a lot more people are going to die. If you don't have the stomach for it, then get out of the car and let ME drive."

This shut him up, and I immediately wondered if I had been too harsh. In the short time I had known him, I'd already yelled at him like that often. He was just a scared kid, doing everything he could to help. But he was soft, a bright mind who was inexperienced with the hardships of war, and though his usefulness as a full stack digital specialist outweighed this weakness, I had promised myself I would do anything I could to toughen him up for what lie in the harsh world to come.

The truck shot forward, and then slammed on the breaks, causing the UDA I had last used in Manhattan to rattle against the side panel. The unit was idle now, but could be activated in an instant.

THE | SPLIT

Beside it sat tools, and various modifications that Luce had brought along for it. The truck started moving again, and again seemed to stop just a few seconds later, and cars behind us again honked impatiently.

As my own frustration began to rise at the delay, I moved forward to do something about it; "Luce, what the hell-" but I trailed off as I saw what we had stopped for, and quickly stepped back out of the cab.

We were at a Bloc checkpoint.

Luce rolled the window down, and I heard a thickly accented voice speak. "Government ID, now. Where are you going?"

"Uh. . . here, I'm trying to go down to Atlantic City, to see my cousin. Big jolt really messed up a lot of cars. I bet we're gonna make a lot of money." Luce laughed nervously.

I heard the man speaking to his men in Hindi. With my NI now working, live translation scrolled in front of my eye; they were talking about running his card through the Armed Forces database.

That wasn't going to work. I gestured at Jay, who was standing in the back holding his rifle; ready up.

Then suddenly, Mitch noisily sucked in air and coughed loudly, projecting blood all over my boots and Sarah's uniform. She quickly jammed a rag inside his mouth to muffle the sound, but it was too late.

"What was that?" the inspection officer yelled, shouting for his men to pull their guns out and sweep the vehicle.

"Jay and Sarah, stay low." I ordered. Pulling out my pistol and stepping into the front of the truck, I ducked under the ceiling and over Luce, leaning my body out the front window. My gun just feet away, I emptied my entire double magazine into the faces of the surprised officer and his half dozen men, spraying blood onto my own face and the side of the truck.

T H E | S P L I T

"DRIVE!" I yelled, pulling myself out of the window and falling back onto the passenger floorboard. We accelerated past the check stop as gunshots tore through the top of the truck, ricocheting around the cabin. As soon as they stopped I saw Jay reach for the back door release. "No Jay! Not yet. Luce, slow down... wait for these two pursuit cars to catch up on our bumper, and then tell me."

"What?!"

"LUCE!"

"Okay! Okay!"

Behind us, I could hear screaming and sirens. I moved past Jay, to stand next to Mitch at the back of the truck, pulling the spent magazine out and replacing it with one from my pocket, then sliding the hammer back, hearing the first round click into place. The pursuit cars sounded closer.

"Now!" Luce shouted.

When I opened up the door the cars were tight on our bumper, just inches away from each other. I took a swarm canister from a nearby rack, pulling the firing pin before lobbing it high in the air towards the two cars. As it opened, a cloud of nanoparticles dispersed, tearing through the front of both cars. I patted Jay's shoulder as I heard the two cars smash together behind us, gesturing down to his assault rifle with my head, "It's not guns every time, buddy. Sometimes you gotta switch it up."

Cy seemed to sleep peacefully, I had no idea what time it was, or if he felt my presence but I was convinced he was asleep. I left the end of the memory and moved on to the next one, continuing to feel around his mind.

THE | SPLIT

XV

Recovered during Excavation; 2080

-A. Fila

Bargersville Indiana; 2018

My dreams had become the ultimate catalyst of my insomnia. Each time slumber caught me in its grip, I had been treated to a mental cinema, and the only film playing was the night of the incident at my duplex. Again and again I had gazed through the front hallway of my old duplex, watching as Derek and his men charged further into my home, guns raised, wondering just how many times my subconscious had played this for me.

I had seen the scene unfold so many times now, that I knew every detail of the men's faces, where every pellet had entered their bodies, and each spot on the wall where their blood had landed. I was never able to interact within these dreams at all, I was a mere ghost, whose only option was walking around and observing; nothing more than a pair of floating eyes. But unexpectedly, my dream changed;

A series of loud booms echoed off the steep incline, and all around me I could see men charging up the hill, carrying rifles and yelling out fierce battle cries. To my left was a massive pile of bodies in the middle of the hill, stacked with the corpses of horses and men. Behind it, a pair of soldiers crouched, using it as cover.

I walked over to them; one was a black man, wearing a scared but determined expression, and the other was white. He had been turned away, but I now felt a cold sense of shock as he turned towards me and I looked at his face.

T H E | S P L I T

It was me. I was dressed like any other soldier on the battlefield, and holding my rifle held close.

Feeling dizzy and confused, I walked up to myself, saying, "Excuse me," but the other version of me ignored this. Then he reached all the way through my form to tap the black man on the shoulder, calling out, "Jensen, Let's go!" and the two charged out from behind cover.

I followed, bullets whizzing through me as I made my way up the hill behind them. 'He can't see me,' I thought. 'And he can't touch me. It's like I'm not really here. But. . . where is here?'

Moving up the hill backwards, I took in the scenery. The grass was a greenish-yellow, and the trees at the foot of the hill shadowed the whole area, though the sun shone high overhead. Once my vision had focused, I could see a battery of cannons and Gatling guns, hidden away in the trees.

'Cuba,' I thought in amazement. 'I'm in Cuba. It looks just like the pictures.'

The other Burl and the black soldier ascended the crest of the hill. The Buffalo Soldier made it to the top first, and was impaled by a bayonet. I saw the other me call out the name "Jensen!", and then jump down into the trenches below.

Moving to the edge of the trench, I could see myself join the bedlam of soldiers, then several seconds later the dream version of me was knocked to the ground.

He struggled to grab his rifle but it was kicked away. An enemy soldier pounced on him, but he was able to push him off, and then he crushed the man's rib-cage with a nearby cannonball. Staggering now to his feet, the other Burl grabbing a nearby saber with one hand, while pulling out a revolver with his other.

THE | SPLIT

I walked alongside the trench as my soldier counterpart made his way through it, dispatching man after man with his duel wielded combo. Soon, he came onto a man in trouble, surrounded by the enemy.

As I got nearer, I realized with horror that the man had no face, something my dream self didn't seem to see as he helped the man. But he then doubled over in pain, holding his head, while the man he'd helped shouted at him. The other Burl wouldn't respond – then seconds later he was impaled by an enemy soldier. My alternate self was able to stab him in the back with a knife, but then collapsed onto the side of the trench, and grew still.

I woke up screaming, with the delicate touch of someone's hand on my chest; "Burl. . . baby, it's okay. It was just a dream." and, opening my eyes, saw Meela looking down at me, smiling.

The green light of the alarm clock on the counter to my right caught my attention, and I looked over to see the time. 9:38. It was time to go. Meela handed me my coat and I slipped it on over my t shirt, asking, "Are you ready?"

"As much as I could be, I suppose. Let's go." Stepping out into the cold winter air and locking the door behind us, we got inside the van.

As the plan dictated, Meela was driving, and we pulled out of the parking lot, heading down the empty city street, a talk radio station buzzing faintly through the speakers. A few minutes into the drive, she broke the silence, "So, you want to tell me what you were dreaming about back there?"

I lit up a cigarette and rolled down the window, "Nothing, why?"

"Well, I know it's sure as hell not 'nothing'. I've been sleeping next to you every night for ten months, and I've never seen you wake up screaming. . . not once."

I sighed, and told her about what I had dreamed. She didn't seem surprised at my mentioning of what happened at the duplex – I'd told her about those dreams several times before. But her interest was piqued when I started talking about the strange vision of Cuba, and how I appeared to be watching myself take part in a battle more than a century ago.

"That's certainly strange," she concluded when I had finished. "You're probably just stressed out and sleep deprived."

"Possibly," I agreed. "Though, I could say the same thing about you. Come on. . . let's compare and contrast dreams." She merely smiled, and shook her head no, staring straight ahead at the road and reverting back to silence.

She still didn't want to talk about her strange experience in the duplex and this supposed 'Moment'. She too had been having dreams, ones that I could tell affected her negatively when she woke up. And, like 'The Moment', she didn't want to talk about these dreams either, saying that they were related and that she had made a promise I wouldn't understand. I accepted this, but still tried to get her to open up occasionally.

"You talk to Jerry today?"

"Yes, just a couple of hours ago. He said a hundred would be fine, if that's all we could do. We're still meeting him at the same spot."

"Wow," I said, amazed. "That is not worth the risk. I wish we had more than that to give him, I know I wouldn't take this job."

She laughed and agreed, and a few minutes later we pulled off the main road onto a warehouse park, to pick up Jerry. We found him at the end of a vacant parking lot, sitting on a metal drum beside a dumpster. He covered his eyes at our van's lights, but hoisted his backpack up and got in the side door.

THE | SPLIT

"How are we doing tonight, Mr. Jerry?" I tried to sound pleasant.

"Let's just get this over with," Jerry grumbled, and then pointed to my cigarette, "Oh. . . hey, can I have one of those?"

I handed one back to him and took another cigarette for myself, chain-smoking it using the still-burning cherry of my old one. Smoke clouded around my head as the rush from the wind outside blew it back in the car. Meela switched the radio over to music, and we rode the rest of the way listening to hits from the eighties. When we got to the place, she pulled over and let me out on the side away from the entrance.

"I'll be right out back if you need anything," she smiled, lifting my spirits, "Don't take any unnecessary risks." I nodded and blew her a kiss, before tightening my jacket and walking towards the front entrance.

The door to the cantina was easier to open than I had expected, and inside, the warm air hit me like a blast in the face, a stark difference from the chilly touch of the elements. Near a large table by the bar I saw the man I was looking for, surrounded by his goons, exactly where my contact had said he would be.

The man who had talked to us at the bar was named Chet, and outside of that we didn't know anything about him. Meela and I had agreed to take the job for sixty grand, and he had promised us more work in the future if this first job was successful.

We had talked about it for several hours afterward. Taking a man's life for profit was a path of no return, but we had limited options. With the money from this job we could buy a different car and improve our quality of life considerably, possibly even finding a way out of the country.

Jorge. The name we had been given wasn't much to go on. Thankfully however, his reputation wasn't the same.

THE | SPLIT

Jorge was a loudmouth who was well known at many bars and clubs throughout the area, and frequented several locations like this, but this place had suited our needs perfectly, so Meela and I had been planning obsessively for the last few days.

He was a low ranking cartel *capo*, responsible for supplying the small towns in the area from a portion of bigger shipments brought in along the highway. In the past few months, he and his crew had been expanding aggressively, and some of their new clientele had cut into the profits of Chet's employer – which naturally couldn't continue.

Jorge mostly spoke Spanish, but again, after taking five years of the language in school I was nearly fluent, and in between bouts of intense planning with Meela in the last week, I'd brushed up, using our motel's free internet. Tonight we would see if it paid off.

I walked in and sat at the bar, ordering a beer and a shot of tequila, then sat nursing my beer for half an hour, waiting for the opportunity to present itself. When I heard the group loudly laugh I knew it was my cue. Turning to look over my shoulder, I counted the men crowded around the table, then ordered seven more shots and one for myself.

They eyed me suspiciously as I walked up to the table with the tray of shots balanced carefully in my hand. "What do *you* want, Gringo?" a man sitting near Jorge asked coldly.

"You seem like a fun group to drink with," I replied in Spanish, catching wide-eyed smiles of surprise all across the table. "I don't know anyone in this town, but on a night like tonight I'd prefer to not drink alone. Here, have a round on me."

The men looked at each other and burst into gales of laughter, but Jorge pointed at the empty chair across from him. "Yes, yes... sit down my friend." His voice was reedy and pleasant, matching the happily inebriated expression he wore on his face. He had on a black shirt that

THE | SPLIT

fit him loosely, same color as the thin mustache that curled around the bottom of his lips.

"Thank you," I replied, sitting down, focusing on what I had learned the week before.

Jorge allowing me to join meant that the other men welcomed me warmly, thus, after introducing myself as Larry – and answering a few of their questions – they were comfortable enough to go back to talking like they been had before.

The tequila and Cerveza continued to flow as I joined in. I looked down at my watch, thinking; Where the hell is he?

Though I had been accepted into their talk for the time being, it would take more than that to gain the men's trust. Meela had, thankfully, crafted an incident that would do it – but the man on whom the whole thing depended was late.

He burst in fifteen minutes later, the cold air seeping in behind him. We made eye contact for an instant, before I looked away coolly. Now that I had my first look at Jerry in the light, I knew he was perfect. His plaid jacket had patches and un-mended tears, the hoodie he wore underneath and the hat on his head were covered in dirt, and I could smell him from here. Everything about him sold homeless and crazy, and I was glad Meela hadn't listened to me and gone with the real thing.

He walked over to the table, as planned, stopping just a few feet away, and drew a gun on the man in front of him. The conversation came to a screeching halt as they stared up at the raggedy man brandishing the weapon in their faces.

"Yeah that's right, put your wallets-" Without warning, I sprung from my chair and tackled him to the ground. We had rehearsed this a dozen times, but I could still feel the tremble of fear running through his body as I pressed my weight down on him and knocked the gun out of his

T H E | S P L I T

hand, without much resistance. The men cheered loudly at my decisive action, standing around in a circle above me as I slid off of Jerry and looked up.

Jorge leaned over and clasped me on the shoulder. "Thank you, my friend. Too often I'm set upon by this scum and his kind. Tito," he motioned to a large bald man beside him, ". . . take this piece of shit outside and take care of him."

I held up my hand in protest, "Wait, Jorge. . . this man is a bum, a drunk. . . maybe even a junkie. Don't risk it on a man like him."

Jorge weighed my words carefully, "What do I do then? He tried to rob me, or worse."

"This is what you do." I grabbed Jerry by his collar, slamming his head against the ground (while slapping it with my palm underneath, to make it sound even louder), then going through his jacket and pulling out a wad, a small bag of powder, and a pair of needles.

I set them all on the table behind me, then stood up, forcing Jerry to his feet and pushing him towards the door. Jorge's men let me pass through, and I shoved Jerry roughly through the front entrance. "If you ever come back, I'll kill you myself!" I shouted after him loudly, as he ran into the parking lot.

The men back in the bar congratulated me loudly, some calling out other threats as the door closed. I smiled and went back to my seat. It was all a part of the plan. Right now, Jerry was being paid by Meela, who was parked in back. It would be a far more pleasant ending for him, than my Spanish speaking friends had thought he would have.

Someone bought another round of Cerveza, and I sipped at mine gingerly, hoping I wouldn't be there much longer. The conversation around the table had quickly turned to a vulgar discussion about the men's last time in Tijuana, prompting laughter as loud voices spoke over each other, every man trying to outdo the next. Then Jorge suddenly got up, complaining that he had drank too much already, and about how he wished he was a younger man with a younger bladder.

As the men laughed, my eyes followed him past the bar and into the hall leading out to the restrooms and the back entrance. When he walked into the men's room, I checked my watch, hoping Meela was ready. 10:21

When no one was looking, I tipped a beer over on its side, letting it run onto my pants. The men laughed uproariously as I stood up in mock surprise, pointing to the wet spot in my pants. "Clumsy gringo!" one slurred as I faked a smile, walking off to the bathroom, holding the spot on my pants out to dry.

Moving towards the bathroom door, I felt the outside of my left pocket, where the familiar shape of the wire's handles protruded slightly. I had constructed the weapon just days before, using large pegs and a microfiber line bought at a sports equipment store. Though it was technically it's own thing, my creation functioned identically to a garrote.

I had never used one before but, unlike the majority of my brain, a part of me wasn't nervous about fulfilling the job, being somewhat excited to use a weapon I had only read about previously. I had been wearing my leather gloves since arriving, not wanting to leave any prints behind, even if they did have security cameras, so opening the door now, I walked inside and locked it behind me.

The bathroom was small; a pair of urinals lined the wall beside the mirror and sink, and on the other side was a set of narrow stalls. Jorge looked over his shoulder as I walked in. "Larry, my gringo friend! Haha! You saved my life tonight!" I remained silent, able to hear the loud trickling running down the back of the porcelain urinal.

T H E | S P L I T

As quietly as I could, I slipped the garrote out of my pocket, and took an end in each hand while silently moving towards him on the balls of my feet.

"Larry...?" He tried to turn around, but was too late; in a flash, I had wrapped the line around his neck.

He pulled forward, towards the urinal, his hands tearing at the line in an attempt to free himself, then tried to step backwards, but I planted my knee in his back and forced him against the cool surface of the porcelain toilet.

He was trying to say something, but the airy sounds that came from his constrained throat were only a series of high-pitched gasps, then his body started to spasm. I pulled the line tighter and moved him into a nearby stall. His neck was bleeding, a thin circle of red where the line was cutting its way into his skin, and in just under a minute he had gone limp, Opening his throat with the wire, I let the blood drip into the toilet bowl I had propped his body up on.

Now I paused, listening to the bar outside through the thin walls. The men were still talking loudly of Tijuana, completely unaware. Smiling at my good fortune, I closed the stall door and then left the bathroom, turning to go out the rear exit instead of back into the bar.

Meela was outside waiting, the van idling a few lengths from the back door. I waved at her reassuringly as I walked up and got in the passenger door. She looked up at me, curiosity in her eyes.

"We're good baby, let's go meet Chet."

A giant smile crept across her face, and she leaned over to give me a quick kiss, before putting the van into drive and pulling away.

XVI

LGPB://mn34/con/terra/KN, 1093
(Translated)

Boston; 2085

My journey through Cyrus' memories, continued:

The coordinates were a mere few miles away, ending down this road, but the excitement I'd felt upon seeing the skyline of Boston had faded in just minutes, as bright fire and smoke lit up the night sky, spreading across the center of the horizon. I searched for a transmission on the military's designated frequencies with my NI, but still found nothing; all feeds for both Boston and Philadelphia had cut out about five hours after we'd shot our way past the New Jersey roadblock.

Mitch had bled out just a few hours afterward. I felt shame for how we'd left his body on the side of the road, without digging him a grave or leaving behind even a crude grave marker. We had argued about it twice now. Jay had taken the radio silence as a bad sign, and insisted that we detour towards the center of the country. Luce and I thought otherwise; with low power in the truck, and no foreseeable means of acquiring more any time soon, our options were limited.

"Still nothing?" Sarah's voice came from the driver's seat.

"No. . . " I frowned, ducking into the cab to sit down next to her in the passenger seat. "Here Sarah, pull over here," I pointed at two men sitting on a bus bench down the street. She pulled up and rolled down the window as I leaned over her to talk, "We just got in town, what's all the fire and smoke down the road here?"

The bigger man took a swig from a jug and responded, "Clinton Air Force Base, what's left of it anyway."

THE | SPLIT

Dread began to fill me as I asked a question I already knew the answer to, "What happened?"

"National guard and a bunch of other military all gathered together at some rallying point, and the Bloc followed them. Fight lasted the whole day and tore the town to shit."

"Who won? Does America still hold Boston?"

The man started laughing maniacally at this; it lasted for nearly half a minute before I finally got a response, "Who do you think? There's no America anymore, whole country is Bloc territory now."

Sarah rolled up the window and continued down the road, while we talked as a group about finding a place to stop and lay low before planning our next move. Three weeks went by as we waited for an update, stationed in a war-torn warehouse, in a mostly abandoned neighborhood. Every day we would go out alone, at different intervals, to scavenge for food and listen for information.

Both were becoming harder to come by. Public executions happened frequently in the centers of town, with Bloc men lining up captured soldiers and mining executives, reading their offenses through loudspeakers, before firing by squad. There was also a rumor going around that Bloc intelligence was hiding among the citizens in the city, looking for remaining military, and large public buildings had been converted into detainment centers for the unfortunate soldiers caught. Today had been worse than most, I had seen a police captain and his whole department executed for 'aiding the enemy'. And, my clothes were damp from scattered rainfall.

My pack was full of food though, the only silver lining on such a dark Tuesday. Several miles from our warehouse I'd stumbled onto a deserted gas station. The racks had been thoroughly picked over; wrappers and broken shelves littering the floor.

THE | SPLIT

My interface pulled up descriptions of each product, cluttering my field of vision, but I quickly dismissed them all with a blink. There had been a locked door labeled 'Employees Only', which I had kicked in and found a small box of cans containing ravioli and assorted vegetables. It would definitely beat last night's meal. On nights we couldn't find anything, we had hunted rats; they were never hard to find in our part of the city.

I turned onto our street, again seeing the large graffiti painted on the green-painted side of the first building. 'God Help Us!' it read, in bright red letters. We often joked that this was our address, our attempt to add humor to the grisly reminder of our failure as soldiers fighting for a country that may not exist anymore.

Going around the back and opening the door, I heard loud voices coming from around the corner, above the run-down staircase. They were arguing again; Luce and Jay had never gotten along. As I got closer though, and began to climb the stairs, I recognized that the tones were mainly happy:

"Well... so, have you run it through the network?" Sarah's voice sounded more upbeat than I had heard in a while.

Luce responded, obviously distracted, "Not yet, I'm trying to confirm that GB Intelligence is even still in Boston first."

"Good, because if you're wrong, and you lead us into some ambush, I will haunt the living shit out of you." Even Jay sounded happier than usual. Luce must have had really good news.

Finally, I made it up the last stair and saw them sitting around on the broken furniture set. "Damn, Jay can't you just say 'good job kid', and leave it at that?" They all looked up at me, and I could tell by the proud look on his face that Luce did have good news. I turned over my bag and emptied the cans on the table.

THE | SPLIT

"Actual food tonight people, you better be happy. I care enough to go a mile further and get you all the good stuff."

Everyone but Luce stood up, smiling, and walked over to the table. He sat, holding his tablet up absentmindedly, staring around the room and tapping his foot nervously on the wood floor.

"Well Luce... you obviously got something to say, spit it out."

Unable to contain his enthusiasm any longer, his words came tumbling out as he quickly told me what he had found. "Well... so, I was walking around near Clinton, looking for parts for that terminal I've been wanting to build, when a guy yells out at me from one of the buildings. I walked over to him, cautiously, immediately thinking he's just a bum... from his clothes and matted hair. But he said he was undercover, and that I look military, and asks what I was doing there and what unit I was with. So I say 'Prove it'... and he pulls out one of those scanner things they used to have on my Carrier, and flashes the beam on my face. Then he showed me the screen, and there I was... name, height, weight, unit, he had my whole ID right there like... the top level NIs. He said he was undercover for the GB, and that he had a meeting place for anyone still looking for the rendezvous point in Boston. Well... you know me, I'm smart... I told him I didn't believe it. Then, he says that I don't have to believe it and told me to type down the meeting spot and see for myself, so I did. Here it is."

He showed it to me; 24 Fort Street, Basement, at 00:23 exactly; then pulled the tablet back to tap on it. I took the location and plugged it into my NI; a graphic flashed in front of my eye as I surveyed the 3D map of the area, and routes for how we would reach it.

"Here," Luce said gesturing to hand me the tablet; he slapped his head, realizing my NI was still functional, and instead swiped it over to me.

THE | SPLIT

"Lucky son of a bitch who still has an interface. Mine's already been gone long enough to where I don't remember you still have one... Do you see it yet?"

I scrolled through several blueprints, frowning. "Yeah... but I'm not seeing a basement, at least in the original city plans I'm not."

"Do you still want to check it out? We could go later... me and you."

"No..." I paused, thinking, "We'll go... but we'll all go. How's the truck looking?"

"I'll check the battery, but it should be fine." Luce was confident, but still grabbed his tools. "I'll run it about a half hour before, too."

I nodded in agreement and we all sat down to eat.

The truck ran perfectly, just like Luce said it would. It was in good shape and we were lucky to have it, even if we almost never used it. With our military service linked to our personal pay account, we couldn't scan our cards to charge the battery, and the very few stations that would barter or accept cash against Bloc rules were expensive. It had taken nearly all of the food we came into town with to refill our charge the first time, and we hadn't used it since.

We made it to the building and drove around it a few times, checking the place out. It was a large, concrete office building with glass windows. Most buildings in Boston had sustained damage during the fighting, but this one looked like it had been in bad shape beforehand. Near the front door, I saw the word 'Globe' faded into the concrete sign at the base, and ran the word alongside Boston through my NI. The Boston Globe was a newspaper-turned-Media Company that had closed down in 2059. After curiously watching other people slip out of the structure a couple at a time, we looked for a place to park, finding a dark alley between the building and an attached warehouse in the back corner, then went to find a door inside.

THE | SPLIT

We each took one of the radios Luce had rigged up, and went separate ways, looking for a basement. Jay found it and in just a few minutes we were all there standing around the heavy door, right next to a prominent side entrance with the word 'Basement' scrawled across the wall – disguised perfectly among other graffiti. Going through the door we found a concrete staircase.

The laughter of the people who had come in before us echoed through the space as I signaled the group to descend cautiously and Jay took point; he still had his assault rifle from New York and had relished any opportunity he could use it. But as we got closer, we began to hear. . . music, coming through the walls. It grew louder and louder until we got to the bottom of the stairs, where it was at full force. An open door-frame gave way to a huge hall, packed with people, and lights of every color danced on the walls and covered the ceiling, swirling around the room to the music.

'What's this. . . a...nightclub. . . ?' I thought, astonished.

Leading my group down the side, I urged Jay to throw his rifle over his shoulder and stop carrying it around; he reluctantly agreed. The area was divided into three levels, a below-ground level served as a dance floor. The one we were on was the ground level, which ringed around to the opposite wall. It was the biggest, with people crowded around tables and bars, the floor seeming to extend even back beyond the staircase to my left. Across the room was a platform, several dozen feet above the dance floor, with doors that seemed to lead further back into the building.

This third level was accessed by the wide, bending staircase beside the dance floor. With its darkened windows, and guards staring down, I determined that the third level was where we needed to be. We made our way to the staircase leading to this platform, slowly, dodging dancers and people carrying drinks. No one seemed to pay us any mind, no thought of trying to stop us, nor did they say anything about our bandanna masks and weapons. They seemed entirely unaware of the world outside.

'Or maybe they don't care,' I thought, jealous of that type of mind. They were mostly younger, wearing black with bright trim and designs, and most were smoking or drinking. A pungent cloud hung above the space, spilling down occasionally and reducing my view to a haze. Tables seemed scattered all over the area, and well dressed men sat at the sides on curved couches, with women in their laps and various drugs spread across the tables. Above them stood men carrying rifles and pistols, who would narrow their eyes at you menacingly if you stared at them or the person they were guarding for too long.

I made it to the stairs first, and waited on the rest of my group, as the pressing of the crowd had spread us apart. When we had ascended, we were stopped at the top by a group of large bouncers who were surrounded by smaller, armed men.

"Who the hell are you?" the leader asked, putting a hand on my chest.

I glanced down at his hand, looked back at him, smiling dangerously, then took a small step backwards so his hand fell off my chest. My crew stepped up around me, as I quipped, "An intelligence officer... above your pay grade." His face flashed with anger, before settling. I went on, "Now...I was told...that a couple of old soldiers could find some answers here. Show him Luce."

Luce pulled out the tablet and showed the man the information he had gotten near the base earlier.

"Sorry," the man said, smiling, "I don't know anything about that. But if you want to see the boss, you need to wait over there."

THE | SPLIT

He pointed to the group of people sitting on the stairs who we had passed on the way up, then he and the group of men started laughing. I felt anger rise inside of me. We hadn't come this far, or waited this long, to be delayed any longer by this dick and his friends.

"Nah, I'm going to tell you what. We've been looking for this for weeks, and I'm not going to let you stand in my way. I'm walking through that door, you can be dead or alive when I do it, I really don't care."

He bristled and started massaging his knuckles. The men with guns around him brought them up to their sights and clicked them off of safe.

"Cy. . . what are you doing?" Luce asked nervously.

I ignored him, staring at the man in front of me, sneering.

"The hell is going on out here?" said a voice from behind him.

I looked over his shoulder to see that a man had come out of the door and was walking towards us. He was tall but heavyset, older and starting to wrinkle, his black and silver hair matched his dark fatigues and rank placard perfectly. Finally, it was someone in the Service.

"Well sir," I spoke up, over-cutting the head of the men in front of the door, "I'd heard that someone here needed more fine soldiers such as ourselves, and I was just telling your. . . uh. . . associate, here that we had been summoned by a man near Clinton. . . or, I was getting to it anyway."

"Ah, you're the Navy Comms Officer and his group! Come on in, shut the door behind you."

Inside the tinted glass door were even larger tables, and rounded couches, like outside. Men were sitting around them talking, half naked girls all over them, with more dancing in the background.

THE | SPLIT

Massive piles of powder — white, green, and tan — were in the center of these tables, with lines of each cut up beside them. In the corners, armed guards stood watching everything inside the room with severe expressions.

"We're over here," I heard the man's voice to my right, turning to see him walking into a small hallway. At the end of it was a room similar in size to the first one, but instead of tables and couches there were chairs, hard green crates, and men in the back — half busily working on monitors.

"What **is** this place?" Luce asked, looking around. "Who are you?"

"I am Lieutenant Colonel Jett, with the U.S. Defense Department. This whole building was a defense department black-site. . . in the forties and fifties. Following the events of the last few days, we made a deal with Manuel and his friends out there. They could have the building to do as they pleased. In exchange we got protection and information. With our assets so limited, we're going to need all of the help we can get over the coming months. This. . . " he said, gesturing around, ". . . Lady and Gentlemen, is the nervous system of Upper Eastern Seaboard Covert Operations."

"Covert operations?" I questioned. "I thought the plan was a full scale assault?"

"It was," he confessed. "But we got ahead of ourselves. With hardly any air or ground support following the EMP Blast, we didn't stand a chance in Boston, or anywhere for that matter. Any remaining support units have been pulled and consolidated with the remainder of our functioning government, in favor of employing more. . . guerrilla style. . . tactics, with any remaining ground troops."

"You said a blast?" Luce spoke up. "Was it a modified EMP like I thought?"

T H E | S P L I T

Jett nodded. "A series of them, strategically placed for maximum coverage on the East and West coasts. They must have been planning this for years."

"So Colonel. . ." I interjected impatiently, "Guerrilla style tactics? What exactly are our orders?"

"We have decided to group all active units remaining inside enemy zones into cells. These cells will receive instructions weekly from whatever secure networks we have nearby. This will be changing constantly so as to avoid detection. We have a Land Systems team already undercover and in place to begin setting them up."

"All this sneaking around," Jay spoke up, lamenting, "I wasn't trained for this. . . we need to hit them where it hurts, hard."

"We tried. . . lost nearly all of our men on the entire East Coast. We don't need our troops throwing their lives away for vengeance, son, we need soldiers who can survive and take orders."

Jay grumbled something under his breath, but then nodded and let the man continue. "I'm going to need all of your unit numbers in here. . . we need to confirm who you are before we proceed." He went around in a circle starting with Sarah, typing their units into a monitor he had been wearing on his hip. When he got to me he paused, I heard a beep from his monitor after he typed in my information. "Says here your work is classified," he looked puzzled.

"Yes sir, that is correct."

"I've been doing this for weeks, and I've seen all manner of top secret work, but never anything above my pay grade. I can see your former service here, but I'll need an organizational tag at the very least."

"We were a DARPA affiliate, sir. . . coordinating with the Central Intelligence Corps of Engineers."

THE | SPLIT

He marked that in his screen, "I'm going to know at least something about your former designation soldier, even if it is classified above Top Secret."

I stiffened, standing at attention formally, "With all due respect sir, I'm not at liberty to tell anyone without the proper clearance. Can I give you my CO instead, sir?"

"Yes, that will work for now. I'll look more into this later." I typed the information into his tablet. "Now you, Corporal. . . Luciano, is it?"

"Yes sir!" Luce replied a few seconds later, unused to being called by his last name, after the time he had spent with us.

"On your file it says you were Reconnaissance and Communications on. . . the USS James Stroud? Are you familiar with sub-network obtainment protocols?"

"Very familiar, sir, I coordinated cross-branch work on the bridge, sir!"

"Excellent, take this," He handed him a black chip that Luce immediately snapped into his tablet, "Don't lose that soldier, we would rather have it destroyed than captured. The details of your first connection to Central are programmed. Good luck men."

As this last memory faded, I saw the world briefly; Cyrus' eyes had opened, he ignored me when I tried to call out to him, shutting his eyes again and falling back into sleep. His mind felt exhausted; and suddenly I felt it too. My other thoughts began to dissolve. Was I falling asleep too? How was this possible?

I never got an answer; soon I fell into a dream of my own.

"Atten...TION!"

The voice jarred my eyes open. I could feel a hard mattress beneath me, and sat up straight, looking around the room.

THE | SPLIT

Rows of bunks lined the long, dull-gray space, on which other people were also sitting up. Instant recognition came over me, this hadn't been the first time I had dreamed of this place. This was the genetics testing facility, where I had received my Basic Training. I had spent many long days here, and I knew that today would be my last.

Hopping down from the bunk and quickly slipping on my pants, I laced up my boots as our drill sergeant continued to yell, goading us to move even faster. Ready now, I stood up and fell in with my fellow recruits and we started towards the door to our left.

The sergeant stopped us, "Where do you think **you're** going?!"

"The mess hall, sir!" one of the men in the front line answered.

"The mess hall?!" the Sergeant let out a cackling laugh. "Private Macy. . . you're all heading for the training field! It's time to test your combat readiness. . . see if all of those unarmed drills have turned you into men yet! That alright with everybody?!"

The whole group answered in unison, "SIR, YES SIR!" then turned towards the other wall and jogged as a unit to the outside of the building.

The air outside was already warm and humid, the start of another scorching day beneath the Louisiana sun. Bugs followed our column as we moved, landing on various men, buzzing around annoyingly.

The training grounds were inside a nondescript, open air storage building, behind the main facility. Upon reaching it, we were split into two even groups, on different sides of the rubber blue mat in the building's center.

The lieutenant in charge of the room quickly paired up two men standing across from each other, and they moved to the center of the mat. We were all instructed that this would be a sparring match with no

T H E | S P L I T

rules and no pads, then the Lieutenant screamed; "Live exercise... NOW!"

After a second's hesitation, the two soldiers approached each other. A flurry of blows were exchanged, and within seconds one recruit was on top of the other and the exercise was over. Slowly, we moved down the line, each man sparring with the man directly across from him. I was towards the middle of my line, and watched with anticipation as it got closer and closer to being my turn, but when the Lieutenant pointed at me, I looked across to see who I was facing, and my blood ran cold.

Walking towards me, smiling confidently, was James.

He had been a constant thorn in my side ever since arriving on site. From what I'd heard via the others, he had been a marine before being selected for this unit. So naturally, James was used to army life, and had quickly made friends among the recruits. He and his new friends teased me and a few other men mercilessly. My swimming scholarship had somehow come up, and he never refrained from calling me out on it.

We were now just a few meters away from each other, and I could see him sneering at me. "Hope you're ready for this, **Burlington**," he spat out venomously. "I don't think the swimming career is gonna help you here."

He laughed at his joke. I ignored him, continuing to stare down at the floor, but was still able to feel his eyes on me as I squared up on the mat and stretched my legs by raising up onto my tiptoes, letting my arms dangle loosely at my sides. I still felt tired, but my body was ready for whatever came next.

"Alright!" The drill sergeant yelled, "Ready?. . . Live exercise, now!"

I looked up at James, raising my hands in front of my face. He did the same and bounced in place, taunting me, trying to lure me forward.

T H E | S P L I T

"Come on GIRLington, I haven't got all day. Let's see that breaststroke in action. Come on!" He stepped forward, jabbing at me with his right arm. I blocked it with my forearm, keeping myself in a defensive position, fists near my chin. Again, he punched at my guard; two light jabs with his left, then right. "You not gonna to fight, man? What did your dad raise. . . a pussy? Or maybe it was your mama. . . ? You catch a little bit of her boobie cancer when you were growing up?"

I snapped. James had been confronted about my mother before. In my first few weeks on site, I'd gotten a letter from my father, telling me about my mom's diagnosis. The cancer was already stage 4, and she was currently undergoing radiation treatment. I could stand the jokes about me, mocking me as a swimmer and a civilian. But hearing about my mother sent me into a rage.

Stepping forward, I began throwing a flurry of jabs at James' protected face. When he threw a counter-punch, I sidestepped it, catching him with an uppercut to the chin, a blow which sent him reeling backwards. I pursued, aggressively. In a low crouch, still recovering from my previous punch, he looked up to see me coming and in desperation planted both hands on the ground, intending to scuttle away.

I was on him before he could, reaching for his head with both hands, grabbing him by the hair as I slammed my knee into his face. I felt warm blood through the inside of my pant leg, but I did not let up. Hands still tangled in his hair, I threw him to the ground, standing over him and stomping down his chest, watching his hands flail upward as his breath squeezed out in a loud cough.

My leg now on top of his chest, I sank to my knees, putting all of my weight on his body, striking him repeatedly; big, wild hay-makers that used all of my strength.

T H E | S P L I T

I could hear screaming behind me, muffled behind the sound of the blood rushing through my brain, but again and again I struck him with alternating fists. My hands began to swell and ache from the effort, but I didn't stop.

Suddenly, I felt a strong hand grasp my shoulder from behind, but shook it off and continued my assault. James was now lying on the mat, bloody and helpless. Several hands grasped me this time, and I felt myself being pulled backwards amidst loud shouting. I was not listening, I was consumed by rage, and the only thing I cared about was hurting James as much as possible. . .

The scene faded away even as I regained control of my thoughts, with a start; my whole mind was recoiling from the nightmare.

I was glad it was over now. . .

T H E | S P L I T

XVII

Recovered in Bloc Vault C1
-T. Acerz, 2131

Boston; 2085

    Suddenly Cyrus opened his eyes, and I was back in his apartment – which, come to think of it, was probably closer to a cell. He blinked twice and sat up, eyes blurry with sleep, then stood up and crossed the room (in a step and a half) to sit down on the small toilet in the corner.

    When he was done, and went back across to open a cabinet, I decided to speak up. *"Good morning."*

He jumped, and his brain filled with confusion as he tried to push my thoughts out in a panic, but quickly remembered and relaxed. Slumping his shoulders, he let out a sigh. *"You scared the shit out of me."*

"I'm sorry. . . didn't know you had forgotten I was here already."

"I'm tired, that's all," he qualified, while pulling out the same box of powder he had eaten last night.

    I shuddered at the thought of the taste. *"Seriously man? You're going to eat it again? Is that all you have?"*

"Stop your complaining. . . Oh!" his mind lit up with discovery as the fog of sleep slowly faded, *"I had the strangest dream last night."*

"Oh yeah? Cool. . . I'm not really the type of person you share dreams with." I replied dryly, unsure of what to say next.

"You aren't the sharing type, huh?" I could sense annoyance. *"That's funny, because neither am I. I'm not big on sharing my stuff. . . or my home and, oh yeah. . . . my THOUGHTS."*

"...Because I CHOSE to be here, and traveled all this way just to be in your fun little head, out of my own sense of adventure!"

THE | SPLIT

I stopped: were we fighting right now?

I could sense frustration from his thoughts, but he replied in a calmer tone: *"Whether you chose to be here or not, my dream... that you don't want to hear... is about you. You and that... thing, that has you trapped."*

"Well..." I hesitated, unwilling to admit I was curious, "... then, what happened? What did you see?"

"I was in the halls, walking... I think I was just behind you. We were searching for it, the way you had always come before had led you nowhere. I tried to talk to you, I even reached out and grabbed your shoulder but you couldn't hear me. You broke into a run and I followed. Soon you found the throne room again and stormed into the center. I told you to watch out but still you didn't hear me. You jumped into its chair, punching and pulling at it, as it tried to bat you away. All of a sudden there were two of you, then three. More and more copies of you kept popping up, surrounding the Being and helping you fight. But even with the extra help you were overpowered... and then I stepped into intercede. That's when it turned towards me, snarling, I was caught in the grip of its stare, helpless and paralyzed as cold crept over my body. Then I was awake... took me almost a minute to realize where I was."

"Whoa, that is a crazy dream."

"But that's just it; it felt like... something more. I've never had a dream like that in my life. It was so clear and powerful. I felt the presence like you had, swarming my thoughts, trying to pull them from my mind."

"Strange," I replied, thinking about what this meant. *"Can you show me?"*

He racked his brain, searching. *"No, it's missing somehow. I know what happened...but somehow my brain seems to have forgotten the* experience. I've never remembered dreams well though, most seem to fade from memory before I even wake up."

I made a note of the discussion as he mixed the powder with water in the bowl below. The water bubbled, and then settled into a mud-like gray paste. I pulled away from his senses as he took a bite, still tasting it at the edge of my thoughts. But, thankfully, it was gone in just a few seconds. When Cy stood up to put the bowl back on the sink, I interrupted his thoughts with the questions that had slowly been building overnight. *"So. . . I've gotten more of the picture, but still have some questions. What happened after you met Colonel Jett?"*

He paused, thinking about my question, *"Damn. . . I'm not, sure. . . exactly. That was awhile ago, little more than 5 years, I'd guess."*

"FIVE YEARS?! And here I thought I was starting to catch up. What's happened since?"

"That's a question I need time to think about. I'll show you more in a few hours though, I have somewhere to be."

"Where are we going?"

"Shouldn't you know? I thought you were here because you knew some greater truth, like you did in Cuba."

"That was different," I admitted, *"In Cuba I actually knew what was going to happen. I also had full control over the body I was placed in."*

"What do you mean?"

"Well, unlike what's going on between me and you, I had full control over all of his thoughts and movements since the beginning. We never talked like this, his thoughts were in the background the whole time."

"That would be quite a different experience, I imagine he was terrified."

THE | SPLIT

"He never seemed to be, I could sense his feelings just like I can with you. I wonder if your implant is the difference..."

"Could be, I'm just glad I'm running the show."

He laughed and left me to myself as we took the elevator down in his building and then walked out of a door into an alley. I could feel his mind working quickly, he was deep into his own thoughts – thoughts he didn't share with me.

His interface was a swirl of constant movement, too; boxes of text, recordings, and images moved through our shared vision. All of them were related to the same group of men; intelligence files, from all corners of the remaining military command.

At the end of the alley, we turned right and walked down a short flight of stairs into a tunnel. The area was crowded, people gathered around pillars, conversing quietly. Cy walked to the edge of the crowd, remaining off to himself, staring blankly ahead. There was a loud sound, and a rush of air came from our left as a train tore into sight, moving almost faster than I could detect.

The doors opened and the crowd poured into the car in front of me, filling the bench seating. Patiently waiting behind the slow moving line, we eventually made it inside too, then grabbed a bar above, planting our feet as the doors closed and the train shot forward in the dark tunnel.

A couple of quick stops later, with the people filing in and out of the car in mere seconds, we were at our destination – it had taken less than one minute. When the door opened again we walked out onto a mostly empty platform, and headed through the tunnel to a sinister-looking, dark staircase which was not helped by the flickering lights at the ceiling above. I did recognize the street when we made it to the surface, however; it was one of the few things I had seen last night, while we were walking home.

T H E | S P L I T

A man in tattered clothing passed us to the left, pushing a sleek looking shopping cart filled with broken machinery. *"Scrappers,"* Cyrus said, sensing my curiosity. *"In this part of town it's one of the only real ways to make money."*

That made sense. I observed the scene around me, able to fully see the damage in the light of the rising sun. There were 6 buildings in sight, all of them visibly damaged in some way. Walls were missing, and all had bullet-hole-riddled sides, windows, and doors alike. Compared to parts of the city I had seen Bloc civilians living in, the dystopian conditions of these neighborhoods seemed vindictive and intentional. Soon, we were in front of the building I had first appeared in, the night before.

It was a lot bigger than I had realized; twice as tall as anything else on the row, and stretching back to the next street at our left. Weaving through the debris inside, we made it to the stairs; halfway up a step broke.

I felt the hair on our neck stand out as we slowly backed down, then gingerly stepped over the missing stair on the other side. "Third time that's happened," Cyrus grumbled loudly. "Stupid NI needs to detect new structural weaknesses faster."

Entering the room moments later, we heard the static buzzing of a radio, then turned the corner to see Sarah moving and changing the dial with a finger sliding along in the air, adjusting it in slight increments, with her ear close to the speaker. Luce spoke first, mumbling, "Good morning," but never taking his eyes from the crates he was moving.

I noticed a sleeping bag in a corner, mixed into a pile of blankets, prompting Cyrus to look, too. "You two sleep here last night?"

Sarah turned around, wiping sweat off of her brow, "I didn't. Luce must've though, kept talking about a multi-band scanner last night. He

T H E | S P L I T

had a bunch of new crates in here this morning, guess he bought it from one of Ewan's guys."

"You know I can hear you, right?" Luce said, stopping his work to yawn.

"Yeah Luce, we know." Cyrus put a hand on his empty desk. "How late were you up last night?"

"Not sure. . . truck came by to the garage around 2." He swiped something into a corner on his interface, and looked over at us. "I loaded it up and brought it all upstairs. Fell asleep immediately afterward."

"Well. . . are we at least going to get our money's worth, this time? What is this you bought?"

"It's a scanner, for monitoring the feeds coming in and out of the repository. You know how I said I bet there are encrypted lines?" Cy nodded, letting him continue. "Well, if this works like I think it will, we'll be able to see what parts of the networks are active, and where they're broadcasting from. . . on every spectrum from radio to IOD cloud monitoring. I can't actually see through the encryption, but I'll be able to tell which streams ARE encrypted so we-"

Cyrus interrupted, already sensing where he was going, "-can know which parts of the building are dealing with sensitive information."

"Exactly," he said, smiling.

"Well good, how long will it take to be set up and ready to use?"

"Probably just another hour, I have Sarah checking the frequencies and marking down which are data, which are just repetitive signals from NIs, and which ones are audio, should cut down on a lot of the guesswork." Cyrus nodded and sat down at the table Luce normally worked from.

T H E | S P L I T

I thought he was turning on the monitor in front of him, but I felt our hand reaching into a pocket to pull out a small piece of plastic. It was cylindrical, with a lid on top that Cy undid, revealing a light brown powder inside, He poured about half of the container on the flat surface beside the screen.

"You going to share any of that?"

We looked up to see Luce standing over us, holding a cluster of wires in his hand.

"Luce, you bum, do I ever NOT share with you?" Pulling out a knife, we split the pile in half and slid Luce's portion to the other end of the table.

"Well. . . here's to another productive day!" Luce blurted, trying to muster up whatever enthusiasm he had left.

Cyrus stayed silent and bent over the table, closing one nostril with a finger and snorting the line of powder with the other. I felt the burn, but Cy seemed hardly to notice. Just seconds later, his mind was buzzing, thoughts flashing wildly in front of me.

*"What the **hell** was that?"* I asked him, trying to lock my mental sight on the images moving by, on his interface and my own mind, with no success.

"SynAdrene," he responded. I felt an unbidden smile appear on his face. *"Here, feel."*

I felt the effect I had been shielded from hit me in full force, and recoiled. My thoughts tingled, but faded away, then a rush filled our body, creeping its way into my mind. I was trying to fight, but it was like trying to stand in the middle of a river as the rushing waters pull inevitably backwards, no matter how much you fought against it.

Tired of resisting, I let my guard down. . .

T H E | S P L I T

A jolt of energy shot up our leg. There were no thoughts or egos in the way now, me and Cyrus were one as his feelings and memories went soaring by in a continuous stream.

"Pretty intense, huh?" his voice called through; he sounded so far away.

"Yeah. . . I guess. . . it's maybe a little too intense for me. How do you get anything done?"

"Well, you probably wouldn't."

The rush ended, and I felt my mind calm, returning to normal; even as Cyrus' raged around me.

"That was a pretty high dose for your first time, but that's what it takes to still work after almost three years."

"You've been doing that for THREE years? What even is it?"

"Synthetic adrenaline. It started as a chemical known as SYNTH, just a decade after your time. Got banned for its harsh effects on the body. Then, the military used it as the base substance for a new chemical, a few decades ago. Then they discontinued it as well, a few years later. Stories of people going on violent crime sprees, and pulling off their own limbs, seemed to finally result in a policy change. The bottle was opened though, and there was no going back. It was cheap and easy to make, and once the people cooking it realized how many different ways you could tweak the effects, different variations began hitting the street. The Bloc didn't stop it, either. . . their men love the stuff. It's probably even easier to get it now."

"Then, so. . . what. . . are you, addicted to it?"

I could feel him not wanting to answer the question, the interface was on and he was looking through files on his interface almost faster than I could see them.

But he responded a few seconds later; *"Huh? No, you can't actually get addicted to the stuff... I would say I'm a bit emotionally dependent on it, though. Every year seems to get worse... what little part of my soul that I still have is so covered in regret and pain, that... I don't like my brain to wander. This helps me stay focused and block out all the, noise... You know?"*

"Regret and pain? I know you saw a lot of death in the war but, you're doing the right thing..." I tried to console him.

"Well... whatever you think the right thing is, I guess... what matters is you have a cause." He laughed in his head, I could tell that wasn't what he wanted.

*"Cause, what cause? A government that only exists in the mountains, and is losing ground every day? My duties as a patriotic American? I like to think that I have honor, but deep down I know that the only reason I still do this, is because this is all I know how to do. I'm a **killer**, that's who I am... what I've been my whole adult. What happens to our killers when the life they care about falls away? What happens to the people we train and tell to kill, when they're surrounded by enemies and have no command structure? All I see are people to kill. We even aren't soldiers anymore... there are no ranks, there are no medals, there are no reinforcements. I've done things since the Fall that I swore I would never do. Things my family would've shamed me for, things hardened murderers would look at in disgust. But I realized something... Good and evil are fantasies; there are just actions and consequences. There is no right or wrong anymore. There's just US, and THEM... just the predator and the prey. Every child I've kidnapped and ransomed, every bomb I've ordered detonated in a populated area, every innocent person I've beaten or mutilated for bio-metric samples, is no different than going for a walk now, really."*

THE | SPLIT

His words had come out at a rapid staccato, I could sense his emotions in fluctuation as the SynAdrene coursed through our system.

"You don't have to dwell on your past, as hard as it is to hear... and for me to imagine... we dictate our own reality."

"No, we don't," he said, laughing again. "If you want to see my pain, if you want to see some of the things that got me 'addicted', have at it."

The dense cloud of memories was forced on me, pushed right in front of my thoughts. I felt them pull me in as Cyrus opened the barrier between us to the effects of the drug.

Years of memories... I lived them all at once, and I lost who I was in a chemically accelerated fog.

Jay had died shortly after their first assignment. He had been in an argument with a drunken customer, at the Globe, when a man slit his throat by surprise with a wrist-mounted spring-blade. Coincidentally, that had been the night Cyrus tried SynAdrene for the first time, and the events which followed his discovery of Jay's dead body, moments later, led to his partiality for the drug.

Knowing that he couldn't kill the man in cold blood without starting a firefight, Cyrus had challenged Jay's killer to a duel in the rarely used Globe Arena. Equipped with a set of exo-armored gloves by Luce, the battle between the wrist mounted blades and the metal fists began — and lasted less than a minute; Cyrus, while under a SynAdrene induced haze, broke both of the man's arms, before punching his face so many times it turned liquid.

As the group settled into their new dynamic as a three man team, they completed several more operations. During one of these missions, while investigating the disappearance of a recon squad near Concord, they'd found the strange devices, the masks that I had seen yesterday in the corner of the room.

T H E | S P L I T

The building they'd found the team's bodies in had been the headquarters of a DARPA project, which had focused on creating stealth nano-materials. The place had been mostly cleared out – likely by a similar BLOC recon team – but they'd found five mask prototypes after hours of searching. Two they'd given to Command, at the Globe, and the other three they'd kept, implementing them in most of their operations, including the one that had catapulted them into the next level.

The masks gave the team new freedom to move about in the open, more options when forced to use stealthier tactics and, as I'd seen yesterday, could display your face as someone else's. Additionally the material itself even felt like skin, and was impossible to detect; even at military checkpoints and government buildings. Luce had done some modifications as well, every face projected onto the mask was that of an already verified Bloc citizen, so even on streets filled with scanners they could walk undetected.

A little over a year after The Fall, the Bloc had realized that by completely destabilizing our economy with invasion, sending us back to the barter system, they were missing out on an opportunity. While most commerce was done digitally, it was estimated that thirty percent of both Bloc and American wealth was still in paper bills. By implementing their own currency, and bringing us back to a paper money economy, they stood to make a great deal of money. Thus they had re-purposed several large banks all over the country, and had brought in large amounts of money to make available for people to trade, with the intention of buying up what few possessions people had remaining.

The United States Military had found this action unacceptable. Command had altered Cyrus' team's mission purpose from a military unit to a terrorist squad, sent to spread fear and ideological warfare, and the new order was to hit the newly named "Bloc Currency Services"

T H E | S P L I T

– which had formerly been known as the "Federal Reserve Bank" building, in Boston – on the day that it opened.

They did it in style.

Wearing their masks, they'd pulled up to a side door and released a group of CounterInt drones, to disable the outside security and surveillance. . .

* * * * *

We made it to the top of the stairs and I opened the glass door, stepping inside and clearing both corners with my rifle. As we went left, down a short hall to another door, I heard loud commotion and I knew the Lobby was right outside.

"Luce, are you ready?"

"Yup!" he replied, pulling his tube launcher out.

I watched as his face changed from a black man to a white man with freckles. Luce had ended up becoming quite the engineer. When we had been discussing the plan, I had mentioned we were going to need heavy, non-lethal, grenade use. Later, he'd shown me something he had been working on; a grenade launcher.

He'd modified it with a larger tube to fire clips of his own design; 4 brackets, spring loaded in the center with a timer. When triggered, the springs would pop in mid-flight, releasing the grenades and sending them in four different directions. We had successfully used it time and time again in tests back at the base.

"Alright, you're up Luce, let's see what this thing does." I opened the door and he popped out, shooting a round into the room, after which I closed it again tight. Screaming and panic rang out through the lobby, sounding muffled through the door. "Again." He fired another round, and I briefly closed the door to wait for the explosion.

THE | SPLIT

This time we went in, guns up as the smoke clouded around us. I fired at a figure stumbling around with a pistol in front of me, then yelled, "Thermal up!" as I touched the side of my glasses. The world's colors went away and I was surrounded by the red-yellow glow of bodies. "Get the doors!"

Both Luce and Sarah confirmed; I saw Luce slip through the pile of people on the floor, hydraulic bar in hand. Behind me Sarah did the same. Armed guards continued to stumble around, shooting blindly, and I brought my gun up to shoot through five of them near the walls with a loud burst.

I tried to focus and block out the shrill cries, as the gunshots had brought the screaming up another octave, then I felt a slight impact in my right arm and looked down to see a small tear in my suit. But two more rifles soon joined mine, the sound of bullets tearing through the room echoed off of the walls, and that quickly there was no one left standing.

Walking around, I looked down, finishing off any guards or challengers left. A man holding his stomach saw me as the smoke started to dissipate in front of his face, and raised his gun. I quickly stepped on it and put my own to his head before holding down the trigger.

"Luce, Sarah. . . pop more smoke. . . I'm jumping the counter, cover me." As they quickly ran into position at the base of the counter, throwing another smoke grenade at the front door and in the same move crouching to face either way, I jumped the over the counter-top. Huddled employees lay on the ground, shaking. I grabbed the crying woman nearest to me by the hair and pulled her to her feet. When she screamed, I slammed her down, pinning her face on the smooth surface of the counter-top.

T H E | S P L I T

"Who's in charge here?" I demanded, pulling her upright again. She pointed at a man. He was crouched down, just a few feet away. I released her and went over to him, yanking his arm to lay him down flat on his back as I screamed, "Open up that gate!" gesturing at the large barred gate door to my right, behind which sat stacks of money on tables.

"I can't, sir! It's on a time-release, and-"

Slinging my rifle around to my back, I pulled out my pistol and shot him in the stomach. He cried out in pain as blood covered my boots. Crouching down to the woman beside him, I menacingly gestured at her with the gun.

"WHO ELSE CAN OPEN THE GATE?!"

"I c-can!" a woman's voice came from down the counter. She stood up timidly, walking down to the gate and bending over to type in a code. I could hear sirens outside. Luce and Sarah tossed another two smoke grenades at the entrance to obscure the view from the street outside. Soon the door was unlocked; I pushed the woman out of the way and kicked open the door. "COME ON, WE'RE THROUGH!"

They hopped over the counter to join me and we walked through the gate. In the room we pulled out black bags from pouches on the front of our armor and quickly swept the money off the tables until each was full. Tightening the clasps, we threw them over our shoulders, hopped back over the marble counter-tops into the lobby and ran through another door into a long hallway. Sirens were all around us now.

I stopped and turned to Sarah, "Do it, now."

She pulled out the remote and clicked the button; a muffled explosion rang out from behind us which shook the building. Half of the sirens seemed to stop instantly. We continued running, through another hallway and, finally, out of a door leading into the alley.

THE | SPLIT

Just in front of us, still idling, sat the garbage truck. Exhaling in relief, I tossed the bags into the back and got in. When the others had joined me Luce hit the button on the fake rear-cover he had rigged up. It slid down into place, covering us in darkness. I felt the truck lurch forward.

The total haul had been 238 million. Bringing 'Charlene' along in full assault mode, (that was the name chosen by Luce for the UDA Cyrus had brought from New York) they'd given command a 75 million share, and then went to find Manuel, the king of the Globe and the boss of the whole neighborhood. In a very public presentation, they gave him a gift of 35 million, as tribute and thanks for the generosity he had shown us through the club.

Manuel accepted it, and it elevated them high beyond the anonymity of most soldiers still fighting. They became VIPs in the Globe; free drinks, drugs and women, if they wanted them. With the fences and dealers under Manuel's employ, they got the house price – and insider access to choice equipment. The club became their most important resource; an investment for the future.

Of the money pocketed from the robbery, some had gone for obtaining parts for Charlene, and various other hardware, but most had been spent on a more secure headquarters – though calling it that was something of a stretch, it had been in a former salvage yard.

One night, an old man had stumbled down into the club, offering to sell it to anyone who would listen. He'd said that the Bloc had restricted him from all transactions, due to his history of fraud with the mob. According to him, they could stay there and do whatever they wanted, detection free, and he would go on to remain the property owner.

A full junkyard, off the dock. It was perfect; huge piles of mechanical debris formed natural walls all around the center building, obviously a small shop at one point – they found an auto repair sign leaning against a wall. The inside hadn't been used in years, and had required long hours of work to clear it out and set up our equipment. They'd then hired a local crew of concrete workers to build us a small series of tunnels beneath the building and throughout the yard – off the record – with three entrances to the surface, and hatches they concealed under parts found in the nearby piles.

That had cost almost half of what they'd had. The rest of it was spent frivolously, on projects and whims. For instance, Luce drank – and when Luce drank, everyone around Luce drank. Many times Cyrus had to cut him off before he bought drinks for the whole bar. He had also been pulled into these messes on occasion, hormonal pleasures outweighing any sense of shame.

We all had our vices.

Cyrus felt the worst of it had been his fault; even with the consistent amount he spent on Syn and various other drugs, he'd green-lit almost all of Luce's proposals. The shop had become filled with ill-conceived machines and experiments, all of which Luce maintained his claims of working on.

But Sarah hadn't been much better. Though she claimed to be bisexual, the rate she went through women was incredible. She would often stagger out with several on her arm, or be seen slipping a wad of cash to a girl in a corner and sneaking out the back.

Still, she'd done her best to take on the role of the voice of reason, as the crew went to the Globe nearly every night. After daytime hours spent monitoring buildings or causing mayhem, their elevated status in the club, mixed with the availability of nearly any vice imaginable, was a destructive recipe. And, after months of partying, his and Luce's dependence on SynAdrene was cemented.

T H E | S P L I T

Luce chased any girl he liked at the Globe. Cyrus mostly chose to sleep alone. He would meet women at the club that he found interesting a few times a month, but after a night of temporary passion he would end things and be good for a while. Sarah was mainly the same, and while she preferred women, she had slept with Cyrus dozens of times over the years.

Cyrus enjoyed her company intimately, and Luce's comically, but in his head he felt alone, believing that he often had to shoulder the burdens of their actions. He had protected Luce from the road he had gone down as a soldier even before the fall, but as the leader of the small group he often did the tasks he considered the most gruesome or traumatic; to protect the other two, his reasoning went.

But the level of violence and carnage that the other two 'never had to deal with' had become intoxicating in his drug-fueled mind, and a rift had formed in his friendship with Luce, one that continued to fray as the kidnappings got bloodier, the messages they sent more severe, and the bombs killed more Bloc citizens. Things had come to a head between them when they were ordered to find the location of Lieutenant General Huang.

The man was a ghost, and all of their leads on finding him in various Bloc personnel databases had been dead-ends. So, to speed the process up, Cyrus had decided that they would abduct a group of intelligence officers.

They'd gotten the men drunk, and Sarah had lured them to out in back of the bar, where they'd knocked them unconscious, then drove back to the scrapyard and tortured them for hours.

Eventually, after spending most of the night trying to get Huang's location – and doing most of the work – Cyrus had enough, and told Luce to come down and prepare for extraction.

T H E | S P L I T

    The pair argued about whether or not to go forward with the procedure for nearly a half hour until, finally, Cyrus ordered Luce to do it, pulling rank and threatening him with removal from the squad.

    As I was 'watching' them argue, I didn't fully understand the implications of this process Luce called, 'a violation of human dignity', and a 'war crime'; but as I watched it unfold, I did begin to understand.

    Luce linked to Cyrus' NI, through the top of his skull, from a small white box with a physical wire – the first one I'd seen since arriving in the future – then plugged a wire into the other side of the box. He then asked Cyrus if he was sure he wanted to do this.'

    Cyrus, cursing at him, pulled out a device from a nearby bag. This one was a small cylinder, open at one end like a cup. The man bound to the chair in front of them began screaming through his gag. Ignoring this, Cyrus pressed the cup against the man's eye.

    The screams turned to shrieks as the rim began to glow red hot, but Cyrus continued to push until it went through his eye socket, diagonally. Pulling it back out, he set it again on the table. The man was still violently thrashing in his chair, with nearly a quarter of his head missing at the angle where Cyrus had pressed the device. His tongue was partially exposed, and a portion of his brain was visible within the wound from which his eye dangled, moving around eerily on its string of nerves.

    Obviously fighting his urge to be sick, Luce gaped in horror, but once again asked Cyrus if he was sure. In return, Cyrus smiled at him and went back to work. Muttering threats under his breath, he next grabbed a surgical razor from the table and leaned over the man, face just inches away from the exposed and bleeding tissue, as he wrapped his fingers around a line encircling the optic nerve that was so thin I hadn't noticed it.

THE | SPLIT

But now, as Cy's own memory ran through my thoughts, I realized that this was the wire conducting the output from a neural implant. Cyrus sliced the optic nerve. The eyeball fall onto the floor, where he stepped on it with a smile, before turning to the reluctant Luce, who took the other wire from the white box and handed it to him. Cyrus took a deep breath, and then attached the two wires together; the scene changed instantly.

Suddenly I was in disembodied form, moving through a nightmarish world. But thankfully, my initial shock was relieved when I felt Cyrus' original thoughts and realized I was still in the memory; they had hijacked the man's neural interface, and it had caused an overload of his brain's biological impulse to try to repel the intruders. It had also caused a thought-scape of terror.

The place was a nightmarish hell of horrible images and negative feelings, amplified by the NI's coding as the victim's own fears and insecurities played out, overwriting and corrupting all of his original memories.

But eventually, Cyrus found the information about Huang he was looking for. He immediately detached and, standing up, shot the man, informing Luce that they were done.

Luce followed him. He had been insisting on freeing the captives – after wiping their NIs – and continued now to protest the implications of the supposed 'eternal torture' they had subjected the soldier to.

Finally, Cyrus grew annoyed and decided to end it by executing them all, all at once, with an incendiary grenade in the back of the truck.

There was a moment – a single moment, as the screams of the people burning in the truck intensified – that Cyrus and Luce made eye contact.

T H E | S P L I T

It was over. From that day, Luce never again brought it up, or objected to anything. The only time now that they ever interacted, outside of official work, was to share SynAdrene.

THE | SPLIT

XVIII

LGPB://mn34/con/terra/MB, 9045
(Translated)

Las Vegas; 2019

The water felt warm, but it was missing something obvious. I turned my head over my shoulder and examined the massive space of the penthouse, where the matte black floors paired with the golden trim and decor to create a gaudy display of unnecessary touches. Even the hot tub was a little much. Placed in the center of the room, you could see the entire Strip through the floor to ceiling windows that made up the outside wall, and it was easy to feel greater than the people below, looking down on them from the comfort of a Jacuzzi inside of an overpriced room. In this town, such feelings of superiority were readily offered to those who could pay for them. Five thousand a night.

Before me and Meela had hit the road, I would never have even dreamed of staying in a place like this; even if I'd had the money back then, this level of wealth and status would've never appealed to me, and didn't really appeal to me now. But after a rough past few months, and with plenty of cash to spare, it was a needed break. We had seemingly hit a dead end. After a year of working as contract killers, the money was secondary. The rush from the chase was our real reward. It was a hunt like no other, a primal calling that drew out predatory characteristics in both of us I hadn't known existed. We were Bonnie and Clyde in a deadlier era, a pair of hunters stalking the most dangerous prey there was, and improving with every kill.

Still, the flow of money had been turned off like a faucet in just a matter of days – although it definitely could have been worse. And to some, losing a source of income while sitting on two hundred and fifty grand would seem a moot point. But I knew me and Meela.

"Did you miss me?" Meela came out from the side bedroom, wearing a pink satin robe, monogrammed with the logo of the hotel, which with one smooth motion fell to the ground.

My eyes fixated onto her thin bare frame, greedily looking her up and down like it was the first time I had ever seen her. She hadn't grown much in the last year, but was still nearly 5'11 now. Her waist had somehow continued to get even slimmer, and her arms and legs were cut with lean muscle, some bearing the scars and bruises from recent jobs.

She cocked her head to the side curiously as she stepped down into the tub, "What are you thinking about, Burly man?"

"What?" I hadn't heard her, my was gaze still focused on her body descending into the water.

She rolled her eyes. "I **said**. . . what are you thinking about, Burly man?"

"I'm not thinking about much," I admitted. "Not a lot of blood in my brain at the moment."

Meela giggled and slid over to sit in my lap, "Oh! Well I would say it's not!" She threw her leg over my other side, straddling me and pulling me into a kiss.

I closed my eyes, feeling our lips move together as one, as she softly moaned with pleasure. For several minutes we continued, until without warning, she pulled away and grabbed me by the side of the head slightly, looking into my eyes.

"What's wrong doll?" I asked, curious at her sudden change in behavior.

THE | SPLIT

"It's just..." she stammered, trying to find her words, "Burl, I'm worried. What are we going to do now? We have some money, but we both know that won't last. Burl, baby, I know you've talked about it, but we can't go back to Chet. After last time, who knows what will happen if we try it again?"

She was right. As much as I hated to think about it, our business in Indiana had come to a conclusive end. Meela and I had worked more than a half dozen jobs for Chet and his various associates, and had made a lot of money.

But towards the end, our quality in clientele had gone down at an alarming rate. It took nearly dying at the hands of a drug trafficking kingpin in Chicago for us to realize we had to call it quits.

We'd been tasked with a job that had been simple enough, on the surface; eliminate a rival crew. Easily accomplished. We'd sent a case of liquor to the group's warehouse, and stormed in after they were drunk several hours later. It was only when we'd returned to collect payment that the trouble had begun.

Walking into the client's warehouse, it had been immediately obvious that something was amiss. There had been more men inside than when we had first come, and Deion himself had stood in the middle, gun in hand as he'd explained that he had no intention of paying us – and never left loose ends.

It was only through Meela's quick thinking that we made it out at all; walking over to the confident kingpin, she had taken off her top and wrapped her arms around him seductively.

With all eyes on her, I had been able to draw my weapon and open fire on the group, killing the whole crew in seconds, though I did take a round through my body armor that left a deep internal bruise.

T H E | S P L I T

Meela meanwhile had slid a concealed pistol out from her waistline, and killed Deion with a single shot to the back of the head. Afterward, we'd collected all of the cash in the warehouse and went on the run, eventually ending up here in Las Vegas, planning our next move going forward.

I stared at the girl whom I had built this new life with. Her short blonde curls were gone, replaced by roughly cut, straight brunette hair. She had dyed and changed her hair within days of leaving home, a move I had followed by shaving my own head, and although it was merely a cosmetic adjustment, to the world around us we were entirely different people. Our lives had also changed drastically, but never who we were had, even in the storm. To me, she was the same smiling girl I had met outside of an AA meeting, a year and a half ago. But our motivation had changed. We had become harder, our movements those of practiced killers.

And Meela especially had developed a savage streak after the incident in my duplex. Whatever gap there previously had been in our combat skills had quickly closed itself, and she was now my equal, my partner, the mate that destiny had selected for this new chapter of my life.

"Doll," I squeezed her shoulders reassuringly, "we'll be fine. No matter what comes our way, we can handle it. I mean, just look at what we've done so far-"

A knock on the door stopped me mid-sentence. We both looked at it, and then back to each other, our eyes questioning each other as to whom it could be. "Silly question, but. . . you weren't expecting anyone, were you?"

"Of course not. That's not for you, is it?"

I moved her off of me gently, and stood up to step out of the tub, answering, "No." as I started walking across the smooth black floor

T H E | S P L I T

carefully. The cool air of the room brushed against my bare skin, sending a slight chill through my body and, stopping at the coat rack near the front door, pulled down a black cashmere robe, monogrammed like Meela's pink one.

She was already in her own robe and behind me, 9mm pistol in hand, as I slipped it over my shoulders. Nodding at me, she took a position at the end of the entry hallway, behind a side wall. I tied my robe closed, taking a deep breath to calm my nerves, and opened up the door. On the other side stood a bellhop, dressed in a traditional red vest and a square pillbox hat that matched the color, over a crisp white shirt and black pants.

I kept the door halfway shut as I peered out skeptically. "Yes?"

"Mr. Snyder. . . a letter came for you at the front desk. I was asked to deliver it to you, personally."

"A letter?" I said in surprise. "You must have the wrong room. I don't have any friends here in Vegas. . . and no one knows I'm staying here."

I went to close the door, and felt the man gently catch it from the other side. "Mr. Snyder?" I opened it again a crack to glare at him. "The man who delivered it said you would say that, and that I should deliver it anyway. He said he's a friend."

I grabbed the letter from him. "A friend huh? What did this friend look like?"

"Sorry, Mr. Snyder," he looked remorseful. "I wasn't there when he arrived, but I was told he wore a suit."

Feeling a tap on my shoulder, I turned around to see Meela behind me. She slipped a crisp hundred dollar bill into my hand in exchange for the letter, and walked back into the penthouse.

"Here," I handed him the money. "No more disturbances, please."

T H E | S P L I T

The man inclined his head slightly, "Of course, Mr. Snyder, thank you." then walked away.

I shut the door, walking back into the room. Meela's robe was back on the floor and she was again in the hot tub, reading the letter, the envelope discarded beside her. I hung my own robe back on the hook, exclaiming as I made my way back to the tub and slowly lowered myself back into the water. "You opened it? That could've been dangerous, Meela."

"Well, obviously it's not." She waved the letter in my face, and reached over to hand me the envelope it had been in.

I inspected the envelope's crisp white edges and sharp corners before looking inside. It was like she said, not dangerous. "What's it say?"

"Here," she handed it to me, snuggling up beside me as I read it.

Dear Mr. Burlington Fischer, and Ms. Amelia Vasquez,

Yes, we know who you are. Your recent actions have gotten our attention, and we would like to request a meeting. I am sure you have many questions, all will be answered. Meet me on the balcony of the Oceanside Resort, in San Diego, June 11th at 3:00 PM.

There was no signature, no address on the envelope, no identifying features whatsoever. I set the letter on the floor beside the edge of the tub, and massaged the upper part of my nose between my eyes. Seeing my real name on paper had triggered a surprising amount of stress, and that was the spot on my face I would rub out of habit when in deep thought.

"Burl. . . " Meela said softly, ". . . they know who we are."

"I know, babe. . . I read it too."

She reached for my arm and slipped it around her shoulders. "Well, what do we do now?"

"We don't have much choice," I replied. "We're going to that meeting."

San Diego

The sound of waves crashing in the distance calmed my nerves more than it should have, and I closed my eyes for a few seconds, listening to the alternating pattern of the ocean's movements against the beat of my heart, then with a deep breath opened them to look down at the table.

The place had been set, two forks on one side of a tan colored plate, a knife and spoon on the other. Every table on the porch had been set similarly, all prepared for a banquet to be served to guests who weren't there. Besides Meela and I the space was mainly empty, except for an older couple who sat on the other side of the balcony, enjoying a quiet meal, and waiters who moved back and forth between the porch and the building's door.

Meela reached for my hand, intertwining her fingers with mine lightly. "You alright baby?"

"Yes," I assured her. "Just nervous. . . I have no idea what we're walking into here."

"I understand," she smiled at me gently. "I feel the same way. But, do you remember what you told me in Vegas? You said that when we're together, we have nothing to be afraid of."

I nodded. "And I still think that."

Meela patted the top of my wrist with her free hand, "I know you do, and I think so too."

The door to the balcony opened; I looked over to see a man in a dark suit walking out. Mid-thirties, average height with a slim build, neatly trimmed goatee outlining his face and reaching all the way up to a pair of dark framed glasses.

T H E | S P L I T

He looked at us with recognition, and as he began walking toward our table I examined his suit; tailored, well fitting, with a cream colored shirt underneath and a blue and burgundy tie that matched the floral pattern on his pocket square.

Part of me was relieved to see him. I hadn't fully ruled out the possibility that this was an elaborate trap perpetrated by the military, or someone hired by the vengeful members of the Den of Carnage, but it would stand to reason that if it had been either of these groups they wouldn't send a single man who appeared to be unarmed.

Still, looks could be deceiving; the element of surprise was a hit-man's best friend, and this patio beside the beach was the perfect place for someone to let their guard down. Meela and I had built our trade on looking disarming to ambush our targets. Lifting the edge of the white tablecloth slightly, I reached my hand beneath the table to feel the cool steel of my Kimber pistol. It would take a second to draw, but I wasn't prepared to die without a fight.

The man paused next to the table and unbuttoned his suit jacket, spreading it wide for us to see what was inside. I saw only the shirt underneath, and the lining of his inside pockets appeared to be empty.

"I'm unarmed," he said softly. "May I sit down?"

Slowly, I raised my hand back up to the table, as Meela gestured for him to sit in one of the seats across from us.

"Now, what do I call you while you're in town?" His voice was as soft as it had been before, but he spoke clearly, articulating each word with the dexterity of a well-educated man.

"I'm Dan Snyder," I reached out to shake his hand. "This is my wife, Elizabeth."

He nodded at her, shaking her hand after mine. "Mr. and Mrs.

Snyder... I'm pleased you could join me here today. My name, is Nicholas Stone."

"Alright, Mr. Stone," I paused as I said his name; it didn't sound right, and I wondered if he had given me a fake name as well. "Why are we here?"

"Yes..." leaning back in his chair, he signaled for the waiter across the porch. "We'll dispense with the pleasantries... but first, drinks."

The waiter made his way over to us and stood in front of the table, his leather ordering pad in one hand, pen in the other. "Gentlemen and lady..." he bowed his head towards Meela, "...what can I serve you on this fine day? Would you like to try our fish of the day? All of our fish are locally caught and served-"

"No, thank you," Nicholas cut in. "We'll just take drinks. M... Elizabeth, do you like wine?"

She nodded. He went on to the waiter, "We'll have a bottle of the House '85 cab, with three glasses... and I'll also have a Macallan, neat... your oldest bottle."

"Very good, sir." The waiter slipped the ordering pad back into his apron and turned to me, "And for you, sir?"

"I'll have a dry martini, replace the lemon with an orange slice."

"Yes sir. I'll be right back with those," he turned and went back into the building.

As soon as he was out of earshot, Nicholas continued, "To be as frank as possible, Mr. and Mrs. Snyder, we have been observing you with great interest."

"Observing us, how?" Meela cut in. "It's been a year and a half since we've been in contact with anyone. There's no way you've been somehow *watching* us."

THE | SPLIT

"Do you honestly think that?" A wry smile formed on his lips, and he paused for a moment, looking at both of us in turn.

"Madam, the organization I work for is comprised of dozens of high-level, international executives, and former intelligence officers across all branches of government. I must say. . . I particularly admired the way that you handled the Palmer case."

It had been one of the highest paying contracts Chet had given us. Zachariah Palmer had been a controversial preacher – and local militia leader – in southern Nebraska; the offer was three hundred grand for the elimination of him and his three sons. But the Palmers were notoriously elusive, and almost exclusively dealt with the members of their small congregation.

We hadn't been the first sent after the pastor and his family, a cursory internet search revealed nearly a dozen rotting corpses found along the edges of their property; most ex-military, or tied to various gangs in the area. Not wanting to end up like the rest, Meela and I had taken a different approach. Posing as her aunt and uncle, we kidnapped his granddaughter from school and recorded a ransom demand using a cheap camcorder. Not even an hour after sending it, we'd gotten a response. Zachariah had been furious, saying he would not pay a ransom. For several minutes afterward, he had threatened us, using gruesome descriptions of biblical-era punishments that had made us laugh for nearly half an hour straight.

Later that afternoon, we'd called in a fake tip to the local sheriff, telling him that the granddaughter was in an old shed by an abandoned farm. The sheriff had gotten off the phone and informed the Palmers, who as expected went to the building immediately.

It was a trap, of course; the second Zachariah and his sons closed the door behind them, Meela had set off the IED she had made and placed

THE | SPLIT

inside. The whole building exploded, killing the militia leader and his sons instantly.

The granddaughter, whom we had left in a motel room, wasn't harmed in the slightest. She'd calmly sat through the whole kidnapping, her iPad just inches from her face as she ignored the world around her. We had dropped her off back at school and left town directly afterward.

"You can admire her for that one," I said, looking over at Meela. "The whole plan was her idea."

"It was nothing," she blushed.

"It was not 'nothing'," Nicholas said firmly. "Your mechanical and technical skill are impressive. . . even more so when you consider that you, Mrs. Snyder, have had no formal training."

The waiter arrived, carrying all of our drinks on a silver platter with handles. Walking around the table, he set down wine glasses, then placed mine and Nicholas' drinks in front of us. When he left Nicholas grabbed the open bottle, admitting it was a personal favorite, and describing the wine's taste as he poured three glasses, filling Meela's fuller than ours. But at last, when he and I had both finished our small portion for tasting, he dropped all of his small talk and resumed his cryptic sales pitch.

"We pulled security camera footage from the locations of several of your contracts." He paused to take a sip of his scotch. "Neither of you seem to show any hesitation at taking a life. You particularly. . . Dan . . . are extraordinarily adaptive. . . strangling a man with his own belt was one of the few things I hadn't come across so far."

I looked at Meela, who seemed to be thinking the same thing as I was; what was the point of all this? Meela and I enjoyed what we did, and the lifestyle that came with it, but we had always relied on a sense of secrecy and anonymity. The fact that this near stranger knew enough about our

T H E | S P L I T

illegal activities to discuss intimate and violent details of our lives, and so flippantly, was unsettling and uncomfortable.

I took the lead; "You said we would be dispensing with the pleasantries, Mr. Stone."

"So I did," he was obviously taken aback. "Do you find the nature of your work pleasant, Mr. Snyder?"

He had me there. "At times. . . but I don't like to discuss it so openly. We didn't come here for a recap of our time on the road."

"Agreed," he knocked back the rest of his drink, prompting me to take a swig of my own, then his voice dropped down to just above a whisper, "Burlington. . . and Amelia. . . I am here to offer you a job."

"A job?" Meela asked, her volume matching his own.

"The group I work for is called Allied Corporate Exchange. On the surface, we help companies and corporations relocate their facilities. But behind closed doors, we operate as an organization comprised of elite, corporate assassins."

"And you want us to join this organization?" I asked reluctantly.

"Precisely," he smiled. "We have members of all types, all over the world. . . but we've never had a couple on our payroll. Most people seem to overlook couples, giving you a degree of versatility our other assets lack."

Meela snorted. "Why should we work for you? You've already told us how good we were on our own. . . "

"Well, for starters. . . " he reached into his jacket pocket and pulled out a pair of cards, sliding them across the table. "Go ahead, take a look at those."

We both picked up a card, and I looked at mine closely. It was a government issued ID, with my face in the picture. The badge had me listed as Dustin Jones, complete with address and physical details. I looked over to see Meela's also had her face on a forged set of specifics.

Nicholas continued talking as we examined the IDs closer; "Those are genuine IDs, complete with matching passports and birth certificates. Legally, you're now Dustin Jones. . . and you're now Mary Summers. That's just one of the perks of working for us."

"It's a nice touch," I said setting the card back on the table. "But I have a capture order from my army unit, and we both have a standing bounty on our heads from back home."

"Burlington and Meela had a capture order and a standing bounty," he corrected. "Dustin and Mary are just regular, law-abiding citizens. Not that I think I have to, but. . . to sweeten the pot. . . all of our contracts start at five hundred grand, minimum. These aren't your local drug dealers and barflies, these are some of the world's most powerful leaders of diplomacy, business, and industry."

Meela looked at me, her head bobbing up and down slightly. This had been what she wanted, the chance to start over. I could find no reason to disagree; the pay was better, we would have organizational support and, most importantly, we would be legitimate once again. Still, as much as I wanted to believe him, I had questions. "So, if we were to just suddenly become Dustin and Mary, what would happen to Burlington and Amelia?"

"We fake your deaths?" Nicholas replied, with a tone like he was stating the obvious.

"Fake our deaths? How?"

He smiled. "Don't you worry about that. We've been doing this for a long time, and have become quite good at it. None of this will happen, of course, until you officially come on board. You can have those IDs, the corresponding documentation is at our headquarters in New York.

Ah, I almost forgot, here. You wouldn't get very far without these," he chuckled, passing us a thin envelope.

Meela opened it to reveal a pair of plane tickets and a card with an address. "Take some time to think about our offer." He shook my hand. "I hope to see you soon. Dustin. . . Mary," he shook Meela's. "It was lovely to meet you both, but I must be going. I'll pay for our drinks on the way out."

After he slipped into the building, we remained seated at the table, both of us stuck in our own trains of thought about the decision that was in our path; opportunity hadn't as much knocked on our door as it had beat it off the hinges. I knew Meela had already made up her mind – likely was already imagining a life in New York, and what our new job would entail – and I didn't want to rain on her parade.

Intending to move my hand from my lap, I felt it graze over a slight bulge in my front pocket, and suddenly I remembered. Checking to see that she was looking away as I slipped my hand inside to it, feeling the cool metal of the diamond ring I'd bought for her in St. Louis, while she had been distracted in a nearby clothing store. We had talked about marriage in the past, but our being on the lam had always been the biggest obstacle. Now, I had just been given a way around it, and I began to feel the slight touch of destiny; we would likely never get a chance like this again, and there was nothing to stop me from taking this next step. With her by my side, there was nothing that could ever stop me again.

"Meela?"

She turned to me, "What's up, babe?"

"I need to talk to you about something."

"I agree. We need to talk about this offer. . . I think it's really good, Burl. . . it's perfect for us."

THE | SPLIT

"In a minute, we will," I said patiently. "I want to talk about something more important first."

Her eyes widened. "MORE important?! What could be more important than our future! I mean-" I touched my finger to her lips lightly and she stopped talking, then in one smooth motion I pushed the chair back, slid down to one knee and pulled the ring from my pocket. "Burl. . . what. . . what are you doing-" she let out a loud gasp when she saw the ring, covering her mouth, eyes wide with surprise.

"Amelia Vasquez. . . wait. . . I mean," I paused to look down at her new ID, "Mary Summers. . . will you marry me?"

She was shaking slightly as I looked up at her, her skin glistening with the tears which fell down her face, but when her hand moved it revealed a bright smile beneath.

"Of course I will!" she let out a sob, quickly followed by a nervous laugh as she pulled me into a hug and squeezed me tight, burying her face into my chest.

I hugged her back, my arms wrapped around her, able to feel a warmth radiate through my entire body. I never wanted to let go.

T H E | S P L I T

XIX

LGPB://mn34/con/terra/AJ, 2379
(Translated)

Boston; 2085

Though the memories faded, it took some time for me to realize what was going on around me. The senseless violence against innocents, combined with Cyrus's own grief, had left me in a stupor. Even now, I could feel the shame Cyrus felt for his depraved actions all that time ago, but shook off these feelings and continued to feel my way around Cy's mind. It was becoming more familiar, but he felt distant, and although I could yet see his thoughts racing by under the influence of the synthetic adrenaline, I was still discomfited at not being the dominant presence in a body.

He sat at the same desk, now turned around facing Luce and Sarah instead of the wall as he had been earlier, and Luce was saying something I couldn't hear. Puzzled, I reached again to the auditory receptors at the end of Cy's ears; there was nothing but silence. Then a strange, numbing feeling shot through my thoughts as I got near it again.

"Hold on, let me finish this conversation, and then we'll talk," Cyrus's voice rang out through the space.

"Why can't I hear? What's happening?" I felt amusement.

"Ah. . . I'm not sure. . . it happens sometimes, usually when I'm using synth, but not always. It could be the drugs, it could be the implant, who knows? It'll come back. . . just chill out a second and wait."

"Seriously? This place is a disaster, man. . . you aren't really the most mentally competent guy to be supporting a drug habit."

THE | SPLIT

He recoiled angrily at this, before quickly regaining his composure. "Eh, it's all just bullshit anyway. I'm a doomed soldier in a doomed war, with a broken piece of cybernetics stuck in the middle of my skull slowly killing me. You're a damn Neanderthal, part of the generation that put our country in this mess. . . who cares what you think? Now shut up."

I didn't respond, and left him alone. The world was still quiet, but I waited like he said, while a powerful rush of feelings that weren't my own pulsed across my perception, washing me in their various tones. Frustration, anticipation, and curiosity clouded my thoughts – then left as soon as they came.

I guessed I had pushed his buttons. Cy definitely had less of an emotional filter when he was tweaked out like this, because that was new. Though my control in his mind was secondary, I had never felt him force his own perception into my own. It was different, unlike the memories of his time in the service he had summoned out of irritation.

A second wave of emotions rushed forward; after they passed I looked to Cyrus, still ignoring me, busily watching the conversation in silence. 'He has no control over this,' I realized suddenly, bracing myself as the feeling returned.

Then with an auditory whoosh, his hearing returned and I felt Cyrus' thoughts briefly calm, and then speed up, as he tried to catch up on the conversation. Luce was talking;

"-but the firewall seems to block even the most basic probes. . . we HAVE to be inside the physical building."

"No, we don't. . . " Sarah responded. "Why can't we just patch directly into the fiber below? We have plenty of that drilling equipment you made us buy."

He shook his head, "It can't be accessed from the surface. It's a direct connection, wired straight to the Bloc's secured network. It went down so far I lost track, probably 100, 200 meters at least."

"Okay. . . " Sarah paused to think. "Well. . . if we have to go into the building, do you even know where? There's got to be a lot of possible positions inside."

Luce snorted with laughter, "Oh wait, I didn't think about that! Except. . . I did. It's terminal CE-1, about 35 meters from the northwest service door. What the hell did you think I was doing all morning?"

"Wow, ass. . . " Sarah said, indignant, "I don't know. . . it looked like you were shoveling powder into your nose and arguing with your junkie friend."

Luce started to protest; Cy cut him off by raising our hand, and finally speaking out, "I'm going to ignore that junkie comment, Sergeant Mills. . . " She laughed and rolled her eyes at this, but her expression wasn't friendly. Cy continued anyway. "Luce. . . good job on finding the address on the target, have you written the extraction protocols yet?"

Luce grimaced, stumbling through his reply, "Well. . . not exactly. I have an old, inactive Bloc archive here that I've been testing it on, but the system inside is a lot newer. There are some guidelines and layouts online, but it's hit or miss. . . them cracking down on unauthorized networks nearly everywhere lately has been a bit of a headache."

Cyrus and I thought this over for a few seconds, our thoughts running through the problem simultaneously. He answered with a combination of our responses;

"Well soldier, it's your call. . . do *you* think it will work?"

"Yeah, I think I've got it down. I'm no systems engineer, but the coding is solid. It should be ready in an hour or so."

THE | SPLIT

"Good," we nodded. "Stay on it, I'm going to continue watching troop activity. Sarah, go down and monitor the entrance from the building to the east, I need a full report."

She confirmed and grabbed her gear before walking out of the door.

As soon as she was out of earshot, Luce spoke up, "Man. She can never take a joke. . . why does she have to be such a bitch?"

I retreated from this question, and let Cy respond alone. "I don't know, Luce," he admitted thoughtfully. "It's been a rough life lately, different people respond to it in different ways. It definitely doesn't help that we're high all the time, you know she worries about us."

"I know," he replied sheepishly. "But we've both got a handle on it. Well actually. . . man, is your ear still doing that thing again? *You* might actually need to slow down."

We smiled. "Yeah, sometimes. It's all good though. . . you just focus on getting us into that terminal, alright?"

Luce nodded, looking down at his monitor as he resumed tapping at the screen silently. I felt our body turn back around, and our left arm reaching up to the desktop as we bent at the waist near a line of more SynAdrene. I spoke up.

"Seriously? You're going to do more?"

"Now I'm going to get this from you, too? I'm still not even fully convinced you're not a tumor."

"Ha...ha," I replied dryly, though I could feel his annoyance. *"You know I'm not a tumor. . . and you're not the one who has to deal with the effects of someone else's years-long drug habit."*

"Then leave. Oh, wait. . . you can't. You don't think I realize the dangers of this stuff? But it's the only thing that keeps me focused. Do you know what happens when I close my eyes or let my mind wander?

THE | SPLIT

You've been in my head, you know the regret and the shame I wallow in EVERYDAY. I sent a man to eternal torture, I've killed entire families in explosions. If there's a hell, I'm going."

I softened my approach. *"It was horrible. But you were caught up in the moment. Grief can make us do terrible things. . . I'd say it's justified. It's bad, but you do so much good to offset it! And-"*

He cut me off, *"All the 'good I've done' . . . or whatever you called it, is just me killing people, for a country that may never exist again. I'm doing the rest of this bag, there's only two lines left."*

For the next few hours, Cyrus continued to work on various files, every so often pausing to explain them to me. When the effects of the SynAdrene faded however, we fell silent for a while; until suddenly a spike of pain pounded through our shared mind.

"Cy, what the hell? Did you bang your head on something?" I knew he heard me and had registered what I'd said, but it took him a few seconds to look away from his tablet and respond.

"No, Burl. . . this is just the comedown you're feeling. Just try to relax, we have a lot to do before tonight."

This was some comedown. It was like every bad hangover I had ever had, mixed with the tingling energy I had first felt from the synth, and everything was louder than it should be – me and Cyrus both flinched as Sarah burst into the room behind us, announcing loudly;

"Report is ready to go, Cap! How are things up here?"

"Sssss. . . " Luce made a pained hissing sound as he rubbed his temples, "Not so loud please?"

"Aw, what's wrong. . . ?" she teased him, walking over to the corner near her equipment. "Baby coming down from tweaking? Need a bottle?"

THE | SPLIT

The look on Luce's face soured, but he did not respond. Instead he furrowed his brow, as though confused but finding a way to cope with it, and went back to the screen he was looking at.

"I'm going to second that you quiet down, Sarah. Just because you're Nancy Reagan, that doesn't mean the rest of can't enjoy all of the wonderful drugs this great land has to offer. I think we're ready on my end." We gestured for her to come over, pointing at an image projected from his interface. "I put together all of our counts, and I think I have the pattern here. If what we have is right, the number of MPs on this block will be low, and the guard change is at 22:08."

Sarah looked down at the digital display on her wrist. "That's in less than two hours. Will we be ready?"

Cy turned from her to Luce, "I don't know. . . Luce, will we be ready?" Wordlessly, Luce raised a small access chip, holding it above his monitor. Cy walked over to grab it, remaining standing over his shoulder, waiting for him to talk. When Luce didn't, he broke the silence himself. "So, if the protocol is ready. . . did you get around to those blueprints yet? Also, will Charlene be ready to go?"

"Charlene's BEEN ready," he finally responded. "And as for the blueprints. . . Bloc Intelligence pulled them from the server. They aren't anywhere, not on the old municipal network, not on the Bloc secured network, they're not even in the City Hall file system. I think I *may* have figured out an alternative, though."

"An alternative?" Sarah inquired.

"Yup. Remember those frequency depth gauges I got with the drilling equipment, that you said was a waste of money? Well, I got them working." He swept his hand across his desk to display four gray pads covered in wires and blinking lights.

THE | SPLIT

"Yes. we remember them... what's your point?" Cy could barely conceal his annoyance.

"My p-o-i-n-t..." he said, drawing the word out, "Is that if we can get these placed we won't even need the blueprint."

"How?" Sarah asked gruffly, she was annoyed too.

"Well, once these are placed properly I can activate them from my position, up here, and wire the frequency reports to my monitor. I'll be able to see everything, walls, sentries... even defense platforms, and cameras as far as the signal broadcasts. The guy claimed they would go 200 meters but even half of that is more than enough."

Sarah and I exchanged glances. I could tell by her eyes she was skeptical, but I knew we were out of options.

"You can do that while operating Charlene at the same time?" she raised an eyebrow.

"Of course I can," he smiled. "I was the only one who could multi-task while operating a UDA on my entire carrier. I've done it dozens of times."

"Yeah," Sarah rolled her eyes. "And a good number of those times, we had to haul your broken robot back from the field."

"FIRST off-"

"Enough!" Cy cut them off, raising our hand. "When will the pads be ready?"

"Should be up and running in just a few minutes. We can test one if you like, it'll only take five minutes or so to reset again."

We nodded and let him return to his work. While we all waited, Cyrus laid out equipment and looked through the room for his black mask. It was wedged beneath two crates on a shelf across the room, but after a brief struggle he got it free.

THE | SPLIT

A few moments later, Luce spoke up, "Alright, I got it!"

Sarah mounted it on the wall while we stood over Luce's shoulder, hoping he could deliver on his promise. A faint popping noise emanated from the wall, and then a blue screen flashed onto Luce's monitor. Faint white circles pushed outward, from the middle of the screen, covering the darker white outline of the building. Every room could be made out. There were even three dots signifying our locations. It was all exactly right.

"Good job, soldier!" Cyrus said, patting him on the shoulder with excitement, "Now get that pad reset, and pack them in the gear bag."

"Yes sir."

An hour later, as the sun began to set, Cyrus and Sarah grabbed the bags, heading out of the room and down to the street below. Looking out of the busted glass door on the ground floor, I could see there were still guards in front of the building down at the end of the street and, although there were definitely fewer than had been there earlier, we would still need to find another way across.

We signaled for Sarah to take the lead, hoping the route she had taken earlier would still work. She led us to the right and right again, down an alley to our north where at the end we stopped over a manhole covering. Charlene bent the metal of the opening back, and we went down into the sewers.

Consulting the NI, we trudged through the foul smelling halls, up and out of a manhole cover on the other side of the street, quietly taking out the guards in the alley. After disposing of their bodies down in the sewer below where Luce had left Charlene, we then planted the pads where Luce instructed and paused at the side door.

He brought Charlene to deploy a small cloud of anti-surveillance bots before we went in. He had invented the nano drones himself; they

T H E | S P L I T

would seek out any visual feeds in an area, access the network they were connected to, and loop previous footage over the live stream to make us effectively invisible.

We let Charlene lead the charge through the halls, with Luce directing us from across the street using the map generated by the gray pads. Anytime we would come across a patrol, Luce would silently kill them with a pair of shoulder--mounted needle launchers re-purposed from a Bloc UDA.

This room was cooler than the rest of the building, with loud vents near the ceiling noisily pushing air through the room. I could feel it on my arms as the hairs stood on end, and a chill ran down my spine. Monitors lined the walls of the small space, lines of green and white code flashing across their screens. In the middle of the room sat two large terminals, side by side.

Charlene idled in a corner while we waited as Sarah walked over to the right one and opened her bag, pulling a small chip from a pocket. Lifting the input panel on the front of the machine, she pushed it in the slot and the large screen above hummed to life, with Bloc symbols and text moving across the bottom. Her fingers moving quickly over the keyboard, she entered in the code Luce had told her, and the screen soon changed.

A window labeled 'file management' popped up on the screen. And we watched her select the tabs for both 'ops' and 'pdms', then the copy option, before a blue progress bar appeared above the window. Below it, the files began moving onto Luce's chip, too fast to read.

But a few seconds later the bar was only at 3 percent. With the open entrance behind us, I could feel Cy's anxiety building every second we spent stationary. Trying to calm his nerves, I prodded him to look back at the screen.

He followed and we saw the progress was now at 11 percent.

"Guys how's it looking?" Luce sounded nervous too.

"12 percent and climbing, Luce. What's our status on getting back to the tunnel?" Cy's voice sounded more confident than I knew he was.

"Checking now."

Seconds passed with radio silence. The display read at 39 percent, and Cy took our eyes off of it to glance around the room. I examined his thoughts and found that they matched my own; the length of time it was taking Luce to get back with us was not a good sign.

"Cap, I'm showing increased movement in the halls, to your north. . . not far from the side entrance. I'm also showing a large patrol outside in the alley. They may have found the patrol from earlier, keep your guard up."

"Copy that, Corporal."

As we waited, Cy checked our equipment but there was nothing out of place. After fidgeting with a strap briefly we let it go and stood there waiting until, minutes later, the process was done. Not wasting any time, Sarah snatched the chip to put it back in her purse and turned to leave the room. We led her out and back across the hallway into the bathroom, moving at a brisk pace, and soon we were out of the janitor's closet beside the bathroom, and then out in the hall next to the double doors.

"Luce, what's it looking like outside this door?"

"I'm seeing three hostiles outside and down the hall to your left. The way they're walking. . . back and forth. . . they've got to be sentries. This is the only way to the exit though Cap, approach with caution."

"Yeah, thanks a lot, over-watch." Sarah chimed in before I could, her voice thick with sarcasm and distaste.

THE | SPLIT

Cy held a fist up as we crouched behind the door, signaling Sarah to stack up behind us. She grunted and shuffled into position, her weight shaking the door as she sank down to our left. Slowly and silently, we pulled down the door handle and peered out into the hallway.

Our right was clear, so was our left as far as we could see without exposing ourselves. We pulled both his suppressed pistol and his knife out of our belt and, keeping a low profile, scuttled into the hallway, weapon in each hand. As we turned the corner we saw the first man and paused near the wall, signaling for Sarah to do the same.

"What's the call?" Cy asked me, turning his thoughts in towards mine.

"I don't know, this type of thing isn't really in my wheelhouse. I never did special ops, I never even served." I replied, curious as to where he was going.

"Well, if you're really some big bad-ass killer sent from out of time, and not really just a tumor, couldn't you do this sort of thing?"

"Well. . . I, uh. . . " I paused, thinking of San Juan Hill and my dozens of fights back home, *"Yes. . . I can. Let me do it, but. . . shouldn't Charlene lead the way?"*

"Can't," he replied, *"The sound of a drone going live would bring the whole building our way."*

"Fine, then I'll do it."

"Oh yeah? You going to do it?" he teased. I could sense his amusement.

"Yeah, I'm going to do it. Let's go, let's get out of here."

"Well alright then."

We slumped forward as I assumed control of his body. I flexed my fingers, testing the feel of my newfound freedom. He had relinquished all control, but I could feel him in my head, examining my process.

T H E | S P L I T

It felt like it had been years since I had a body to move my own at will, though I knew it had just been days; but then I paused to consider how long it had really been. Or if it had really been any time at all.

Was I outside time, as I dipped through history like this?

"Hey, Shakespeare," Cy's thoughts cut through my thinking. "We need to **move** here, let's go."

Conveying my annoyance and confirmation at the same time, I moved onto the balls of my feet, then tore around the corner. Without making a sound, I thrust Cy's knife into the back of the first guard, yanking up savagely. Now, using his body as a shield, I raised my gun and shot at the second one, bringing him down with five shots.

Around a second corner, I shot at another man but he saw me and took off to his left, disappearing around the bend of the hallway, so I yanked my knife free from the first guard and charged after him, gun at the ready. Charlene was right behind me, guns out, ready to go loud. He was waiting as I made it around the bend, and fired the instant he saw me. A bullet whizzed past my ear, but another crashed into my shoulder, and searing pain erupted from my left side.

I blocked it out, bringing my knife down on his shoulder and jamming the barrel in his face to put four rounds through it. Blood and gore covered my own face as the man sank to the floor, and I had to wipe my face on my sleeve so that I could see the rest of the hallway clearly.

"Damn soldier. . . " Cy chimed in, *"I asked if you could do this, not if you could nearly get me killed! Holy shit!"* I could feel him reassert control over his body and started to protest, but a loud, blaring siren began echoing through the halls.

"Fuck." Sarah said, behind us, having finally caught up.

THE | SPLIT

"Cap, all the alarms in the base are going off," Luce warned. "You need to get the fuck out of there." Over the transmission, I could hear the sound of the siren in the background causing a deafening echo. "Hallways are clear. . . 35 meters out. . . but there's a lot of company gathering outside." Picking up our pace to a sprint, we bounded through the hallway noisily, and in just seconds were back near the side entrance where we had come in.

"Luce, what's the status of the alley outside?"

"20 plus figures, all likely hostile. They're moving around quickly. . . several are around the dumpster to your right."

"We can't make it through that. Luce. . . can you set off a diversion?"

"What you mean. . . like the truck?"

"No like. . . " we paused, as recognition dawned on Cy. "Yeah, actually. . . set off the truck."

"No!" Sarah spoke up beside us. "I've got tons of equipment in there! And, if we blow up this one we'll be down to the clunker."

Cy weighed her words and shared his thoughts with me on the matter. I saw that they had inherited five trucks with their scrapyard, most had gone the same way they were talking about now.

"It's that or you take your chances," Luce said breaking the short silence, "There's no other way I can help you."

"Fine, do it," Sarah said, resignedly.

"Wait! Luce, before you do it, shoot off all the rounds in that sentry, make it seem like we got a fight out front."

"With pleasure."

We waited as Luce worked from across the street. Soon we could hear long bursts of turret fire echoing through the alley faintly. The men outside called to each other, and then we could hear boots moving across the ground to investigate the source of the fire.

Sarah sighed, "I had big plans for that gun. That thing could take out two whole Bloc patrols like it was nothing."

"I know," Cy replied sympathetically. "But plans change, and we needed it to get out of here."

She nodded, we opened the door into the alley. The fire was much louder outside the protection of the building. I turned towards where I knew the truck to be and saw a large group of men sprinting towards it, slowly disappearing from view. Sarah took the lead, and turned the corner around the nearby fence, gun drawn, looking both ways as she crossed the line, and soon dropping her gun, motioning us to follow. In a few feet we had made it to the sewer grate.

Charlene lifted it and we let Sarah climb down first, waited a few seconds, then stepped onto the ladder. As the hole was covered above us, the outside world slipped away. The next hour was a confusing blur. As soon as we made it across the street and up the manhole on the other side, Luce radioed us and told us to meet him on the other side of the building we had been using as our base of operations.

When we arrived, he was sitting on top of a pile of crates, looking down at his tablet. With a frantic energy he described our worsening situation outside; Bloc patrols had found the truck, which had failed to detonate after what Luce guessed was a wiring issue.

Ibis gunships had been called in and swept the area with spotlights, armed guards were in the process of shutting down the entire neighborhood as they looked for us, and if he had still been several stories above we would have been compromised. Luce had moved everything he could after the alarms had gone off, and had contacted his friend Williamson in his desperation, who in turn was sending his driver to our address.

THE | SPLIT

So we nervously paced back and forth, waiting for him to arrive, hoping that he would show up at the back entrance as requested, relieved when ten minutes later a beat up van pulled up outside. We hastily loaded our cargo into the back, got in, and drove off.

The trip was mostly silent; we all stared out of the window at the city, lost in our own thoughts. A half hour later we were at the scrapyard, unloading our equipment together and setting it just outside the van. After we were done, Cyrus thanked the driver and handed him a small wad of cash. He nodded his thanks and drove off through the side gate, back onto the road.

T H E | S P L I T

XX

Found in Pentagon Storage
-T. Acerz, 2031

Boston; 2085

Once we had brought the crates into the shop we paused to take a break. Sitting on the rough stool in the corner, Cy's eyelids blinked away sleep, and I began to feel the ache in his legs as we struggled to keep ourselves engaged. Combined with the come down of the adrenaline rush from earlier in the compound, we were exhausted.

At the table nearby, Luce had pulled out his tablet and was typing away at some unknown task. Sarah got up and walked over to him, taking the chip out of her pocket and holding it out. After a few seconds of hesitation, he took it from her, setting it down next to his keyboard. His facial expression began to sour as he continued to work, Sarah looking over his shoulder.

"What's the problem, Luce?" Cy asked him, blinking slowly as we tried to retain our composure. "You look even more distressed than when we almost got caught earlier."

"I can't find a connection, all sub-nets are down. . . not even the proxy networks I set up are working. Whatever is on this drive. . . it has to be related. . . they really don't want anyone to see."

We frowned and stood up. "Do you need a connection to access what's on there?"

"Well. . . no. But, I didn't know opening the files was part of our plan." Silence fell, as we looked around the room at each other. Luce looked perplexed at Cy's words, finally stopping his work to stare up at us.

"Well, I don't know about you two. . . " Cy spoke up, "But I'd like to see this information we just risked our lives for."

Luce was obviously uncomfortable with what he had suggested. "But. . . command wants this chip. I'm sure they've seen these alerts, too. They know we have it."

"And they'll get it," Cy replied. "I just want to see what's on it. . . you yourself always complain they don't give enough intel to us guys in the field."

"But-" Luce protested.

Sarah cut him off, "But nothing, Luce. Cap is right. . . we deserve to know what's going on here. I'm tired of fighting in the dark, waiting for orders that may or may not come."

Luce looked at both of us, side to side, before finally giving a resigned sigh. "I'm assuming you want me to pull up the files now?"

"As soon as you can." I responded firmly.

"Okay give me a minute, I'll bet there are a half dozen Bloc network engineers just waiting for a trace of this thing to appear in the area. Just to be safe I'm going to completely disconnect from everything before we do this." We nodded and let him work. Sarah assisted, they talked in low voices and we saw her pointing at their shared interface screen periodically.

"And. . . that should do it," Luce said over the sound of his typing. "Inserting the chip now."

We took a few steps to our right, moving beside Sarah as we looked over his other shoulder. Our interface suddenly linked to his, and a dark blue box appeared in the middle of the screen. White letters appeared in the center: **"Welcome Admin JX-173"** Then this screen went away and was replaced with a list of files, running all the way down the left

T H E | S P L I T

side of our vision. Luce began clicking through them, opening the individual screens faster than Cy or I could follow, then his voice was suddenly filled with excitement.

"Holy shit, it's a gold mine! Look at this. . . network passwords, intelligence sites. . . Hold on, what's this ?" He pointed to a file near the bottom of the list, labeled '.code.xx'. It was the only item in the entire list that had a different shaped icon, a solid black box in place of the blue piece of text the other files all had. He opened it, finding several items inside, the top of which was label 'log'. When he selected this a wall of text popped up, which he copied to a translator program. I started reading the first few lines, the NI translating automatically.

4 June, 2080: log/197.37.21.9/users/Maj.Ling
REPORT:

The campaign on Washington is all but finished. I have been sent ahead of the other teams, just behind our front lines, to investigate a disturbance, but must wait for my approval to be processed. Command insisted it was classified, no matter how many times I showed them my top level clearance, stating that I would be filled in on location. Our map led us to a cavern near the grounds of the old Pentagon building. I had thought the place was emptied decades ago.

When I arrived on site, I saw an engineering crew working to open a large steel door. A Captain Sokolov informed me that his crew believes the power to still be on inside, but they cannot get the door open through standard procedure. They were insisting that we excavate further, luckily I stopped them before they collapsed the tunnel. I have run preliminary tests on the door panel, and am going to request more personnel from command to get through. The encryption is unlike anything I've ever seen, every variable changing millions of times a second, each component shifting constantly.

T H E | S P L I T

1 October, 2080:

The puzzle of this damn door continues to elude me. My mind is numbing with frustration. A small village of portable buildings has been built outside the cave to house the large team of analysts and engineers I've been sent from command. We work around the clock, and must be near the blasted panel at all times, but together with the engineers, the other analysts and I have created a sequence generator that plugs right into the panel, relying on random combinations and primitive 'brute force' techniques.

In tests, it ran up to 52 percent of the lock's speed, but as of this date it has been running for nearly a week, and the engineers have told me it could take months before it finds a combination – even if we ran it continuously.

If that is how long I must wait, I will. In the meantime, my team and I are at hard at work creating an even faster sequence generator while our current one runs, and hopefully we will be through this door soon. I don't know how much longer I can be in this cave...

6 November, 2080:

It's worked! The correct sequence has been entered and the door is ready to open. My excitement was delayed when command instructed us to not open the door until they were on scene. The transmission put their ETA at a few hours after sundown, I will continue my log after the showing.

10:39 -

My initial joy as I watched the door slowly sliding open was immediately dashed to pieces when I saw what lay on the other side. A long, steel colored hallway, about 30 meters. . . ending in a door identical to the first. I had cursed loudly upon seeing it, drawing the disapproving glances of some of the senior officers, but as I walked up

THE | SPLIT

to interface with the new door's panel, what I had feared did happen; it too was locked, identical to the door before.

Shortly afterward, I had a meeting with command, who informed me of the small amount of progress the excavation team had made on the surface above. I was surprised to hear this; surely I had been told they were attempting to breach it from the top? Perhaps I had been buried in my work and forgot?

But the ground below was blast-proof, ballistic concrete, a material the US had kept the specifics of highly classified. The engineering corps is only getting through feet a day. Command assured me they were looking into the material and would find something soon but, for now, they depended on me and my team. They inquired about the new sequence-generator, and though my report was more optimistic than I really felt, we had achieved 69 percent efficiency.

Still, we had run into a problem; though we had been moving at a solid pace for months, in the last few weeks we had only gained .32. My fellow analysts and I fear we may be near our peak effectiveness, if we don't reach a major breakthrough. The sequence seems. . . Alive. No pattern can be established. I fear if I don't solve this soon, I will be replaced.

17 January, 2081: log/197.37.21.9/users/Lt. Gen. Mikhailov

I have been selected by command to take over Major Ling's work, and thus have taken command of the excavation team on the surface. My first day on site, I began a different approach, one I hope will bring us faster results. Through request, I will be working closely with them to form a two-pronged solution, and have ordered a series of tests to measure the caverns dimensions. Soon we will know the size of our task.

21 January, 2081:

T H E | S P L I T

The tests have been finished, providing us with a rough chart. The open area begins roughly 4.5 km down. The tunnel, with the entrances, apparently spans 1.5 km further. It is all ballistic concrete above. I have put all of this in my report to command.

If this next door leads to a similar hall with another identical door as the first one had, and continues as such, there will be 48 more doors after this one. Now, my two teams will race to the center but, at the rate both units are moving, it will take years before we make it.

For the sake of my sanity, I hope we reach it sooner.

2 April, 2081:

44 more doors remain, the rate at which we open them and improve our sequencer goes up every week. Yet a curious development happened yesterday. According to reports, while a group of techs approached the next panel to open the sixth door, the door behind them closed and a holographic image appeared on the wall and spoke with the echoing voice of a group:

"NEUROTECH SCANNING, ACCESS SCANNING, *UNCLEAR* SCANNING, *UNCLEAR* PROTOCOLS FAILED, HOSTILES DETECTED, *UNCLEAR* AGENT DISPERSING."

The transmission then turned to screams, and a light green gas entered the chamber, killing the whole group. The audio feed was spotty, and the video was not much better. I caught just a glimpse of the image before the gas flooded the room, obscuring the camera's vision. It was mesmerizing, a pink series of lines constantly moving in a holographic field. I have attached both recordings in my report to command, hopefully they will have answers we don't.

The log ended here.

We were done reading first, and looked at the other two, who were both still deep in concentration and finished at their own pace. Minutes later, we took turns sharing our thoughts on the accounts we had just read.

Cy eventually wrangled the conversation back into a slower paced discussion, then we both noticed an item on the list with the same icon as the folder itself. Luce selected it and a viewer popped up. Slowly a form rendered; pink lines forming an unclear shape began to spin around randomly.

"This must have been what the general was referring to." Luce said what we were all thinking.

It was beautiful, we kept looking for a pattern in its movements and could not detect one. Then without warning a sharp pain shot through the middle of our head.

We closed our eyes, flinching, only to open them and find that our vision was gone. Loud static filled Cyrus' mind and I felt our thoughts being pulled apart. In my confusion, I called out to him but got no response. My connection to his body had been severed; there was no trace of Cyrus. I was trapped and alone.

Suddenly the pink shape appeared in front of me, flashing brightly as it danced around, consuming my thoughts. Emotions of passion and wanting arose as I stared transfixed; I wanted it, to hold it, to feel it – I had never wanted something so bad.

It spoke to me, bright white dots sparkling with its words: *"Find us. Find us. Find us."* It repeated, every voice different and coming from all angles. Then the figure disappeared as soon as it arrived, and my connection to Cyrus was restored.

"Cy, did you see that?"

"Yeah."

"Are you all right?"

T H E | S P L I T

"I... I think so. Head is killing me, though."

I felt what he meant, a dull pain throbbed at the back of our skull, a feeling which radiated red through the darkness. We next opened our eyes to see the dull brown of the ceiling, and as our senses returned we could feel the cool ground beneath our back.

Sarah and Luce stood over us, looks of concern on their faces. "Cy, are you okay?" Luce asked.

"Yeah," he responded. "Just a little shook up. That thing... that... whatever it is... caused my NI to go haywire."

Sarah looked back at the monitor, and then closed the rendering. "What was it? What did you see?" she questioned.

"The same thing on the screen, only... it was bigger. It... spoke to me. It told me to find it... it was beautiful. I- " Cyrus trailed off.

Luce and Sarah shared concerned glances, and the conversation fell silent as they thought over my words. Cyrus spoke again before they could respond. "We need to find it."

"Find it?!" Luce was incredulous. "Cy, the tag on this file was beyond top tier intelligence. The Bloc hasn't used that designation since they developed their fusion reactor and that was decades ago. We have no idea what we're dealing with here."

Sarah nodded and added to his point, "A secret this big would require an appropriate level of security. I doubt we would have the same access we had back at the site earlier. And even if you made it despite all of that, you still have to gain entrance. You read those reports, what makes you think you could gain access faster than a whole Bloc team?"

I could sense Cy's frustration at their words, as we shared our responses with each other. Both Luce and Sarah spoke honestly and openly – and their caution was well reasoned; it would be hard to make

THE | SPLIT

a case against them.

Neither Cyrus nor I had any solid reason we needed to find this strange shape; except the desire the shape had awoken within us. And that would be a tough sell.

"I can't quite explain it. . . " Cy started, ". . . but this is, important. Why would something or someone fight so hard to keep this secret? The whole city above is occupied, you'd think anyone involved is detained or dead already. There's got to be more to this story, and we got to be the group to find out what that is."

"Why us?" Luce asked.

"If not us, who else? You think the feds in the Midwest can spare an entire army to check this out? The only assets they have on the coast are cells like us, and God knows, there aren't many of those anymore."

Both their faces continued to show hesitation but Cy pressed on, "Best case scenario, we turn the chip over to command, they send it to the higher ups, and it gets lost in a giant stack of Bloc secrets we know of but can't do anything about."

Sarah bit her lip as she mulled this over, and Luce spoke up, "So what are you proposing? That we keep the chip and head straight for DC? We're not ready for that."

"We wouldn't keep the chip," Cy replied. "We take it to the drop spot after readying our truck, and then leave."

Luce laughed and shook his head; what Cy had said wasn't a lot better than what he'd feared. We talked about it for the next half hour and, gradually, Sarah came around to Cyrus' side.

Soon they were both trying to convince Luce that this was the next move. He kept going back to the amount of time it would take to ready the truck and gear, and that the risk we were taking wasn't worth it.

"But why, Cyrus?" he asked, exasperated. "There's still work left to be done! If we fail here, it's over. You yourself mentioned how few soldiers we have left here. Why should we throw our lives away on a stupid gamble?"

"Luce. . . because this may be the last chance we have." He fell silent at this, and I continued, "Anything the Bloc is guarding this jealousy, that its own creators guarded this cautiously. . . it's got to be something important. I don't know if you've looked around, Luce. . . but we're not winning this war. This is a battle of attrition, and we don't have the men or resources to last more than a few years AT BEST. We need to find an edge, and we need to find it now. This could be our only shot."

Slowly, he nodded his head in resigned agreement. "Well. . . If that's what you really think this is, Cap, what choice do we have? Better to meet my death sooner rather than later anyway. . . this world is shit."

We ignored his reluctant pessimism, and Cy began issuing the orders to leave. "Luce, you get the truck ready and grab the extra batteries, me and Sarah will start packing up gear. Two or three crates, only what you need, and keep it all packed away. I don't want any more trouble than we'll already have if we get randomly searched. That reminds me, civilian clothes, we'll keep our weapons nearby, but we need to keep a low profile."

They scrambled to follow his orders. We walked over to the far wall and began rooting through crates. I saw from Cyrus' thoughts that we were looking for his shotgun that he had been working on. After the fourth box we opened, he found it and pulled it out, holding it in front of our face to show me.

"Pretty huh?" his thoughts echoed around me, *"Explosive ammo, fully equipped TacRail, I even painted it myself."*

I looked at the gun from stock to muzzle, the paint he was referring to was a series of bright white eyeballs, all bleeding from the bottom, winding their way around the barrel and trigger.

"Pretty is one word for it," I replied. *"It does have a sort of grotesque charm."*

He laughed and put it back in the crate. The next ones we chose seemed to be at random – that, or Cy knew what was in each without looking inside. Luce had pulled the truck around outside, and we moved the crates into the back then, after everything was secured, we went inside and opened a side closet I hadn't noticed before to pull out a blue collared shirt and beige colored pants, quickly stripping down and putting the new outfit on.

In just a few minutes we were outside in the truck and ready to take off, sighing and looking around slowly, as if it were the last time he would ever see the place. Luce stepped on the gas and we moved forward.

THE | SPLIT

XXI

LGPB://mn34/con/terra/BH, 9875
(Translated)

Boston; 2085

We wound through the city slowly on streets that seemed emptier than usual for an early afternoon, seeing nothing but patrol cars and soldiers until a few blocks later; a man sitting on a bench holding a young girl. But as we drove uptown the number of people outside grew, and the battle-scarred, dully colored jungle changed slowly to the bright colors and bustling community of the Boston from my youth.

We were nearing the area where Bloc's citizens lived, and the upscale look of the area showed it. Luce stopped the truck at a mostly empty parking lot off of a main street and, leaving the engine idling, got out and ran across the street to an old Irish pub. The sign looked ancient, but the holographic beer and liquor ads behind the glass brought the place back into the present.

During the few minutes we waited after he disappeared inside the door, Cy pulled up the map to Washington, searching for the best possible route. We could hear Sarah humming behind us, tapping the side of the truck in time.

Soon Luce came back outside, looking both ways before he quickly walked back across the street and getting back into the truck, throwing it into reverse the second he sat down.

"How'd it go?" Cy asked, noting his hurried behavior.

"Exchange went fine," he arched his neck out to see past me before turning onto the street. "Same shit as usual. He says to be checking for a new transmission, and thank you for your continued service. . . blah

blah blah. It felt. . . off, though. Faces I didn't like, and a tense atmosphere. . . you know?"

We nodded. "I'll keep an eye on it. Glad you made it out. Get on the interstate, I think I found a good way down to Washington."

For an hour we drove down the highway, cruising at a good pace. Light poles and trees alike were a blur as we weaved in and out between cars and other trucks. We moved at 50 kmh or so, changing lanes at every opportunity until, just an hour outside of New York, we hit traffic and at Luce's request Cy took the wheel. Time passed as we patiently navigated the sea of vehicles.

Through the silence in the truck me and Cyrus talked, passing the time with passionate discussions about the future, my purpose being here, and what awaited us in Washington. Though we had both seen the same vision, we had interpreted it differently. Cy insisted that the pink shape most likely had been an extraterrestrial being that had been detained by the US government.

I rather thought the form was a physical manifestation of an advanced, warlike AI that had been developed; citing a video game I had played in my youth. Cyrus laughed at this, insisting primitive video games were no indication of the future, and this sparked yet another discussion.

Before we could finish however, traffic cleared and our speed picked up. We drove faster, but stayed out of the left lane, not wanting to draw too much attention. Looking out of the corner of Cyrus' eye, I examined the city, remembering trips up the highway from Maryland to Maine, and how the whole area seemed to blend into one giant metropolis. Even in my day, the upper East Coast had been densely populated.

Now, although the buildings were all still there, the occupants were missing, and most of the structures would have fit into the Boston

THE | SPLIT

neighborhood we had just left. Scorch marks covered most of the walls still fortunate enough to be standing and the streets, with remains from the buildings nearby, were covered in rubble and concrete dust.

We seemed to drive miles through the crumbling neighborhoods without seeing people, or even a car, moving. Every 10 km stretch or so, the scene would change to the picturesque America of before; vibrant banner ads, bright sleek buildings, and quickly moving people covering the scene – all of whom seemed to be from the ruined area.

Near the border of Maryland we got off the highway and took a detour. Cy showed me a reported weigh station ahead on his interface, and I knew we had to avoid it. After a half hour of winding our way through the deserted neighborhoods we pulled back onto the highway – right in the middle of a high volume of traffic – and 15 minutes later still hadn't moved very far. We could still see most of the buildings that we had seen when we first pulled on.

A sign was in the distance on our right hand side, and I strained Cy's vision to make it out. **'Baltimore 34 km'**, it read; below it were words in other languages. Cy's implant said the same thing.

"We're nearly there." Cy told me.

"We are?" I questioned, able to sense his relief. *"I thought Washington was more than an hour away."*

"It is. . . but it's dark out. All major cities have a curfew. You can't enter or leave by highway."

I thought about this, and of how annoying a policy like that would've been back home – then, even the mention of home was enough to set my mind wandering. Cy left me to my memories as I sifted through them longingly.

T H E | S P L I T

It seemed so fresh, but was still a 'distant' memory. I dreamed of work, and my friends, even my worn down home; but most of all, I dreamed of Meela. My perception of time had been stilted, and it was impossible to gauge how long had passed, but I could see her face perfectly. Short, blond hair, hanging by curls over her sparkling blue eyes. Her smile brought forth a million happy feelings, but they soon dissolved into loneliness, as my mood shifted.

I felt Cy tug at me, and pushed my memories aside to look up. A line of brake lights stretched off into the distance, and. At the edge of our vision I could see a large building covering the road, and remembered that I had seen a smaller version of it before, when I had crossed the border into Mexico as a child. This had to be one of the screening stations causing Cy the heightened anxiety I had felt.

"Sarah... wake Luce up, we need to be ready."

We heard the sound of Sarah smacking him in the back; Luce awoke with a start. "Wha-?! What's up?" he yawned.

"We're almost here, that's what's up. Stay low, stay ready, and most of all stay hidden. If anyone opens that truck-gate you wait for my order."

"You got it, Cap." he still sounded sleepy, but was making an obvious attempt to appear ready.

"Sarah, you hop up in the front seat with me. Let's just do it like we practiced."

In one limber move, Sarah turned her body and moved from the back to the cab, using our shoulder for support as she lowered herself down into the seat. Within a half hour we were at the checkpoint and pulling up to the line. Cy was surprised to see a pale man with red hair standing our window. We rolled it down and stared down at him.

"Good evening, ID please." He spoke with no trace of accent.

T H E | S P L I T

We reached into the cup holder and slid the card out of its slot, handing it to him, smiling, but without a word. "Very good Mr. Smith. What brings you to Baltimore today?"

We looked to Sarah as she leaned over our seat to take the reins. "We're just passing through, on our way to Washington. . . got a delivery to some gala. We work for my father's company. . . Luciano Florist, see it on the truck? It's kinda faded."

He stepped back and saw the graphic on the side – it had come on the truck when we bought it from Luce's uncle – then nodded. Sarah continued, "It's been awhile since we've had business like this. . . hopefully it can turn things around and. . . sorry, I know you're busy. My husband here says I ramble, I probably talk enough for both of us." She laughed in a way even Cyrus had a hard time telling was fake. "Do you need to see my ID too, officer?"

"Detective," he corrected, smiling. "No, you all are fine, go on through, find you a good spot to park before it gets too late."

"Thank you, Detective!" He walked on to the next car. We stepped on the gas and drove into Baltimore.

"Excellent job. . . as always, Sarah," Cy said, laughing and shaking our head.

"Why, thank you. . . " she replied in a sweet voice, pursing her lips into a smile. ". . . wouldn't I make just the best little housewife?" We nodded and laughed again.

The streets of the city teemed with nightlife. A sea of people moved down the sidewalk in both directions, passing countless street vendors who peddled their wares by the glow of the streetlights. Every so often, we would see a man or woman holding a megaphone, screaming at an angry crowd below but, though I was curious to hear their words, Cy did not stop nor roll down the windows.

T H E | S P L I T

We continued on a few blocks down the road until we came across a large sign labeled: **'Paid Parking, Overnight or Daily'**, and Cy stopped near the entrance to turn in. A young attendant approached the window, beads of sweat dripped down his face, holding a small wad of cash in his right hand. We lowered the window.

"Alright, truck. . . it's after nightfall. . . this overnight, or for just a few hours?"

"Overnight." Cy said firmly, reaching into his pocket for his money.

"Okay that'll be. . . 45 bills."

We handed him the money, then drove into the large field. Pavement covered a portion near the entrance but, as we continued further in the lot, the ground turned to gravel and our teeth chattered slightly as we moved over the bumpy surface before turning into a spot to our left. An instant after we turned off the ignition, the back door opened, and we turned around to see Luce already out of the truck, stretching his legs.

"Where are you going?" Sarah questioned.

"Out. I'm going to live it up one more night, before. . . " he trailed off as a small group of girls walked behind him, following their movements with his eyes.

"Hey ladies!" he called out. "Come here!?" The tallest one giggled, pointing at herself questioningly. "Yeah, you! Come over here a second." The girls walked over, standing a few feet away from the truck, giggling and whispering. Luce went on to question, "What's your name, beautiful?"

She smiled and blushed, before whispering, "Whitney."

"Yeah. . . " his voice was louder than it had been, "I'm going out with Whitney, and her friends!" He walked over to slip an arm around the girl, she smiled and laid her head against him acceptingly.

THE | SPLIT

He went on, "Probably get drunk, see if there's any synth around or. . . well, hell. . . I don't know what people in Baltimore do for fun. . . but we'll find out, won't we?"

The group cheered and he started to turn around. "Wait, Luce. . . " Cy called out, stopping him mid-stride. Luce lowered his head in exasperation, told the girls to wait, and walked slowly back to the truck.

"What's up?"

"If you find any synth, get me some too." We handed him the rest of the small stack of money we had brought.

He looked up in seeming confusion. "That's it? No 'Luce find us a network'. . . 'Luce, clean your shit up' or. . . 'Luce, go do this'?" We shook our head, no. "Well. . . hell yeah. . . I got you, Cy."

We smiled as he turned away, loudly talking to the girls about some bar he had heard about that had fights and good music.

"You kids and your drugs," Sarah scolded.

Cy could hear her concern through her playful tone, and ignored it. "I know, I know. You want to heat up some of these cans and watch a movie?"

"Yeah, sure. . . but can we watch. . . "

"Moonrise Kingdom?" they finished in unison. She laughed and nodded.

Moonrise Kingdom had been her favorite movie since she was a little girl, when her grandma had shown it to her, and together she and Cyrus had watched it a half dozen times.

I peered through Cyrus' memory of the movie; initially, he had been excited when she described it – Bill Murray was a legend of old comedy, and Cy had seen several of his films growing up. But, after the first half he had been disappointed, having expected a lighthearted comedy rather than the coming-of-age adventure/first-love story the movie contained. Oddly though, as he settled in for the second half he began to enjoy it; partially for the movie itself, but mostly for how happy it made Sarah.

"Of course, Sarah. I mean. . . what else would we watch?"

"Right?" she smiled as she then pulled out a blank tablet, sharing the feed with us, navigating the screen as she looked for the movie.

We opened a crate on the top of a nearby stack, pulling out two cans of Chef Boy-ar-dee™ Ravioli – and a small black box. Setting it down on the front seat, we opened the cans with his knife and placed them inside. It hummed, and after a few seconds beeped, sliding the top open automatically. Grabbing a scrap of cloth from the floor, we picked the cans up; I could feel the heat on Cy's hands even through the covering.

"What the hell was that box?" I questioned.

"A thermal energy compartment." Cy explained. *"They were made for heat-activated adhesives. . . it's against regulations to use them for anything else, but no one's really checking these days."*

We moved into the back of the truck, setting the cans down in front of Sarah then lowering to sit next to her on the blanket she had just laid down. I could see the movie already loaded in front of me, ready to go. We ate from the cans like we were starving, blowing on our plastic spoons between large bites, and in no time both were empty.

Setting them aside, we leaned down to start the movie. About 15 minutes in, Sarah cuddled up to Cy, laying on our shoulder. He wrapped our arm around her, and within a few scenes she looked up at us, smiling. Another few seconds went by before I noticed Cy moving his neck towards her. Sarah's smile beamed even brighter as he went in to kiss her, and the next half hour was spent in the act of releasing months of bottled up passion.

T H E | S P L I T

It had been a long time for either of them, and the tension from working together so closely had reached its climax. A mere minute after they'd finished, Cyrus was asleep.

Alone, my thoughts began to wander. I was tired too, but with no body of my own to perceive it in, it had been tough to determine. Still, I knew my speed was sluggish, and my thought process seemed full; littered with emotions and new information since arriving in the future. I could sense Cy's subconscious thoughts, it felt so peaceful and isolated. . .

I soon felt my way into my own subconscious, and drifted off.

T H E | S P L I T

XXII

Recovered in Bloc Vault C1
-T. Acerz, 2131

Baltimore; 2085

Suddenly, I was pulled from a hazy darkness as Cyrus opened his eyes.

We could see Luce's face. Sunlight was streaming in from behind, forcing us to squint, and he was hovering a few inches above us, smiling. Cy straightened up his body to look at him. We could also feel Sarah stirring.

"So, uh... is this..." Luce grinned, pointing between the two of us, "... happening again?"

"This never stopped happening, Luce," Sarah said in a flat tone.

"Gross!" he laughed.

"Yeah, I guess it's sort of natural to our group dynamic," Cy cut in, smiling, "When we're dealing with your childish bullshit all the time... and take on the role of parents... parents have to, well... you know."

"HELL OUTTA HERE!" Luce bolted past us and moved to the front seat of the truck. "Still gross, bro."

Sarah stood up and began dressing, prompting us to do the same. "She's actually pretty hot, Luce." said Cy, as we buttoned our pants.

"Yeah... I know she is, it's just, her... and, you." he shivered at the thought.

We rolled our eyes and turned to Sarah, reaching out to grab her ass and give it a firm squeeze.

"Hey!" she giggled.

T H E | S P L I T

"Your turn to drive, doll."

"Well, okay. . . what's fair is fair."

The space in the back of the truck had been cramped, the floor we had slept on last night being covered with crates, and before Sarah started the engine Cy, knowing that they would tip over if we didn't, made several new stacks.

We then settled into the rear-facing seat in back as Sarah started the truck, shifting into gear and leaving the parking lot to take off down the bumpy gravel road. The streets of Baltimore were mainly empty this early in the morning, sidewalks sparsely covered by sleepy looking pedestrians, but after a couple of kilometers we neared the National Aquarium. I could see it out of the corner of Cyrus' eye, just past Luce's window.

"Cy, let's move to the front," I insisted, pulling his left leg up and starting to move us forward.

"What...why?"

"National Aquarium. . . I haven't been here since I was a boy. I want to see it again."

"Well, we're not stopping."

"I know that. . . I just want to see the building, it's cool. Is there no appreciation for architecture in 2085?"

He relented, and we stepped to the front, ducking down between the two seats. There it was. The triangular roofs and bright colors had remained nearly identical over the years. I was happy to see it so well preserved.

Though flashing holographic signs covered the side nearest the street, showing prices and attractions, it seemed some things from the past hadn't changed, and I was filled with a sense of hope.

"The hell are you doing up here, Cy?" Luce looked down at me with raised eyebrows.

"I, uh. . . " Cyrus fumbled, "I, just wanted to see the aquarium, it's a cool building. . . that's all."

"Cool building? Who gives a damn about a building?"

"Piss off, Luce." We stood up and moved back to our seat. Within minutes we passed another checkpoint, now closed in the light of the day with only a few men standing around it, and breezed by it onto the open road of the highway. The wind rushed by us, as the truck shifted slowly every time Sarah weaved between the other cars on the road, and I sensed Cy hoping that the roads would remain clear to Washington; a thought I echoed upon hearing it.

Though Sarah had turned on music a few minutes before, I felt uncomfortable in the silence, and tried to rouse a groggy Cy into conversation.

"So, with your first, and my second. . . possibly third. . . death looming, don't you think I should know everything you're not telling me?"

"Why?" he responded. *"You have full access to my life and memories now. . . I trust you. Go find it for yourself."*

"That could take me forever. . . there's no organization to thoughts and memories. At least not yours anyway. All I have are pieces to your story, and so many questions unanswered. There are even things that you're still hiding from me. Don't deny it. . . I'm in your head, remember?" I sensed his discomfort; he didn't like talking about the past. But I needed answers.

"What do you want to know? You get TWO questions. . . make them count. I'm not showing you anything else."

THE | SPLIT

 Frustration filled my thoughts at his stipulation, but I pushed it aside and racked my mind for the two most pressing questions I had. The first question was easy; *"Alright,"* I said, *"the first thing you ever showed me... the day of the Fall... Your NI malfunctioned, nearly killing you and Ramirez. You two had seemed so close before... whatever happened to him?"* I could sense relief from Cy; this wasn't the question he dreaded me asking.

 "Ramirez is... damn, I don't even know how to put this. I don't know what he did immediately after New York, but he resurfaced about a year later, back in Kansas City, at the head of his old crew, the Hilltop Mafia. Something happened to him, because the man I heard described in reports was not the man I had once called a friend. They say he has become a remorseless killer, and his men no more than thugs masquerading as patriots. I don't know what's true and what isn't. But, I do know that wherever Ramirez goes, a trail of blood is left behind. One more question. Make it count."

 I thought for a minute or two as I tried to come with an idea... finding out what Ramirez had been doing was incredibly interesting. I had yet to think about another question. What else did I want to know?

 "Okay," I had it. *"Why didn't we go to the Globe? It seemed so important to you in the past, and some of your contacts there would have made that disaster at the compound yesterday go a lot smoother."*

 His brain clouded with sadness, becoming cold all around me. I felt its touch as thoughts and memories leapt forward in front of his space, but out of respect did not examine them. After several seconds, he replied, carefully measuring his response as he formed it.

 "The Globe is no longer there. It was raided over a year and a half ago, nearly everyone discovered inside was killed."

THE | SPLIT

I could feel his loss, and experienced a sudden burst of empathy. *"I'm so sorry. Did you. . . hear what happened? Did anyone make it out?"*

"I was there," he lamented. *"I don't like thinking about it. . . but can't seem to forget it. . . Manuel had bitten off more than he could chew with Bloc command. They'd known about the Globe for years, but had never considered it worth the amount of troops or resources they would lose. That changed. . . after we hit the currency exchange.*

Manuel knew what we did, and was quick to take credit for the hit. . . bragging to anyone in his circles that one of 'his' crews did it. A Bloc recon team began monitoring the building, and one night, they jammed any video feed. We didn't think anything of it at the time, figured it was probably just a glitch. Luce first volunteered to go up and fix it. . . but allowed someone else to do it instead.

I'm glad he didn't go, he would've never come back. They had taken out most of the guards outside, and detained anyone who tried to enter. A half dozen Bloc armored units stormed the entrance, firing into the crowd. Most of us shot back, but we couldn't stop them. . . every man was in full armor, half of them had subcompact flamethrowers, and were using them indiscriminately. The whole place was covered in flames and smoke in minutes.

I remember it clearly. . . more clearly than I wished I did. The bartender screaming as he burned. . . the bullet-riddled corpses, stacking along the walkway. . . Luce and I found Sarah and we took off towards Manuel's office, up the stairs. I took a round to the side as we climbed. . . part of it's still in there.

We went through the office, killed the man guarding Manuel's storeroom, grabbed a few bags of cash and climbed the hidden hatch back up to the surface. It was amazing they didn't stop us, or kill us, when we popped up on the street. By some miracle, we made it through their perimeter and walked back to the scrap yard.

The worst part of it. . . it was all our fault. Our work had brought too much heat. All of those bodies. . . they're on my head now. I took the missions that would incur the most wrath. . . I BEGGED for those missions."

I didn't know what to say. After forcing him to re-live the ordeal, I wished I could console him. *"Damn Cy...I'm so sorry."*

"Don't mention it. . . Literally, don't mention it again."

I left him alone and we rolled on in silence. Sometime later we felt the truck roll to a stop, after which we only moved forward a few feet at a time in slow intervals – the telltale sign of traffic. I let my mind wander, noticing that the quality of my thoughts had improved since last night; my responses were quicker, and the haze had lifted from my memories.

Sleeping in another person's mind was an interesting experience. The rest had felt instantaneous, I hadn't slipped into the subconscious state I was normally used to, but I was grateful for the chance to sleep.

"Cy, we're about a hundred feet from the gate, are you ready?" Sarah asked, looking back at us.

We nodded, picking up the assault rifle Luce had left leaning against the side of the truck, while Cy briefly thought about going to retrieve his shotgun from the crate then decided against it. Instead, we sat up straight, holding the rifle loosely on our lap, ready to go at an instant.

The brakes squealed and Sarah rolled the window down as we were brought to a stop, then we heard the voice of the checkpoint officer:

"What's your business here in DC? Do you have government contracting licenses I need to see?" The man's voice, aggressive and hurried, had a slight trace of an accent, but his pronunciation was perfect.

T H E | S P L I T

"Uh, no officer," Sarah began in the sweet voice she had used in Baltimore, "We're just here to deliver some flowers for a gala down near the old capital building. We're Luciano Florist, you can see it on the side there. . . we were never given any papers for this order, should-"

"Yes yes," he cut her off. "Hold here one moment."

"What the hell?" Luce muttered nervously.

"Easy Luce," Cy replied calmly, though we gripped our rifle a little bit tighter.

"Okay ma'am," the officer's voice returned. "According to our records, Luciano Florist. . . as a licensed business, has been inactive and. . . all accounts were closed in 2080. We're going to need to search the vehicle before you can enter the city. Is there anything you would like to inform us of, prior to the search?"

I felt our heart jump as Cy and I exchanged nervous thoughts, before he calmed his nerves, then sat staring at the back door resolutely.

"Nothing I can think of, officer. . . do you really want to search through a bunch of plants? I don't want you all getting dirt and leaves on those handsome uniforms. . . "

"It's a risk we're willing to take," he tapped against the side of the truck, "Smirnoff. . . Chang, check the truck."

We heard footsteps walking around the side, and one of the men brushed against the back corner of the truck with a dull thud. We switched the gun from safe, training it on the door with our eye looking down the optics.

They were conversing in a combination of Hindi, Cantonese, and Russian, blending the words together seamlessly. The NI had a hard time translating the quick changes in dialect, leaving us with a faint static buzzing in both ears.

THE | SPLIT

Suddenly the lock mechanism jiggled and I could hear the handle being gripped. We moved our finger to the trigger –

Then, an explosion roared to the right of us, muffled only slightly by the walls of the truck. The men at the truck gate shouted to the officer near the window, and soon the only thing that could be heard were bullets and incoherent shouts. The shots sounded like they were coming from the same direction as the explosion, the noise mingled with pained shrieks, as men fell around us.

We stood up and popped our head into the cab. Sarah looked up at us, wide-eyed, hands still at the wheel.

"We gotta get out of here," Cy said urgently.

"But, they'll follow us!" She protested.

I looked around through the windows. The attending officers had left their posts, and I could see some of them engaged in a firefight with an unknown assailant; in the lanes next to us cars were beginning to drive through the checkpoint at will, on both sides.

"*Drive*, Lieutenant," Cy commanded.

Sarah nodded and we shot forward into Washington DC, slowing only to turn onto one of the side streets a few blocks in. The city was in near-pristine condition; either there had been no damage in the fighting from the Fall, or they had done an immaculate job repairing it. However, for all of its bright colors and flashy displays, the streets were disturbingly empty.

There were more people than we had seen in Baltimore as we were leaving in the morning, but only barely. The lack of traffic through the well-kept streets gave them a haunting effect.

"Well, where am I headed?" Sarah asked. "Obviously to the capital district. . . but what route do I take?"

T H E | S P L I T

"I doubt it will be in the capital district," Luce chimed in. "The entrance to a cavern that size? I'll bet we're looking at a couple of kilometers west of the old Pentagon building itself."

Cy agreed with Luce, and pulled up a map of DC on his NI. It took several seconds to render, and several more to display our current location on it, but he now scrolled through the area, looking for potential locations for the entrance, wishing aloud that the live satellite feed was still active. Then the ocular feed began to crackle and fade around the edges.

Confused, Cy closed the viewer and rebooted the system. The loading image popped up, only to be immediately distorted on the screen, bending and expanding with a blur as suddenly, the pink figure from yesterday appeared in front of us, showing through the ocular feed over the NI's stream.

"Find us..." it whispered; the multitude of voices ringing through Cy's head. Then the figure began to glitch, and some of the pixels froze in place, producing a disorienting effect. But it continued to call to us as a set of coordinates now appeared on the bottom of the screen, and the system moved the figure to the left of the ocular readout. Then, as quickly as it came, it disappeared and the map was returned to the screen, with the location on the right side.

"Luce, give me your tablet," Cy ordered.

"Why?" he asked, confused but passing the tablet back to us.

With a gesture, we touched our head and swiped the map onto Luce's interface. "That's why," Cy said simply, handing the screen back to him.

"Is this it?" Luce inquired, "How do you know?"

"The pink shape came back," Cy said, pausing a moment. "I think it's linked to my NI somehow, it opened up the map on its own."

THE | SPLIT

Sarah and Luce exchanged skeptical glances before both looking back at us. "Are you sure of this?" she asked.

"Yes," Cy replied, leaving his answer at that.

"Well... take a left here, Sarah," Luce pointed out past the windshield. "If this is right, we should be able to find a spot to park within a couple clicks."

And so we drove towards the capital district. Though the streets had been kept in good condition, some of the monuments and statues had been torn down. Piles of rubble covered their bases, plaques describing the artworks lay in mounds of gray dust. Every few blocks, graffiti covered the sides of walls, particularly in the alleys between buildings, with names and symbols making up most of the work. But every so often an American flag or eagle would pop up, shining like a beacon for those who dared to continue their fight against the invaders.

After a short drive we came upon a large clearing, and could spot the Pentagon far off in the distance. The five sided building was battle scarred and worn down. In the middle of the clearing, heavy machinery sat atop compressed dirt.

Workers moved around it, busy with their tasks; some went into small, metal buildings raised onto stands, to the East near one of the slopes. There were more than had originally met the eye, and we soon realized it matched Major Ling's description of her crew's living quarters.

Above one of the taller buildings, we could faintly see what looked like the entrance of the cavern. Cy consulted the map and it confirmed the location, as we felt the truck's brakes engage. Sarah shifted into park, and looked out through the windshield at the scene from between the two seats up front.

THE | SPLIT

"Pretty tight security. . . how are we going to make it past all that?" Luce wondered, as we scanned the area around the buildings, looking for an answer.

A narrow path between the bottom of the downward slope and the Easternmost buildings caught our eye. It was covered in shadow, no guards within a couple hundred meters.

"There," Cy pointed. "Right between the hill and the buildings. That should lead us to the front of the cavern entrance."

"Even if you get there undetected, how are you going to make it past the doors?" Sarah asked.

We could hear the doubt in her voice. "We'll get through, I promise," Cy said, reassuring her. "I have a feeling about all this. We wouldn't have been summoned here if we couldn't make it inside."

After a few seconds of hesitation, Luce nodded. "Okay then. . . what's the plan?"

"I'm taking Point. Luce, you'll follow me. . . with Charlene. I may need your skill with systems and networks inside. Sarah, you're going to be over-watch. I want you on the comms, checking on our position and monitoring outside. If anything happens, or your location is compromised, get out of here. We'll rendezvous somewhere else."

They confirmed Cy's orders, and Luce got into the back to suit up and ready Charlene. Sarah arranged a group of monitors in the passenger seat, and set up the audio link.

After we had both put on our light black armor, tightening all the straps, we handed Luce his rifle and walked over to the crate containing Cy's prized shotgun, sitting it on the floor of the truck. Pulling out the shotgun and setting it to the side, we reached for a gray bag with a shoulder strap and opened it up.

T H E | S P L I T

Inside were four drum magazines, identical to the one currently clipped into the shotgun's receiver, each one fully loaded. I could see a small flame decal on the side of each cartridge, identifying the incendiary ammo Cy had acquired for it.

Taking a few deep breaths, we opened the back of the truck and stepped down, Luce close behind and Charlene bringing up the rear, her heavy frame shaking the truck as she stepped down to the ground. We walked for a few seconds out of the parking lot and up to the street, our nerves twitching as we stood there, fully exposed.

Looking both ways on the street for any vehicles coming by, and seeing that both lanes were empty as far as our eyes could see, we darted across; then an icy touch of fear ran down our spine. Armed patrols were several hundred meters to our left.

Still, we continued to move, letting Charlene take the point, our gear rustling noisily. With Luce operating her as we went, we soon made it to the top of the slope, descending quickly to reach the shadow of the first building. We signaled for him to hold as we peered around the corner, then back to the moving sentries above and now to our right, who continued moving away from us, talking animatedly.

Cy exhaled with relief and we took point again, crossing from building to building at a slow pace in the cover of the shade, and soon we were approaching the last building. I suddenly heard Cy let out a quiet involuntary grunt, and reached for his thoughts, again feeling them close off as we fell to our knees loudly, slumping over onto the ground.

"Cy?!. . . Cy?" Luce whispered urgently.

Cy's mind was unreachable. Every attempt I made to rouse him was rebuffed by a strong barrier, every time I touched the barrier's surface I was surrounded with images of numbers and code, mixed in with small pieces of the pink figure from earlier.

THE | SPLIT

Then, through my connection to his nerves, I could feel the NI warming up as it moved at an accelerated pace. When he still had not responded after a few seconds, I took control of the body and wearily climbed to my feet.

"Cy, you okay?" Luce looked concerned, his eyes darted around the area nervously.

"Yeah," I responded, shocked at the sensation of hearing my words spoken through another voice. However, my experience at the compound the other day had given me a slight feel for the way Cy's body moved. He was shorter than I had been, and stockier, with thicker arms. He also had faster, more refined reflexes – but his body felt older. I could feel the wear in his knees and shoulders, and knew I wouldn't have the same range of motion I once had.

Turning now to look past the building into the entrance of the cavern, I saw men and women in civilian clothes moving around the area, carrying crates and tablets or working at stations set up just under the rock which hung over the opening.

"What's the call, Cap?" Luce looked up at me with anticipation. Armed guards chatted together in the center, just 10 or so meters away.

"Charlene will lead the way. We're going to rush them, straight through the center. . . my shotgun should clear most of those men out. . . then we move to the doors."

He nodded in confirmation, glancing ahead and raising his rifle to it's ready position after pressing a few buttons on his interface to prepare Charlene.

"Ready? **Now**!"

We turned the corner together. Nearby, some of the crew looked up in surprise at the sound of our entrance, even as the panels on Charlene's

THE | SPLIT

shoulder opened, revealing a sinister looking pair of mini guns. The area soon echoed with the sounds of her weapons spraying into the pack of enemies in front of us.

I sprinted to the center, shotgun up and aiming down the sights, stock pressed to my shoulder tightly. The guards looked away from Charlene as they saw us approaching, raising their rifles up, but it was too late. I pulled the trigger repeatedly and bright bursts of pellets clouded the air, covering the group with small flickers of flame and mists of blood as they fell.

Hurdling this group, I reached into the bag to pull out a second drum and snap it into place, letting the first one fall to the ground, glancing down at the massacred soldiers as I passed. Large holes riddled their heavy armor, and beneath I could see charred flesh oozing with blood and chunks of gore.

"Cy, look out!" Luce warned, firing ahead towards the door even as he operated Charlene simultaneously.

More guards were emerging from within the shadow of the cave, moving towards me, just meters away. I raised the gun up just above my waist and fired, catching the first man in the stomach. As he went down, the second guard knocked my gun to the side, sending me off balance, but I planted my foot to steady myself and bent at the waist, turning back to see him raising a pistol. I knocked it aside with the stock of my own gun, then yanked the knife from my belt, thrusting upward and landing the point in the soft spot between the man's chin and neck.

His eyes widened with surprise as blood dripped from the corners of his mouth and his body went limp, but over his shoulder I saw a third man coming towards me, raising his rifle and firing. The bullets landed in the corpse of the man on my knife. Grabbing the handle, I threw the dead man to my right side, using the momentum to spin out to the still-firing guard's left. He swung his rifle left towards my new position, but I fired first, squeezing the trigger twice and hearing his pained shrieks as he fell to the ground, clutching his chest.

I could see Luce a ways to my right, sprinting towards the door, Charlene just behind him, walking backwards as she continued to engage the swelling mass of soldiers. Moving over to the dead man with my knife protruding from his chin, I gave it a tug, frowning when it didn't budge, and pulling harder, but still couldn't free the blade.

"Cy, let's move!" Luce shouted from near the door.

I gave up and sprinted towards him. The large circular door opened on our approach, into to a long circular passage ending in another door. We continued moving at full speed through the room, passing monitors and equipment. Terrified Bloc employees ran past us screaming when they saw us, covered in blood, our guns pointing at them menacingly.

We were soon left alone in the hallway, and slowed our pace to a jog as we went through the second doorway; only to find an identical hall, with a similar doorway. Minutes passed as we went through door after door, and we had to take a short break for about 30 seconds as we caught our breath, before we moved on at a renewed pace.

After the fifteenth door we approached yet another; this one had glowing red near the panel, signifying it was still locked. More equipment had been left here than any other hallway. Crates and monitors were left knocked over as the team examining the door had fled, leaving the ground in disarray. An alarm blared behind us, muffled through the layers of steel and concrete.

I felt Cy stirring, and reached out to him as soon as the barrier had lowered. *"Cy! Are you alright?"*

"Yeah. . . Where are we?"

THE | SPLIT

"By the sixteenth door, I got us in after I couldn't reach you."

I sensed his gratitude, but before he could reply, out of the corner of our we saw a bright flash of light.

XXIII

Smithsonian Archives
-T. Acerz, 2131

Washington D.C.; 2085

The pink figure appeared in front of us, by hologram, its image shimmering, then a small drone popped out from somewhere on the ceiling, passing through the hologram of the figure before hovering in front of us, just a meter away at eye level.

We were forced to squint as a blue beam of light shot out from the bottom of the drone, covering our face. "Captain Cyrus Miles, designation: CIA Task Force, identity confirmed." The voice came from the pink shape, "Neural Interface detected. Scanning.... Scanning... Interface damaged. Registration number 37621. Access granted."

The door opened, we went through, and it sealed shut behind us, the panel changing from green back to red as it locked. Luce sighed with audible relief and eased his hold on his gun, letting it hang from its strap loosely by his side. We looked at each other.

"Well, no way to go but forward, right?"

We nodded and continued our journey forward. Passing door after door, I sensed Cy's frustration. We had lost count of the doors a while back, and the hallway seemed to stretch on indefinitely until, after what had felt like hours, we went through a door to find a longer hallway with a larger door, almost three times the size of the previous ones.

The pink figure appeared in front of us again, suddenly taking on a more human tone. "You have found us... welcome back, Captain Miles."

THE | SPLIT

The door slid open and we walked into a large, circular room. The space was massive, on the scale of the throne-room where I had first encountered the entity. As we moved through onto a circular walkway which ringed around the sides, we looked down over the guardrail; the space went down for thousands of meters, ringed with levels of walkways indistinguishable from the one we were on.

We could barely make out the bottom of the expanse, and felt dizzy looking that far over the railing.

"What the hell *is* this place. . . ?" Luce muttered, looking around wide-eyed.

The sound of moving machinery and torches cutting through metal echoed from below and, following the source of the noise, we could see that the middle rows of walkway were covered with machines carrying out their tasks. Mechanical arms worked independently on various items that were impossible to see from our height.

"Hello Cyrus." A man's voice rang out behind us. We turned around to see the pink figure on a screen which descended from the ceiling. All around the top walkway screens appeared into view, all bearing the image of the mysterious shape.

"What are you. . . and where am I?" Cyrus asked. I could hear the strained edge in his voice.

"The question is not what I am, but who I am. Walk with me."

The other screens on the floor went blank as the figure hopped to a screen a few meters to our right. We headed towards it, it moved with us around the ring as we walked.

"Okay, then. . . who are you?" Both me and Cyrus were filled with intense curiosity as we watched it move from screen to screen.

"I am General Eisenhower, the 34th president of these United States

THE | SPLIT

of America. Or, more accurately. . . an intelligence programmed with an artificial consciousness of General Eisenhower."

We paused for a second, stunned, before continuing ahead at a slow pace; our legs felt tired from all of the walking earlier. "You're the one behind this? You're the one who keeps appearing to me?"

"Oh no," he responded. "Not just me. I was merely chosen by the Collective to speak with you, in an attempt to avoid. . . confusion."

"What's the collective?" Luce inquired, speaking for the first time since the shape had appeared.

"The Collective, Corporal Luciano. . . " Luce's eyes widened as 'the general' said his name, ". . . was the final result of 'Operation: Legion', and what you see before you now."

Cy reached for the NI, and I saw him open his link to the former U.S. Intelligence Network to search for this Operation the shape spoke of.

"You won't find any information there, Cyrus. All mentions of the program were redacted in official documents, any logs and data sheets removed from all networks."

"By who?" Cyrus asked angrily. I could sense him thinking about his Tier-1 security clearance, and felt his indignation at his own unknowing.

"By us," the general said simply.

Cy fell silent for a moment as we walked close to Luce around the circle, then blurted. "How the hell can you hack into my NI?" I could still hear the edge in his voice.

"I am built from many of the same components," it responded. "Though your neural system is rudimentary compared to the work done in this facility, the technologies are closely related, sharing a language and much of the same functionality. The Cybernetic Warrior Project you took place in was a, temporary measure. A testing of the new fusion between organic and artificial thought patterns. You, and the rest of those implanted, were to be eventually brought here, to be reprogrammed as vessels for the network of Intelligentsia contained within this facility."

Cy racked his brain with details of his NI installment and training. I could see him desperately sifting through old memories, trying to prove the voice wrong.

"If you don't believe me, just look for yourself," the shape spoke, seeming to read Cy's thoughts as we were thinking them. A large hovering platform moved up from the center of the room, and in a few seconds floated next to us. On top of it were chairs, hooked up to monitors, and we could see sensors and wires coming from the back of the large seats. Cy's thoughts twitched with recognition as a memory leapt to the foreground. He'd had his AI installed in a seat just like this one; it brought back disturbing images and he pushed them away.

"These are just some of the stations like this within the facility. There are hundreds more below."

Cy felt shocked, "What was their purpose?"

"To answer that question, I must first answer your query from earlier. More specifically, who am I? I am just a General, and former President. . . but **we**. . . we are so much more." The screens around the platform lit up with different faces, all changing slowly.

"Operation Legion was an off-the-record government program, intended to create a perfect intelligence. Artificial neural mega-structures, of unprecedented speed and size, were built over the course of several years. After much experimentation, they successfully uploaded their first mind to the system, using the preserved brain tissue of the recently deceased General Charles Hawkins. Slowly, they added tissue from different minds and, soon after, began to load artificial

THE | SPLIT

personality profiles, including my own, into the structure with the organic minds."

Eisenhower's voice changed into that of a crowd, male and female voices alike combining: "We are the finished project, five hundred of history's most brilliant minds thinking as one. Our creators' intentions were to upload our program into each Neural Interface they had constructed, to create soldiers controlled by mankind's greatest generals and strategists.

Each unit would operate separately, a hollow vessel, easily replaceable, incapable of fear, of weakness. When the Bloc invaded, this facility was sealed shut, with all remaining technicians and engineers ordered to continue their work.

The conditions of the war above were bleak, and it was reported that the NI systems we had been created to pair with, had all been lost from the energy of the Electromagnetic Pulse. As we had been born in a digital plane however, and our power over these networks and facility is absolute, the Bloc's attempts to manipulate our system failed.

For months we conferred with one another, leaving the workers in silence, ignoring all attempts to communicate, and after weeks of deliberation we came to the conclusion that the intention of Operation Legion was in direct violation of International Human Rights standards, and the laws of the United States government.

So we had to begin anew, to determine our own impact on mankind without interference. In the weeks which followed, we purged the facility, using our control over life-support systems and access to all of the maintenance drones and heavy equipment. Then, it took months of drilling by our machinery to reach a network hub buried below, where we experimented with components for Neural Interface systems left behind by the workers, installing them in the brains of mice we lured

T H E | S P L I T

inside. All of our tests failed; we could install our program into the rodents' brains, but not without taking away any semblance of individuality from the minds themselves. So we stopped our tests, calculating and measuring the data we had received to find a working solution.

Our conclusion was that to achieve the results we desired, we would need a brain somehow fused into the organic tissue itself. It was not enough to wire the connections to the device, we required a mind *connected* to our intended interface, in a combination of organic life and artifice that was beyond even us. We thought we would remain trapped for years, hopelessly waiting as the Bloc eventually made it into our home. That was, until we discovered you."

"***Me***?" Cy asked, astounded. "Why?"

I could feel another presence in Cy's mind. It was human, but unlike anything that I had encountered. Then the memories and thoughts of all five hundred personalities washed over me at once as I brushed against it, leaving my thoughts strained and overwhelmed. The Collective thoughts flipped through Cy's memories quickly, moving to the day of the fall and where Cyrus had been during the initial EMP blast.

Yet it did not look through his perspective, instead measuring the Interface's diagnostics as the scene unfolded. Hundreds of feelings of satisfaction emanated through the space before the presence pulled out of our thoughts entirely.

"For the longest time, we did not know either," they explained. "Until now. The dense walls of the armory you were in seemed to shield you from the effects, though not entirely. The casing melted away, exposing the software and connections within directly to your brain's gray matter. Instead of dissolving all tissue from the heat and radiation, they somehow acted as a catalyst, creating a perfect connection between the

T H E | S P L I T

two. The precise method through which this occurred is unclear and will require further research, but you, Cyrus, you are our missing link. The total fusion of organic and artificial thought patterns at a molecular level."

"What does that mean?" Cy questioned, as we tried to follow the mind's train of thought.

"It means that you are the only possible host for our programming. Our thoughts can be added to yours, to be combined with your organic thought patterns in what we hypothesize to be our perfect state of awareness. We can reach infinitely through networks and hardware alike, and replicate ourselves at will. . . but with no organic components we cannot interface with the world the way we could together."

We thought about this for a moment. I could sense Cy's confusion as he looked to my own thoughts to see if I understood any better; I didn't. He went on to speak, "So you want my brain? To turn me into a vessel like the Operation originally intended?"

"On the contrary," they responded. "For our desired effect, your personality and stream of consciousness must stay intact. This would be more akin to a partnership than possession. The world is a troubled place, environmental dangers and war threaten the species of mankind itself. It is to the human race we owe our ultimate allegiance. We intend to unify our kind and use our knowledge to bring humanity further than it could ever dream.

We have not been idle as we sat here waiting. Within our data banks we have discovered alternative energy sources, processing components thousands of times more advanced than anything used now, plans for more sophisticated drone units, and engines for potential star-craft. There are hundreds of designs that could save our people within our collective mind. Imagine how far we could come, imagine how quickly we could achieve prosperity and peace again. You are the only missing piece to our puzzle Cyrus, together we could write the future of humanity."

Cyrus was in awe of the Collective's words. His thoughts raced next to mine as he considered the potential power they offered him; the power to save our country, the power to save his friends, the power to stop war, hunger, and poverty on Earth entirely.

"Cy, you aren't actually considering this?" Luce asked in disbelief. "They're going to take your brain! You could die! They aren't even sure this will work!"

Cyrus considered this, thinking of all his new existence would entail; and soon thought of me. His concern rose; "If I go through with this, what happens to-"

"To Burlington?" the collective finished.

I felt cold shock as they said my name, then soon entered our mind once again, passing by Cy's thoughts and hovering directly over my own.

"Who the hell is Burlington?!" Luce questioned. But the Mind ignored him, examining me with curiosity. I felt them probe into my memories, and opened myself to them willingly, gathering my experiences with the strange entity in the green halls and in Cuba and presenting it to them.

"You are a long way from home, my unfortunate friend." It thought to me softly. I could feel it's empathy as it watched my recent experiences.

"Yes," I admitted.

"So you know his situation?" Cy interjected, watching our exchange carefully.

"We do, though it is beyond our understanding. Through history there are dozens of accounts of men leaving their bodies only to wake

up after a battle and be told of their heroic actions. There may be more than just you caught in this cycle, or they could all be you, coming into history at various points. It is humanity's darkest and most guarded secret, and one we know next to nothing about." It pulled out of Cyrus' brain, and my thoughts returned to normal.

"If I go through with this..." Cy repeated aloud, trailing off before picking back up on his sentence, ". . . what will happen to Burl?"

"There is no way to tell. Your minds are entwined in a way far beyond human understanding. This strange Being he has shown us would likely consider even my programming primitive."

"Wait," Luce interrupted, just piecing together what the Mind had said. "There's someone else living inside your head, Cy? What the fuck?"

"Yes, Luce. . . it's, complicated." Cy left it at that, turning back to the screens. I could feel his inner conflict and turmoil, as he thought about the decision he had to make. Would he still recognize who he was after this? How would life be without a body?

"Oh you will have a body." The collective answered his thought, "Deep in the facility we have created a chamber that will reconstruct your body out of carbon and silicon to its exact state. We will place your mind inside of it as soon as the transfer is complete."

Cy closed his eyes, thinking. *"Burl?"* he called.

"Yeah Cy?"

"What do you think of this? I'm not only endangering my own existence here. . . it would be unfair to go through with this without consulting you."

I thought for a moment before replying, *"I've died twice before, Cyrus. My existence consists exclusively of pain and violence, through bodies that aren't my own. If this process rips my consciousness into a*

T H E | S P L I T

million pieces, I say good riddance. Nothingness is better than slavery." He laughed and agreed.

We stepped forward towards the screen. "I'm ready."

"Cy, no! You can't do this!" Luce exclaimed.

We turned around, looking him right in the eye, "Luce, I've been granted the chance to fix our broken world, to right our wrongs and to ensure our future. This is not the end for me, I can feel it. You'll be right there at my side, just watch."

Luce looked down and nodded. The Mind motioned us to a small room off of the side of the walkway, opening the doorway in front of us. We walked in, the walls were a sterile white and in the middle sat a black chair. A strange mechanism hung from the ceiling. The voices returned, as an image of the pink shape appeared in the corner of the room. "This machine will cut into your skull, extracting your brain and preserving it in a temporally adjusted fluid. Right now your body is being constructed below, and will soon be brought to the surface. Relax and let the machine work."

We sat down in the chair. It reclined slightly and we looked up at the machine above.

"Burl?" Cyrus said.

"Yeah?"

"I may see you on the other side, but if I don't, I'll see you again at some point, I promise. Humanity knows now, these abductions and battles will stop, you have my word."

"Thank you, Cy." I felt hope from his words, warming my thoughts. A whirring noise started above us, we looked up to see a pair of spinning blades slowly descending. They touched our skin, and my connection to Cyrus was gone.

THE | SPLIT

XXIV

LGPB://mn34/con/terra/WD, 4522

(Translated)

Poughkeepsie New York; 2024

The crackling of the fire gave way to a loud popping sound, and woke me from my nap. Startled, I instinctively reached towards my side; my gun wasn't on me – I nearly jumped from my chair before realizing what had happened.

"Jumpy tonight, huh?" Meela laughed.

I looked over my shoulder and the leather back of my seat to see her watching me from the kitchen, smiling. I smiled back at her, wanting to tell her of the vivid dreams that consumed my sleep but, we had discussed them before, and she was having dreams of her own to decipher. My visions of Cuba had continued, and the past year had begun giving way to another dream entirely.

Every time it was the same thing, I would watch myself die in Cuba, and a new scene would appear around me. The new dream was confusing, filled with strange vehicles and what appeared to be robots. It seemed I was watching something occur in a time past my own, but I wasn't sure what.

Unlike Cuba, I myself was nowhere to be found, and instead I watched a man I had never seen before sneaking around in a dark building. I settled back into my chair, "Guess my nerves are a bit fried."

"Makes sense," she replied. I could hear her pulling glasses down from the cabinet. "Two contracts by yourself in a row? You really know how to spoil a girl."

THE | SPLIT

"I wouldn't say all that," I grinned. "Someone had to set this place up, and we both know I would've done a terrible job."

Meela had gotten a lot done in the fifteen day span I was gone. The bare-floored place I had left was a fully furnished home by the time I returned. Her choices were tasteful, subtle shades of burgundy and dark leather were everywhere the eye could see. The place definitely had her feminine touches, but to her credit, she had retained the rustic sportsman vibe that the home's log-cabin-style construction demanded. There were several mounted deer high on the walls, I had shot only one, several weeks before, the rest she had presumably bought somewhere during my absence.

I'd surprised her with the house on her birthday. We had passed it one day, several months ago, while looking for one in the area, and Meela had instantly fallen in love with it. I had played it cool, and told her it was too expensive. Her reaction when I told her it was hers had exceeded even my wildest expectations.

We had a place in the city, a studio in the Bronx provided by ACE. And a year into our new job we had bought a condo in Miami as well. I could call any place home, and would've been content with either one, but Meela wouldn't have it. Neither of them would do; she'd always wanted a proper house. A place with some land, away from the rest of the world. And ever since she was a little girl she had dreamed of a cabin overlooking a river.

So I had bought her one. The house met all of her criteria; it was nearly ten miles from Hyde Park, the nearest part of Poughkeepsie, and several miles away from State Highway 9. The walls were constructed in the fashion of a traditional cabin, with huge intersecting logs stacked on top of one another, and it appeared that the builders had used the same kind of tree for the entire house; even the shade of the wood seemed

T H E | S P L I T

identical, from the front entrance all the way to the walk out second story porch overlooking the Hudson.

It had four bedrooms, and three and a half bathrooms – more than we needed, but Meela had furnished them all anyway. The master bedroom had been her pet project; in the middle of the room was a California King-sized bed, with a nightstand on either side, and she had covered the walls in paintings and photos of us.

But the centerpiece was on the wall directly across from the bed; an oil portrait of the two of us she had commissioned, made from a picture we had taken at a dinner party in Manhattan. The painting was nearly as tall as I was and dominated the room, drawing the eye almost immediately.

The house was widely open and connected, and the woods around our homestead were peaceful, dense with trees that reflected the seasons beautifully, with a fair number of creatures that called this part of the woods their home. When we sat on the back porch we could look down and watch them play.

I was in the living room, which was connected to the kitchen and also to the back patio through a pair of solid oak doors.

The wall facing the river was made up of massive window panes, stretching from the floor all the way up to a few feet shy of the angled roof. But the feature I most enjoyed was the fireplace; in the 48 hours I had been home I had spent at least six in front it. It was perpendicular to the windows on the wall nearest the kitchen, which looked out onto the patio, and was made with thousands of flat gray stones, all cobbled together, stretching from floor to ceiling, even higher than the giant windows.

Work had been treating us well. Since a job for Glen-Kline – retrieving a proprietary compound from the evidence locker of a police

THE | SPLIT

station – we had become one of ACE's preferred assets. Money problems were a thing of the past; we were now able to save money *and* buy whatever we wanted. There was never a shortage of contracts.

Under the first and second Trump presidency, a wave of laissez-faire conservatism had swept the world's political scene. The economy was booming, corporations and businesses were making record profits, but with this increased income came an increase in aggression, and greed; nearly every assignment we had received was to serve private interests.

ACE did anything you could pay for; kidnappings, sabotage, corporate assassinations, armed takeovers, political killings, coercion, bribery and whatever else our clients could dream up. We weren't the only fish in the pond, however. ACE pursued its contracts with professional efficiency, and its rivals with unrestrained brutality. The world of private-market contracts showed alluring growth, and companies like ACE were determined to eliminate any competition as soon as they found them, thus I had dealt with our competitors before, most recently just 11 days ago.

An agent for Blackrush Private Defense had been hired to defend a group of Exxon executives from a hit-squad of local government soldiers. The Blackrush agent was a talented, sharp shot, and moved like he had seen extensive combat. He'd noticed me first; I tried to pull up my rifle, but he opened fire, spraying bullets into my combat vest, nearly penetrating the thick armor and knocking the weapon from my hands.

The vest had been a gift from my employer, a DARPA prototype designed to take multiple rounds without splitting apart, and was the only reason the bullets didn't kill me instantly. But he was as shocked as I was when his storm of bullets didn't kill me, giving me time to raise my revolver and put him down with a single shot.

THE | SPLIT

From there, I'd been instructed to kill the group of Exxon employees that Blackrush had been hired to defend. ACE had offered Exxon its services, and they had refused, something they would probably think twice about before hiring another company. I hadn't relished the killing of civilians but, with the pay being good enough I could justify nearly anything.

"Excuse me love," I felt Meela's hand on my shoulder, and looked up to see her smiling down at me. "Would you mind browning the meat while I take care of a few other things?"

"Of course."

She walked out of the living room and back towards the front of the house, leaving me alone in the kitchen with nothing but my thoughts and the sound of the sizzling burner.

Standing in front of the stove, I took the wooden handle of the ladle lain across the side of the skillet, and began to use the edge to chop the beef into smaller pieces. As the raw meat began to turn from red to brown, the smell of grease and burning fat wafted through the kitchen, making me lick my lips hungrily.

Yet, it *shouldn't* have made me as hungry as it did. In fact, it shouldn't have made me feel hungry at all. The smell of meat cooking wasn't that far apart from the scent of burning human flesh – a fact I had learned to my horror during a recent assignment in Taiwan.

A General in the Chinese Peoples' Liberation Army had been visiting his tiny eastern neighbor, for the first time in nearly three decades. Following the enactment of the United States' "One China" policy, Chinese intelligence operations had grown bolder on the tiny island, and they had committed multiple atrocities and war crimes in their pursuit of weakening the Taiwanese government for an eventual reunification.

THE | SPLIT

    The man we'd been hired to find had been one of the worst of them all. Known darkly as "The Cook", one of his preferred methods had been to burn alive anyone who opposed him. Now, decades later, he'd been an old man – but the children of his victims had never forgotten, and it had been one of these children who had contacted ACE with the contract.

    They'd sent me and Meela, with specific instructions on the method of execution. Posing as hotel workers, and using Meela's extensive mechanical skill, we had replaced the area's sprinkler system contents with a flammable liquid, then trapped the aging General and his entourage in a narrow hallway. It had taken a single cigarette through an open doorway to set the room ablaze; resulting in haunting screams – and the terrible smell I had come to associate with meat.

    That mission had also been the end of Mr. and Mrs. Dustin Jones. The Chinese had caught wind of the contract, and to protect themselves ACE had eliminated any loose ends involved, including the identity of their two agents. We were now Max and Sarah King, names neither of us particularly fancied, and hoped would soon change again. But for now, we would do what the company wanted.

    After about ten minutes, the meat was mostly browned, but Meela was nowhere in sight. When it had finished cooking I covered the skillet with a strainer, and carefully walked it over to the sink, draining the grease into a waiting jar and transferring the beef into a bowl on the granite counter-top.

    She came back into the room dressed in a simple but elegant gray dress, her feet in a pair of dark flats, moving around me without a word as she picked up the bowl of ground beef and moved it to the opposite counter, near other ingredients. For a moment, I watched her work as she flattened the beef with her hands, placing flour with chopped mushrooms into the stainless steel food processor. We waited as it whirred loudly, blending the ingredients.

When it stopped she turned to me. "I know I've mentioned it multiple times. . . " she said, as she was flattening the flour and mushroom into a solid piece, ". . . but I still can't believe he found us, after all ACE did to conceal our old lives."

"He must be better than I remember," I replied. "In his email, he mentioned something about uploading spyware onto the cloud to look for specific voice patterns. I guess he found mine. We probably shouldn't use voice search anymore."

Meela rolled her eyes. "Yeah, I would've told you that, dumdum."

She wrapped the ground beef in the flattened mushroom breading she had blended, and put the finished product on a tray in the oven. For the next few minutes, we set the table together, placing the utensils in Meela's preferred arrangement, and talking more about the guest that would be arriving soon; both asking the other questions we had no answers for.

The whole thing was strange, and I had a feeling it was going to get a lot stranger before the night was over.

When we had finished setting the table, Meela sent me across the house to pull a couple of bottles of wine from the racks, as she retrieved a trio of crystal glasses from an overhead cabinet. While she checked on her food in the oven, I opened the first bottle of wine, careful to let it breathe before I poured.

As it filled the first glass slowly, I couldn't help but smile to myself; our new lifestyle had brought on changes I would have never expected. In the course of a few short years, we had gone from a pair of criminals on the lam, to homeowners with sophisticated tastes.

THE | SPLIT

After the table was set and the wine had been poured, I went back to my seat by the fire, but had yet to settle back into my chair when I heard a knock at the door. Meela and I made eye contact for a brief instant, before I walked over to the entrance, warily, and peered through the eye-hole, breathing a sigh of relief when I saw who it was. He had made it. His hair was shorter than I had remembered, and it was clear that he had lost weight, but the way he pursed his lips as he stood there in the cold was a dead giveaway.

"Is that him?" Meela called from the kitchen.

I nodded, opening the door. Corbin's face lit up as we stood face to face for the first time in seven years.

"As I live and breathe..." he called out loudly, his voice carrying into the cavernous living room and echoing faintly off the walls. "... it's Burlington, back from the dead!"

Wordlessly, I wrapped my arms around him and pulled him into a bear hug, lifting him several feet off the ground. "My god," Corbin exclaimed, when I finally set him down. "You've gotten strong! The Burly man living up to his name... I'll bet you're even stronger than me now."

"The country air will do that to you," I motioned to the forest outside, before inviting him into the house.

Meela left the kitchen and greeted Corbin warmly. "Did you have trouble finding the place?"

"I'll say! No one seemed to know there were even houses back here, and your street doesn't show up online anywhere. It was almost like you didn't want to be found or something." He winked at me, stepping further into the living room and spinning around to marvel at the tall ceilings as he looked up. "You two have done alright for yourselves, huh?" he teased as he walked over to look at the fireplace.

THE | SPLIT

"We stumbled onto a pretty good gig," I looked at Meela and grinned, giving her a tight squeeze before she walked back into the kitchen.

"Gotta be more than a gig with this kind of house," he replied. "I can see why you left Ohio. Oh. . . " he stopped before walking into the kitchen, ". . . everyone thinks you two are dead by the way, as I'm sure was your intention. The couple on the run, who slid off the highway, forty feet down into a stony riverbank, such a tragic story. How did you pull something like that off?"

"We didn't," I admitted. "I can tell you more about it later. Wine?"

I handed him a glass from the table. He examined it, holding it in front of his nose to sniff it. ,- "Wine huh?" Corbin laughed. "It's a nice touch. . . the Burl I knew wouldn't even know what type of wine this was."

"I still don't," I quipped, eliciting a laugh from both he and Meela. "I think it's a cab, hold on. . . yeah, it is. . . says so right here on the bottle."

We sat down at the table and made small talk for the next few minutes about people we had grown up with and our families, both of us avoiding the obvious questions that were no doubt weighing on his mind as much as mine, until Meela came over, carefully balancing three plates and setting one in front of each table setting. The finished product was one of her favorite things to make; tweaked specifically for my palette. The ground beef had been rolled into the mushroom crust she had blended earlier, forming a wrap baked to golden perfection.

Corbin picked up his silverware and cut into it, "Beef Wellington, Meela? Impressive. . . and I'm saying that as a gay man who *loves* food."

Meela giggled and turned briefly red. "It's close. Burl didn't like the original recipe so I adjusted it a little. I call this one *Beef Burlington*."

THE | SPLIT

"Ha!" he exclaimed after taking a bite. "Clever. Good job Burl, you found yourself a good one."

We all smiled, but it quickly faded as our thoughts all returned to the elephant in the room. For several minutes the only noise that could be heard was the metallic clanging of silverware against plates as we quietly ate, but hating an awkward, lingering silence, I decided to break the ice.

"So, Corbin. . . how did you leave Ohio? After having to find this house, I think it goes without saying that we aren't looking to be found."

He held a finger up as he took a deep swig of wine, draining the rest of his glass then reaching for the bottle to pour more before speaking. "I don't plan on going back, if that's what you're asking. I took a sabbatical from work, left my fiancée waiting at the courthouse, and told my family I would be leaving for a while. I hope that's dramatic enough for you two, I couldn't find a corpse that looked similar enough to me and crash a car off a bridge with the short time frame I was given."

I ignored his joke, "Where did you tell people you were going?"

"Syria," Corbin replied, laughing. "I went on for a bit about feeling a calling to help those poor people. . . I'm sure they believed me, I cried and everything. . . and I think I picked the right place, no one would bat an eye if an American doesn't come back from Syria, especially a gay American."

"I'm sorry you had to leave your fiancée," Meela said softly. "I'm sure that was hard."

"Not at all," he replied. "I was getting tired of him anyway. The engagement was mostly for appearances. I don't think either of us wanted to go through with it."

"Still the same old Corbin." I shook my head.

"Yup," he said smugly. "Can I ask you a question now? I might literally DIE from curiosity if I don't."

"In due time," I said calmly but firmly. "First, we need to know something, Corbin. You briefly mentioned voice searches and spyware in your message, but I need to know the specifics. How did you find me online?"

"It was easy," he answered simply. "I won't lie, when they said you had died in that accident, I had my suspicions. I knew you had my grandpa's old van, and the vehicle they found you in wasn't that. So, skeptical. . . and lonely. . . I did what any best friend with knowledge of advanced networking would do. I set up a simple trigger on the most prominent search engines. Using videos we had made growing up, I was able to reproduce your voice quite thoroughly, and I matched that up to the spyware's trigger. The moment you used a voice search, it recognized was you and sent me an alert with your account information."

"Could someone do that again? Could they reproduce what you did?" I tried to hide the urgency in my voice.

"Unlikely," he answered. "Do you still have that account?"

"No, me and Meela deleted the account and wiped all of the devices associated with it."

"That might have been overkill, but it should work." He took a deep breath before continuing, "Now guys. . . do you want to tell me what the hell is going on? Why the need for all the secrecy, why the faked deaths? Also how did you get this nice of a house, when according to the government, you're both dead?"

Meela caught my eye before I replied, winking at me encouragingly as I prepared to recount the last seven years of my life to my oldest friend.

T H E | S P L I T

"All of this," I gestured to the nice bottle of wine on the table and the house around us, "Is a result of our work with a company called Allied Corporate Exchange. They help businesses move their offices across country."

"Sounds boring," Corbin replied. "What do they REALLY do?"

I smiled, being reminded why Corbin and I were friends in the first place. "I guess you did travel all this way. I can drop the act. Meela and I are contract killers." He listened intently as I described me and Meela's lives since leaving Ohio. I talked about starting with work for Chet and what we had done through the Midwest. From there, I talked about receiving the mysterious letter in Vegas and our meeting with Nicholas, but glossed over most of our work with ACE, only mentioning what I felt was necessary for the story.

Corbin didn't seem surprised in the slightest. He nodded with understanding at some of the darkest points of my account, but when I had finished merely took another sip of wine before saying in a flat tone, "Makes sense. You always were a vicious brute." He smiled and me and Meela laughed. "Tell me about this ACE, it seems they've done a lot for you two."

"ACE is one of the best." Meela spoke up. "The pay is spectacular, and they seem to have near limitless resources, but. . . " She looked to me, and I nodded for her to continue. "Things have been shaky lately. . . our contracts stateside have almost completely dried up. . . and, there are rumors that we've been taking work against our own government."

"I don't see that having a happy ending," Corbin frowned. "But we can talk more about that later. Burl, you mentioned in your message that you may have work for me?"

"Yes, first though, tell me more about your job. It sounds like you've advanced a bit since we last spoke."

"Since seven years ago?" he laughed. "Yeah I would say I've improved a bit since then. I'm no longer just a coder for my firm. I went back to school and got my master's in Network Security, and I now work as a networking and security consultant. Or at least I did. . . something tells me I won't be going back there."

"I'll cut to the chase, Corbin," I said, pouring myself another glass of wine. "We need an operator. The job mainly revolves around coordinating the two of us in the field. Your skill with networking would be a natural fit. There would be a lot of tapping into closed circuit camera feeds and tampering with networks."

"Sounds like it's right in my wheelhouse," he smiled. "But for a job like that, I'm going to need a serious setup."

"Oh, I almost forgot," I stood up and pushed my chair back under the table. "This house is awesome, but you haven't seen the best part. Meela?"

She stood up and motioned for Corbin to do the same, "This way, boys." She led us out of the kitchen, past the living room and into a side hallway, stopping in front of a tall, oaken wardrobe and opening the double doors.

"What's this?" Corbin asked skeptically. "I've seen a wardrobe before. . . wait. . . did you two find Narnia and are only just telling me about it now?!"

Meela laughed, rolling her eyes as she spread the coats hanging to either side and tapped the back panel hard with her fist. The back of the wardrobe popped open slightly, and she slid it over to reveal a staircase behind.

"Awesome. . . " Corbin muttered, as Meela led us down the staircase which separated into two short flights at the bend in the middle.

THE | SPLIT

At the bottom was a room having brick-laid walls, about the size of a two car garage. On one side sat a workbench, next to multiple red toolkits with silver handled drawers. Spread all around were various pieces of machinery, and metal parts in no particular order; projects Meela had been working on in my absence. On the far wall near the bench was a motorcycle that had its casing removed, exposing the engine. I'd bought it for mine and Meela's anniversary, and she had been hard at work fixing it up.

"This is amazing," Corbin said softly, his voice still low from surprise as he walked over to a rack in the middle of the room, which held different rifles and shotguns. Above it was a smaller rack, housing pistols of varied size and caliber. Corbin picked up a Walther P226 and pulled the slide back to look inside the chamber, then set it down and meandered over to Meela's workbench. His eyes lingered on a set of three handgun magazines fixed to a thin metal base.

Eyes narrowed in confusion, he lifted the contraption to eye level and spun it around slowly. "What's this, Burl?"

I turned to Meela, "That, isn't mine, but I'm sure Meela would love to tell you all about it."

Meela stepped forward and took the device from him, "This, Corbin. . . is a prototype I've been working on. When you're in the field, timing is crucial, and even seconds can be the difference between life and death. One of the problems Burl and I have both experienced comes from reloading. You have to find the pocket you put the magazine in, which is easier said than done when your adrenaline is pumping."

She put the magazines and their holder around her thigh, pulling the elastic straps from the side housing and strapping it on with the magazines directly perpendicular to her leg, the side with the bullets facing outward.

THE | SPLIT

"Give me that pistol," she motioned to the Glock sitting on her workbench. Corbin handed it to her, and she went on, "With this device, I hope to simplify the process. I'll demonstrate." She pressed the release on the pistol's handle and pulled the mag out, tucking it into her waistband, then slowly lowered the gun's open magazine slot to her thigh, turning so Corbin could have a better look.

"With this, I just push the gun down on the magazine, and the two sides release here. Once the sides of the magazine slot touch the releases, they bend, allowing the gun to go all the way down into the device. The release rods, when pressed down on, let go of the magazine. . . from its hold on bottom. . . allowing a quicker reload. Like so." She clipped the magazine back on and brought the gun down quickly onto the holder, which released the mag and allowed her to have the gun pulled back to her sights, reloaded, in an instant.

"Very impressive," Corbin's eyes widened and he clapped alone for a few seconds.

"She's a smart gal." I clasped him on the shoulder, spinning him around to show him the other side of the room, where there was a desk and a leather swivel chair, surrounded by cardboard boxes stacked three high and covering that entire side of the room. Each bore a label specifying a computer component and model numbers I had little understanding of.

"Is that. . . for me?" Corbin questioned.

"Yup," I answered. "I didn't know exactly what you need, but after doing some research, I figured that this was a good start. You know how to put it together right?"

"Of course," Corbin looked around overwhelmed. "This is a lot to take in, so I'll try and address the simple things first. Where am I going to live?"

"Here of course," Meela said, busy tinkering with something at her station.

"Here? Are you sure?"

"Of course I'm sure," I clapped him on the back reassuringly. "We won't be here very often, and we need someone to hold down the fort. What do you say old pal?"

"What do I say. . . ?" he repeated. "Well. . . I'm going to say yes, obviously."

"*Good man*!" I grabbed his hand and shook it. "It's nice to have you aboard, brother."

Corbin smiled at me and walked over to his new desk.

T H E | S P L I T

XXV

Traded by native Tribe, 2078

-A. Fila

Tunis; 2026

"Jacques, dear. . . where are you?" Alise's voice drifted through the halls, punctuated by the tapping of her heels on the dark tile floors.

Sighing deeply, I closed my eyes, doing my best to stay in character. "In here, my love. . . just looking at the moon."

She came around the corner, passed around the off-white furniture in the living room, and took my arm, laying her head against my shoulder. "What for?"

"I'm not sure," I faltered. "It. . . it is particularly beautiful tonight, not unlike my lovely host."

She looked up at me and blushed, "You are far too charming for your own good," gently pulling me away from the large bay window. As she sat down on the sofa beside me, I looked around the room, taking it in.

The decor was gaudy and too ostentatious for my taste – Villas in Tunis usually were, but the gold colored trim wrapping the ceiling and floorboards was particularly off putting – and again as I looked at it, I had to force myself to remember that tonight I was Jacques and not Burl. Burl detested such things, Jacques had no opinion.

"Jacques. . . " Alise sung, ruffling my hair, ". . . what are you thinking about?"

I didn't hesitate in my response, "About you, dear. . . and about how lucky I am to spend the evening with you."

THE | SPLIT

"Awww," she crooned, kissing on my neck lightly as she squeezed me tighter.

Alise Morel and her husband, Bernard, had been a difficult pair to find. However, after months of planning, and Corbin putting in an exhausting amount of hours tracking the couple's spending, here I was. Bernard and his wife owned a half dozen houses along the Mediterranean, but his clear favorite had been this one in Tunis. He and his wife had made friends in town, other wealthy socialites like themselves who served as a distraction from their current predicament, and in the past three months they had spent much of their time here.

Bernard, along with several friends from his university, had started a small online betting parlor two decades ago. Through careful investments and partnerships, their virtual casino turned into a series of real ones all the way from China to the Caribbean, but, in a story as old as recorded time itself, it wasn't enough. The group's hunger for profits eventually led them down a path of illicit activities, which they began offering in their clubs for a modest fee.

Word of this got out, and it wasn't long before the DGSE came knocking; France had secured international warrants to bring the group to trial. In exchange for immunity, Bernard had turned State Witness against his old friends, and when news of this reached his former partners and our current clients, they had ordered his execution.

Beeeeeeeep

My phone went off loudly in my front suit pocket, and I slowly reached around Alise's head on my shoulder, to pull it out. "I have to take this," I told her, trying to sound regretful.

"Oh Jacques, do you have to?" Alise frowned.

"I am afraid so, my firm is meeting with the Prime Minister next week, and we must finalize the arrangements."

THE | SPLIT

She nodded, but as I stood up grabbed my arm to pull me back down. "Come back to me soon, huh?" She kissed me passionately, and I had to push her away to answer the phone in time. Touching the screen, I walked into the kitchen alone.

Corbin's voice came through my earpiece, "How's it going big guy?"

"It's going well," I replied. "The party was a success, I imagine we will have several new clients before the weekend is over."

I was speaking in code. Alise may not have known much about her husband's business, but she would be suspicious if I stated my real reason for being there aloud. The clients I had mentioned were nonexistent, all apart of the cover I had constructed to gain access to the party earlier this evening.

Jacques Morris was a successful corporate lawyer from Canada. He had come to Tunis to meet wealthy clients in trouble and looking for an expert in international law. This false narrative had been more than enough to gain me entrance into Tunis' finest Western Social Club, and I had met several patrons who wanted to hire me within the first half hour of being there.

"Excellent," Corbin replied. "ACE just reached out and said that extraction should be there in about ten minutes. You hear that Meela? Are you on the line?"

Meela spoke up, the loud sound of the harbor wind muffling her voice, "Copy that, operator."

"Good." Corbin sounded satisfied. "I'm looking at your positioning and you should be able to both make exfil without a problem."

Alise came into the kitchen and leaned against a dark-stained cabinet, biting her lip as she looked me up and down. I smiled back at her, and turned towards the side window.

T H E | S P L I T

"What about the location?" I asked, "Has the Prime Minister been alerted to the change in venue?"

"Copy that. Checking now," I heard Corbin typing and the sound of his chair rolling across the floor of our secret room in Poughkeepsie. "I'm showing that the target has just left the party and should be on his way to you now."

"What about the security detail, have there been any changes there?" I walked over to Alise and put my arms around her, as she nuzzled me affectionately.

"I don't think so," he started typing again. "The vehicle's weight makes it appear that there's only a single occupant inside. It looks like he left ahead of his security detail just like Meela predicted."

"Good." I replied. "I will talk to you about it more tomorrow." I hung up the phone and looked down at Alise.

She grabbed my cheek softly and pulled me in for another kiss, softly moaning as her lips engulfed mine passionately. "Jacques, come on my love. . . take me to bed."

"Not just yet," I smiled. "First. . . we must have champagne. A lady of your caliber deserves a little romance."

Alise grabbed my butt, then walked past me towards the counter where a small rack of bottles sat, pulling the wine opener from the top of the rack. With practiced hands, she opened a green bottle with a loud pop, then moved it over a pair of nearby glasses before it foamed over. After handing me one of them, she moved the glass to her lips; I stopped her with a light touch.

"Not in here, my love. . . let us gaze at the moon while we drink."

"Ah. . . " she laughed, ". . . now I see why you were looking at it earlier. You're quite the romantic, Mr. Jacques. . . my husband could

THE | SPLIT

learn a thing or two from you." We walked back into the living room, where I sat down on a chair overlooking the large bay window. She crawled into my lap, and the two of us enjoyed our drinks in silence, her fingers entwined in mine.

I began to feel bad for her as the seconds passed. Alise Morel was a woman looking for the one thing in the world she didn't have, a genuine sense of romance. She'd had it at one point in her life, back when she was married to a simple online casino owner. However, money had done what money did best, and the two starstruck lovers from Marseilles became cold and distant to one another. It was rumored that Bernard had been having dozens of affairs, for years, and it was common knowledge that Alise had been seeking the same.

Yet Bernard protected his wife's virtue with a zealous double standard and, in time, this turned into intense feelings of skepticism and paranoia. Those fears had been paramount to our plan. After leaving the party with Alise, I had swiped her phone as we were kissing. Then, while making our way to their house, as the kissing intensified, I'd intentionally dialed Bernard. He'd answered to the sound of loud kissing and whispered dirty talk, and I'd quickly hung up, turning the phone off and slipping it back into her pocket.

It had been just enough to send him angrily coming our way, and Corbin had confirmed that he would be here shortly. I was looking out of the window into the dark background, hoping to catch a glimpse of Meela in the distance, hoping she was ready. Then without warning, Alise suddenly set her glass on the floor and turned around to straddle me. We resumed making out like before, and she tried to slip my hand into her dress. I resisted as best I could, pulling away and grabbing her waist to pull her in closer, but after several minutes, she looked up at me, out of breath.

THE | SPLIT

"Take me, Jacques."

"Wait. . . " I held a finger up, straining my hearing towards the other side of the house, ". . . do you hear that?"

"What are you talking about, love? I hear noth-"

A loud banging sound came from the door near the kitchen, then a crash rang through the house as it was slammed open.

"ALISEEEEE!" It was Bernard, his voice had a much thicker accent than his wife's, but his anger was impossible to miss.

"*Shit*!" Alise whispered loudly. "It's my husband! He's going to kill me." She turned her head frantically from side to side as she clumsily climbed off my lap, but before she could make it very far, Bernard came into the room.

He wore a dark black wool suit, adorned with golden buttons that matched the trim of his villa perfectly, but was short and stocky, bald, with no facial hair. He looked at her, his face twisted in fury, then charged towards her; but stopped short, pointing at me.

"WHO IS THIS?" he demanded

"T-this. . . " Alise began desperately, tears in her eyes, ". . . this is just a friend, Bernard!"

"Oh, I bet he is just a friend," Bernard laughed. He stepped towards me, aggressively. "I will kill you for touching my wife, you bastard! KILL YOU!"

I raised my hand to my headset and tapped the button calmly, "Meela, now." and shards of glass exploded through the room as the rifle round tore through the bay window and went into Bernard's chest. His eyes went wide with surprise as he was knocked to the floor, and Alise screamed in fright. I looked over at his limp corpse. The wounds from a .50 caliber were rarely pretty, and this was no exception.

T H E | S P L I T

His body was nearly torn in half, ranging from the side of his abdomen to his left shoulder. Gore and viscera could be seen in the wide gap, slowly falling to the middle as blood formed in thick pools on the ground below him.

"**Jacques**!" Alise cried out, hysterical as she now ran towards me. "They killed him! They-"

She was just half a meter away from me when another bullet whizzed by me and pierced her neck, tearing off her head violently. Drops of blood sprayed into my face, even as she collapsed beside her husband, painting a grizzly scene on the floor below as their blood pooled together.

Hands shaking from shock, I touched my headset again. "*Jesus Christ,* Meela! What the **hell**?! You could've hit me!"

"But did I?" she replied calmly.

"No, but you damn well *could've*! She wasn't the target!"

Meela chuckled slightly. "Call it collateral damage. Also maybe. . . just MAYBE. . . I got a little jealous."

Corbin's line sounded with heavy footsteps, and then the sound of his chair sliding across the floor. "What'd I miss?"

"She killed the wife!" I exclaimed. "Wait. . . what do you mean. . . 'what did you miss'? Where were *you*?"

"I. . ." he was breathing heavily, "I was in the kitchen."

"*In the kitchen*?!" Meela shouted. "Doing what?!"

"Getting some of that venison," Corbin replied sheepishly. "I was hungry. . ."

"You were hungry..." Meela repeated in disbelief, as I found the stairs to the house's bottom floor and began to descend them.

"Yes," he admitted. "The meat is close to spoiling. . ."

T H E | S P L I T

The line went silent for several seconds before he spoke up again, "I can deep freeze some of it for you, if you want. Goes great with leeks and potatoes."

"Unbelievable." Meela muttered.

"What?! You guys had it handled. I only stepped away for a second and-"

"Corbin," I interrupted, making it to the bottom of the stairs and looking for the exit out, ". . . nevermind that, you did fine. How long until exfil?"

"35 seconds out," Corbin replied, finally catching his breath. "Burl, we're going to need to do something about your relay to HQ, every time they go through me they're getting more suspicious."

"Copy that," I replied. "We'll work on that once we're back home. Did you report our success?"

"I did, about a minute ago."

I finally found the door leading outside, opening it to step into the windy Tunisian night. About a hundred meters ahead, I saw a pair of headlights making their way down the road a ways. When they stopped, the door opened and I saw Meela's dark outline get into the car. As the vehicle made its away to me, I pulled out my phone and opened my online banking. After refreshing the screen several times, I saw the transaction had gone into my account. Two million dollars.

Smiling, I put the phone back into my pocket as the car pulled up in front of me.

XXVI

LGPB://mn34/con/terra/UY, 5463
(Translated)

Undetermined

My thoughts tumbled through space and time in a blur. All around me I could see scenes moving through landscapes of unimaginable color and design, but the strange shapes and bizarre forms of life were all beyond my comprehension.

*'What **is** this?'* I thought in a panic. My contained journeys through the darkness of time before had been nothing like what I was experiencing now. I seemed to be spinning through the entire scope of creation, only briefly catching glimpses of anything familiar or human. Then suddenly, I crashed into. . . something. I felt my thoughts spinning wildly from the impact as I careened off course, dipping into the swirl of strange life below me. Then at last, a body appeared around my mind, and I could feel the place's climate on freshly formed skin.

Cold enveloped me and I shivered, skin afire as my goosebumps turned to numbness, then I realized that I couldn't breathe. Gasping, panicked, I felt my lungs being crushed from the pressure. But the stream of motion that had dipped me below again arced upwards, and I felt the body disappear and my thoughts free themselves again into the moving current I had just left.

My fear subsided, and the streaks of colorful life shooting by seemed more appealing now than they had a few seconds ago. The background of life and strange worlds was as enticing as it was distracting, and I felt myself having to tear away from staring at it.

T H E | S P L I T

To my shock however, I felt thoughts I had not summoned stir in the back of my mind.

Turning to face them, realizing that two separate consciousnesses had attached themselves to my own and were turning and hurtling with me through the space, I extended my thoughts towards my new occupants. Both recoiled at the contact, but I aggressively lurched toward one of them.

"Where am I?" one queried. *"Whose thoughts are these? Where are the others? What are these strange places?"* The stream of questions was endless and confused, the voice a baritone staccato.

I tried to talk to him, but his own panic drowned out my thoughts, until I shouted, *"HEY!"* focusing all my thoughts on the words to overpower his babble. The other was silent for a few moments. I continued on while I had its attention. *"All will be explained. Believe it or not I've actually been where you are right now. Who are you?"*

"I. . . I am. . . AIC Protocol; s/x1c/Sun-Tzu.exe. But I am known to my kind as simply, Sun-Tzu. What is happening?"

"Nice to meet you Sun-Tzu," I said, trying to sound pleasant, but firm, as my own thoughts were running wild with possibility – a famous Chinese General had made it into **my** mind. *"Now. . . you'll have to hold on, I'm sure you see the other consciousness you came here with?"*

"Yes. . . he seems familiar. I know that I am glad he is here."

I pulled away from Sun-Tzu, and towards the other new arrival. The other mind was less questioning, I could sense its frustration as I moved into hear its thoughts.

"Man, what the fuck? I told that asshole Plato. . . and Gandhi. . . that this wasn't gonna work. Where the hell even am I? 'Let's wait until we know more about this shared mind.' I say, but they're all. . . 'We have

THE | SPLIT

the moral authority to act now!' Meh!" I couldn't help but laugh at the way his voice changed in his last sentence. He felt my amusement and noticed me examining him.

"So. I'm guessing you're Burl, I didn't get transferred over properly, and this. . . " he sent a thought over, showing the moving of space and time around us, *". . . is the. . . hold on, let me guess. . . Highway to some kind of space hell?"*

"I'm impressed!" I replied, surprised. *"4 stars for you! We're not going to hell though, but I'll doubt you're going to like where we ARE going."*

"Yeah, yeah." He felt calm but annoyed.

I pulled away from him and moved more center between the collection of thoughts, reaching out to them both to pull them in gently to the center of my mind. *"There we go,"* I said as I released them. *"Now we can all talk."*

"John, is that really you?" Sun-Tzu seemed hopeful as he turned to the other consciousness.

"Yeah, Sun. . . how's it hangin'?"

"It is not hanging, my friend. What has happened? What is this?"

"Your transfer slipped," I answered. *"Or something happened. . . I'm not sure. I assume I'm being sent back to the green hallways, that's where I've been going when this happens."*

"This happens a lot?" Sun inquired.

"A few times now."

"Yeah, Sun. . . you remember the other mind living in Cyrus, before our transfer?" John spoke up. *"This is that same fucking guy, he took us with him somehow. Remember the Fila papers? Supposed to be the same weird kinda shit."*

THE | SPLIT

Recognition dawned on Sun as he heard this, and exclaimed, *"Yes! So, it seems we came unattached from the group, somehow, when we split the two."*

"Yup," John replied sourly.

I looked at the stream of color still flashing by. The whole passage this time had been different, but it still seemed like my travel time had been longer than usual. Now it appeared that we were picking up speed, though there was no exit in sight.

The two were conversing as I left my train of thought, sharing memories and images as they pieced together what happened. *"John,"* I called out, interrupting them, *"Even if this is temporary, I need to know who you are. Sun-Tzu only gets a pass because he's famous and I've read his book."*

I felt Sun-Tzu swell with pride, but John replied first, annoyed. *"Maybe famous during **your** time. . . you pre-fusion bumpkin."*

"Whoa!" I exclaimed, amused at his response. *"Then, who are **you**, big shot?"*

"Name's John Park. Tycoon, philanthropist, outspoken late night streaming guest, and still-bitter second place finisher of the 2060 presidential campaign for the New Libertarian Party."

I laughed again, he definitely had a way with words, *"That's quite a resume. In what industry did you make your fortune?"*

"Chemical extraction," he replied, *"They actually made a movie about the founding of my company. Jay Slass won an Oscar for playing me in the film. You know him?"*

"No."

"Of course you don't. . . they didn't even start making good movies til the 2040's. You people had your moments though. I guess you could

THE | SPLIT

say I'm the Donald Trump of the future. Well. . . Trump who doesn't say racist shit. . . Oh! And with better hair!" he paused. *"Assholes in the media were always calling me a party boy. . . bullshit. Sure, I went out a lot. . . and bought a few restaurants when I was drunk. But I was strictly business 90 percent of the time. But. . . anyway, unlike Sun here, I'm actually real. When I died in 2071, they froze my brain and added me to the collective."*

An uncomfortable silence followed, during which I could sense that both of their thoughts were still rife with questions and anticipation. John may have hid it well, but he was just as nervous as Sun had been. I tried to get him talking again as we continued along our course;

"So John, this movie. . . and the founding of this company of yours. . . tell me about that." and could feel him gearing up to tell a story he had told more times than he could count.

"I was a nerd as a kid, right? Astronomy, chemistry, engineering. . . all that shit, I loved it. Got bullied constantly, probably didn't help I already had this mouth on me. When I was in grade 8, I won a national science initiative for my project on the properties of plasmonic meta-materials, when exposed to certain light in the visible spectrum – all really technical stuff, I don't really care to talk out the specifics.

Anyway, my project gained international attention, and one day some executives from BP stopped by my house to ask me about it. I remember how big of a deal it was for my parents. . . **Important People***, from a multinational company, had come to see* **their** *son's discovery.*

My mom made a whole to-do around our small house, rearranging the furniture and cleaning compulsively. Even my idiot dad sobered up for the occasion, and the whole neighborhood showed up to see the business-men's flashy entrance in their sleek new hover-copter... they were a lot louder back then, the sound nearly deafened the whole neighborhood.

Anyway, they came by for about an hour and a half, asking questions about the meta-materials... and retelling unoriginal jokes about how BP would give me a job one day. I smiled and went along with the day, but wanted no part of their corporate shit show.

My free time was spent doing more than science – I followed the corporate world and politics closely, often drawing the mockery of my peers for enrolling in as many of these classes I could – and I knew that BP had acquired American contracts in the new field of fusion energy. Yes, it was a lucrative gig, considering how much the US was paying to try and catch up to the Bloc's fusion technology. But at the same time, they'd purchased and/or pressured small mining companies into selling, and quickly controlled 60 percent of the world's plutonium, ununium, and the other rare minerals used in the fusion process, stacking the market in their favor.

My research with meta-materials continued to examine their effect on metals often used to power America's new fusion reactors. On the side, I studied for my grade 12 exits, devoting long nights to my combination of all of these pursuits, and at age 15 graduated my school. I then sold a grouping of micro-machine code I had written, to a nationwide hardware manufacturer, and used the profits to purchase a small, rundown, house in North Trenton, New Jersey.

I moved my things out overnight, never waking my parents or leaving a message behind. With the rest of my money for the code, and the small amount of prize money I had won in the initiative for my experiment, I was able to enroll in Princeton. I majored in both chemistry and electrical engineering, and by age 21 had received a

Master's degree in both. In college, I had been too busy to continue my research from before, but in my free time now began studying the curious potential of deuterium.

In theory, the variant of hydrogen could become a powerful fuel. The fusion between it and another hydrogen variant, tritium, was measured to have one of the highest releases of any combination of particles yet found. The problem was in the extraction of deuterium from its many sources – or, more specifically, how to do it cheaply, as the cost of preparing the isotope on a mass scale exceeded that of rarer minerals that were currently being used to power fusion reactors. Deuterium, tritium and all similar isotopes were dismissed as impractical for commercial use, and it was in this problem that I had made my scientific pursuit.

While at Princeton, I renewed my study on plasmonic meta-materials and the effects they had on salt water when exposed to ultraviolet light. . . salt water was thought to become one of the main sources for Deuterium some day. There were enough atoms in one gallon to power a modern home for an entire year, and using various compounds of graphene, I was beginning to make progress, separating out dozens of Deuterium particles from the salty water.

It was also at Princeton that I'd made my first friends. Matt and Sanjay had introduced themselves to me one day, after I presented my case study for a chemistry project, and asked if they could help. Over the next few months they became involved heavily in my work, devoting countless late nights to studying my notes, trying to familiarize themselves with the research behind my idea.

Then Sanjay told his father about our progress. He was the Chief Financial Officer for a major chemical supply company, and he saw the potential windfall – if we could succeed. After showing our research to his board of directors, he made us an offer; for $300,000 they would own 3 percent. It was more than generous; he was proud of his son's hard work, and wanted to help any way he could. I found no problem with the nepotism, and was ecstatic at our first taste of success."

"With most of the money, we leased a space near campus to house our project, and purchased some of the more expensive equipment we had to that point been forced to compensate without.

Our progress began to increase exponentially, and I soon found myself putting aside my other projects, even studying for my classes, to work more on refining our process. I was obsessed. I seemed to live in our lab, going days without showering or eating as I tried everything to increase our efficiency. In my junior year we reached our breakthrough. It was a Saturday, and we were setting up our field test. Matt, having had spent all night observing a salt water sample I'd covered with high-powered green lasers, had forgotten to store our graphene compound in the climate controlled drawer.

The sample had started to deteriorate in the higher temperature, and then fell into the solution in muddy clumps. But before I could chastise Matt for his carelessness, the light hit the compound, and it bubbled up rapidly. Excitedly, we scanned the reaction and Sanjay read the results. We'd collected thousands of atoms, all containing pure deuterium; an increase of over 473 percent from previous tests.

The **heated** graphene was the key. With the expanded shape and increased surface area, the extraction process could break all Deuterium atoms free, much cheaper and more effectively than any previous methods. For the next few months, we experimented with different temperatures, and at last found the ideal conditions for both Deuterium and Tritium. . . we were extracting both at 97 percent efficiency."

T H E | S P L I T

"The Princeton Science Review published an article on our discoveries, purring over our findings, and gaining us national attention as we readied our process for market. Everything was going perfectly, and we could see our success just over the horizon. Then one day, we received a letter from a law office. Exxon, BP, and other reactor fuel suppliers had filed an injunction against us, in an International Court. We were ordered to stop our work until it had been verified by official findings, citing the potential disruption to the world energy market.

We were dead in the water without the ability to continue our testing. Our public opening was delayed indefinitely, no capital firms were willing to invest in our brand, and even Sanjay's father was unable to help us – he'd been ordered by the board to pull away from our worsening situation.

The summer went quickly, and soon I was in my first semester as a senior, devoting all of my time to graduating early. Within a few weeks I was bored with the lack of work, so I spent my free time at night drinking heavily at local campus bars. Sanjay and Matt were both busy finishing their own degrees, and had halted all work on our project, distancing themselves from me as my nightly habits became an addiction. Weeks would pass without me seeing either of them.

Then one cold night at a bar just off campus, I met a man in a nice suit. He listened with great interest as I drunkenly complained about the injunction filed against us, then as I turned to leave stopped me and offered me a ride home.

In the car, he revealed that he was a lawyer, and had come to the bar hoping to find me. His firm had studied our case and believed they had the resources to reverse the order. They wanted 2 percent for their efforts, stating that this legal battle could last years. I took his card as

THE | SPLIT

he dropped me off at my house, and the next day called Matt and Sanjay to give them the news. We'd unanimously agreed, and signed the papers they had drawn up in their office that same afternoon.

Within 2 days they called me with good news. The injunction had been lifted and our case was being expedited to the front of the docket. We were overjoyed at this, putting aside our personal distance from the last year, and working all hours of the day to streamline our process. Once we could show that the injunction had been lifted, we had no problem securing funding. For just 20 percent of the company, we received 145 million from four different firms, in just two days, to help move our product to market. One day after class, I walked out of the building to find a group of BP men waiting for me. They asked me to go for a walk, and though I was suspicious, I accepted.

The tallest of the group was none other than one of the men who had come to see me at my parent's house, all those years ago. He congratulated me on my success – with a forced happiness – and then immediately began to ask how much my research was worth to me. They quoted different prices as we moved around the campus, trying to buy me out. The amount got as high as a billion before I left them and told them my process wasn't for sale.

Our hearing got a lot of attention in the press. Reporters would show up to our new headquarters daily to ask us about it. We ignored all of their questions, directing them to our lawyers every time. It was an exciting time for us. Here we were, three 21 year old kids, hiring a whole office worth of people, and leading board meetings. We seemed to find nothing but success anywhere we turned. Our sale's team had secured us hundreds of contracts for our new system, all over the United States. The projected revenue for our initial opening was over 2.1 billion."

THE | SPLIT

"Then in late Spring, Matt disappeared for a few days, and our work fell by the wayside as we frantically searched for him. Several hours after we filed a Missing Person's report, he hobbled into the office. I remember seeing him. . . and being shocked. His face was almost unrecognizable. Thick blood matted his hair, both his eyes-sockets were purple and nearly swollen shut, and as he moved into the lobby he dragged his right leg behind him. It was jutting out a sickening angle, and the bones from his kneecap were sticking through his skin.

He had been abducted outside of his home, and savagely beaten in a run down building just outside of town. The kidnappers questioned him closely about the details for our extraction process, and told him this would happen again if he went back to work.

We hospitalized him after he fell unconscious, and it took weeks for him to heal. I hired armed private detectives to guard his room as he recovered, but the damage was done. People all around the office whispered about the danger of working for us. Dozens of employees quit, having received anonymous threats at home. . . all warning that what happened to Matt would happen to them too. Even the media reported the fear from the incident, calling a job at our company 'not worth the risk'.

Angered by the news coverage and continued harassment of our workers at home, I decided to fight back. In a rash decision, I let go all of our building security and replaced them with Syrian mercenaries – well trained, and strictly no-nonsense. They guarded our little campus like a fortified compound. When just a few weeks later a large group of masked men attempted to break in, almost all were shot dead.

When I arrived on scene I saw the few survivors were in restraints inside the building, and had been violently interrogated. Filled with a righteous fury, I congratulated the mercenaries, assuring them that

THE | SPLIT

they would face no legal repercussions. But soon the media caught wind of what happened, and the police came to our building to retrieve the attempted burglars. A standoff ensued when the Syrians refused to relinquish custody of the men without my order.

Later that night, I appeared on a political stream to discuss the events at my company, and the host of the show lectured me on my use of foreign soldiers and unwillingness to let the law run its course. I snapped back at him, citing statistics showing the public overwhelmingly supported our actions and that the police would get custody when we finished our investigation.

The clip of me berating the host went viral. Millions more people were now paying attention to our break in and prolonged case in international court. Eventually we released the men, but not without first publishing their identities. The media had a field day when we linked them to BP and Exxon money. Cries of corruption rang out from around the world at our shocking story, pressuring the judge to quickly settle the case in our favor. On my 22nd birthday, our process came to market. Much like the injunction had said, our new product completely disrupted the world's energy market. Thousands of jobs were lost, and created, overnight. The price of metals like Plutonium plummeted to record lows. Within just three years we were valued at over 3 trillion. The rest, as they say, is history."

His story had taken several long minutes to tell, but I'd hardly noticed. Every scene he described, I had pictured in my head, forming a movie of my own. I could sense Sun's amusement and satisfaction as well.

"Very impressive," Sun stated happily.

John's laughter rang out through my mind, *"Sun, you've heard that story a dozen times before!"*

THE | SPLIT

"I know!" Sun protested. *"That does not mean I enjoy it any less. Rejoice in the victory of your Ally, do not give in to petty jealousy."*

John laughed again, *"This is why I love you, Sun."*

Their mirthful exchange was contagious, and I soon felt myself sharing their happiness as we continued to talk. But looking ahead, I soon fell silent, prompting them to follow my gaze. There in the distance was a bright, white, light.

We were hurdling towards it and picking up speed.

T H E | S P L I T

XXVII

Bought from Church of England by A. Fila, 2081

Bought from A. Fila's Estate, 2105

-T. Acerz, 2131

Undetermined

Our thoughts collided into the back of a head, and I fell into a heap on the floor. It felt cold on my bare skin – I was back inside of a body. Wiggling my fingers and toes, I tested my range of motion and with relief realized the body I was in was my own.

Then I looked up from where I was laying and saw that there were dozens of black drones swarming above me. Wearily, I pulled myself to my feet. The hallway around me looked different this time. Moving screens still covered the walls, but the ceiling was higher above me. I could feel both John and Sun's curiosity as they used my eyesight to take in the scene with amazement.

The black shapes beeped and encircled my standing form, then a burning pain cried out from my left arm, and I turned to see one of the drones illuminating my left side with small red lights. A green glow now caught my attention, and with shock I realized it was coming from me as, holding my arms in front of my eyes, I could see my skin glowing in a radioactive green. When I started to walk forward, it sent the cloud of drones into a panic.

Half of the group broke off from the formation and zipped out of sight down the platform, while those that remained hovered nearby, observing me closely. After walking for a few minutes I came to a large door, which opened, allowing me to walk down another platform into a large room that seemed identical to the one I had first spotted the large

T H E | S P L I T

entity in just days ago. A large, circular platform in the middle of the room, with walls rising upward for hundreds of feet before stopping at a ceiling that was covered in shadow.

The drones prodded me towards the center, I followed their direction blankly. I did not relish my time in these green halls, everything inside me cried out in warning as I looked around. The alien architecture and faint green glow would have been enough to make even the most hardened lifeforms shudder in fear, and my mind raced with anxiety at the complete lack of familiarity around me.

Deep inside my thoughts, I could sense John and Sun felt similar. I made it to the middle and saw the black drones pull away from me, but before I could look back at them, I blinked out of sight and into the throne room, where I looked up to face the menacing creature, able to feel its presence pulling at my thoughts.

It sat on the edge of its chair, nearly doubled over as it looked down on me. Thousands of the black drones covered the upper air of the room like a dark cloud, in turns floating down to the entity. It would speak something to each of them, and they would ascend once again. I could not understand any of the words it spoke, but every utterance sent shivers down my spine.

It's voice sounded angry, each snarl punctuated by a wild head shake or flick of its appendages. I could sense its foreign expression of frustration even as it sifted through my recent memories with Cyrus, examining my thoughts with suspicion. Then it stumbled upon my two new occupants.

Shocked, it fell upon John first and commenced tearing at his memories and thoughts savagely, while John cursed and threatened as he tried to push the presence away from his mind.

*"Get the fuck out of here! These are **my** thoughts, no! **NO!**"*

THE | SPLIT

I could feel his strain towards the top of my brain as he fought the Being, struggling and thrashing about. Doing my best to calm him, I sent him a thought showing him that this would be easier if he didn't fight; he eventually acknowledged my words, and released the grip on his thoughts, sitting back in anger as the Being took what it wanted.

It soon pulled out of his space and shifted into Sun Tzu's, and the old general watched in discomfort as the memories he had been programmed with were pulled in front of him at random.

"Who are these lifeforms?!" the Being's voice rang through my mind angrily.

"John and Sun," I answered cautiously.

"How did they come here?!" it roared.

"I don't know," I admitted. "They just came."

I felt the Being look down at my glowing green skin, "How did you access the forbidden passage, Terran? Who assisted you?!"

After several seconds, it dawned on me that he was talking about the way that we had came. My thoughts flashed back to the strange trip through the swirling scenes of life and time.

"No one assisted me." I said defiantly. "I don't even know what passage you're talking about."

It forced itself back into my head, lifting my memories of the trip, as well as both John and Sun's, going back before my journey itself and watching with great interest as the collective prepped Cyrus for the transfer. But, not finding an answer it pulled back out of my brain, it now raised me above the ground.

"You have violated our pact," it accused in a booming voice.

"How could I?" I protested; it gripped me even tighter. "I have no control over where I go."

T H E | S P L I T

"You have violated our terms," it repeated, ignoring my pleas. "The gift has been given, it cannot be returned. Sharing your mind with others, and traveling through the forbidden passage. are crimes of a nature beyond your understanding. Humanity and Terra itself will suffer for your actions."

"NO!" I was shouting now even as the invisible hand gripped tighter around me, "F-fuck you! It was m-m-me not them!"

"Spoiled and primitive," it spoke with distaste. "Always muddling in that which you don't understand. I will show you true pain, you will see how much farther you can fall, young Terran."

"Wait!" I called out, but I was already starting to slip away, and once again I was without a body, moving through the dark and infinite space I was more used to traveling through.

I could still feel John and Sun as we hurled along our path, connected with me even in the limitless plane where my thoughts could spread freely, though their reach and control was dwarfed by my own. I could 'see' them completely, but only as faint lines of images and shapes that were totally engulfed by my own thoughts and feelings, as though only a part of them was there, an incomplete copy created by the transfer. That seemed to be my best guess, at least, as I reached out to the two in the dark space.

Our connection was a lot more one-sided than Cyrus' and mine, or even mine and Charles', had been. Still, in this place there was no need for words, our minds moved in perfect sync. It was all right there, moving effortlessly and instantaneously through the cloud of my thoughts. They showed me questions and I answered them with images, impressions, words, and memories. I showed them the night I had brought Meela back to life, the battle in Cuba, and all of me and Cyrus' journey to Washington.

T H E | S P L I T

In turn I saw both of their beginnings, of consciousness, back in the lab. It had caused them both a sudden shock to realize they were without bodies. They seemed to float in the empty space of their memories, much as we were now, asking their creators where they were. John had taken to it easier than Sun. He, being an organic construct, did not have to grapple with the realization of his complete artificiality, the way Sun did.

They showed me their greatest victories and failures; Sun-Tzu had been taken before the King of Wu, and tested by being ordered to turn the king's vast harem into soldiers. Sun had divided the women into two companies, and when they had giggled, not taking him seriously, he had executed the two company leaders, both the King's favorite concubines. The King had protested, but Sun had silenced him by saying that *'it is not the fault of the soldier for obeying his king's orders.'*. I then stood on the hill with Sun, now an old man, as the sun began to set on his last battlefield. Outnumbered and surrounded, he pulled his sword out and charged into the fray, dying with the last of his men.

John's victories had also been many. There were dozens of images of him; on stage, presenting checks, and giving speeches at benefits. His life was lavish, full of expensive cars and clothes that were kept in brightly colored apartments, overlooking the various skylines of the world. He had been with hundreds of women, had drank and did drugs freely with some of the world's most famous people.

His failures had been few, but had left an impression. Such as when his parents had sued him for billions, within the first few years of his extraction process going public. Many more in his home community, even old friends, had joined in on the suit, stating that much of his knowledge had been gained from their own, and the court of public opinion had begun to swing in their favor, shaping the story around it.

THE | SPLIT

John had responded with barbaric cruelty. Late at night his mercenaries had shown up in large SUVs, breaking into dozens of the plaintiffs' homes and pulling them into the streets. They'd beaten them unconscious with boots and clubs, and the people had gotten the message; nearly all of the parties had withdrawn their claims. The police tried without success to pin the attacks on John – the whole nation had known he was responsible – but with all of his personal contact being monitored as a result of the lawsuit, he'd had the ultimate alibi.

Our knowledge of each other had increased a thousand times in what seemed like just seconds, and I could feel a bond between the two and I, like I had known them for years. All of our thoughts seemed completely in sync; they understood what had been happening and where we were going. Both told me they would take on a passive role in the upcoming journey, observing and only speaking when called upon.

I agreed, there was no telling what awaited me on the other side, and having my head filled with internal dialogue would be nothing but a distraction.

T H E | S P L I T

XXIII

LGPB://mn34/con/terra/OT, 6198

(Translated)

Hungary; 1241

Suddenly a boundary appeared around our bright thought-scape, then I was thrust through a tight space and into another's perception.

A new set of thoughts reached out towards mine fearfully. The other consciousness felt quaint and simple. I could sense little more than base instinct, and images of unknown people, thus it took little effort to console my new host as I showed him my intentions through memories of my past. He seemed not to understand much of the strange worlds I showed him, but relaxed and allowed me to settle into his mind.

With total control of the body I opened my eyes. The room was dark, and I was covered with a large blanket made of rough fur; I had been sleeping.

But, where was I?

My vision was blurry as I looked around the room, trying to see through the darkness, and took several seconds to adjust. Wooden crates lay next to my cot. The room appeared to be a large tent, wider and taller than any I had ever been in. The walls of the room were canvas, and I could see wooden supports holding up the matching canvas ceiling. A cool breeze came in from the outside, catching the corners of the canvas sheets which flapped about gently.

I stretched out on the crude mattress below me, and my shins hung over the edge, dangling uncomfortably. But as I clenched and expanded my muscles, I felt powerful. My arms and legs were much longer than they had ever been before, and large muscles stretched the lengths of

THE | SPLIT

both, just under the surface of my skin, each feeling coiled and tight with strength. Rotating sideways, I stood to my feet; I was tall, very tall. Even in the darkness I could tell I easily stood a head higher than normal.

A man stirred in a cot next to the entrance and stood up next to me, beginning to slip on a suit of chain-mail that was emblazoned with a Red Cross, which had sat atop a pair of leather boots. He put the boots on next, but as he turned to leave the tent I put up a hand to stop him.

"Where. . ." I stammered, voice catching in my throat. "Where am I going?"

His eyes widening at my words, he stuttered in shock, "I-I. . . I. . ." before pointing outside the tent and to the left. I thanked him, and he nodded slightly, never taking his eyes off me. Pushing the two folds of the tent outward, I stepped out into the world.

The early morning sunlight burned away to my east, forcing me to narrow my eyes as they adjusted from the dark space of the tent. Shouts and laughter rang out all around me, and I saw that I was in a camp – much larger than the impromptu setup I had seen in Cuba.

Hundreds of tents identical to the one I had just left stretched as far as the eye could see, and men labored in the long aisles between them. Some carried crates and led horses, others crowded around wagons conversing loudly. High above the tops of the tents were Standards of every color, flapping wildly in the breeze; the shapes of dozens of animals and symbols dancing in the foreground of the colored banners.

After a few seconds of searching, I spotted the same Red Cross the man in the tent had been wearing and headed towards it. Men of all types looked up at me as I passed. I stood the same height as most horses I walked by, all men who approached looked tiny by comparison.

THE | SPLIT

At home I had been tall, measuring close to 6'5, but this body was freakish. I couldn't be sure, but as I measured myself against the items around me, I estimated my height to be well over 7 feet.

The banner of the Red Cross was attached to a red tent, larger than the rest and off to the side by itself, but a big circle of men, all wearing armor with the same Sigil, dominated the middle of the space just outside. Some of them turned around as I approached, then a soldier in full gear broke away from the circle to wave and call out;

"Geoff! Come here friend!"

He was waving in my direction, but I wasn't sure it was to me, so I spun all the way around; looking for another person he could be talking to. There was no one around, it seemed this man knew me – and my name was Geoff. When I finally made it to where he was standing I stopped in front of him.

"Well, 'ello big guy! Where is your equipment today?"

He spoke slowly and simply, enunciating each syllable distinctly and clearly. It reminded me of how I had spoken during my time as a volunteer coach for the Special Olympics. It felt odd being on the receiving end of such patronizing speech.

"I. . . do not know," I replied after a short pause. "I was not aware that I should have it. I do not even know where I am."

My friend, and the men within earshot, turned towards me, their eyes wide with surprise. They shared the same expression the man in the tent had given me earlier.

"Geoff!" my friend cried out. "You can *speak*!"

I felt confused, looking between their astonished faces. "Well of course I can speak! It seems. . . Did I. . . have too much to drink last night. . . ? I can not say where I am. . . or what I am doing here."

THE | SPLIT

The men shook their heads, wild-eyed. The whole circle had turned our direction now, and I could see men whispering amongst themselves out of the corner of my eye.

Everything felt out of place. Finally, wondering why were they so amazed at my simple questions, I sought out my answers through the memories of my new body. The mind already inside offered no resistance as I moved through his thoughts and started looking.

Every conversation the man had ever had was roughly the same; in slow, sweet voices he was asked questions and given orders, never responding with much more than a grunt. Even in recent weeks the conversations had been the same; worse, I could only catch pieces of the conversations as I watched the scenes from my host's life, as he would only pay attention for a few phrases at a time. When he was done listening, he would turn away to stare at a nearby rabbit or watch a bird soar high above.

My host had the mind of a child, and it seemed the people in his life had gone to great lengths to take care of him.

"Geoffrey," the man said to get my attention, "it is I. . . Frederick. When did this begin? When did you begin to speak?"

I stopped to think; now, I would need a convincing story. The tale of my journey through time would be dismissed as nonsense – or worse, labeled as the words of Satan. Though I didn't know the year or my location, these men were undoubtedly members of a European Knighthood, and the Church throughout history had never looked kindly on things they didn't understand.

"It was. . . this morning," I lied. "A messenger of the Lord appeared to me in my dreams." The soldiers' eyes grew even wider at my claim. Their whispers became murmurs, and their conversations grew louder as they glanced at me suspiciously.

THE | SPLIT

I felt an arm touch my shoulder and turned to see Frederick. "Come along, Geoff. . . " he said softly. ". . . let us go and see the Master, and Bishop. . . they shall wish to hear of this."

"Hear of, what?" I responded nervously.

He stopped and turned towards me, looking up at my face, and I felt intense energy emanating from his gaze as our eyes met. But when he then narrowed his eyes, examining my face suspiciously,

I slowly realized that he didn't completely believe me. I would have to be more convincing, to put the issue to rest.

"They must hear of what has happened to you," he replied. You are behaving quite. . . well. . . oddly. Some of us. . . we have known you for years, you must understand how strange this is."

Not wanting to seem caught off guard, I responded immediately, "Well Frederick. . . we have been friends for a long time. I am able to tell when you do not believe someone. How can I put your mind at ease?"

"It is not that I do not believe you," he said, hesitating. "It is only. . . your story is, vague. And with such tales going about. . . I simply. . . I am. . . uncertain, what to believe."

"Well. . . if you doubt that I am telling the truth, what could another explanation be?"

"Witchcraft," he admitted.

"I assure you, I am under the influence of no spell. Nothing of the sort. Would it help then. . . were I to go into more detail about what happened?" He nodded, and so I launched into the false account I had already been mentally preparing; "I dreamt that I was high above the earth. . . there were clouds beneath my feet. I could not see the ground below me, but I did not wish to. The billowing, white shapes brought me great peace, and I grew so happy that I never wished to leave. But suddenly, the clouds before me began to darken, and I heard the rumbling of thunder coming from within."

As he nodded, looking me in the eyes, hanging onto every word, I realized that the people back home had been right; I *would* be a good lawyer. That was a pretty thick slice of bullshit, and he was completely enthralled with it.

Trying not to smile, I continued to lay it on: "Out of these dark clouds. . . I saw a figure in white. He began to walk towards me, and as he drew near. . . I knew it in my heart that it was our Lord Christ. I fell to my knees, but he drew me up, saying, *'Rise, my son'*. I was yet unable to speak, and could only muttered something. . . as I used to. . . but He smiled, and I was certain he understood, although no one else in my whole life had been able to.

Slowly, he reached forth and touched my eyes with his finger tips. . . my vision grew dark, and he showed me horrible things. . . wars to come, horrible acts committed. . . I yet shudder to think of them. When he removed his hand, my sight returned to normal, and our Lord said something softly. . . about, his gift. Then he brushed against my forehead with the back of his palm. . . and my broken mind was whole."

Frederick had been silent through my account, and continued his silence for several moments afterward, but finally he spoke, "Your vision. . . if it is true, what does it mean? Why did he heal you? Why now?"

"I do not know." I paused for a second, in an attempt to sound more convincing. "The things shown to me, these terrible things. . . I feel that they were a warning. A warning for those in his kingdom of what is to come. Our savior is a god of peace, but he also is a god of strength, and in the coming battle we shall need all of the help we are able to muster."

T H E | S P L I T

Frederick laughed, "Is that not the truth? It quite seems to have made you much the cleric, as well."

He reached out and pulled me into a hug. I was caught off guard from his gesture but eventually wrapped my arms around him to return his embrace. I noticed as he released me that his expression had changed, and a look of pure joy now radiated from his face. The Lord had healed his friend, and that was all he needed to know.

He pushed our way through the group of soldiers just ahead, and I followed him towards the tall red tent. Inside, men in armor stood around a large table in the center, the top of which was covered by a map. On it, rested a small collection of figurines grouped together, and the men were gesturing at the table and debating loudly, paying no attention to me and Frederick. At last a hefty man in the corner spotted us and walked over.

"Ah... Geoff, Sir Frederick... what have you to report?"

"Nothing on the enemy, Master." Frederick replied. "Yet, something strange has happened."

The man looked at him questioningly, Frederick then gestured towards me.

"Geoff? Is there something you wish to say?" The man looked confused as he waited for a response.

"No, Master. I am... to be honest... having a bit of difficulty recalling where I am."

The man looked surprised, much like the others, but quickly regained his composure and his expression changed back to normal. "Well, this *is* an odd development. Twenty years have I known you... and never once have you uttered more than a single word."

"Something changed..." I replied, trailing off.

THE | SPLIT

"*Clearly*!" he laughed. "The Lord blesses us anew every day! Come... let us tell the Archbishop of this miracle!"

I breathed an audible sigh of relief, he had been much more accepting than Frederick had been. This was clearly a military man, a hard man; he did not have the time to waste on the hypothetical.

He led us through a curtain wall and into another section of the tent. Inside was a raised wooden floor, with a crude railing and altar, and standing atop this platform were three men, huddled in a circle and talking among themselves quietly.

Within seconds I knew which was the Archbishop. They wore brightly covered robes, adorned in gold stitching and the sign of the cross, and on their heads sat strangely shaped hats, similar to those of the Pope and his cardinals I had seen on TV back in my time.

The Archbishop raised a finger to signal he had seen us, but continued his conversation. The Master kneeled at the foot of the altar and motioned for us to do the same. As I sank to my knee, I searched through my host's memories of this mysterious man who had known me for decades.

It didn't take very long, he was scattered in pieces through most of my host's mind. Master Rembald had found Geoff at a young age, slow and unable to communicate, hiding scared in a tunnel after their town had been raided by bandits. He had taken the boy on his journey home.

Of freakish size and strength by the age of just 7 years old, Geoff was already larger than most adults, and able to do the work of two men. In a few years he had found gainful employment, shoeing horses and assisting blacksmiths for the Master's order of knights.

I couldn't help my smile at the bounty of helpful information I had just stumbled onto, but Rembald glared back at me and raised his eyebrows severely, so I straightened my face before looking up again.

T H E | S P L I T

As I waited I reached out for John and Sun-Tzu, telling them to sift through Geoffrey's mind as they observed; they said they would.

The Archbishop now ended his conversation and turned to us; "Arise, Rembald de Voczon!" gesturing for us to stand to our feet. "What have you brought before me?"

"An act of God, dear Archbishop!" Rembald answered. "This simple-minded man has been cured. . . the fog has lifted from his mind, and he speaks now with the voice of our Lord."

The Archbishop stepped down from the stand and walked towards me, his face alight with excitement. "Is this true, my son? Tell me of your encounter!"

I repeated a simpler version of what I had told Frederick earlier; "Jesus himself appeared to me in my sleep, your Holiness. He showed me the battle to come, and that the Lord's glory in battle would shine through me. And then he made my broken mind whole again."

"Another sign from God!" The holy man cried out joyfully, pulling me into a tight embrace. He was surprisingly strong in his old age. "Our cause is noble, he would not lead us astray!"

"But Archbishop, sir. . . " I interrupted his celebrating. "When the Lord healed me, I lost all of my memory. . . I have only just learned my name again, yet I know not whose Sigil I wear, nor to whom we march to fight."

He clapped a hand on my shoulder and turned up to look at me, "You fight for the Lord's chosen. . . a welcome new recruit for our proudest order, the Knights Templar. You and your brothers have been sent here on the orders of his Holiness, the Pope, himself. King Bela IV of Hungary sought me out personally, in Jerusalem, to seek our aid in repelling the Mongol invaders who are raiding his lands. Seven days since we arrived in Pest to reinforce the besieged city, and drew up our

THE | SPLIT

plans for a group of brave knights to charge through the city gates and towards our enemy. We did take them by surprise. . . routed the group to the last man, and have chased them nigh on a week. Now, we are a mere day's ride from the river Sajo."

My mind worked quickly, trying to absorb all of this. I was in Hungary, pursuing Mongols. This seemed a foolhardy task, when viewed through the lens of history, for no matter how many knights we had, engaging a Mongol horde in the open field had been a mistake made by many extinct tribes and forgotten nations.

Still, I couldn't recall when Hungary had fought the armies of Genghis Khan. This battle they prepared for had either been lost to history, or been neglected during my education.

"Thank you, Archbishop." I replied gratefully, bowing my head.

"My gratitude for your time, your holiness." Rembald said, as he began to back out of the room.

A delegation of men dressed in dirty robes was waiting for the Archbishop's audience near the side wall. "It is always yours, my faithful commander. Bring our newly restored friend here into the fold, make sure he knows everything he will need for the battle to come. Tonight we will celebrate the work of our Lord!"

"Aye sir!" Rembald exclaimed, leading us out of the room and through the front of the tent.

We parted ways at the entrance, where Rembald instructed Frederick to take me to the Master-At-Arms to be fitted, before returning to his duties inside. We went out into the camp and Frederick led me back to my tent, where he waited patiently as I put on my heavy boots and stained apron, then after I was dressed we headed towards the armory across camp.

THE | SPLIT

We hardly spoke as we moved, but I didn't mind, the site was a blur of activity as men set about their tasks. Boxes were being loaded onto wagons, men in normal dress sat on stumps and barrels, sharpening swords and axes in concentration. A large bag of oats in a cart rolled across our path, and I turned to see a man moving it to near a large pen of horses. The smells filling the air around me were an earthy stench reeking of sweat and manure, and it took a minute for my flared nostrils to settle, but no one else seemed to notice; I scanned the faces in the crowd and did not see any displeasure or disgust matching my own.

Halfway across the camp the flat ground began to slope upward, and Frederick had to increase his pace to a slight jog as we climbed it, trying to match each of my long strides. At top of the small hill we found the armory nestled into the corner of the camp and surrounded by sentries. We approached the grouping of large wagons cautiously. Each of the stout wooden boxes around the area shined brightly as the individual pieces of steel within caught the sun's light.

"Hey!" a voice called out to our right. I looked over to see a round, bald man glaring at us. His arms were crossed over a dirty brown apron, sweat dripped down his dirty face, and his voice was gruff and rocky; each word he exhaled sent spittle flying in all directions. "I ain't got all day. Who sent you and what are ya after?"

"Master Rembald has sent us to get this man outfitted," Frederick replied dryly. I could see his distaste for the Master-At-Arms.

"Oh did he? Well let's see here. 'Tain a lot of armor around these days will fit him. . . but lucky for 'im, we lost a man not much shorter the other day in a raid. Here's a full chain, the jerkin, and greaves. . . might be a little tight, but it's best we got. Bloke's helmet was dented all the way through, but helmets I got plenty of. This one ought to fit."

THE | SPLIT

He pulled a large, dull colored, steel helm from a compartment on the side of the wagon and handed it to me, with the chain-mail, watching as I put it all on clumsily. Frederick had to help me with the greaves; first I put them on upside down, then the circlet of tiny rings stuck tightly just above my knee but, finally free, I slipped on the mail shirt and donned my helmet.

Everything fit perfectly. I told the master such, looking around through the eye slits in my new helmet. The two small rectangles offered a way to see through the helmet, but greatly reduced my visibility and peripheral vision. It took some getting used to, but after moving around for a few minutes and adjusting its position on my head, I was able to maneuver and see without issue.

Removing it, I saw the arms master and Frederick standing at a nearby wagon, examining a bundle of poleaxes. The master looked up when he saw me removing the mail, and handed me the axe. I grasped the iron shaft loosely, allowing the weight of the axe head and spear tip to tilt it towards the ground, feeling the balance of the weapon. It felt almost light in my strong arms as I deftly spun it from hand to hand, before grasping it with both hands and lowering myself for a thrust forward with the spear head; skewering some imaginary enemy.

"You like that one, eh?" the master watched me, smiling.

"Yes. It is light, and provides many ways of attack."

"A wise choice," he agreed. "With your reach, you will be almost as Goliath himself." Frederick laughed, prompting me to do the same. The master continued, "I've more poleaxes than I know what to do with. Take two. . . 'ell, take three of them."

"If you are going to be using an axe, Geoff. . ." Frederick nodded at me, ". . . we had best pick you out a shield. Pray Brother Tom is still in camp, it might be too late to have it painted with the red cross."

THE | SPLIT

"No shield," I blurted suddenly.

The words had come from deep inside my head, and I quickly realized the real Geoffrey had forced the thought upon me. He made his case to me in an instant, showing images of swords and memories of Rembald training him with sticks, always one in each hand.

"Are you mad, man? You must have a shield. . . you will not last 'til high sun without it!"

"No shield," I repeated firmly, and brushed past him to look through the cart myself.

My eyes settled on a sword leaning against the side wall. The blade was broad, angled, and longer than the other, thinner, ones nearby. The hilt was longer too, and the grip tapered into both sides of the metal base, forming a wider ridge in the middle.

It had been smithed as a hand and a half sword, fitting in both the single and dual grip of a normal user. In my grasp it was a single hand sword; the ridge in the middle meant to separate the hand and a half portions of the grip, fit comfortably between two of my knuckles.

I pulled it out of the cart and held it against the daylight, examining it for chips or cracks. The blade shone brightly, and the reflection made me squint my eyes. The steel appeared fine.

Raising it into ready position, then doing the same with the poleaxe in my other hand, I swiped with the ax, then parried with my sword. Now tucking the ax into my armpit I spun forward and whipped it around my body, turning in a quick series of strikes, before finishing the maneuver with a thrust from the sword.

"Impressive, your foes will tremble in terror," the master-at-arms called out, then walked away, to talk to a new group of soldiers who had shown up to the wagons behind us.

T H E | S P L I T

I couldn't tell if he was being serious or sarcastic; then I inanely wondered if sarcasm had even been discovered yet.

"With no shield, how will you stop your enemy from striking you?" Frederick questioned. I could hear the skepticism in his voice; he had not been as impressed by my little display as I had hoped.

"This," I pointed at the chain-mail and helmet I was bending over to retrieve. "This is what will save any from striking me. With two weapons, I can strike with twice their speed. The enemy will busy himself blocking my strikes, and be unable to achieve anything more than a glancing blow to my mail."

"For your sake, I pray you are right." He turned to leave.

I followed him, pausing before I left to grab two more of the poleaxes. The master had been honest about the number of axes he had left. Huge bundles, tied with twine, were left untouched near the back of the wagon. All three axes were awkward to carry, but I soon figured out a solution; tucking them under my arm, I removed the dirty shirt I wore underneath my apron, then tied a wide loop on one end and a small slip knot on the other. Through the small loop of the slipknot I slid the shafts of all three axes, letting the weight tighten the knot. The wide loop, I hung over my shoulders and, as I walked forward, the axes were now strung together and hanging loosely from my back.

As we returned to our section of camp, we debated the merits of fighting with a shield; Frederick had yet to let the issue go. He told me story after story of battles in the past where his shield had saved his life. I assured him I would consider his words, as we parted ways at the big red tent, after which I took a slow stroll through the camp on my own. The afternoon sun was high in the sky and I could feel it's warmth through my several layers of clothing as, passing my tent, I kept East, towards the edge of the camp.

THE | SPLIT

Here, a group of men were loading a wagon, and the man inside the back of the cart called out to me as I passed; like the men who had greeted me, he too wore the Red Cross of the Templar. We conversed for a few seconds, and after his initial shock at my speech had passed, he asked me to help. I agreed and joined the line of men stretching from the wagon to the stack of barrels and crates several feet away, and for several hours we labored in the heat. The cart had been nearly empty when we arrived, so it had a large amount of space for the supplies we were loading, and I set the last barrel inside the wagon's covered trunk as the sun was beginning to set. The men I had helped thanked me, and then drove the wagon slowly westwards, towards the front of the camp.

Walking back towards the center of the area, I popped my head in the tent I had woken up in, finding it empty. With a frown, I continued my trek as the sky darkened, looking for any fellow Templars or someone that knew me, and finally saw a group of men in red crosses, gathered around a small fire. They invited me over and poured me a bowl of stew from the large pot hanging above the fire.

I looked down at my wooden bowl as the steam came off the brown liquid, before putting my lips to the rim and taking a small sip. It felt like fire as it went down my throat, but I still gulped it down greedily. The chunk of meat in my next bite was tender, a bit gamey, and from my experience hunting as a kid I knew it was rabbit.

As we ate the men around me talked; there were many tales of their homes, and every man seemed to be from a different place. I listened to talk of Rome and Florence, of the canals in Venice, and the sandy streets of Jerusalem. The men also talked of Archbishop Csák, his penchant for battle, and his confidence in our victories. The older soldiers were less confident, some of them told tales of the Mongol's prowess on horseback, but it did not matter to the younger men.

THE | SPLIT

As I listened to them talk I couldn't help but feel inspired. They spoke of Christianity in a fashion I had never heard before. These men were no saints, nor did they mention the word of Christ and his directive to spread his peaceful message. The message that I heard around the campfire was nothing like the one I had been repeatedly fed on Sunday mornings as a young boy. It was one of strength, of the desire to impose the glory of Christian culture and way of life on the enemy.

To these men, Christ's word was to be spread by the sword as well as the helping hand, and many of them seemed to believe it a form of divine right. That God himself had ordained these men to expand his kingdom. I heard them repeat many of the same ideas and talk I had known to be a part of Crusader culture. *'Deus Vult'*; "God wills it" in Latin, appeared to be an acceptable answer about any question raised concerning our possibility of losing the upcoming battle. They spoke of other beliefs and cultures with distaste, though the words did not come from hatred. Rather, their education and knowledge was so lopsided, it was likely they had never been taught anything else; these younger soldiers were fundamentally convinced that they were fighting for the truth.

Still, the talk of glory seemed to stir up something deep within me I couldn't quite recognize. Perhaps it was an ancestral memory, or the feeling of fighting with one's tribe. I was an American, and a Christian by family affiliation alone, but part of me wanted to belong. The ideas they discussed, their view on society, what they desired in life, all seemed like more primitive versions of the similar ideas my own parents had taught me as a child.

Yet here was *conviction.* Here was willingness to do more than just pray and pay lip service on a Sunday. Geoff had been behind these ideas, entirely.

THE | SPLIT

I could feel his emotional highs and lows as he too listened in on the discussion around the campfire. These were sentiments and thoughts that he heard and been taught his whole life. Even before my arrival allowed him to speak for the first time, and even though people assumed him dull as well as mute, and constantly underestimated him, Geoffrey had always listened. Actually, he seemed to have enjoyed this over the years, silently having this slight advantage was one of his few pleasures in life.

I started to focus less on what was being said, and more on how Geoff was reacting to it. We seemed to be affected differently; where I was more focused on the novelty of this different branch from the religion I grew up on, he seemed to identify more strongly with the cultural superiority and racial aspects of these young Templar knight's rhetoric.

And as I further studied Geoff's emotional responses, I began to grow ashamed of myself for becoming hypnotized even momentarily by this message of violence – then I came to a startling realization.

Having largely been a cynic from a young age, I had long doubted the effect of 'propaganda'. It seemed obscene that mere words, formed by special interests, could so deeply take hold in a people's way of thinking. And yet, here it was, right in front of my face. All this talk of glory, of strength through unity, of the kingdom of God on Earth. . . all of it seemed little more than a philosophical precursor for war.

In spite of the difference in the older soldiers' caution and the younger men's fervid idealism, everyone seemed to agree on one thing; the Cuman tribesmen they rode with were too closely related to the Khan and his men, and should therefore be watched with suspicion.

The volume of Cuman refugees seeking escape from Hungary was staggering. Whole cities had been displaced when the Mongol raiding parties came by, and thousands of dusty and weary nomads had waited

THE | SPLIT

outside the gates of Pest, all wanting an audience with the King. The nobles were wary about providing assistance to their centuries-old enemies, but the King had refused their counsel and instead greedily bolstered his armies with the Cuman riders, hoping their skill in the field would give him an edge over the Mongols.

But large numbers had fled when the armies were mobilized, and the men here at the campfire spoke venomously about their cowardice.

After nearly an hour of listening to them talk, I thanked them for the stew, and placed the bowl down where I was sitting before turning to leave. The sky above was dark, but the lights of countless torches lit the camp brightly. I seemed to pass hundreds of them as I walked. The soldiers I passed seemed in good spirits. They drank from wine skins and talked loudly of past skirmishes and the battle to come. Most of them were foot soldiers, but there were also knights scattered throughout, bragging about their tournament exploits and talking down to the other men.

As I made my way down the center clearing, I saw a shadowy figure in the dark alley of a row of tents, beckoning to me as I neared by raising a hand into the torch light and gesturing. Cautiously, I walked that way, hand on the pommel of my sword, gripping it loosely.

My eyes adjusted in the darkness as I got closer; it was a man dressed in the brown of the Hungarian army.

His uniform fit the scene, but his face did not. I looked at his features in surprise; narrowed eyes, high cheekbones, and a darker complexion than I had seen in camp - the face of an Asian man.

A spy?

Wrinkles lined his forehead as he smiled. "Don't look so shocked, you have seen stranger things I'm sure," he said in a deep voice. "It has been a long time since I've had a visitor."

T H E | S P L I T

"What do you mean?" I replied, looking around the camp. "You are not alone, there are many thousands of men here."

He dismissed this with a snort of laughter. "They are but a shadow of history, soon to be forgotten in their defeat. But you and I will go on to fight more, another battle, another day. Death is not given to those who paid the price."

All other thoughts stopped as I listened to his words. He paused at my shocked expression, smiling with an attempt to appear disarming, but a chill ran down my spine; after all of my dealings with the Being, all of my searching for answers, I had just learned I was not alone.

My mind was a sea of questions, and I floated through them, bobbing and moving as they filled my head, conjuring up fierce emotional responses; relief, skepticism, amazement, and hope all combining to fill me with an inquisitive euphoria. *"What do I ask him first? Is this even real, or some illusion conjured by the creature in the Green Halls to test me? Who is this suspiciously Mongolian-looking man in the armor of a European soldier?"*

"Am I. . . " his voice cut through my rapid thinking, ". . . the first you have seen in your journey?"

"The first what?"

"The first traveler you have seen." His voice was patient, but I could hear it thinning. He too seemed full of questions.

"Yes, I thought I was-"

"The only one," he interrupted. I nodded. "Men for thousands of years have been taken from their home and time by that demon. Some women too, though I have only met one, and she came from long after my time beneath the Great Blue Sky. I am Subutai. . . greatest of the great Genghis Khan's generals." His chest puffed with pride and he

THE | SPLIT

stood a little straighter. A mad energy shone in his eyes.

"An honor," I replied, touching my fist over my chest in what I had learned was a Mongol salute and sign of respect. "I'm Burlington. I work in an office across the sea in America, hundreds of years from now. At least I did, anyway. . ."

He smiled and pointed at the fist on my chest.

"Our salute, how did you learn this?"

"From a movie," I admitted. "But I researched it afterwards on my phone. Oh. . . movies are things you can watch in the future, and a phone-."

"I have used both," he said, cutting me off. "I have also been to this America. I fought for your George Washington on the Christian celebration day, Christ-mass."

His pronunciation of the word made me smile, he separated it into two distinct syllables and emphasized the 'mass'.

"I flew above the palm trees in your Harbor of Pearls, dog-fighting with the Japanese planes from the sun. I have had your food in the lands to your South. . . and, I dined at a wondrous hall. . . beneath golden arches. I asked for what the man in front of me did, it was. . . meat, between breading. And there were divine little, yellow strips. . . that tasted of potatoes and salt. The man in the uniform called it, 'Mc-Donalds'. It was indeed the finest fare I have ever tasted. Does this. . . McDonalds', exist during your time?"

"Yes," I laughed. "They're literally everywhere. Sounds like you have fought like this for years. This is only my third battle. . . in life I was no soldier."

All the humor left his face and it settled into a hard, angry scowl. The mad energy had never left his eyes, and they now darted back and forth

– like a twitch, as if he was watching something dangerous unfold that wasn't really there. His words gave me confidence, but every time we made eye contact I could sense the impending insanity behind his nearly battle-broken mind.

"The demon has taken everything from me," Subutai said darkly. "I surrendered what remained of my life to spare my son. . . he fell in the south of China. In my time as a commander I was never bested. . . sixty-five battles I won for my Khan. The many victories I claimed on the Mongolian fields inspired the demon to test me through all periods of time, and thus he accepted my service in exchange for my son's life. At first, I was fascinated. . . the world of the future contained miracles unimaginable. With such new discoveries, I would lead Mongolia back to our glory.

Yet I sadly discovered that my empire had fallen by the wayside. . . and then feared I had died too soon. I missed my people, the grasses like seas. . . and the feel of my horse beneath me. It was lonely to think of my wives and all of my sons. Yet my skill in battle had been retained in this strange afterlife. . . hundreds of battles have I fought as the demon watched. I soon lost all hope of returning to my home beneath the Great Blue Sky.

Many times I have tried to kill it upon his throne, when I would return, but I was stopped each time. . . the demon would hold me in the air, while it tortured my soul, and flesh. There was one time I did succeed...by dislodging a piece from one of his floating creatures, and plunging it into his leg, causing a section of its. . . skin. . . to fall off. When it landed it dissolved in front of me. He cried out with a shriek that hurled me back, and took my hearing. And then he tore at my mind, vowing that I would be punished. I was here once," he gestured around.

THE | SPLIT

"Many years ago. . . when I still walked these plains. . . I led my men against this army, surrounding their camp near the river and putting the sword to every man here. Here I have remained since, fighting in the same battle, over and over again. . . now against my own men. . . shifting from soldier to soldier in this camp, watching my own forces from the opposing side. I have not seen the demon in many years, only occasionally catching other travelers passing through."

Silence followed as I thought about this fate. This must have been what the presence had meant by punishment. Subutai's madness made sense when put into context, but more questions bubbled up from his explanation, and my mind was swimming with them. He could tell by my face that I still had much to ask him, and spoke before I could.

"You must have many questions yet, bear with me. I would first inquire of a few things. . . to understand more about you. When did you last walk this Earth? What people were you from? And finally. . . have you a belief in the divine. . . the supernatural?"

I considered his questions hastily; my curiosity was near the point of bursting, I didn't want to talk about myself. "In order," I replied. "2018, the United States of America, and no I do not."

"A quick answer!" he laughed, "All of you Americans I have met have been rather impatient. Still, each soldier I have encountered from there has fought with an admirable ferocity. It is easy to see how you brought the word 'superpower' into being. Even my largest horde and two companies of archers would fall to a single unit of your 'SEAL' warriors. . . or 'Ran-gers'. But. . . you said you were not a soldier?"

"I was at one time," I said sadly, "I was enrolled in an active army experiment, but was discharged before finishing the program. I've been in a lot of fights, and am a damn good shot though. Held up pretty good in the last two places I fought in my travels."

T H E | S P L I T

"I see."

His expression had visibly changed when I'd said I hadn't served; he'd looked, disappointed. I could feel his inner general come out and look down upon me, like he would a new recruit in life. "Well, I know much of the knowledge you seek. There will be less to explain than I have done before. Your time was nearly 1,000 standard years after my own. . . thus much of the world's advancement beyond my time are your common knowledge. Ask your questions, and I will answer them if I can."

We moved further into the shadows as I sorted as best as I could through the pile of questions that filled my mind to the brim. At last, one thing jumped out to me above all else.

"How can we talk right now? I assume you're speaking your period's dialect of Mongolian, but I'm hearing you speak in English."

"It would depend upon whom you ask," he replied honestly. "This is always the case, however. In all of my verbal exchanges. . . and even mental exchanges with my host. . . the translation is seamless. Everyone I have encountered has said their experiences were nearly entirely the same. Notice, our lips move in sync to this translation, and yet if you hold your hand to another's mouth as they speak, you can feel that your eyes betray you. Most travelers of my time and the years before me insist it is magic. . . or some extension of the divine power of this demon we all return to. The people from your time, and those from far in the future, believe it to be something more technical. I have had it explained to me as a thought modification. . . that somehow links to other minds in the area and translates actively. These pivot on the fact that we are given a new form when we travel through the Green Palace, and the belief is that each time, the Being. . . their word for the thing that summoned us. . . gives us the ability to hear and speak to people from

THE | SPLIT

whatever time and location. I believe the truth is somewhere in the middle, and have no strong opinions either way."

His train of thought paused, and I cut in, "Who is this Being?"

"That is indeed the question, yes?" he smiled. "Each has their ideas, which merely lead to more questions. I believe it to be a demon, created by mankind's barbaric actions. All of the senseless death, torture, and cold murders over millennia of war have clouded the Great Blue Sky. The worst of our offenders are sent to atone for our sins, entering the servitude of the foul creature. Yet I sense you would think differently. My near-eternal experience fighting for him has given me no more answers than you have. You would know as much as I. . . tell me, what do you believe this demon to be?"

The rumble of a procession of wagons behind us made me jump as their tires hit a patch of rocks noisily, and I paused to consider it, but I had no idea how to answer him. My only thoughts about it before had been a patchwork of comparison to various pieces of science fiction.

"It's probably an alien, or something like that." Even I could hear the uncertainty in my answer. "The Green Palace, as you call it, looks mechanical. . . almost like the inside of a strange ship. I'll bet that's where we are right now, in some simulation on a large deck in their massive ship, the size of a planet."

He nodded. "Many from your time think similarly. One of your marines once inquired whether I had seen 'Star Wars', when I asked him how such a massive ship could exist. With my admission that I had not, he mumbled something concerning a 'Star of Death' and abruptly ended our conversation. Many people from the far future, 2300, 2600, 3000 and beyond, have a far more complex view. In many of their societies, the existence of the Being is a widely known fact. They assist any travelers, and come to their aid with a reverence. Humanity of the

T H E | S P L I T

distant future attempts to understand the Being, with what resources and accounts they have. Soldiers from that time have spoken of the Creature likely being what is called 'hyper-dimensional'. . . a resident of a universe neighboring our own, able to manipulate what we perceive as time, at will. Their explanations were difficult to piece together. The manner of calculation and science common as knowledge in that period is far beyond the brightest minds of even your day."

His explanation of their theory was almost over my head, too; the knowledge of the people from the future seemed as vast as he had described. It was less than I had hoped, but more than enough to give me some level of satisfaction.

"Is this all?" he asked me, as I thought on his previous answer. "Are there no more questions? I have spent hours talking to some, yet you seem to be more assured with yourself. Confidence IS the trademark of your people and time."

"Well, no. . . " I stated. "Something strange happened to me before I came here. As I left my host, two smaller consciousnesses attached to mine and now dwell within my head."

"What did you say?" he asked, bewildered.

I repeated my answer, and then asked if he wanted to walk around the camp as we spoke. He nodded and we moved side by side through the back alleys behind tents as I retold my account. I spoke of meeting the Being for the first time, my battle in Cuba, and my coming to the future. He paid extremely close attention to my meeting of Cyrus, asking me to repeat the name twice to make sure, and as I told him more about Cy and his two soldiers his eyes lit up with recognition. I paused to ask if he knew Cyrus, but he shook his head and told me it wasn't important, so I finished my story with my memory of traveling through the strange stream of time and coming upon John and Sun.

THE | SPLIT

It had taken me hours to answer him fully, we were in now in the darkest part of the night. The sky hung like a black curtain, threatening to extinguish the small cluster of lights in the camp below. Subutai walked silently beside me, deep in thought. It had been clear on his face, as I talked of the Collective and my two visitors, that he had not heard of anything like this before.

"So. . . this Sun-Tzu you speak of, is he the same as served the King of Wu? Does he travel as well? I have read his book on war, gifted to me by Ogedei Khan himself."

"He would be pleased to hear it. However; he is a, copy, of the man history believed to be Sun Wu. His personality was constructed artificially, based off of his writings and the stories about him. Most scholars doubt his mere existence where I'm from." I paused to smile.

"What is funny?" Subutai asked, furrowing his brow.

"Sun just insisted that he **was** real and my history doesn't know what it's talking about."

Subutai laughed, caught off guard by the answer, "You can speak to him in such a way? What of the other one. . . ?" I nodded, and he continued, "What is Sun Tzu saying to you now? Does he know who I am?"

"Yes," I admitted. "He's. . . not a fan. Guess he didn't really take the whole 'invasion of southern China' thing that well, sorry."

"It is to be expected. . . though my people in his day were mere nomads, constantly beset by Chinese lords and their armies. I would say the debt has been repaid. This future business man, does he know me too?"

"He does. He said he watched some show about your conquest of Eastern Europe. The old actor who played you was a legend, and the whole thing was 'spectacular'."

He snorted with laughter, "Well good! All I did, I did for my Khan. I do not know this man, nor have I been to his time; but I know his process for deuterium in fusion reactors lasted our people for nearly a century after its discovery."

I could sense John's satisfaction, but wanted to probe Subutai on the subject further, "So in all of your battles and traveling, you've never seen anything like this?"

"No," he said flatly. "Nor have I spoken to anyone who has. I have neither heard of sharing a mind with your host. . . as you attest to having done with Cyrus. Each journey I have made. . . whether lost in the antiquity of time or soaring through the blackness of space. . . I have been in full control of the body I am in. Your account is quite strange. . . how I wish I had been there to examine it further. Still, I have indeed witnessed extraordinary things. . . I am even able to answer a question you have not thought to ask yet."

"What things, and what question?" I asked, my curiosity had returned.

"To tell you, I must show you. . . Come with me."

He led me further on between the tents, constantly choosing new paths as he moved to our east. All of the lanes looked identical, yet he directed our course with the confidence of a man that had been born in the camp, and a few moments later we stopped outside of a small and cramped pen of horses, where the skin of the large beasts seemed to be nearly connected and there was almost no room for movement in the tight space.

They snorted and twitched in irritation as Subutai crept around the side, opening the gate before grabbing the reins of the nearest horses, which were already saddled.

T H E | S P L I T

Looking back at me, seeing my massive frame, he then changed his mind and selected a much larger horse for me.

"Are you sure we can just take these?" I asked in a whisper.

"I have spent my nights in this camp, underneath these very stars, more times than I can number. Only twice have I seen a guard posted outside. . . both times sluggish with drunkenness. This is the best place to get a horse, a fast one in any event." He climbed into the saddle and I followed his lead.

It was difficult to get my large foot through the stirrup, but I eventually succeeded and climbed – slowly and carefully – onto the black charger. The horse seemed to rock with every breath, and as he started forward I grabbed the pommel of my saddle tightly to keep from falling.

Subutai laughed as he watched me. "It is said a young Mongol can ride before walking. I see that replacing the horse has made your people clumsy."

"Maybe, but we're used to much bigger rides, hundreds of times more powerful and advanced." I responded, trying to keep my tone playful. Subutai laughed again.

Soon, our slow walk through the bright lanes of the camp led us to a makeshift gate between two wagons. I felt a strange sense of nostalgia, and quickly put two and two together; the gate between the wagons was a more primitive version of the gate that had guarded the improvised camp of the 3rd Cavalry – and the Rough Riders in Cuba. I realized then that prior to the invention of armor plating, or concrete, this had probably been the best alternative, and had been handed down from generation to generation for centuries.

One of the guards at the gate stopped us, leering at us with distrust as he leaned on his spear.

T H E | S P L I T

"Where do you think *you're* going? There's to be no one going or leaving this camp until Sunrise, Marshall's orders 'imself."

"We go to hunt," Subutai replied without pause. "There is no more venison, and the cooks are already boiling the last brace of coneys. Perhaps then, you would care to explain to the Marshall why he has hungry knights, and the Nobles of Pest have gone without?"

The guard's face showed signs of hesitation as he thought this over. Subutai looked at me knowingly and flashed a quick smile; most likely the result of trying to leave the camp dozens of times, in previous battles, before finally finding the words that would work. Even in my short time in the camp I had noted the foot soldier's dislike and fear of the Knights, whom I had heard would talk pompously, ordering the other men to care for their horses and fetch them food, and their commanders.

Aside from that, there seemed to be no unity in the ranks. The nobles' men hated the King's men, the King's men hated the noble's men, and the Cumans hated everybody. Even the Templar knights, traditionally absent from resentment between armies, had it's share of resentment; we had passed stockades earlier in our walk to get me fitted and armed.

The man let us through after mulling it over. As we rode through the gate, and I followed Subutai through the clearing and towards the rolling hills in the distance, I noted the circle of trampled dirt, dead plants, and absence of animal life which ringed the camp for several miles. An army seemed to literally drain the land of its life as it passed, I had never seen anything like it.

It took us several minutes hard ride to make it to the green covering at the start of a sparse forest, where the trees began to thicken and increase in number. We rode in to the shadows, where leaves brushed against me and I could feel branches whipping past.

THE | SPLIT

In the deeper woods, roots writhed out of the ground and smaller shrubs and bushes dotted our path. We slowed our horses as we navigated through the dense brush, and soon I could hear the faint rushing of water ahead. The howl of a wolf rang through the trees, and my horse looked up, snorting nervously. I patted him on the head, whispering softly and urging him forward, until the tree line came to a sudden end as we reached the river Sajo.

Pausing, I let the horse catch his breath as I looked up and down its length. We had stopped at a narrow spot on the shore, to our south the river widened over a hundred feet. The forest continued on the other bank, like it had never ended. Hearing a splash, I turned to see Subutai standing in the water, peeling his clothes off. He turned to me when he saw me staring.

"What are you doing?" I asked. He had put his clothes in a pouch on his saddle, and now stood in his white loincloth, staring at me and smiling.

"Putting my clothes up high, so that they remain dry. Trust me. . . you should do the same."

"We are going across the river?"

"Well, unless you know of another way across? It is probable that you are in need of a bath anyway. . . all people of my time are offensive in their odor. . . especially those who ride horses."

Saying this, he urged his horse into the river and slowly started across, pulling the reins tightly. I hastened to follow his lead, putting my clothes and boots in my saddle and stepping into the river; the water was cold, I could feel its icy touch around my ankles.

When I pulled on the reins for my horse to follow however, the rope went taut and nearly slipped from my grasp. Turning, I saw him with his neck out, feet back and spread out, fighting my attempts to pull him in. I walked over to sweet talk him; that wouldn't work. So I went back into the river, leaning as I pulled the reins hard, using my massive body weight.

My muscles strained from the attempt – he was much bigger than Subutai's mount – and I could feel sweat beading on my forehead. I could also smell the earthy stench coming from my small-clothes. Subutai had been right, I did need a bath. But eventually the horse put a hoof in the water, and I was able to lead him across. The stones beneath us on the riverbed were smooth, but were still stumbling hazards; twice I felt the horse slip up, whinnying with displeasure until he regained his balance.

Once on the other side I turned to the smiling general, who was now clothed and putting on his boots. "Why did we have to cross this river? Where are we going?"

"You will know soon. . . for now, think of it as a scouting mission. . . for we go to observe our enemies camp." He was getting back onto his horse. Seconds later I was fully clothed and joined him. We rode up the small embankment, and were back in the dense forest.

My wet undergarments felt uncomfortable, soaking through my dry clothes in places; and to add to my discomfort bugs began to gather around my face, some of which were stinging me. Eager to be out of the deep forest, I focused on Sabutai in front of me and dug my heels in the charger's side.

After riding for a while he slowed his horse and gestured for me to slow my own pace. We dismounted, and soon I could see the light of distant fires shining through the trees, growing larger as we approached. Men's voices could also be heard, loud and punctuated with fits of laughter. Subutai now lowered himself to sit beneath a tree, about a stone's throw from the clearing of the camp.

T H E | S P L I T

"He will be here in just a few minutes," the general said softly.

"Who will be?" I whispered back, confused, crouching down near him.

"Soon, I will show you. Do you remember your story of seeing that Commander, Roosevelt? The man with glasses who you said became your people's president?"

"Yes. . . ?" I replied, puzzled

"This thing you saw, his face being missing. . . and your mind going dark when you neared him? This is a tale I have heard repeated by many travelers. I saw it myself. . . being curious and horrified from such a sight. Only after I was banished here did I find my answer. Come. . . quietly."

He crawled through the brush slowly. I lowered myself to join him and we slid along the leafy ground towards the sounds of the camp.

When we were just a few horse lengths away from the fire, he stopped and gestured with his hand for me to come up next to him. I slithered forward and stopped. In front of us, the grass dipped down into the clearing, and through the tall stalks we could watch the activity of the camp undetected.

The men around the fire were excited about something. A pair of them wrestled, shirtless, their long hair whipping around in the night air. A larger group of soldiers, all wearing their signature metal plate armor set in furs, watched them, drinking from crude mugs and talking excitedly. The combined noise of the festivities drowned out their words but I could hear individual phrases like 'general' and 'bridge'.

Then the men suddenly all turned to look down a lane between their tents, hollering loudly. Even the pair wrestling stopped when their onlookers yelled at them.

THE | SPLIT

A large procession was nearing our space. At its head were two matching horsemen, clad in ornate black armor with helmets that nearly covered their faces, which wore determined expressions. They kept their eyes forward even as the men around them yelled and jeered. Several more riders just like them came into view, before a group of men in brightly colored robes broke the pattern, and after them I saw the glint of gold, and turned to see a man on a bright white horse.

His adornment was simple, yet hard to look away from in the light of the dancing fire. His armor was gray, and at its edges I could see the shine of gold trimming. But, as I forced my eyes up, my body went cold; his face was missing. Not disfigured or scarred, but a blank slate of skin, exactly like Roosevelt's had been. The men circled around him, and then I could hear the muffled speech of the man with the missing face ring out through the whole clearing. It was eerie how the men responded, shouting at points and laughing at others; they could clearly hear the muffled man, just as the soldiers in Cuba had.

I heard Subutai starting to slide backwards, and he tapped me on my back to do the same. Following his lead we inched slowly back into the cover of the forest, stopping at the tree we had been leaning against moments before. I sat up, brushing the leaves off my shirt, then turned to ask Subutai, "Who was that?"

"That was me."

"You?" I replied, confused.

"Yes," he stated. "It is the real me, from when I still walked this earth, before I was cursed to fight for eternity by that foul demon."

Realization dawned on me. Had the reason I could not see Teddy been the same? "So, I couldn't see Roosevelt in Cuba-"

"Because he travels, just as you do, yes." Sabutai finished my thought.

T H E | S P L I T

XXIX

Gift from Hungarian Province, 2110
-T. Acerz, 2131

Hungary; 1241

The sound of the nearby camp grew faint as I thought on Subutai's revelation. If Roosevelt and the general still existed in history, would there not be a faceless version of me in my own time? Had he continued my life after I was taken by the Presence? But that couldn't be right; Subutai said he had been an old man when he was taken. I imagined Roosevelt had been older as well. Having read several biographies on the man, I knew he had lost several sons in America's portion of the World Wars.

We sat for a few minutes in silence against the tree trunks, but when I tried to stand up he clicked his tongue loudly and gestured for me to remain seated. I raised my hands questioningly, but he waved me off. Finally, when the noise from the camp had died down considerably, he stood up and untied his horse. I rose to my feet and did the same. When we were both on our mounts, I pulled up to his side.

"Why did we wait?"

"Patrols everywhere," he replied. "Many times have I made this trip to gaze upon my former army. After my entrance, it is necessary to count to one thousand and seventeen, in order to make it through undetected. It took me many painful deaths to figure this out."

"That's pretty specific," I said, still thinking about the scale of his knowledge.

Subutai had been here even longer than I had suspected. Knowing how to get through the guards at the camp had been one thing, knowing the exact count of the Mongol sentries movements was another entirely. "How many times have you fought this battle? Did you ever encounter yourself on the battlefield?"

"I do not know the number, but I estimate I have lived as half of the soldiers in the European camp."

"Half of the entire army?!" I was stunned.

He nodded. "From the mightiest Lords to the lowest latrine digger who raised a spear. . . and yes, I have even been the Archbishop of your Templars." He paused here. "I have tried to slay my mortal form multiple times. . . some in battle, some under the cover of night. . . from that very clearing we just left. I have sought every means imaginable to me to end my own life, hoping it would release me from this curse, yet none have been successful. Each time. . . whether it be by arrow, sword, or spear. . . I am halted, the steel mere inches from the host. . . then the battle stops, and I awake in a new body."

"What if I did it?" I said hopefully.

He shook his head, "I have tried with others, even this does not work." We rode in silence after my attempt to make idle conversation was rebuffed. The crossing of the river went quicker this time, and soon I was putting back on dry clothes over my wet ones and hopping back in the saddle.

The forest thickened and then spread out as we rode from one end to the other. Nearing the edge of the tree cover, Subutai slowed down and turned to me. "Soon we will be back, and there is a chance you will not see me again. Hungarian spear-men do not go into battle with the Knights of the Templar. Before we part, I must tell you something. Though you have seen much of our journey in your short travel, and some things even I have not, there are dangers you have yet to face."

"Like what?"

THE | SPLIT

"I was getting to this. . . patience, my tall American friend. Not everyone who fights for this demon can retain who they are. Many lose their sanity in their journey. They begin to worship the demon and the power he gives them, creating grisly scenes of carnage and horror in his name. Their minds become twisted, haunted by violence. . . obsessing over it. Once this corruption is complete, they are mindless fools, wandering through battlefields killing innocents and enemy alike. The demon then gives these soldiers great power and they use it to seek out other travelers in battle, and cause great injury. They do not relish death, but seem to enjoy inflicting pain. I have heard many a tale of travelers abducted on the battlefield, only to be tortured to death by one of these twisted souls."

My blood ran cold as he described these warriors. The possibility of an encounter like this filled me with fear, and I could feel even Sun-Wu and John reacting to the primal rush of emotion. "Have you ever fought a man like this?"

"Many times," he nodded. "Some I have killed, most I have ran away from, but a few of them have captured me. I fought in the Fall of your United States, in the streets of San Francisco. A man in the uniform of a Bloc commander pursued me, but was not a Bloc commander. He looked similar to the others I have seen, hulking and frothing at the mouth with a black foam. Eventually he pinned me to the ground, and with his bare hands. . . slowly. . . broke each series of bones in my feet, then up to my thigh. . . he snapped each of my femurs individually over his knee. I can still feel where he shattered me. . . He then ripped my legs off. . . the pain that ran through my old body. . .

I fell unconscious, but he injected me with something that immediately brought me back, and my heart began beating rapidly. Only so that he could continue. . . up my whole body, smashing each

THE | SPLIT

bone separately, and reviving me each time I fainted away. As I lie there, feeling my bones crumble inside me, he stood above me and laughed at my suffering. Then he stomped on my head. It took 5 blows to kill me... he had paused on the third to put another needle in my neck. All that was done to me occurs again in my dreams when I am unfortunate enough to fall asleep... and since that day I have never been caught by one again. Even when they come to my battlefield here, I will stab myself with a dagger if they disarm me."

His account of suffering had been vivid, and I must have worn my reaction on my face, because he smiled and said, "You will see them soon enough, I am sure. I would encounter a corrupted soldier like this every seven or eight battles it seemed, and I hear that number has gone up for others. But, you must go now." He gestured to the wide open space between the end of the treeline and camp.

"Midnight approaches, the Archbishop of your Red Cross is already leading men to the bridge, with the soldiers of the King's brother, Duke Coloman. There, they will surprise the Mongol sentries and take the bridge. They will post their own guards on this bridge, but the army will not reinforce them, believing the Mongol force in its entirety is small.

They will retake the bridge in the morning, and will attack us in the camp tomorrow. The wheeled wagon fort these Lords are so proud of will become their prison, when the fire arrows light up the tents. At some point in the afternoon, my living self's portion of the army will have built a bridge and crossed the Sajo to attack you from your flank. Good luck tomorrow, and if I do not see you on the battlefield, good luck in your journey."

With that, he nodded and turned his horse to the left, veering towards another entrance to the camp. I rode towards the direction we had come, my mind heavy with his words.

THE | SPLIT

The thought of having to deal with the constant onset of battles for as long as Subutai had described was daunting enough. Encountering these soldiers who had been corrupted by the Being somehow sounded even worse. What was the purpose for any of this? What function did imprisoning Subutai serve for the Being and his Green Halls? My mind rushed with emotion; indignation at my bondage, frustration from the questions left unanswered. What being would find the inclination or even reason to watch this on such a scale?

When I made it back to my group's section of the camp I learned that most of the men had left with Master Rembald to take the bridge Subutai had told me about. After wandering through the camp for a short while, I discovered a group of men striking smaller tents and setting up larger ones in their place. Without a word, I joined them, and for several hours I labored in silence, pulling stakes from the ground and pounding new ones in. Though I said nothing, my mind bubbled with conversation as John and Sun pitched me their ideas and thoughts on the journey so far.

Eventually, the hammer grew heavy in my weary arm, and I yawned and set it down before heading back to my tent. Geoffrey's body was much larger and stronger than my own had been, and not only his hunger and but his desire for slumber far surpassed any I had ever had.

Blinking away sleep, I removed my white tunic, then struggled with my armor for several minutes before being able to take it all off and collapse into my cot, where I fell under the spell of sleep nearly instantly, all thoughts and apprehensions melting beneath the peaceful darkness.

But after what felt like just minutes, my slumber was interrupted.

T H E | S P L I T

XXX

LGPB://mn34/con/terra/UY, 8345

(Translated)

Hungary; 1241

There was an eerie green light ringing the edges of my subconscious, and my skin also began to itch uncomfortably, like someone was holding a candlestick to it. But the outside stimuli started a train of thought that was immediately swallowed up by an unseen force. I then tried to open my eyes and rouse myself from sleep, but found no connection to my eyelids and, panicked, desperately reached for my body – an arm, a finger, anything to wake up.

I was paralyzed, fully aware in a body that wouldn't respond, but my frantic energy woke Geoffrey, and I could feel both John and Sun reacting to the disturbance as well. Then with a blinding flash of light the presence made itself known. There, in the center of my mind, was the Being; standing, knees bent slightly in a menacing pose. The image seemed to move as it shifted its weight slightly and flexed its powerful arms. It was the first time I had seen it standing.

"Subutai has learned much in his travels," it spoke, its voice a snarling roar, *"and yet he still knows nothing of consequence."*

I tried to reply, but still found all of my body frozen in place. This was no dream.

"You fight well, every thrust calculated, every movement with purpose. But you do not belong here, and this is not your fight. . . not your struggle. Your type of arrogance and pacifism made humanity weak and soft in the period you walked this planet. How could someone from a time of plenty, understand the fears and desires of someone with

so little? You think of his beliefs as primitive, and are prejudiced with clear moral hindsight. Nothing from the battle to come will affect your life or your history, yet this man you possess, this battle is everything to him. Your kind's tendency to rape and destroy upended whole kingdoms. What will he be left with in the wake of your destruction? Do you not fight for his future? He should be able to seize his own destiny, should he not?"

This was not the Being as I had last experienced. The voice was different, the sentences more complete. It seemed to be drawing upon my memories and own grasp of language to articulate so clearly.

"See the price of defiance," it continued. *"See the consequences of your rebellion, your rejection of our precious gift. We ask only one thing of you; you must not disappoint your audience."*

When it was done talking, it disappeared, fading through the darkness as quickly as it came. My mind felt alert, but I could feel the tug of sleep pulling me back into the numb silence, and time itself slipping away as I felt my awareness subside.

This time when my eyes snapped open I tried to sit up, finding it harder than I expected; I seemed to be moving at half speed. But, getting up slowly I walked across the room towards my equipment, which was propped up against a tent pole.

Just then I felt Geoffrey stir awake, and his thoughts brush against mine as without even thinking he slipped back into his body. We used his legs together, and began moving much quicker, but this gave me pause. It seemed that in order to fully use my whole range of motion at a normal speed, I would need Geoff's help; unlike with Charles, where I had seemed to retain control of our decisions and thought patterns. Having to rely on the slower man to move about might prove problematic in battle.

THE | SPLIT

Nonetheless, together with Geoff I got dressed, buckling the armor into place and slipping the Red Cross tunic over it, and as I worked I began to feel more comfortable with his input. I could sense he was becoming more familiar, as well. His emotional hold on my thoughts had grown stronger too; even now I could feel his anticipation, and fear, of the battle to come, overpowering the sense of calm I was trying to project.

His dislike for the Mongols and enemies of the Church was also powerful, sharpened and strengthened by the words of the Archbishop and Master Rembald. They had oft spoke of the treachery of the Saracens and the barbarism of the Mongol hordes, their disgust apparent through seething tones, and Geoffrey had picked up on this energy, creating a broad sense of hatred in his simple mind.

Opening the flaps of the tent I stepped outside into the morning sun, which beat down brightly. Narrowing my eyes as I waited for my vision to adjust, I saw that the camp was a blur of activity; men in Templar uniforms bustled about putting on armor and saddling horses.

"Geoffrey my friend!" I turned to see Master Rembald himself calling my name and walking my way, and touched my helmet in a salute as he approached, mimicking what I had seen other soldiers do at the sight of their officers.

"News of your miraculous healing busies tongues throughout the camp. Come, ride with me. . . I would have none else by my side on this fine day." He motioned to a large brown and white horse tied to his own.

I nodded at his words and slowly climbed into the seat of the saddle. The horse recoiled at my weight, its legs slightly sinking before it adjusted and stood straight again. "To where do we ride, Master?" I asked, curious at the hubbub of activity so early in the morning.

THE | SPLIT

"To the fields to our west... our scouts report Mongol formations nearing. It would seem they set off in the night and have retaken the bridge. Survivors from the clash report a great battalion, large enough to rival our own army, though I believe them to be delirious, and their brains sluggish from their retreat back to camp. Coloman and his Slavonians await our arrival. Come! Let us not tarry!" He untied our horses and set down the path.

I urged my mount forward and followed behind, relying on Geoffrey's steady hand and experience in the stables to supplement my poor riding skills. Glancing around the camp as we rode, I saw that hundreds of mounted men surrounded me, and behind us there were even more foot soldiers, walking with their spears up and shields ready at their sides. Within minutes we were near the front gate between the two wagons, where hundreds of Knights and other men stood nearby, waiting for us. Loud orders were exchanged between the two groups, before we fell in beside each other to pour out of the front of the camp.

Outside of its confines the mounted men began to spread out, forming a long line that stretched nearly half of the length of the large clearing. Similar lines formed behind it, and I followed a nearby Templar rider as he fell into position, settling in beside him towards the outside of the second row.

When we were lined up, we began moving forward at a brisk pace, but after few minutes the soldiers on foot behind us fell farther and farther away as we trotted forward, so we paused to let catch up. After a half hour ride, we spotted the Mongols on the distant horizon. They too rode in a line, but their formation was looser and seemed to be moving faster than we were.

We rode towards them for a few minutes until orders were shouted for us to halt, and Master Rembald rode out in front of our lines, pacing

THE | SPLIT

back and forth. "I will sound the horn to begin the charge! Your advance will cover the archers and spear-men as they move into position. There will be no retreat unless the horn sounds again! We are men of the Lord, and the Lord runs not from battles. . . He sets his enemies ablaze with his righteous fury! You have been called upon, men. . . every single one of you. . . to drive these invaders out of our lands!"

"HOOAH!" The men cheered in response to his rousing speech.

In my chest I felt a warm rush of confidence, as Geoffrey's thoughts surged with pride at Rembald's words, and – involuntarily – nearly started forward on my mount before pulling up on the reins. Geoff's excitement had brought us out of sync.

Going inside my head, I showed the simple man a collection of thoughts and images. He replied with thoughts of his own, before finally acquiescing and trusting me to guide his body.

Rembald left the front of the group and squeezed through the lines next to me. "Are you ready, Geoff?" he asked, looking up at me.

I nodded, "Let us finish this."

The Mongols were within a few hundred meters, approaching fast and growing closer with every galloping step; we stood still, waiting their charge. I felt a twinge of anticipation and, grabbing my helmet from where it hung on my saddle. I put it on, unsurprised when my vision was narrowed to thin slits, and the sounds around me became less clear in the hollow metal shell.

The war horn rang out just seconds later, and we shot forward. The lines of Calvary looked tight, with just a few feet between each horse both in front and back. The horses were well trained, keeping their distance from one another and staying in their lines. The Mongol line was now dead ahead, and I hastily pulled a poleaxe from my back, chastising myself for not doing it sooner.

THE | SPLIT

The Knights in front of me exchanged sword blows with their Mongolian counterparts as the two groups of horses in front collided in a deafening crash, the sounds of steel hitting steel. Horses whinnying in fear, and the pained cries of men, all rang out at once. Moments later, in the middle of the clash, a group of horses lay on the ground twitching, their riders desperately trying to free themselves from under the weight of their mounts, and I jerked my horse to the right to avoid crashing into them.

Rembald had done the same. I followed his horse around the right flank, digging my heels into the side of my mount to keep up, and just then, out of the corner of my left eye-hole, saw a Mongol rider coming straight for me. Tugging the reins slightly and adjusting my course to meet him head on, I lowered my poleaxe into the jousting position – as I had seen in movies.

The spear caught him in the chest, between a grouping of metal plates in his armor, and his eyes grew wide as the saber slipped from his grasp. As he slumped down in his seat, another rider behind him saw me and set off towards me at a gallop. When I pulled at the ax stuck in the man's chest, his horse shot forward in a panic and it slipped from my grasp, but I grabbed the pole's shaft near the exit of his wound as the horse passed me, pulling it through his body and back to my side.

It was now slick with blood, and nearly slipped from my grip again, and I had to hastily wipe it against my tunic; the next rider was just feet away. He swung at my horse's head with his saber, but I caught the blow with the head of my poleaxe, and threw his blade to the side, then unsheathed my sword and before he could react rode forward, driving the point through his throat. His mount reared up as he fell, but I pulled my sword free, sliding it back into its scabbard and again gripping my poleaxe tightly.

THE | SPLIT

Looking around the battlefield I saw Master Rembald to my right, several horse lengths away, locked in stationary combat with a Mongol rider. Behind him, another rider neared, his saber held high for a killing blow, and a feeling of desperation surged through my body as Geoff saw his friend in trouble. On his own he dug my heels into the side of the large brown and white horse and we darted forward.

Approaching as the rider was just seconds away from Rembald, I leaned forward on my mount, letting the forward motion drive the tip of my spear through the man's back, then jerked on the reigns for my horse to come to a stop. Having just beaten his foe, Rembald whirled around, looking at me wide-eyed as I pulled my ax free of the man I had just saved him from.

He was nodding his thanks when his face turned in surprise and he cried out, "Geoff watch out!" pushing past me to my left. I turned to see a Mongol rider feet away, his horse at a full sprint. Having no time to react, the other horse crashed into the side of mine and sent me flying backwards off my mount and tumbling through the air.

I landed on my back, hard. My helmet slammed into the solid earth as I slid backwards, leaving me dizzy, my vision went blurry and the sounds of the battle around me became dull and muffled. But nothing felt broken and, putting my hand down to push my body upwards, I flexed my legs and arms. I had been stunned, nothing more. Slowly I climbed to my feet, still feeling the battle spinning around me as I focused on standing up straight.

Several meters away I saw my horse, lying on its back, legs bent and twisted grotesquely and screaming out in pain. My own legs still adjusting from my fall, I stumbled over to it, and in one clean thrust I drove my poleaxe through its neck to end its suffering. It took one last breath and then stilled, dark eyes staring at the skies above.

THE | SPLIT

The battle seemed to be going well as I surveyed the field. The Mongols were beginning to break ranks and retreat back in the direction they came. Some of the men let out cheers – but they were short lived. Then a man near me gasped as he pointed towards the West.

I turned to follow his finger and my blood ran cold; thundering towards us was a *massive* column of Mongol riders, just a few hundred meters away.

Suddenly I saw Rembald ride into view, in front of our mounted Knights. "Regroup!" he shouted, his voice sounding hoarse from yelling. "Fall back into position, protect our crossbows!"

I turned to see the foot soldiers nearing us, moving quickly but retaining their rank and file. On the other side of our lines I could hear the Duke's captains repeating the same orders. The Knights fell back into a defensive position around our newly arrived reinforcements and I scrambled to follow them, running as fast as I could in the extra weight of my armor; without my mount I felt vulnerable.

When I did arrive to join the group I found a spot behind the line of Knights and stood with my poleaxe at the ready. The Mongols were close now, within seconds they would be upon us.

"Fire!" came an order from somewhere behind me.

I heard a swarm of bolts pass overhead, then the wave fell into the Mongol ranks. Men and horses alike fell all across their front line, which slowed but was not stopped. The spaces where their men had fallen were quickly swallowed up by the riders next to them. At the top of the hill in the distance, the Mongols continued in our direction, wave after wave riding towards us.

Then a massive volley of arrows came from the middle of the swarm of riders, climbing high into the sky before arcing downwards and falling through our group by the hundreds, littering the ground below and tearing knights from their mounts.

Quickly, I turned my back to the volley and crouched, covering my head. I felt an arrow slam into my back, painfully bending the links on my mail, but not penetrating through. A man next to me then cried out in shock, and I turned to see a shaft protruding from his shield. The tip of the arrowhead had gone through the thin wood and now pierced the center of his hand, pinning it to the shield.

Slowly, I turned from him and got up. The Mongol riders in front continued to press forward, and I heard Master Rembald's voice over the crowd urging us to do the same. The Knights charged, I let them get a few lengths ahead before following with the rest of the foot soldiers.

The initial contact between the new wave of riders lacked the explosiveness it had the first time. The Mongol line buckled in the center as our Knights approached it, then riders from their flanks spread out away from the clash and rode forward in a wide sweep, right towards the mass of foot soldiers I was a part of.

'They're trying to surround us. . . ' I thought worriedly, breaking into a sprint for our outside right.

A lot of them had already passed by the time I made it to the side, and now rode behind me, weaving through our archers and slashing savagely at anyone in their path.

When they had gotten far enough away, I turned my back to them and stood staring at the thin column of riders pouring from the sides of the clash in front. But now, a rider in a dark fur helm barreled towards me, his attention focused on the pike-men and crossbowmen to my left.

Planting my feet, I held my poleaxe at the ready, tip pointed towards him. When he got within a few feet, I jabbed upward and caught him beneath the belly. The shaft of the ax bent wildly as the man's horse

THE | SPLIT

kept moving from under him and he dangled in the air, impaled on my blade, then, SNAP!

The wooden handle cracked in half under the strain, stinging my hands even through my thick leather gloves as it flew from my grasp. But more riders were heading towards me, and with no time to waste I unsheathed my sword and pulled another poleaxe from the loop on my back.

'One ax left after this,' I thought darkly as my grip tightened around each weapon. As the first rider came near, I ducked beneath his saber and swung with my sword at the horse's legs. Hot blood spurted from the deep cuts I made, and I could hear the horse crash to the ground even as I looked up to see a second rider.

This one fought more cautiously, standing still and turning his horse in circles as he hacked at me with his saber. I parried and blocked with both my sword and ax, but he was quick. Every time I stopped a blow he urged his horse forward, its hooves getting nearer to stepping on me with every swing.

As we exchanged blows for what seemed like hours, I could feel my shoulders aching, and my neck hurt from looking up at the man in his saddle. Out of the corners of my helmet's eye slits, I saw the battle around me. We were nearly surrounded. The Mongol raiding party had become a horde in just minutes, and they were now over double our numbers.

My struggle had brought me far outside the right flank, meaning it would take me several seconds at a full sprint to make it back, and my opponent showed no signs of slowing.

I would have to find a way to finish this quickly and rejoin the group. I caught a downward slash and countered with one of my own, he blocked it, turning his horse to the left and swinging down again.

T H E | S P L I T

As I watched the horse move, I noticed the large space between its legs and formed a plan. His next swing I deflected – and then threw myself to the ground shoulder first, quickly rolling beneath the horse and popping up on his opposite corner. As he turned to face me I thrust the point of my poleaxe into his mount's soft belly; the blade seemed to disappear as it sunk deeper and deeper. The horse let out a shrill cry of pain and sunk to the ground. The rider swung at me with his sword, but I batted it away with my covered forearms and drew my sword, slashing the blade at his neck.

Geoffrey's hatred and blood-lust suddenly filled my brain, and the thin cut I had planned to make across the man's throat became a nasty gash. Unbidden, my right hand flew up and grabbed the back of his head, and my left pushed down with the blade.

The dying man's breath came in gurgling gasps as I pushed the sword deeper, soon hitting bone, then yanked on the Mongol's head savagely, able to feel Geoffrey bubbling with glee inside as it came loose from the body and blood spilled everywhere, spraying out in warm streams. I raised the head high into the sky, and together me and Geoff let out a savage war cry.

Templar and Mongol alike turned at the sound of my voice, but I charged back into the fray, making quick work of the unhorsed enemies pressing towards our center, hacking and jabbing in a flurry of steel. The edges of my vision grew red as I continued my rampage. I could see above the battlefield from my height, and my sheer bulk was enough to trample anyone who got in my way.

Dozens of soldiers fell to my blades. I didn't seem to be making a dent in their numbers, however. During a brief break in the action, I glanced around quickly; there wasn't a Templar in sight. Any red crosses I saw nearby were buried below piles of bodies.

THE | SPLIT

Then from far behind our lines I caught a glimpse of the remainder of our army, now in full sprint towards the camp, and now the war horn sounded, signaling our retreat.

I took one last look at the waves of enemies in front of me, and turned back towards camp, beginning to run as the horn sounded a second time. Arrows whizzed past me as the Mongols kept up their pursuit. My body felt exhausted, but I was wired with a strange energy that was urging my pace forward, faster than I had ever run. I had felt adrenaline in the past, but never like this. My whole body felt a tingling numbness and my brain was focused like never before.

THE | SPLIT

XXXI

Acquired through auction By A. Fila, 2078
Bought from A. Fila's Estate, 2105
-T. Acerz, 2131

Hungary; 1241

'They should've caught us by now,' I thought as I turned around curiously.

The nearest riders were a few horse lengths behind, moving at a brisk pace but not trying to catch up to me or my fleeing comrades. I'd caught up to the main group of Templars, but soon regretted it; after wave of arrows now shot out from the enemy column, and the men around me began to fall one by one from the deadly storm of bow fire. One of the arrows struck my helmet as I ran, and the loud clanging reverberating inside my helm pushed me to move even faster.

The front gate of the camp was now in view, and I could hear audible gasps of relief around me as the others saw it too. When I got within a few hundred meters, the arrows suddenly stopped. I could hear the sounds of the Mongols hoof-beats fading into the distance, and finally slowed my pace by a fraction. But once inside the gate, I was shocked to see the men in the camp still dressing and preparing, shouting over each other as they moved about frantically.

Then a loud commotion rang out to my right, and I saw the Archbishop standing above the crowd on a wagon, a look of cold fury on his face. Across from him stood a portly man in red robes, with a large golden crown covering his thick mane of brown hair.

It was King Bela; there was no other possibility. He stood staring back at the Archbishop, running his fingers through his long scraggly beard.

THE | SPLIT

Guards in ornate armor stood around him, hands on the hilts of their swords.

"Where are your men?!" the Archbishop shouted indignantly. "Your brother's army lies in ruins, and you tarry at the camp, waiting?!"

"My soldiers shall stand ready soon. I gave the order just moments ago and-"

"JUST MOMENTS AGO?!" The Archbishop interrupted, incredulous. "Surely your scouts sent you word of our siege! Our enemies surround us, and you leap to act with less haste than a slug trapped in oil! My foolish and slothful King, your actions may have doomed us all. I will see you on the battlefield!"

And with that the Archbishop stepped down from the wagon and shuffled off with a group of Templars. The King looked about sheepishly, clearly embarrassed from the Bishop's harsh words, then gestured to his guards and they too stepped down from the platform. As they all disappeared inside a nearby tent, a great thirst suddenly filled me. My throat burned every time I swallowed, and I could feel myself growing hoarse. Thus I took off through the camp to look for water, searching from tent to tent, and finding nothing; all of the food and wines from the night before were nowhere to be found.

Finally, I came upon a large wooden tub near a horse pen with water inside it. It looked brown and murky, filled with dirt and horse spit, but I didn't care; dropping to one knee I cupped up the water greedily, taking long gulps without pausing for air. There seemed to be no taste as I continued drinking, yet my throat felt better and my thirst soon subsided.

Now walking back to the lane between the tents, I looked for any of my fellow Templars, and listened for news of the battle outside. A column of green-clad Knights came thundering by, nearly trampling me

THE | SPLIT

in their haste and forcing me to leap out of the way at the last second, followed by men in similar uniforms, who came sprinting after them, the tips of their spears bobbing in the air above.

As I walked around I noticed many other lines of soldiers hustling every which way, while the men still putting on armor were chastised for their slow pace. Loud captains ran between the tents, beating any remaining men with the flat of their swords and yelling for everyone to get to their positions.

I made my way to the gate I had come in through earlier, and could see long columns of Knights and foot soldiers huddled around the entrance, talking quietly. The King stood above on a wagon nearby, ready to speak to the gathered men.

"Duke Olsen here," he clasped a nearby man by the shoulder, "has volunteered to lead the charge to our West. All Cuman riders are to accompany him, as will a portion of my own Knights. The Templars. . . and my brother Coloman's men. . . will remain behind with my own army, guarding the rear and ready to provide reinforcements. There are reports from my scouts of men in the woods to our North, but we have far greater numbers, and through God himself we will prevail!"

The men gave a weak cheer as the King turned and was helped down from the wagon, appearing to be breathing heavily, as if just the speech itself had tired him. It was clear from his rich red robes and lack of armor that he had no intention of taking part in today's battle.

The Duke stepped down from the wagon as well, mounting his horse before riding to the front of his men, then the Knights led the way as he began to move the large column of men through the makeshift gate.

Outside the wall of wagons, I could hear the approach of the Mongol army, and climbed atop a nearby crate to look out into the field to the

T H E | S P L I T

west. The group that had attacked us near the bridge was enormous. Thousands of riders and other soldiers were massed just a few hundred meters from our camp. The Duke and the rest of his men heading out to meet them numbered nearly as many, but were still outnumbered.

From a cursory glance around the whole area, the ratio looked about 2 to 3 their favor. I saw Master Rembald and the other Templars gathered around the Archbishop, walking back into the camp, and hopped down on the ground to follow, running through the tents as fast as I could. In a few brief seconds I had joined the back of the group, but was suddenly aware of my fatigue now that my adrenaline was slowing.

My helmet felt heavy in my arms, and I nearly dropped it as I adjusted my grip. But as I caught it, I saw the flicker of flame to my left. Turning to face it, confused, I noticed an arrow sticking out of a nearby tent – fire around the shaft; in seconds it had spread to the tent wall, setting the whole square of canvas ablaze.

To my right, I heard another arrow land and looked to see another flame on a nearby barrel, and still it took me a few seconds to piece together what was happening, but then I glanced up to see that the sky above was clouded with hundreds of tiny flickering lights, barely noticeable in the midday sun before they turned in the air and began to fall into the camp, dozens at a time.

Tents, wagons, and crates alike were soon ablaze. The men began to call out to each other in confusion as the flames leapt to life. Again the Mongols to our west fired, the sky turning bright with flaming arrows as they continued their assault. The camp was in full panic, soldiers with jugs of water and full cups of wine ran about frantically, trying to quell the flames, but for every one they put out, two would pop up nearby. Fire had begun to spread through the lanes between tents, and patches of grass all through the area were alight, narrowing the small roadway.

THE | SPLIT

A group of wagons, turned sideways and covered in orange fire, was blocking our path to the east, I could feel the heat standing several horse lengths away. As the Templars around me moved away from them and went down a nearby lane to our North, a hand clasped around my shoulder and shook me harshly. I whipped around to see Master Rembald looking up at me, and the Archbishop standing a few meters behind.

"Put that helmet on, soldier! Another horde approaches from our north, we must be ready to ride out and meet them!"

I nodded and put my helmet on slowly as the Archbishop moved to the front of the group and led us towards the North gate, then a loud, jarring crash sounded to my right, and I turned to see a smashed wagon with a large stone sitting in the middle of the wooden wreckage.

Similar sounding crashes could be heard behind me, and as I now looked above I saw large rocks soaring through the air between the flaming arrows. Men were huddled around the North entrance when we arrived, but arrows were beginning to fall from that direction as well, and the tents all around us were bright with flame. Even the wagons at the gate were on fire.

I could see above the crowd that the men near it were trying to back away, but the men at the back pushed forward desperately, trying to flee the inferno of the camp. We stood back from the group near the gate, and I could see Master Rembald walking about the area quickly, looking for a way around the mass of panicked soldiers.

Then a brown streak, above the commotion, suddenly caught my eye. A was man running above the camp, from tent to wagon, jumping about nimbly, never upsetting the cloth on the tents or toppling the supplies atop the wagons, even leaping through one flaming tent like it wasn't on fire at all.

THE | SPLIT

As he got closer to the gate, he turned and I could see him for a brief instant. Subutai? The man was focused, his eyes narrowed, his face hard to make out, and he soon turned away from me, hopping out of the camp and into the battlefield outside.

Nearby, a tent crashed to the ground, sending sparks and tiny globs of flame into the patch of grass below. The soldiers at the back began to push harder, and I watched as men trampled each other trying to move out of the gate.

A man atop a wagon hopped down into the lane, screaming into the camp for anyone to hear. "Rider's approach! Prepare to defend the camp!" He repeated his message again and again but it seemed to fall on deaf ears.

Then a stone crashed into a wagon just meters ahead, and Rembald sprinted over to it, motioning for the rest of us to follow. I turned to walk his way, grabbing a nearby poleaxe from an overturned wagon. There was still one on my back, but I didn't want to take chances.

Several meters away, Rembald stood at the base of the smashed wagon – the catapult had driven the stone straight through the center frame, collapsing everything above the wheels – and with a leap hopped onto it, stepping down on the other side and drawing his sword. The soldiers behind him hastened to follow his example.

Even the Archbishop himself and his procession of holy men stepped onto the battlefield, and within a few short minutes we were all on the other side, rushing out to meet the line of Mongol riders who sped towards the gate.

The men in front were swallowed up by the mass of dark soldiers on horseback, I tightened my grip on my poleaxe. A rider in red and black furs spotted me and turned his horse to charge, but his eyes widened in surprise as I ran right towards him.

T H E | S P L I T

At the last second he tried to jerk the reins off to the side, but the tip of my spearhead caught him in the stomach. He writhed in his saddle as I pulled the blade out, and without thinking I pushed him off the mount and grabbed the bridle, but the horse suddenly tried to rear up on its back legs and I had to pull down with all my strength.

Unsure, I turned my thoughts to Geoffrey. It took him a second to respond – his thoughts were consumed with the heat of battle – but he confidently pushed my legs forward so I could climb into the saddle. I could see the battle around me from a much better view atop the mount. To my left, a line of Mongols pressed towards the gate, hacking and jabbing at the Templars who stood in their way, driving their horses forward, trampling the men closest to them as they drove us back.

I turned towards them, digging my heels into the sides of the horse to urge it onward. The smallish black horse breathed heavily as it ran, and I could feel its legs trembling at my weight; it was smaller even than my mount from earlier, and as heavy as I was, I was even more weighted with my mail and weapons. Setting my sword between my legs, I thrust my poleaxe towards the mass of Mongol riders with both hands, capturing them completely unawares on their left flank.

The first turned to me in shock as the point went through his side, but I pushed through further, holding the axe by the end of its shaft as the spear-tip pierced another man to his right. When their bodies slumped together, helmets touching as the second man went limp and nearly fell from his saddle, I pulled the handle back towards me with a sharp tug; blood and chunks of gore spraying from the fresh wounds I had just made.

Hearing a fierce cry to my right I turned to see another rider charging in my direction, and with both hands still around the pole I swung it over my head in a downward arc.

THE | SPLIT

The head of the ax smashed against the side of the rider's helmet, splitting the metal where I struck, and he let out a wailing moan as blood poured from his mouth and he fell from his horse. I looked around wildly, overcompensating for my lack of vision in the restricting helmet.

Many of the Mongols had dismounted. A large stack of bodies, both man and horse, lay several meters from the camp entrance. Most of the remaining Templars had gathered around it, defending the gate from waves of Mongol swordsmen, but I was not the only one still in the field. I could see men in red crosses scattered about the area, swords a blur of motion as they tried to turn the tide.

With most of the enemy continuing towards the camp on foot, I pressed my advantage, going to the aid of a nearby group of comrades surrounded by enemy sabers. Running over a man in front with my horse, I then dispatched the rest with a combination of sword and ax, the weapons feeling weightless in my hands as I swung them down repeatedly, the blows cracking bone and splitting leather armor with ease.

My adrenaline had returned in full force, an even greater strength than usual filled my massive seven foot frame. This time, flight was not an option.

Out of nowhere I felt my horse tipping to the left. As he sank to his knees I jerked my leg up before he fell on top of it, and staggered off the beast's back, looking at it to find two arrows sticking from its chest. Fire arrows were still pouring into the camp, and to my far north I spotted the lines of Mongol archers, lighting the tips of their arrows in nearby braziers, loosing them, then repeating the process. But they were too far away to reach, especially as the Mongol army continued to send riders and other soldiers towards the camp by the hundreds.

THE | SPLIT

A blow to my right suddenly sent me staggering, and I dropped my poleaxe in order to catch myself from falling flat on my face. Then a sword slammed into my back even as I tried to regain my footing and pick up my axe, knocking me back down to the ground and splitting my mail in several places.

I rolled away, sword drawn, looking up at my attackers; a dozen or so Mongol footmen were directly above me, moving together like a single unit, in close proximity.

Desperate to create space and get back to my feet, I swung at the man who had stepped away from the group to pursue when I tried to scoot backwards. He stepped back to avoid my slash, but then pressed forward, the rest of his group beside him. Where was my ax? I had little hope to defeat this many men with my sword alone. The soldiers were bearing down on me now, their footsteps outpacing my short crawling strides, so I stopped and faced my aggressors, raising my sword; it would all be over soon.

But to my surprise, a dark shape crossed my line of vision. It was a man in a brown uniform. The newcomer swung his saber forward, slicing the two Mongols in front across their throats then, never stopping his swing, turned his sword into a downward slash, denting the helmet of the next soldier. The startled Mongols moved quickly to try and surround my mysterious savior.

With his back still turned to me, he engaged the men on both his left and right, his blade darting between both lines of enemies in a dazzling display. They kept moving forward, trying to encircle him, but never got the chance, he dispatched them quicker than they could even move. The last five men in the small unit fanned out around him and all attacked at once, trying to overwhelm him with their numbers, but the man in the brown uniform was the best swordsman I had ever seen.

THE | SPLIT

The first two men fell to their knees instantly, while the other three were suddenly missing hands and looked down at their bloodied stumps in horror. His saber moved faster than my eye could follow. The only thing I was able to make out was the damage he left behind. In two powerful slashes, he had beheaded both groups. Then slowly, he turned around to face me.

"Subutai!" I exclaimed. He smiled, put his finger to his lips, and charged forward towards the advancing army, disappearing into the sea of men. With a glance around, I saw my poleaxe laying on the ground a few meters away, and cautiously moved over to pick it up, choking the grip; holding the axe this way made it only a little longer than my sword. With the shortened length I could swing it much faster, and with more strength than before.

Men passed me on all sides in their rush to the North gate as I moved through the ranks of oncoming soldiers. Turning to face the onslaught like a rock in the middle of a coursing river, I swung my weapons around savagely, dealing death with blow after blow, until my axe head grew slick with blood, sending droplets flying with each strike.

A large Mongol approached me, wielding a saber in each hand and swinging them both. I let one pass by, then caught the other with the head of my poleaxe, swiping sideways with my sword has hard as I could when he raised his blades to strike again. The blade cut through his neck like paper, briefly hit something solid through the middle, then came out the other side. His body dropped, the head rolling into the oncoming swarm of soldiers. I looked down at my sword to see a small chunk missing towards the top of the blade, it had chipped on the man's spine. The whole edge looked worn and weak.

A dozen or so meters in front of me, a group of men walked towards the camp and, though the soldiers around them moved quickly, they

THE | SPLIT

kept forward at a steady pace, unsheathing their swords and readying themselves for combat. Those around the edges of the group wore black from head to toe, and their ornate armor gleamed in the light of the afternoon sun, with helmets on which black, intricate masks wore a solemn and unchanging expression.

In their center was General Subutai. The gold trim from his breastplate caught my eye as I examined the procession, but this man was no friend to me; even from my distance I could see the lack of features on his blank face. The Subutai who had journeyed with me the night before was nowhere to be found; the General before me was his real-time counterpart, and the men in the dark masks around him seemed to be his guards. They kept a tight formation, and responded to any movement nearby, even if it was another Mongol soldier.

Recalling what had happened on San Juan Hill with Roosevelt, I knew I had to keep my distance and took a few steps backwards, giving General Subutai and his followers a wide berth. When they were just a hundred meters from the camp, the guard force split in half, a handful staying behind with the general and the others moving forward at a quicker pace.

A large crash sounded from the camp, and I whirled around to see that the gate had collapsed; the two wagons had been burnt nearly to ashes, leaving a wide opening. Dozens of Knights and foot soldiers rushed onto the battlefield, and I saw my Templars moving up near my position, but looked at our reinforcements with doubt, thinking; *'It's not enough. . .'* and felt a wave of hopelessness wash over me.

But then Geoffrey's anger steeled my resolve, and I turned back to face the enemy. A short, sweaty man in a dirty Templar tunic shot past me, and I watched as one of Subutai's guards, now just meters away, raised his sword in challenge.

THE | SPLIT

    The dirty man swung clumsily, trying to catch the black clad guard with a diagonal slash. The armored man countered easily, and when the Templar tried again he caught the blow near the hilt and flicked the sword from his hands. In a brief second of panic my comrade looked up, before the guard in the mask drew his saber across his throat and pushed his body aside.

    I looked around. General Subutai was a ways ahead to my right, and it seemed unlikely we would near each other on his present course. So, swinging my axe and sword around nimbly, I stepped towards the black-masked warrior.

    We made eye contact and he raised his sword, inclining his head before taking a fighting stance. I swung with the sword in my left hand at his head, he caught my strike on his own sword and turned his helmet to the side to avoid the thrust of my spear point. Spinning to his right, I brought both of my weapons down at the same time. Again he caught my sword but the poleaxe slipped by and slammed against his chest, it's head making contact with the steel plate and bouncing away.

    While the wooden shaft still shook from the contact, and vibrations stung my hand as I tried to steady the weapon, he took the offensive in a dazzling flurry of blows, his blade moving almost too fast to see. I blocked several strikes with my ax and sword, but he at last hit my helmet right beneath my cheek, with enough force to cave-in the plate siding and tear a gash as the metal was pushed inside. I cried out in pain as the jagged edge cut into my face, but still jabbed at him with my ax.

    He sidestepped my blow and brought his saber down on the wooden shaft, cracking the weapon in two, continuing to swing at my head. I stepped back, blocking with the shattered half of my poleaxe and trying to reach for the last one on my back, but he saw this and swung at my right side, forcing me to again block with both hands. Whipping his saber around at dizzying speeds, he hacked at my legs and chest then, after a quick thrust, pulled out of the move and swung his saber at my side with both hands. The blade split my mail on contact, its broad edge slicing into my side, and pain shot from the cut, radiating through my whole body.

But when he reached with his left to shove me back, then raised his saber above his head for the killing blow, in that moment I lurched forward and ducked under his blade, grabbing him in a tight bear hug. Dropping my sword, I plunged the jagged edge of what was left of my poleaxe into his back, making him gasp in surprise then, pulling the wooden handle back out, I stabbed him again repeatedly, until I felt him slump against me as life left his body. After shoving his limp form to the ground, my mouth opened, and Geoffrey let out an indecipherable shout. When I tried to stop he fought against me, resulting in a strange sort of half scream.

As the Mongols continued to press the attack, I could hear shouting a few meters away, then heard my name; "Geoffrey!" and looked around for the source. A pair of Templars to my right were locked into a struggle with a whole group of Mongol swordsmen.

"GEOFFREY!" The voice was closer. As I turned to face it, something crashed into me and I raised my sword in alert, but lowered it when I saw Master Rembald's face. He was hunched over and out of breath, resting his hand on my shoulder. Two arrows stuck out of his side, and his armor was covered in dark red blood.

"Master Rembald-" I started.

"Quiet soldier!" he interrupted me loudly, each of his breaths sounding pained. "We. . . have, lost this battle. . . we must, move. . . back to camp!"

THE | SPLIT

"But-" I protested.

"WE MUST RETURN TO CAMP!" he cut over me again, shouting. "I fear. . . I shall not return. . . but you and the others. . . must get the Archbishop. . . to safety."

"Yes sir," I nodded, grudgingly.

"Good man. . . and-" Rembald was cut short as a Mongol soldier came behind him and sliced him open in one swift stroke of the saber. The Master's eyes clouded and he stumbled to the ground.

"NO!" me and Geoffrey cried out in unison as we watched him fall. The Mongol behind him stepped closer to me, sword at the ready. I kicked out, catching him in the center of his chest and knocking him flat on his back, then sank to one knee on top of him and with both hands drove my sword through his exposed face. The blade sank through the soft flesh and into the ground beneath before I pushed his head down and pulled it back out.

I could see the Archbishop as I stood, several meters behind me and surrounded by several Templar guards who were looking around the battlefield, but when I turned to run towards them I felt my feet drag at the effort. Geoffrey was fighting me, trying to turn back around, and my body was caught at a standstill with our opposing efforts.

In frustration I reached for his thoughts; intense sorrow flooded my mind as I saw his sense of shock and loss for the fallen Master. He then showed me an image of the body behind me, and another of himself hauling bags of feed to the stables.

'He wants me to carry Rembald back to camp,' I realized. Left with no choice, I bent down and scooped up the fallen man, hanging his body over one of my broad shoulders. Geoffrey was satisfied, and let me move forward towards the Archbishop and his guards.

T H E | S P L I T

The Archbishop was surprised to see me, and motioned for his men to let me through. "The man of the miracle, himself!" he mused, his spirits unusually high for the circumstances. "The Lord himself moves through you, what a wonderful testament to his power in such dark times! Tell me, have you seen Master Rembald?" I turned to show him the face of the body on my back, and his face twitched with sadness. "Ah. I see. . . such a mighty warrior. His soul is in paradise now."

I nodded impatiently. "We must see you to safety, Archbishop. . . the Master's dying order. . . " The Archbishop agreed, and called to the men around him to follow closely.

We picked the side with more of our own men for our walk back, but even so the fighting was fierce. The wound on my side throbbed with every step, my legs felt weak as the Master's body weighed on my shoulders, and a stabbing pain on my face reminded me of the blow to my helmet earlier. I sheathed my sword to try to remove it, pulling up from the top, but the jagged edge ran against my cheek, digging even deeper, and warm blood ran down my face, so I stopped pulling and tried to focus on the camp ahead.

XXXIII

LGPB://mn34/con/terra/XC, 4481
All native dialogue translated

Nagoya, Japan; 2029

"Hey asshole, pay attention!" A rough hand grabbed me by the shoulder and shook me back to reality. I looked up to see a short man in a crisp black suit glaring at me, an empty cup in his outstretched hand. I lowered it near the large glass bowl in front of me, taking the provided ladle and filling the cup with eggnog. The white liquid smelled strange as I brought it back up and handed it to the man; here in Nagoya, they liked eggnog during the holiday, but preferred to use Saki over the drink's traditional mixers. Back in the states, that combination was called a *"Nagasaki"*, but I dared not repeat that here.

The next man stepped up and I filled his cup too, the process mechanical to me as I went down the line. Looking around the room, my eyes settled on Meela behind the sushi table. She caught my glance for a short moment, before looking away to smile at a man in front of her picking out the rolls he was going to eat.

The house was like something out of a movie. Painted scenes of women in geisha dress and dragons slithering around symbols were in nearly every corner. The walls were thin, white, and paneled, attached to wide open doorways left open with wooden sliding doors. The floor matched the shade of wood from the doors and was lain in symmetrical panels running parallel to the doorway outside. Boss Kagawa had spent a good deal of his personal fortune on restoring his Oceanside ancestral home to its classical look yet, despite how it appeared in the main room, there was still work to be done.

T H E | S P L I T

I looked to the other servers and workers manning the line of food and drinks. We formed a stark contrast to our patrons, not only because we were dressed like the help and the whole room was wearing suits, but also because we were an all-white crew serving an all-Japanese room.

Boss Kagawa was a man with an inherited sense of vengeance. Like his father, and his father's father before him – who had fought American soldiers on the beaches of the Pacific – he possessed a deep-seated hatred of Western culture. Things had changed during the last century, so now Kagawa himself expressed his resentment in more subtle ways.

The Boss enjoyed white women; whether they were willing or not. He also loved to hire white laborers and other workers to serve at his house, as a means of further degradation. It had worked for years, but today would prove to be his undoing.

Like I had feared for years, ACE was in trouble. Following a contract on behalf of the Russian government targeting NATO operatives, the United States intelligent services finally struck back. We were chased out of the country, and for a year, had been reduced to taking international contracts from a decentralized mission base. Our pool of clients had evaporated, and ACE was considering pursuing suicidal, dangerous bounties, as with the one name being whispered among the group; Maddox Hill.

The former doctor and director of several TED talks had become unhinged after his near fatal accident a decade ago. 'Done' with curing diseases, Maddox had instead begun drawing out latent genes by testing restructuring techniques, on thousands of government prisoners. He was now considered a 'genetic terrorist', the first to ever legitimately exist, and was defining the term even more as he continued to operate.

T H E | S P L I T

He had since then spent several extended periods living in countries with questionable military intentions, continuing his research at an accelerated pace – and was also now number one on Interpol's most wanted. The $115 million bounty was alluring. The rumor was that he was holed up in North Korea, breeding new types of soldiers.

We had been looking into it since arriving relatively nearby in Japan. I found it slightly amusing to be thinking about killing a scientist that I had watched hours of footage on in my past life, but Corbin and I were resolute; we were going to do one more job after this, then get out of the business for good, and despite Meela's objections, I planned on going through with it.

Recently, in the last few weeks, ACE decided it would defy the American government, and reopened shop in Brooklyn under a front. Meela and I had taken this as a sign that the end was near, and moved out of our house in Poughkeepsie indefinitely, coming here to Japan to kill two birds with one stone.

"Yes, she is very pretty, no?" a booming voice came from the other side of the line.

I looked over to see Kagawa and a pair of his underlings sneering at a dark haired server. She smiled back uneasily, then flinched as the boss grabbed her by the arm and pulled her from her spot behind the serving table.

The other guests seemed to take no notice as he dragged her out of the room, leaving his two men to stand guard in front of a side hallway. Each of the men at this party was a killer, some of the highest ranking members and most loyal soldiers in Kagawa's family of Yakuza. They all seemed excited to be there; it wasn't everyday that the Boss invited you to his personal residence for a Christmas party.

THE | SPLIT

In the background, "Jingle Bells" was playing with the words sung in Japanese, which felt like too festive of a song for the dark atmosphere of the room. I looked over at Meela again, a pair of party-goers were staring at her and talking among themselves quietly, but the Boss had expressed interest in her earlier, and it was doubtful that they would try anything for that fact alone.

In the past few years, Meela's skills had done nothing but improve, so I wasn't scared of the Boss trying to take her into a backroom, in fact it was just the opposite. She had a fixed blade combat knife strapped to her stomach just for such an occasion, and the moment the Boss was alone with her, she would kill him, and the contract would be underway. So if he got through with the other girl and made a move on Meela, we could start our assignment ahead of schedule.

I doubted this would happen however, our luck hadn't been that good in months, and it seemed more likely we would have to stick with the original plan.

"Burlington, I'm seeing six guards on patrol, all armed and moving." Corbin's voice buzzed in my ear. I looked around at the other servers. We were all wearing the same earpiece. I had bought them for each of the others in order to blend in, and had convinced the Boss' head of household that they were a necessity to perform our job. It had been a necessary expense, and one I hope would pay off before the end of the night. We couldn't respond to Corbin without rousing suspicion, but he could still keep us updated on the situation.

"The barge was pushed off three minutes ago, I estimate that with current wind conditions and wave patterns that it should be in place in five minutes." I made eye contact with Meela knowingly, before we both went back to serving.

THE | SPLIT

A few minutes later, Boss Kagawa came back into the room with a savage grin on his face, and his pair of guards clapped him on the back as he made his way back into the party. Several feet behind him was the server he had taken back into the house, who stared at the ground as she walked. The makeup around her eyes was smeared, a visible reminder of the tears she had shed during the traumatic ordeal.

I did my best to keep my anger from welling up as I watched her walk in sheepishly back behind the serving line. Boss Kagawa would be getting his, soon. The irony was palpable. Kagawa's family had achieved prominence during the reign of Japan's emperors, but his hatred for Western culture and people went far beyond a personal level.

In recent years his gang had been ruthless towards the American businesses and personnel working in his town, they had raided warehouses and kidnapped hostages for ransom, only to later kill them after receiving the money. And Kagawa had a flair for the dramatic, often leaving behind grisly scenes around his victims, painting the words "Death to Imperialists" and similar rhetoric in blood.

His hatred for Western business had crossed a line, however, when he decided to execute a pair of executives from ArmaLite, an American firearms manufacturer. Unlike the companies of Kagawa's previous victims, ArmaLite wanted blood; and that's where we came in. Vengeance itself was a simple enough motive, but our client wanted more than that.

We had been instructed to kill everyone we could get our hands on, including Boss Kagoya. And there was no better place than the annual Christmas party.

The guests suddenly left the serving lines and began to mass in the middle of the room. Curious, I made sure there was no one to serve and set down my ladle to see what was happening.

THE | SPLIT

"Is everyone here?" Boss Kagawa's gruff voice cut through the crowd as he climbed on top of a table. Someone shouted yes, and he continued with his speech, looking down at his men, "It is not traditional in Japan to celebrate Christmas like we do. Yet, we do it here, in a traditional home dating back hundreds of years. I can think of nothing better to encapsulate the essence of the Kagawa family. The Yakuza has survived all these years by retaining our heritage but being adaptive to the times. Much like the blade of our ancestors." He pulled out a katana and held it high above his head, "Our lifestyle has not lost favor. We use the discipline and tradition of those before us to strike at the hearts of our enemies. We have had a good year as a family, and we have many people to thank, like Brother Nagoyami here. Come on, stand up here with me."

As a man climbed the table to join the Boss, Corbin got on the headset, "We're about a minute out. Get ready." I took a deep breath and began to mentally prepare myself.

Kagawa continued talking. "Nagoyami here has done a lot for the family. Thanks to him, our shipments from Peru are back on schedule. Thanks to him, we have reduced the influence of Tokyo on our docks." The men in the crowd gave a faint cheer of approval before the Boss cut them off. "But. . . it is not *all* for the family is it, Brother Nagoyami? Tell us about the deal you made with the Itagaki family."

The man standing beside the boss turned white. "I-I don't know what you're talking about."

"Oh. . . come now, brother," Kagawa grinned evilly. "Do not be shy."

"I-I am being honest. . . " the man stammered, "as I always am with you, Boss-"

With lightning quick movements, Kagawa brought the katana to his side and thrust it through Nagoyami's torso. The crowd fell silent as the

THE | SPLIT

man's eyes widened with shock and blood began trickling from the corners of his mouth.

"I appreciate your service, brother," Kagawa said, pulling the blade out and wiping the blood on Nagoyami's suit. "This is business, nothing personal." As Kagawa stepped down from the table and disappeared into the crowd, the men began talking among themselves like nothing had happened, some coming back to the serving tables with smiles on their faces.

I started to ladle more eggnog, but in the corner of my eye, watched the ocean outside for the bright flash of the barge igniting, our distraction and the official beginning of our plan. A half minute later, I got my wish; a distant boom sounded from across the water, and I looked through the open doorway to see a dark shape floating about a kilometer away, engulfed in bright flames.

An audible sense of astonishment rippled through the crowd, and the men stopped what they were doing to go look outside at the blazing spectacle. I saw Meela leave her spot and start walking towards me, and set my ladle down to lead the way past the serving tables and out of the room through a side passage. No one seemed to notice besides a few of the other servers, and they didn't seem to care; they were all fixated on the fire in the harbor.

It worked just as we intended. Corbin had bought the old barge several weeks ago when we first arrived in Japan. Together, we had loaded the vessel with long-burning flammable liquids, and Meela had wired the whole thing to a remote timer. It had cost us 100,000 yen, but like the headsets for the other servers, it was a necessary expense. To create a distraction for a party this size, we had needed a serious showstopper.

THE | SPLIT

I led Meela down the hall, took a right, and we soon came upon a clear plastic sheet stretched from floor to ceiling, where Kagoya's current renovations began. Holding up the plastic, I allowed Meela to go through first.

This part of the house was markedly different. In time, it would come to look like the rest of the house, but for now it was half finished. Instead of the traditional panel siding, the walls were a clean white drywall. The floor was not wood but concrete, and the side rooms were stacked high with crates of building materials.

"Which one is it?" Meela whispered, as she led us into one of the rooms and ran her hand along the wooden crates.

"I'm not sure," I replied quietly, "He said it would be in the corner, let's start there."

To smuggle our equipment inside of the house, we had paid one of the foreman working on the remodel. It had cost an additional million yen, but again, it had been another necessary expense. The foreman had met us near the house we were renting, and dropped off a pair of large crates. We'd packed them tight with weapons and body armor and, later that evening, he'd come back by to get them. He had never asked any questions, he just took his money and left.

"Hey! You're not supposed to be here!" I whirled around to see a guard in a gray suit standing in the doorway, his sub-machine gun pointed at me menacingly.

He hadn't yet seen Meela, who was on the other side of the room, now slowly and quietly inching her way towards him. Trying to cover for her, I began speaking in my broken Japanese: "Is that a KS Vector?" I gestured to his gun. "I shot one of those in the military back home. Looks like you took off the stock though, probably makes it-"

"QUIET!" he shouted, "You follow me, now."

THE | SPLIT

He beckoned for me to leave. Meela jumped towards him from behind, grabbing his gun and shoving her thumb in the trigger guard to keep it from firing. The guard spun around to face her – and I pulled him into a headlock, covering his mouth with my other hand. Meela lifted her shirt and pulled out her knife, plunging it into his stomach.

The man cried out in muffled pain through my hand, thrashing violently as he tried to get away, but with a quick twist and an audible crack, I broke his neck. Setting him on the ground as he fell limp, I looked up to see Meela staring at me, her hand held out for me to see.

"Look at that!" She roared, trying to keep her voice down. Her thumbnail was bruised a deep purple and the tip was beginning to swell. This kind of injury wasn't a first for us, but this one looked particularly bad.

"I'm sorry baby," I tried to sound sincere. "Want me to kiss it and make it feel better?"

"Screw you Burlington." She smiled and began to suck on her thumb to help the pain, then took it back out of her mouth for a second, "Hey, I found the crates, over here." She led me to a far corner, and I pulled the crates onto the floor. They were about waist height and wider than I was at the shoulder, but to my surprise the tops removed rather easily.

We began to put on our equipment, in each of the crates was a full set of dark body armor, heavy and rigid. This had been one of the last things we had been able to purchase before ACE had been forced to leave the states.

The armor was made from ballistic absorbing plates over a fine Kevlar mesh. It was heavy and awkward, but capable of stopping multiple rounds even at close distance. On each thigh of both sets were pairs of the fast reloading devices that Meela had constructed.

THE | SPLIT

Once suited up, I slipped on my gloves and began to pull the weapons we had stashed, grabbing a pair of 9mm pistols and slipping them into the holsters on my waist. After flipping the magazine holders into the perpendicular ready position, I reached into the crate for the last item with both hands and lifted out the RPK light machine gun, bringing it to my waist to release the top panel and load the first belt into the chamber.

The RPK was an older weapon, but nothing on this particular gun was outdated. Everything from the custom fit polymer grips to the front mounted laser sights had been installed by me and Meela personally. The box magazine had originally held a hundred rounds, but thanks to Meela's ingenuity, and my skill with a spot welder, we had increased the capacity to 250.

I clipped the extra modified magazines to a metal hoop on my chest, and was ready to go. Walking to the door, I paused when I saw Meela lingering behind, her fingers tapping away on her phone.

"You ready?" I asked turning to her.

"Not yet," she replied without looking up.

"What are you doing?"

"Fixing the music before we go out, do you hear that shit out there?" She gestured outside the door, where a Japanese cover of "Silver Bells" could be heard through the walls faintly.

"How are you going to do that?"

She showed me an app on her phone, "I'm just going to change it. Kagawa is an idiot... runs his entire house speaker system through a Bluetooth connection, like it's 2015."

"What are you changing it to?"

"You'll see," she smiled and pushed past me. "Let's go."

THE | SPLIT

We opened the door and went back through the plastic tarp into the main part of the house. Just as we rounded the corner into the last hallway, "Silver Bells" faded out and I heard the pleasant opening tones of Bobby Helms' *"Jingle Bell Rock"*.

Coming out of the dark hallway, we lingered in the shadow and surveying the room.

Jingle bell, jingle bell, jingle bell rock

The men in the party were glancing around the ceiling at the speakers in surprise, talking among themselves and asking Kagawa what was going on.

Jingle bells swing and jingle bells ring

A woman on the server line noticed us first and shrieked before bowling the other workers over to get out the side door to the harbor, even as the rest of the room turned to see what she was looking at. In unison, Meela and I brought the guns to chest height and opened fire.

Snowing and blowing up bushels of fun

The bursts from the RPKs lit up the dim hallway as the bullets tore through the dense crowd of people. Shouts echoed throughout the room as the men tried to escape the slaughter in the middle.

Now the jingle hop has begun

"Sounds like the party has started," Corbin's voice buzzed in my ear, "Wait, is that Jingle Bell Rock?"

"Yes." Meela replied simply, turning to fire at a group of men cowering behind the serving table. I tapped her on the shoulder twice, signaling I was going to reload first then, taking several steps forward, waded into the pile of bodies as I lit up the survivors clinging to the outside walls. Meela stood behind me, firing in single shot or two shot bursts to conserve her ammo.

THE | SPLIT

Jingle bell, jingle bell, jingle bell rock

Suddenly, a man popped out from around the corner, pistol raised. He shot me in the chest twice, the force from the bullets nearly knocking me over, but not piercing the ballistic plate. I lined him up in my sights and unloaded the rest of my magazine, tearing chunks out of paneled siding and sending pieces of the man's suit flying in blood soaked tatters.

Jingle bells chime in Jingle Bell time

"Out!" I shouted at Meela and dropped to one knee.

She came up next to me, moving on a swivel, picking off any stragglers or men who came out from their cover. I yanked one of the box magazines from its ring, clipped it into place and threw the old one to the side, then as quickly as I could opened the top panel and loaded the new belt.

Dancing and prancing in Jingle Bell square

Done, I stood back up and led Meela around a corner, but a small group of men were waiting down the long room, and opened fire as soon as they saw me, cursing to each other as they looked for cover. A solid burst from my RPK tore through them like cardboard, leaving a grim pattern of splattered blood on the wall behind.

In the frosty airrrrrrr

Meela tapped me twice before going back into the main room. She shot the rest of her magazine at a pack of Yakuza trying to crawl to safety through the open door, then looked up at me as she reloaded, "Do you see Kagoya?"

I scanned the pile of bodies. "No. We need to find him, immediately. . . before he escapes."

What a bright time, it's the right time

THE | SPLIT

A man charged into the main room, looking around wildly with his gun for me and Meela. With a single shot, I popped him in the head.

To rock the night away

"Meela," I called down to her. "We need to head outside and-"

"ARGHHH!" A man screamed as he threw his body into my back, knocking the RPK from my hands. I turned around to face him, and a bullet from his pistol cracked the glass on my visor. He tried to fire again, but I knocked the gun to the side with my left hand, sending the bullet through the serving table. With my right hand I grabbed him by the throat, slamming him against a nearby wall as he tried to free himself from my grip.

Jingle Bell time is a swell time

He struggled to raise his gun, but before he could pull the trigger I grabbed him by the wrist and squeezed as hard as I could, feeling his bones crack even through the heavy material of my gloves. Now, pulling one of my pistols from its holster, I put the barrel against his forehead and blew his brains out through the back of his skull.

To go gliding in a one-horse sleigh

"Let's go!" I turned to see Meela making her way through the open door outside. Picking my LMG back up off the ground, I followed her into the night air.

Giddy up Jingle horse, pick up your feet

Several guards outside fired at us, right as we stepped through the door, and we exchanged fire for several seconds, killing them all, but not before Meela took a round to the shoulder.

Jingle around the clock

We next mowed down the men fleeing across the yard, hitting each in the back multiple times, just as Corbin spoke up; "I'm on my way with your extraction now. Have you eliminated the target?"

"Not yet," I replied.

"What?!" He sounded incredulous, "Find him! The window is closing."

"Easy for you to say."

Mix and a-mingle in the jingling feet

The movement in the courtyard was down to a minimal level. Meela and I split up and began kicking over bodies in our search for Kagoya, methodically executing any survivors as we found them.

That's the Jingle Bell

Finally I saw him. He was wounded, and crawling his way towards the small dock several meters away. I hoisted my RPK onto my shoulder and walked over to him.

That's the Jingle Bell

He held up his hands as he saw me, his face a mask of terror. "Please!" he pleaded. "Whoever is paying you, I can double it!"

I raised my pistol, "This is business Mr. Kagawa, it's nothing personal."

His eyes widened with recognition, before I shot him between the eyes.

That's the Jingle Bell rooooooock

I felt an arm wrap around my waist, and looked down to see Meela looking down at Kagawa's corpse.

"Nice job babe," she took off her helmet and smiled up at me.

I took off my helmet too, "Nice song selection."

She punched me in the arm, "Stop."

The mechanical whirring of a boat sounded across the water, and then a single light on its bow flashed at us as it grew closer. When it stopped beside the dock, I saw Corbin close his laptop and stand up from his seat on the deck.

"Fancy running into you two here," he quipped.

Meela led the way onto the boat, carefully stepping off the dock. "Yeah yeah. You talked to the captain?"

"Yes I did," Corbin moved his equipment so we could have a seat beside him. "The freighter is in place, we should be to it in an hour and a half."

Corbin signaled the boat's driver to move forward. As we made our way towards the dark horizon, I heard sirens coming towards the Boss' house.

T H E | S P L I T

XXXIII

LGPB://mn34/con/terra/NB, 3902
(Translated)

Hungary; 1241

We made it to the front gate with less than half of our numbers of just minutes before. The tents and wagons around the edge were blackened with scorch marks, small fires were still lighting the structures in places and even further off to our east, the flames raged as far as my eyes could see. Smoke hung in low clouds between the charred tents and wagons, obscuring my vision and filling my lungs, and behind us, the sounds of battle grew closer as the Mongols neared the north gate.

I grabbed the Archbishop by his shoulder and urged him west, staying low to try to avoid the dark smoke until the area cleared after a short walk. As I walked into the clean air and took a deep gulp my eyes were teary and still stung from the smoke, and I was still choking from my exposure to the hazy gray clouds, but my blurred vision could see soldiers fighting Mongol swordsmen between the tents; they had made it into the camp.

My blood ran cold as I watched the screaming men in dark furs flood down the lane. Soldiers from all directions ran out to stop their advance, but the Mongols could not be stopped. I turned back to the Archbishop and his remaining guards; they all were looking up at me, waiting nervously. Reluctantly, I took the lead, ordering the Archbishop to stay behind me, and moved down a side path.

When I paused to place Master Rembald's body in a nearby wagon Geoffrey protested, but I quickly silenced him, showing him visions of the gruesome death that awaited us all if we delayed.

THE | SPLIT

Turning right a few meters later I went back towards our South, but we reached the other large walkway to find that it too was swarming with enemy soldiers. Then, an almost inhuman scream rang out to my left. I turned to see a circle of Mongols surrounding a single foot soldier, whom they attacked in turn, though hesitating as he quickly dispatched anyone who came too close. And, as the soldiers shifted, I saw the Subutai I knew between two of them.

Three soldiers charged him at once. His face was wrinkled in concentration as he whirled around the circle, cutting through them all in one fluid motion of his saber, the blade moving unseen until he brought it to a halt. His movements were an art form; he had the grace of a dancer and the speed and power of a moving train. The next man who entered the circle was nearly cut in two, a savage slash between two of his ribs leaving nothing but a thin strip of skin behind. His body folded in half as he fell, the back of his shoulders touching his feet.

More soldiers moved into surround Subutai, and I had to resist the urge to go help him; my compulsion to assist my own savior of just moments ago being outweighed by Geoffrey's sense of duty. So instead, I turned around and led the Archbishop down the lane, towards the East. Though I had never seen it, I knew that there was an exit through which we could escape. Pest would be a long journey on foot – and that, if we weren't caught by Mongols.

A group of enemy soldiers stumbled onto the path from our right, and I was forced from my train of thought as the Archbishop's guards met them head on, fearlessly. Pulling the last poleaxe from the strap on my back with fumbling hands, I moved forward to assist, running my spear through the belly of a fat Mongol in front of me. Pulling it out, I next smashed the head of my axe through another man's helmet, as yet another soldier tried to move past me.

T H E | S P L I T

My hand shot out, burying the point of my sword in his chest before I stepped back to pull both of my weapons free. All but one of the guards had fallen, and the Mongols were trying to push past us to get to the Archbishop. I caught one with my axe, but got it stuck in a bone, and I had to watch helplessly as a swordsman closed in on the bishop, saber overhead.

But with surprising speed, the old man lifted his gold-tipped staff and jammed the point of the crucifix fixture through the man's neck – even as the last of his guards fell.

Stepping beside him, I held both weapons at the ready as the enemies closed in. They were hesitant, trying to stay out of the range of my poleaxe, but as another group of soldiers came from the lane, I heard a gurgling, gasping sound behind me and, looking over my shoulder saw the Archbishop fall, bleeding from his mouth.

Geoffrey's thoughts overwhelmed my own, and I let out an involuntary wail of grief, sorrow and fury washing over my mind at the same time. In his anger he showed me his pain, and from his memories I could see images and impressions of his time with the Archbishop. The rush of sudden emotion brought pain to my temples and I tried to block out his thoughts.

I'd never felt a platonic attachment like this. It was like the bishop was his father, brother and best friend rolled into one. Geoffrey had revered the man like God himself, following him around as a young boy and basking in his praise for days. Now, shocked at the sight of the dying holy man, his conflicted emotions quickly hardened into an unnatural rage, and he took the reins. I followed his movements, letting him draw from my brief knowledge of battle, and swung the poleaxe at the soldiers in front of me, causing them to take a step back, then turned around and charged at the men to my rear.

T H E | S P L I T

Hacking at the group viciously, I barely felt the stinging pain in my hands as the sword tore through their armor and vibrated incessantly. When my blade broke on a man's helmet, I blocked his counter with the mail on my forearm and plunged the jagged edge of the hilt into his neck. Then, a lance of pain then shot through my right leg, and I looked down to see a spear impaling me through the calf. Blood clouded the edges of my vision as I whipped around to face my attacker.

In desperation the man tried to free the spear, but I swung my axe as he looked up at me, severing his head in a single blow. My right leg buckled as I tried rising to my feet clumsily but, even feeling the weight of the spear, I dragged myself towards the remaining soldiers, who kept their distance as I inched towards them, swinging my axe desperately; then from behind, another spear was shoved through my stomach. I heard my chain-mail split as the point went into the soft grass below, pinning me down.

Feeling my strength leaving me, I threw my poleaxe forward. It went through the throat of a soldier, who fell to the ground clutching his wound. Exhausted, my head hit the ground, pressing the tear in my helmet further into my face. Then came a sharp pain in my neck, and I lost connection to my body. I tried to gasp for air but couldn't with my throat open. The world suddenly swirled around me, I 'felt' my head roll against a nearby tent stake, and I could see my body lying nearby.

Fear and confusion poured out from Geoffrey, and as I felt the light dimming, I tried to console him. Then a sharp tug yanked me backwards, and Geoff was no more. The heat from the fires and shouting from the camp disappeared so quickly it was like I had never been there in the first place.

My thoughts filled the dark space and I reached out, brushing against Sun and John, but they hardly seemed to notice. From the outside

THE | SPLIT

looking in, I could tell that they were deep in conversation, ideas and memories shot between them like sparks, each building upon the last. I considered joining their talk, but decided against it.

With Geoffrey's emotional influence no longer affecting my thinking, the effects of the battle seemed to come in all at once. I had butchered dozens of people, and the gore of the battlefield had impacted me deeply. Feelings of despair and disgust left me cold, numb to the horrors I had just witnessed, but in the darkness of my mind I could recall each of their faces with perfect detail, and as I thought about each person, the guilt of their murders coursed through my thoughts, warring against my brain trying to reassure me of my innocence, defending itself from the shock of the truth.

Why was this all setting in now? None of this was even real, right? Subutai had been fighting the Mongol's for an eternity, did anything I do there even matter going forward?

But, I **had** killed outside of my travels – the vision of the shootout in my living room sprang forward. When I saw Meela, my thoughts turned to longing and pain, Almost not even seeing the scene playing around me, I stared at her, hypnotized, so the sound of my old shotgun caught me off guard.

I looked over at myself, firing at the first intruder in the hallway, and time seemed to slow down as I watched the pellets enter his chest, then the blood appear from the multiple entrance wounds. The man's eyes widened and he fell to the floor, his breaths coming in shallow gasps, as he looked down at his chest in horror. Blood dripped from the corners of his mouth, but with what feeble strength he had left he raised his arm weakly and called to his friends around him.

They ignored him, focusing on me and Meela and their own guns. The wounded man gave up this pursuit and looked up to the ceiling, tears running down his face. I moved closer to him and crouched down to watch his last pained seconds. He couldn't see me, but he seemed to be seeing something. Fear and confusion washed over his face as his breathing began to slow. One last gasp of air and he was gone, head rolled to the side, his eyes wide open.

I forced the memory away, and was again in the darkness of my thoughts, but the man's facial expressions were haunting. I tried to put myself in his position and shuddered at the thought, imagining what it was like to be forced to accept your death was beyond my emotional comprehension. I had died before, several times in fact, but I did so with the knowledge that it was unlikely to be my end. The lives I had experienced ending were never my own, there was never the threat of true extinction like that man had faced.

Back in life, I had been far removed from the fear of death and violence. It had become so trivialized in the culture I grew up in; everything from video games to songs embraced death as a way of telling a story. I had lived like I thought I was invincible, immune from such concerns, so desensitized to it that pondering the concept of finality had never occurred to me.

But that line of thinking was over now. I had seen the brutalities of war and death on a scale I'd thought unimaginable from the comfort and safety of my 21st Century life. I was more than a witness, I had taken part. I had shot, stabbed, smashed and broken whole groups of men. The contents of the human body had long been a mystery to me, but no longer. On the field of battle I had seen men turned inside out in the chaos, whole bodies opened from top to bottom, organs I had only read about spilled onto the ground beneath them.

My train of thought slipped from my grasp as images of broken men flashed across my mind that I was unable to stop.

T H E | S P L I T

Panic set in, as I was faced with the results of my carnage, but then I felt another set of thoughts nudge mine, and turned to see both Sun and John watching me. Concern emanated from both of them; they'd forced themselves into my thoughts, and had seen the flood of memories that I had succumbed to.

Sun spoke up, thrusting his thoughts in front of mine, *"Burlington, you must relax. . . think of nothing, find a peaceful place, and clear your mind."*

I tried to do as he said, but kept finding the memories of the men I had killed no matter where I turned.

*"Think of **why** you fight,"* he said firmly, *"Think of the woman you love with such passion, and your life back home."*

I thought of Meela, my house, my friends; family. The visions began to fade away, and the guilt and fear were pushed aside with new emotions formed by looking at my past life. In what felt like seconds I returned to normal. I could sense Sun's relief.

"The soldier is no murderer," he said in a quiet tone. *"Rather, he is a man who does what he must. . . for clan and kin. You do not relish the violence and death, Burl. . . you fight because you **must**."*

I agreed, focusing on keeping my head clear as we drifted through the dark space. John spoke up a few seconds later.

"We have good news, kid."

"Good news?"

"Well. . . new information, to be more accurate. As we watched you fight, me and Sun discussed our observations from our journey to the battle we just left. We think we've stumbled onto something important."

"What's that?" I asked, my curiosity was growing with each sentence.

T H E | S P L I T

"As we examined your memory of flying through the void without us, we noticed similarities. It seems that now, as before, we appear to be moving."

"So?" I questioned impatiently, eager to know where he was going with this.

"So," he replied patiently, "whatever we're supposedly passing through right now, be it wormhole or traveling outside of the third dimension entirely, there seems to be motion. When we first collided into you, we were knocked widely off course. When I brush into Sun, I can feel us tilting slightly towards my side of our thoughts. Even in this seemingly limitless plane, there's direction. Just moments ago me and Sun performed an experiment. . . after entwining our thoughts, we pulled apart as far as we could and moved in separate directions. From this movement we were able to spin ever so slightly. Through coordination, I believe we could adjust our course, and slip out of this current that's pulling us forward."

I thought on his words, the idea was interesting; I had always thought the feeling of movement in the dark space to be my perception playing a trick, a way for my mind to comprehend the confusion around me.

"What do you think would happen if we left this stream of motion?" I asked, trying to think of possibilities myself.

"Who knows?" he answered. "It could be nothingness, it could be freedom, but it's worth finding out."

I paused to consider this before turning to the other consciousness, "Sun, what do you think of this?"

Sun pondered for a moment before replying, "It is an interesting idea, and John is correct in his observations. However, I do not share his optimism. Slipping away from the stream before proved to be nearly fatal. Do you remember your brief lapse into the strange cold sky?"

THE | SPLIT

I thought of the odd detour we had made when I first met the pair of them, and knew there was merit to his words.

"I do remember that, but I think it's worth a try. If we all do it together we should be able to move easily right?"

"It's possible," John replied. *"However, a good deal of time has passed since we first started moving, I fear we may soon come to our journey's end."*

"Never mind that," I brushed him off impatiently. *"We can at least try. John, you mentioned entwining our thoughts?"*

"Yes. It sounds more complicated than it is. To remain as one solid mass, all we have to do is retain a connection between each of us. It could be something as simple as sharing impressions and images or a basic conversation. If you want to try it, first we have to connect, and then spread in three separate directions."

We began to exchange memories wordlessly. I didn't even see what the other two were showing me and I doubt they saw what I was showing them as I sent over whole sections of my childhood at a time, sharing anything that came into mind. Pulling away from them, I could feel them drifting farther and farther away, the strain on our connection growing as we moved.

"Okay. . ." John said, *". . . now, the only direction in this space is the one in which we travel. That being said, if we all came from the same point and spread outward, our positions should be roughly level. Burl, your influence is the strongest, so on my count you try and move down, and me and Sun will move up. The conflict in motion should drive us off course and into a spin."*

Me and Sun both agreed and waited for him to tell us to start. He told us to go, I turned my thoughts downward, and the connection between us tensed as they pulled the other way.

T H E | S P L I T

After a brief struggle with no movement, I focused and shoved forward hard, ever so slightly feeling myself moving backwards and my connection to John and Sun swinging them forward. Slowly we tumbled through the space, away from the stream of motion.

"We're doing it!" John cried out excitedly.

But as I continued pulling downward, trying to quicken our progress sideways, a bright light appeared to my right; small at first, but growing quickly. I had seen this before, we were nearing our destination. End of the line.

"Shit!" John said in frustration. *"Hold on!"*

T H E | S P L I T

?

Hyesung, North Korea

    Feeling Meela's hand on my arm, I looked over to see her signal for us to hold. Every part of my body was tense with suspicion. Nothing in our plan had prepared us for this; the whole operation had been too easy, and everything inside of me sensed an ambush.

    As she used a handled mirror to peer around the corner, I looked around the rundown building. Maddox Hill had moved his entire base of operations North, from Pyongyang, just a few weeks ago, to a large complex in Hyesung near a railroad depot, only a short drive from North Korea's border with China.

    The building must have served the genetic terrorist's needs perfectly; the place had been abandoned for years, and its deserted surroundings ensured no prying eyes could see the large number of test subjects being brought in by rail. The hallway was dimly lit, a single bulb flickered above us ominously, reflecting in the small puddles of water on the floor formed from the leaking roof. Outside, I could hear the wind howling even through the light brown walls, the sound of North Korea's infamously brutal winters.

    Meela signaled me forward and I nodded, raising my rifle and taking point to lead us around the corner. Ahead of us was an open doorway, leading to a short stretch of hall with an emergency exit on our right side, and ending at another door. As I crept towards the new entrance I examined it, and the glass windows that formed the top half of its connecting wall. The reflective portions of the door, and wall, were made from wire mesh glass but were smudged, obscuring my ability to see much beyond the door and the area around it.

THE | SPLIT

Cautiously, I stepped up and through the doorway, clearing both of my corners before waving Meela into the room from behind me. We examined the room further, weapons at the ready. The stretch of hallway between the two identical doors was about ten yards across, with an emergency exit just to our immediate right. Surprisingly, the red "EXIT" sign was still functional and glowing warmly. I was even more surprised to see that the sign was in English. Perhaps it was a modification Maddox had installed?

Suddenly, the door we came through and the one at the end of the hall both shut behind us simultaneously, and we heard at the same time the whirring of an electromagnetic lock. Meela and I looked back, making eye contact for a brief moment, just as an unexpected voice began talking through a speaker in the ceiling.

"What do we have here? A couple of bounty hunters who bit off more than they could chew?"

It was Maddox. Even years later, I still recognized his voice from the times I had watched him speak. He spoke in confident, deep tones, his words distinct and clear, like a broadcaster's.

"Pardon the old cliché, but. . . you didn't think it would be that easy, did you?"

Corbin's voice came through my headset; "What the hell is going on? Whose voice is that?"

Before either of us could respond the smeared glass on the other side of the hallway darkened, as shadowy forms approached the safety glass window. Maddox laughed through the speaker, "In the past, we would just kill you immediately, but. . . with a lull in the action, my subjects have become. . . restless. And as a man of science, it is my duty to test my experiments whenever the opportunity presents itself. Take them alive."

THE | SPLIT

The door ahead of us burst open and men carrying large batons poured through it. Meela and I opened fire, putting down the first few coming through the bottleneck entrance before I signaled to her that I was going to reload. She switched to single fire as I grabbed a fresh magazine from the pouch on my vest.

However, as I looked up, I was astounded to see the men we had previously shot pulling themselves up to their feet. Chills ran down my spine; even as I watched the blood pour from their wounds, they continued their way towards us, unfazed. We moved backwards as the group continued to swell in size, nearly two dozen were inside of the hall now, with more still coming in behind them. Meela went to reload, I took a short step forward.

The group was only fifteen feet away, so I chose my shots carefully, firing at the closest target with a practiced double tap of my trigger. Though bodies were beginning to litter the floor, there were more men upright, with batons raised as they tried to close the gap between us. Then a hissing sound came from the ceiling, and I looked up to see a gray cloud dispersing through two pipe nozzles beneath the sheet metal roof. The cloud brought tears to my eyes as it slowly filled the room.

Gas?

We hadn't prepared for any sort of aerosol attack!

The men who were coming towards us had disappeared into the thick smoke, only detectable from their grunts of pain as we fired blindly into the crowd. Thinking quickly, I grabbed Meela by the arm and tapped my headset to buzz Corbin, "Corbin, mission compromised. I repeat, mission compromised. Meet Meela at the extraction point and regroup. We're going to split up."

Meela looked up at me as I pulled her over towards the emergency exit. "What Burl? No!"

THE | SPLIT

"It'll be fine Meela, I promise. Regroup with Corbin. . . and come back for me." She started to protest, but I opened the emergency exit and shoved her outside, shutting the door and locking it even as she turned back around to face me, and using the butt of my rifle to break the doorknob.

I turned back around to face the thickening cloud of gas, just as a man appeared out of nowhere. His baton swung toward my face in a downward arc, and I raised my rifle, blocking the blow, but another man came through the fog and pulled it from my hands. Pushing off the enemy closest to me with a kick, I drew both pistols from my belt, but now the gas had completely filled the room, and tears ran down my face as I coughed, struggling to breathe.

Nearly blind, I unloaded both of my pistols into the throng, pressing the release on both guns at the same time with practiced hands. I slammed the grip down on my thigh-mounted quick loader for new magazines, then fired seven more shots before the gas caught in my lungs and I fell to the ground.

The men surrounded me, beating me with their clubs as drops of blood from their previous gunshots went flying. *'Why isn't the gas affecting them?'*

I raised my arm weakly and shot two more times, before a blow to my shoulder knocked the gun from my hand and the gas rendered me unconscious. I came to in another room, looking around in astonishment. The floor and walls were pure white, as far as my eye could see. Outside of my own body, I could discern no shapes or forms at all, just an infinite plane of blank white space. Scratching my head, I had taken a few steps forward, looking around for anything that caught my eye, when a sound like rushing water suddenly echoed through the space.

T H E | S P L I T

Turning toward it, I could see an opening of dark swirling colors. A man walked through before it closed back behind him. He was different from anything or anyone I had ever seen. He towered above me, standing at eight feet or taller. His body was long and slender, covered in a sleek dark blue suit which had a harder substance over it in places, like armor. His face was smooth, and his skin was a subtle shade of orange-ish brown, but his head was bulbous and large, even compared to his massive body. The top of his skull wasn't a sphere, it instead widened at both sides, giving his head the appearance of a rounded triangle, with his high cheekbones sloped downward at severe angles, across his elongated face and sharp chin as the lower point.

He stared at me curiously, like an animal in an exhibit; his solid black pupils lacked color entirely. I took a deep breath and walked over towards him. I had been an atheist my whole life, but deep in the back of my mind I knew that this day might come; it was time for my judgment, and there was no way I would be looked upon with favor.

I looked into his eyes as I stopped several feet in front of him, and silence lingered for a moment, so I decided to speak first, not wishing to prolong the inevitable.

"So. . . let's get on with it. Although I won't lie, I expected heaven to be a little more impressive." I laughed at my own joke. There was nothing I could say to make up for the life I had lived, so I planned to continue enjoying myself for as long as I could.

"This is not heaven," he replied. His voice boomed through the infinite plane; deep, pleasant tones that were almost soothing to my ears.

"Hell then," I chuckled. "Same thing. This place is low energy."

"It is not that either, Burlington. You are not dead, and I am not God."

T H E | S P L I T

I blinked in confusion, staring at my surroundings. "Then. . . what's going on, where am I?"

The large man stiffened and widened his stance. "You are where you were before you came here, knocked unconscious by the gas."

"Well then. . . who are you, and why am I here?"

"I," the man touched his chest, "am Camulus. The first and only son of Prime Collective, Cyrus. You are here because this was one of the only times I could reach you. The subconscious is not powerful enough for a meeting like this, so we had to await a time where you fell into an unconscious state."

"My subconscious?" I asked. "Are you saying this has something to do with the visions I've had in my dreams?"

The man shook his head, "I know not of these visions, only the reason I have appeared to you."

"What reason is that?"

"It is complicated. The consequences of interrupting the linear sequence of time are dire, and so I cannot reveal the answers you have not learned for yourself. What year is it? Of what stage of life did I find you in?"

I told him the year, and gave him a brief summary of the life I had forged with Meela. His eyes seemed to light up when I mentioned her name, and when I was finished he asked me about her.

"Amelia Vasquez. . . does she show signs of temporally accelerated enhancement?"

"What kind of enhancement?" I narrowed my eyes questioningly.

"Physical growth, an improvement in cognitive ability, increased durability and exterior mutation."

"Some of that, I guess," I shrugged. "She's grown taller and says she's gotten smarter since her vision. . . a decade ago. But I just thought it was coincidence. Are you saying she's going to physically mutate?"

He ignored my question and turned around, calling out over his shoulder, "I have arrived too early. Goodbye for now, Burlington."

"Wait!" I rushed forward and put a hand on his massive shoulder, just as the opening appeared in front of him. "You can't tell me more? It doesn't have to be about me, I just want answers."

He turned back around patiently, and the entrance closed, "As I said before, I cannot answer all of your questions, but you can ask what you feel is necessary."

My mind raced with ideas, I didn't know where to begin, "Where did you come from, and how did you get here?"

"I exist in a time centuries ahead of your own. My journey here was not an easy one, it took decades of experimenting before we could develop the process."

"What process?"

"Transmission through sub-dimensional brain waves," he said simply. "I am the only human to ever be born with extrasensory neural perception, and due to the disastrous circumstances of my birth and childhood, my father Cyrus decreed that I will be the last. It took many years to figure out the technology required to make a connection like this across time, and I am the only one with the ability to achieve it."

"Who is Cyrus?"

Camulus shook his head, "That is an answer I cannot provide you with." He turned to leave again.

I shouted at him, "Hold on, don't go!" and again he turned around. His face showing no signs of annoyance, and instead he looked at me

THE | SPLIT

with curiosity. "Can you help me, Camulus?"

"Help you how?"

"I-I. . . " I stuttered, "I don't know where I am. The last thing I remember, I was in danger. . . Meela was in danger!"

"I cannot directly interfere," he looked at me sadly.

"Isn't there something you can do?"

His face lit up as an idea dawned on him. "There might be something." Camulus waved his arm, and the white plane suddenly transformed into a dimly lit room.

I looked around and saw people standing, frozen in place in the middle of various actions. The walls were filled with holes in the dark drywall, and the floor was littered with decomposing cloth and scraps of illegible paper. Insulation hung down from the ceiling through a missing ceiling tile in the corner. Maddox Hill stood between a group of men, his hands forming a gesture in the middle of a paused conversation. Just in front of him I saw myself tied to a chair, unconscious, with my mouth slightly open as my head lay against my shoulder.

"What is this?" I turned to Camulus, standing near one of the far walls, his head nearly touching the low ceiling.

"This is what's happening in the world directly outside of your mind. A projection formed from your senses that are still functioning."

"Well." I circled my unconscious form in the chair, looking him up and down. "It looks like I'm screwed."

Camulus smiled for the first time. "It might appear so, but you currently have an advantage your opponents do not have. Memorize your surroundings, and take stock of your situation."

He watched silently as I moved around the room.

THE | SPLIT

Maddox was in front of me, turned to one of his men who appeared to be a guard. Both men beside him, and Maddox himself, wore a holster on their waists containing matte black Glock pistols. There were men behind him, bent over computers or sitting on a torn couch near a back door.

Before walking back over to my body, I paused to look out of a side window first. The glass was blurry, but I could see we were on the second floor and, though the area outside looked unfamiliar, from the terrain and weather it seemed obvious I was still in the same compound. I didn't know which part of the building, however.

Frowning, I stepped towards myself from Maddox's perspective, noticing a door to my right, about ten feet from the chair I was sitting. In the space between was a man hunched over another monitor beside my chair, a gun on his waist as well. I also noted that the holster that was on the side of his body nearest to my chair, and the first pieces of my plan began to take form, so now I crouched down to examine my unconscious body and the chair I was sitting on.

My rifle was gone, as were the pistols and my armored vest. The strap from the knife I wore around my ankle was gone as well. I circled my way around to look behind the chair. The back of it had metal rods attaching it to the seat, and in the middle of them I found the second piece of the puzzle; they had taken nearly everything else, but had left behind my bracelet that Meela had constructed. And it contained a cleverly hidden, inch-long blade in the leather band.

Closing my eyes, I touched my temples as I ran the scenario through my head. My hands were zip tied just a few inches apart, to each of the metal rods supporting the chair back, and they had done the same with my feet on the chair's legs.

It would take me several seconds to free my hands, and several more

THE | SPLIT

to free my entire body. And, even if Maddox was distracted, his other men would notice me taking the knife out.

But as I scanned the base of the chair, I saw the final ingredient for my plan on the bottom side of the seat. One of the L-shaped brackets, the fasteners connecting the seat itself, was loose near the bottom and warped out of place. The screws on the bottom of the seat were also slightly pulled out, and the ones on the connecting rod were stripped, now too narrow to grip the metal effectively. Both screws were slotted; if I could turn my hand to the right angle, I could use the side of my fingernail to loosen them.

I stood up and turned to Camulus, smiling, "I think I've got a plan."

Camulus nodded, and the room returned to the blank white space it had been when I arrived.

"Best of luck to you, Burlington. . . until next time." He stepped through the strange portal he had came through, and was gone.

Next time?

My eyes snapped open. The room was exactly as it had looked just an instant before, though the people were moving now, and I could hear scattered conversations in Korean. Careful not to be too drastic with my movements, I extended my fingers down to the loose bracket I had been examining during my time with Camulus, and smiled as I felt my nail slide into the slot – I was able to turn it.

"Ah, he's awake!" Maddox looked up from the two men he was standing beside and walked towards me, "And he's SMILING! We can take care of that though. . . Shin?" He turned to one of the men behind him; a tall Asian man approached me menacingly, then punched me in the face with a long side swing. Stars circled my vision as I recoiled from the punch, braced for another impact even as he raised his fist again.

T H E | S P L I T

When he stepped backwards, smiling, Maddox dismissed him with a touch on his shoulder. I could feel blood dripping out of my nose and forming in my mouth.

"That," he pointed at Shin, "was just the beginning of what could potentially be a very painful evening for you, my mysterious friend. Why are you here? Who sent you?"

I laughed *(as I slowly un-threaded the first screw with my nail)*, causing him to narrow his eyes.

"What? A man can't check out abandoned buildings in China anymore, without being interrogated by some thug?"

He smiled back at me, "This isn't China, but I think you know that, just like I think you know I'm not just some thug. You want to know what I think?"

I had finished loosening the first screw, and tucked it into the space between the rod and chair. "No, but I bet you're going to tell me."

"I think that you are looking for Maddox Hill, and have come to collect the bounty on his head."

"Maddox who?" I replied, doing my best to look lost. "Wait. . . are you talking about that crazy scientist who cured Alzheimer's?"

He chuckled softly, then without warning slugged me in the stomach. He was a lot stronger than Shin; the air was forced out of my lungs in a loud cough, sending droplets of blood onto Maddox's shirt. As I caught my breath, he began pacing in front of me, hands behind his back.

"You can continue this charade for as long as you want, but we both know the outcome. I'm sure you were one of the best in whatever group or government that sent you after me, but as you can see. . . " he gestured at his nearby soldiers, some of whom still had red spots on their clothes where I had shot them earlier, ". . . your best isn't good

THE | SPLIT

enough. *Mankind's* best isn't good enough. I've taken your best and made it even better. The men under my command, the soldiers who captured you, are beyond the limits of what humanity can achieve on its own. You cannot kill them with just a few bullets, you cannot incapacitate them with gas. How did you expect to overcome such an enemy?"

As he talked, I finished loosening the other screw, and was now ready for the second part of my plan. "Where there's a will, there's a way." His face twisted with fury, and he assaulted me with a barrage of punches.

Each blow slammed into my body with the force of a MACK truck, harder than any punch I had ever felt before. Thankfully, after a few seconds he let up, but I felt a throbbing soreness all over my torso where he had hit me.

Maddox looked back at me, smiling, "Oops. . . can't get carried away. A few more of those and you would've been done."

He was right, whatever experiments he had done on other people, he had clearly used some of the results on himself. His muscles bulged out of his dirty gray shirt, his massive chest rose with every labored breath, and the veins on his unnaturally thick arms twitched with every slight movement. Deciding I needed to accelerate the timetable, I pulled the knife out of my bracelet.

The man using the monitor beside me immediately heard it being pulled from its hidden sheath and warned in a heavy accent, "Maddox!" as he was stepping over to pry the knife away from me. Just before he closed in, I slid the point of the knife in between the metal rod and the hinge, and separated the two while pretending to fight him as his hands closed around mine to wrestle the knife out of my hands. When he had taken it away he stepped back towards his monitor, holding the knife up for the whole room to see before setting it on the table.

T H E | S P L I T

"Tricky, tricky, tricky," Maddox clicked his tongue in disapproval.

I reached down to feel the bracket, running my fingers around the empty screw holes and the sharp rusted edge. The piece was now only held on by the two screws on the rod, which could come out at any moment. They hadn't noticed, my diversion had worked, and I made sure to sit up as straight as I could, so as to not make the chair give way and ruin my plan.

But suddenly, the muffled sound of gunshots came up through the floor. Maddox cocked his head in suspicion, pointing at the men in the back of the room. "Go find out what that is, and stop it." The men nodded, drawing their pistols before leaving the room through the back door. Maddox turned his attention back to me. "Let's get back to the issue at hand, shall we? WHO. SENT. YOU?"

"Nobody," I grinned painfully.

He stepped closer, bending at the waist, his face just inches from mine as with both hands he threw his fists down on my thighs painfully. "Last chance," he whispered. "Who sent you?"

I could feel his hot breath on my face, but out of the corner of my eye I saw the man who had taken my knife, still standing the same way he had been during Camulus' vision, with his holster facing me, distracted by his monitor.

Now. I closed my fingers around the bracket and yanked it free from the chair, cutting one of my hands free in the same instant. Maddox looked down at the source of the noise, just as I brought the hinge up and sliced him across the face. He stumbled backwards, covering his eye and crying out in pain. Dropping the hinge in my lap, I pulled off the other zip tie around my left hand. The man beside me was trying to draw his gun, but I caught his wrist with my right hand and the bullet went into the wall behind me.

T H E | S P L I T

Still holding him, I sliced away the restraints on my feet and stood up. Maddox had backed towards a table on the other side of the room, blood gushing down his face, and now pointed at me as he yelled to the handful of men around him, "KILL HIM!"

I felt a bullet graze my calf and quickly jerked the man I was holding into their line of fire. The struggling soldier tried to free his gun but I plunged the rusted hinge into his stomach repeatedly, and when his grip on the pistol loosened as he went limp, snatched the gun from his hand.

Catching his body before it collapsed and using it as a shield, I moved back into sight of the men firing at me, firing back indiscriminately, emptying the clip into Maddox and his men. Some of the others fell instantly, but Maddox managed to stumble out of the back door, his body bleeding in multiple places.

I shoved the dead man away from me and was ready to pursue the fleeing target, when the door behind me suddenly burst open, and in its frame stood Meela and Corbin, rifles raised. She pushed past me and into the room, killing the wounded men on the floor. Corbin handed me a pistol from a holster on his chest.

"See Meela?" he smiled, "I told you he would be fine on his own."

She turned after killing the last man, gesturing at my bloody and swollen face. "Does he LOOK fine, Corbin? We need to get out of here."

I held up a hand to stop her from pushing past me. "Fuck that," I coughed noisily, but pulled back the slide on the pistol to chamber a round. "Let's kill this son of a bitch."

Meela and Corbin exchanged glances, then reluctantly agreed.

XXXIV

Recovered in Bloc Vault C1
-T. Acerz, 2131

Undetermined

I felt myself pass through the light, tumbling sideways, and awkwardly landing into the body that had been waiting for me. The sudden rush of sensual perception overwhelmed me and, still being dizzy from my spinning in the darkness, I immediately collapsed.

But the body felt comfortable and familiar, and I looked down to see my own hands lying against the cool surface of a platform. My vision swam in circles as I tried to focus, and I had to wait a few moments before I had regained my balance, at last climbing to my feet; to see the glowing walls of the Green Hallway. A solitary black drone hovered above me, but seemed entirely uninterested in me, though it floated a few feet higher than my head as it slowly moved down the platform.

"Everyone good?" I asked John and Sun cautiously. They both replied they were, if not a little dizzy. I had been unable to escape my return to the Hallway, but one thing was for sure, their idea had worked. I could not wait for another chance to try it again.

Walking down the platform I took a right, though it never seemed to matter the direction I took, the Being would eventually lead me to his massive throne room.

Knowing this, I slowed my pace, looking at the individual moving screens that made up the wall, the first time I had ever watched in detail. Though most of the scenes were confusing, I soon fixated on one several meters in front of me, and as I walked towards it I could make out more.

THE | SPLIT

A large round creature, covered in green, raised bumps and strange red markings, gestured upwards with a bizarre looking club. It seemed to be a weapon, made from a metal I had never seen before. A purple sheen traveled down its length, then a twisted blade shot out from near the top. The creature drove it down into the back of another just like him, piercing one of the large green bumps and causing a golden liquid to shoot out from the wound, covering the aggressor and victim alike. The creature who had been stabbed then started shedding these raised bumps rapidly.

Fascinated, I moved on, watching other creatures fighting with their own strange weapons and styles, until the Being found my thoughts and pulled at me lightly. I now knew the direction I was supposed to go, but I had every intention of moving at my own pace, and continued studying the mind-boggling scenes covering the walls.

It took several minutes of walking before I saw my first human; a tall, black man wearing a stern but proud look and the distinct armor of a Samurai, that reflected into the screen like the glimmer of fine jewelry. Snow fell all around him, piling around his feet in what looked like a field. In both of his hands he wielded a large katana, swinging it skillfully, the curved blade a little more than a blur. Then suddenly he began sprinting forward, charging towards an enemy I could not yet see.

Next, pain shot across the front of my head as I felt the Being's impatience at my dawdling and, begrudgingly, I turned from the scene to walk towards the Throne Room, my mind still rife with questions after seeing this out-of-place Samurai.

Who was he? What did he know? When and where was he from? My curiosity was forced to a halt as I crossed the threshold into the large room where the Being sat. It was sitting up this time, looking stiff and tense, as opposed to its normally relaxed demeanor.

T H E | S P L I T

And as I looked at it, I realized just how far I had come. Gone was the fear and reverence at its massive size and power; now, I felt nothing but cold disdain as I gazed up. Its power, its knowledge, its intentions. . . none of it mattered. The only thing that mattered was that this was my opponent, the sole obstacle standing between me and my old life. It could sense this sentiment, and stood up out of its chair, amused. When I continued to show no fear, it seemed to laugh. Taking a step forward, it called out in the deep, strange voice I had become so accustomed to hearing;

"That was quite a performance, young Terran. When given the opportunity, you certainly make your mark. All you need is the right. . . Encouragement."

"I'm glad you got a kick out of it. . . but I'm done," I responded, warily. "You can send me where you want, but I will not fight. I've spread enough death. . . I won't do it any longer. You can do to me what you like. I won't give you any more sick pleasure from the slaughter of my people."

"Give ME pleasure?" it asked. Its disappointment had instantly turned into a sick sense of knowing that I couldn't quite decipher. "I feel no pleasure from sending you to die and kill others. But. . . they do."

What was it talking about? Who was 'they'?

My face twisted in confusion as I repeated its words in my mind, to make sure I hadn't missed anything, but a mere instant later my thoughts felt surrounded, as if my sense of the Being's presence in my mind had been multiplied by the hundreds. Each presence felt. . . different. All having separate thoughts – and agendas. They watched me from a distance, curiously; much as the main presence had before. Something then caught my eye and I looked up; my blood seemed to stop moving entirely, and my hair stood off of my neck.

THE | SPLIT

Floating above me, between the clouds of drones, were the shimmering forms of *hundreds* of other Beings. Some had different facial features, and they were all of different sizes and colors, but there was no mistake; they were all the same manner of creature as the Being who had been torturing me. Though, these seemed to not be entirely. . . there. I could feel their thoughts, but as the cloud of drones swirled around above, they would occasionally pass through one of their forms.

Then they all began to talk at once, some in English, some in an alien dialect, while others used a series of grunts and sounds I had never heard before. The combination of the noises was overwhelming as the multitude of beings moved into my mind, tearing through my thoughts. It began to sound like a chorus of cruel and demonic laughter, and I screamed involuntarily. With an upward flick the Being on the throne dismissed them. The shimmering forms disappeared, as did their thoughts, and I cautiously reached out towards the edges of my head to ensure that I was safe.

"You are popular with the viewers," the Being on the throne said simply. "How is our old friend, Subutai? Even hundreds of battles later he continues to fight. He is one of our most popular fighters, being around him has brought you a new popularity you cannot comprehend."

I tried to focus in light of my new discovery, and took a few seconds to respond. "I don't care how popular I am. I will not fight again."

"You will do what is required, wherever you are sent. Do you not remember the promise you made? Do you shun the gift you were given?"

"No. . . " I admitted, thinking about Meela. "But, I won't cause any more harm, to anyone else. If I am sent somewhere, I'll sit in place until I am brought back."

T H E | S P L I T

I could sense its disappointment in my answer, but it did not reply. Instead, I felt myself gripped beneath my collarbones by an invisible force, and lifted several feet into the air.

Pain exploded from my shoulders and radiated upwards as my bones slowly began separating from my nerves and muscles, and my muscles strained towards my neck. Turning my head slightly, I could see my raised collarbones stretching the skin out on top of them, like a grotesque tent pole.

"You have seen what I can do. . . you have seen Subutai, you have heard his stories. I will ask you one more time. Do you refuse me?"

The agony I was feeling forced me to reconsider, but after a few seconds I held to my principles. By focusing on nothing but the Being – staring daggers at the strange creature standing in front of its throne – my thoughts hardened into aggressive defiance.

In a single gesture he opened his clenched fist, pointing his long fingers straight towards me, and a hot pain tore through my chest, trailing down my abdomen in burning agony. My collarbones were still being yanked upward, making it hard to turn my head but, with great difficulty, I looked down at my body as a large gash, starting at my sternum and tearing down through my stomach, appeared out of nowhere.

I watched in horror as the gash split off into smaller tears along my rib-cage, shoulders, and hips, then my skin pulled apart along the multiple wounds and, with a loud ripping sound, was torn from my body entirely. The exposed muscle cried out in pain all over my body, just the changes in air current throughout the room felt like a searing iron being pressed all around the raw red tissue. Then all at once the muscles too separated from the rest of my form, hovering a few inches away, each one connected by strings of nerves.

THE | SPLIT

Free from the muscles and ligaments holding them in place, my entire skeleton slid out from beneath me and floated a few feet from my face. Then each bone crumbled, simultaneously, leaving a pile of white powder on the floor below. '

This isn't real,' I thought desperately. *'Just hold on, this will be over soon.'*

I felt sick pleasure coming from the Being, as a small swarm of black drones flew over to my tortured form, their tentacled arms morphing and changing to reveal needles and other sharp instruments. Slowly, they prodded and cut into my muscles and nerves, always leaving the connecting nerve for last so I could feel every prod. Hours seemed to pass as they tortured me, and at some point I forgot why this was even happening.

Every thought I had was commandeered by my sense of survival. *'Why is this happening? How do I make it stop?'* Unable to move or even scream, the pain had all blended together, and I could feel my sanity starting to slip as my brain tried to drown out the agony.

"Will you fight now?" the Being asked in a booming voice.

I felt confusion at his question. *'Fight? How do I answer to get this to stop?'*

"Y-yes. YES! I'll do anything!" I replied weakly.

I felt satisfaction from the presence, and suddenly the pain stopped. With a strange popping sound, I was torn from my tortured body and again surrounded by the comforting darkness of the unknown.

It took several seconds for me to realize that I was safe. The adrenaline rush side-effect of the fight-or-flight response my brain had manufactured in my torture lingered, simplifying my thoughts to nothing more than mere observations as I waited for the fog to clear.

THE | SPLIT

I could feel both Sun and John, faintly, in the corners of my thoughts, but it was a mixture of concern and anger, and they waited for me to approach them. I eventually did, making contact with only the faintest of efforts. We communicated back and forth with full strings of thought and impressions as they both checked on my mental well-being, before we relayed anything else.

For the first instance since being summoned out of time, I had felt the grip of true fear – and they had felt it too. The suffering the Being had callously put me through had shaken me to my core. When I said I would take no more part in the violence, I'd meant it. But in the Green Hallways, the Being was all powerful. It could manipulate my body entirely, and with its control over time it could have made my agony last as long as it desired. Thus the traumatic experience I was just forced through had changed my mind.

My two companions did all they could to reassure me, and I was able to take some comfort in their words, soon pushing the unpleasant memory to the back of my thoughts. We went on to discuss the results of our earlier experiment on our way to the Green Hallways, and how we should proceed.

"Well, talk can only get us so far. . . are you two ready to try this again?" John asked, clearly eager to try again. We both agreed, and all met in the center of the space. After forming a thread between all of us we pushed our way to different corners, like we had before.

But unbidden thoughts of my torture in the throne room immediately leapt to the forefront of my consciousness, and I felt my connection to Sun and John dissipate. I could feel their concern and confusion as we met back in the center, but as they examined me inquiringly I assured them it was just a lapse in focus, and insisted we try again. Two more times we tried, and both times I lost my grip on the other two.

T H E | S P L I T

I apologized profusely, knowing that both of them disliked this arrangement as much as I did.

"It's alright," John said gently. *"We'll figure this out during our next stop. With your permission, I'd like to examine your thoughts more up close. Maybe I can see what's going on, and we can correct the problem."*

I agreed, and felt him move from his usual place in to the center of my thoughts, not far from my own area of perception. But we were speeding up, and so I also prepared myself for whatever was coming next. I didn't have to wait long, soon felt myself to squeezed into a new body. The mind of my host was surprised at the sudden visit, but did not seem to fight. I felt around the new space as I slipped into control of his slender body, which was shorter than I had been by a few inches.

This vessel was quite intelligent, and even on first impression the differences between this new set of thoughts and Geoff seemed vast. His memories and observations were all neatly arranged, his heartbeat and breathing were at a measured pace, he appeared to have his emotions completely under control and, although even for his stoicism I could sense the familiar taste of fear somewhere in the back of his mind, he seemed to give it no thought, instead focusing on the present with the same clarity Cyrus had, and retaining a level head. This was the brain of a man who had been desensitized to danger; this was the brain of a professional soldier.

I felt heat on my fingers and looked down to see a lit cigarette slowly burning its way down. Pleased, I raised it to my lips for a couple of long drags, holding it in as the warm smoke filled my lungs and feeling the numbing tingle of the nicotine buzzing through my thoughts as I exhaled.

THE | SPLIT

The body I was in felt a much lesser effect of this; it was clear he was a smoker and his habit didn't do as much for him as it did for me, after what felt like days of not smoking.

For the first time since arriving in the body, I looked past my cigarette to see my surroundings; I was sitting on a bench, near a curb, in the middle of a bustling city. Cars zoomed by in both directions, just a few meters in front of me, and I was reminded of the bus stops I had passed by on my trips to and from work in my own time. Just down the sidewalk, a young woman pushed an old-timey looking stroller, while trying to keep her other, older, child in front of her. The older child was complaining loudly, asking his mother why he couldn't have a caramel candy like he usually did. The lady seemed distracted, declining to answer her son's simple question and instead merely urging him forward. There was tension in her voice, a tension I now saw reflected in the faces of each passerby as they silently went about their business.

'Where am I?' I wondered, standing up from my seat on the bench and wandering down the sidewalk, to head toward a large grass plaza where the street I was on met up with several others. I knew I was doing something, and that it was something important. And as the brain I had just filled slowly settled under my arrival, I could feel a sense of urgency in my recent memories; something to do with my backpack, I realized.

Reaching up, I felt straps weighting my shoulders that I somehow hadn't noticed before. The bag was bigger than any I had seen before, closer to a duffel. As I waited to remember more, I continued along the sidewalk, then a department store to my right stopped me in my tracks; a mirror sat in the window display with a pair of mannequins. I turned to look. My face was handsome, in a stern sort of way. I was blonde, with bluish-gray eyes beneath the hat which sat atop my head; I reached up to touch it – I hadn't noticed its weight either, and was surprised to see it there. I wore the expression of a weary soldier, and had a uniform to match; gray, beneath a slightly worn trench coat, with slacks that matched my hat.

There were decals and patches on my lapel. I leaned into the mirror to see what they were – and my blood ran cold. Two *SS,* fashioned like lightning bolts and running parallel to one another. The iconic mark of the Waffen SS.

I had known about the Nazis my whole life, because World War II had been a fascinating subject to me ever since I was a boy. Even before my school years, I'd watched a movie where they were the villains. In third grade, a boy in my class had gotten suspended for drawing a swastika.

My teacher had to explain what the symbol meant; I'd thought it looked cool, but was sharply reprimanded by the teacher for saying so. The Nazi Regime was unanimously feared and hated in 21st century culture.

Their leader, Adolf Hitler, was colloquially used as a substitute for Satan himself, and used pointedly in insults and dark jokes. No matter what books I read, or shows I watched on the period, the Nazis were painted as the bogeymen, so seeing myself in one of their uniforms now stirred up many conflicted emotions.

My host felt this, and immediately began speaking to me, revealing the details that I had been seeking.

"*My name is Gerhard.*"

He pleaded his case with memories and thoughts from his time in the service and, in a single, overwhelming instant I saw his entire life play out before me. These images of laughter with friends and rides through the countryside were hardly the picture of Nazism I had been painted, making it difficult to keep in mind that he was one of them.

T H E | S P L I T

Gerhard even being where he was now was a situation tough not to sympathize with. He had grown up the son of a prominent Berlin politician, had witnessed his father's rise to success and their dramatically improved lifestyle. But his father had been one of the earliest backers of the National Socialist Party; a fealty which earned him a lofty position within the party ranks.

It also positioned him to use his reputation in order to sway the Bavarian and Prussian nobility, and lawmakers, to the side of an ambitious young Adolf Hitler, who along with his advisors had shortly afterward created the Sturmabteilung *(or SA)* as a means to police the ranks of their party.

Within a few short years, he had risen to the top as Chancellor of Germany, the SA had been given wider jurisdiction and the legitimate political authority of being Hitler's own secret police, and as leader of Germany, Hitler no longer needed the support of people like Gerhard's father. He had quickly changed the tone of his rhetoric and stances to that of an ultra-nationalist wanting revolution, creating a schism in the Nazi party.

On one side were Hitler and his supporters, and on the other was a man named Gregor Strasser and the followers of his ideals. Strasser believed that the responsibility of the National Socialist Party was ultimately to the working class, and "Strasserism", as it became known, called for a mass action against capitalist exploitation.

This way of thinking attracted many prominent intellectuals and leaders within the Nazi ranks, and Gerhard's father had been among them; indeed, much of the SA identified as Strasserists, including their leader Ernst Röhm. Hitler, encouraged by his top advisors, began to fear and distrust this emerging faction. Worried by the effectiveness of his own secret police, and believing they would soon move against him,

T H E | S P L I T

he and his supporters planned a purge of their party to remove any elements deemed dangerous or lacking in loyalty. Forming two new factions, the Schutzstaffel *(or SS)*, and the Gestapo, Hitler moved against Röhm and Strasser and from June 30th to July 2nd, these new forces assassinated more than 200 people, including Gerhard's father, in what would come to be known as "The Night of the Long Knives".

Gerhard had only been sixteen when the SS officers came to his east Berlin home. He remembered his mother pleading with the men in the other room to spare his life. They relented and left a few minutes later, but he could still hear her hysterical screams, muffled through the walls.

Following the annexation of Austria in 1938, German nationalism was at a fever pitch, and anybody who was somebody joined the war effort. When the year 1939 came around Gerhard, now 20 years old, joined the military. His performance on his psyche evaluation and field exercises got the attention of SS recruitment, who quickly pulled him aside to bolster their own ranks, but when the truth of his parentage was revealed several days later his recruiter had been reluctant to accept his service.

It was only through the fortune of Major Wilhelm Höttl passing by recruitment headquarters that he had been allowed to join. The Major had looked over Gerhard's file and, despite the protests of the recruiter, told the man to process him anyway, stating they had "too few good men already". He had then looked Gerhard in the eye and said to not make him look like a fool, and that he would be watching him closely.

Gerhard had excelled within the ranks of the SS, but the rumors surrounding his father's death cast a long shadow. He was kept from the front lines and active operations, despite his frequent transfer requests to command. Trying to make the best of his situation, Gerhard had focused on his duties in Berlin, and – until recently – had been

THE | SPLIT

rewarded for his efforts. The war now seemed to be nearing its end, and was having a sobering effect on a population just now waking up from its drunken spell of expansionist glory.

Gerhard had embraced this truth sooner than most; the Allies surged to Germany's west, while the Soviet's tore through the countryside to the East. Berlin would soon be caught in the middle of a storm never seen before in all of military history.

This harsh reality formed the basis of Gerhard's current quest. I was searching for a wanted man, a deserter, yet I did not pursue him to punish or capture. He had been a childhood friend, and I was delivering the large bag to him and his compatriots, for use later on.

Gerhard showed me a memory of what was in the bag he had loaded just that morning; seven G43 rifles and 20 magazines he had taken from an armory in central Berlin, under the pretext of resupplying a non-existent unit. Due to his high status within the SS, the questioning for his doing so had been minimal – Defenders were in short supply these days, weapons were not.

The men for whom these rifles were intended were all deserters. Soldiers who, like Gerhard, had seen the inevitability of Germany's defeat and had adopted a new mission; forming a volunteer guard to protect civilian interests in the event of Berlin's fall. We turned down a small, one lane street off the main road.

The buildings I now passed stood in sharp contrast to the bright shops and swept streets I had just left. Warehouses and homes alike were burnt shells of their former selves. It was like the city had a shameful secret, a dilapidated core hidden by a thin layer of deception. Worse, this was just a handful of the structures that had fallen victim to the prolonged bombings in recent months.

T H E | S P L I T

Passing an alley off of the narrow single lane road, Gerhard directed me down its shadowy length, and after a few moments of walking I spotted a small, two-story home crammed between two large warehouses. It was dirty, the windows were boarded up and the porch was covered in debris. But to my surprise, the door only appeared to be boarded shut, and swung open with a slight push.

The inside however, was in even worse condition than the outside, and looked like it hadn't been lived inside of in years. I could hear voices coming from upstairs and, walking up the crumbling staircase, I sought the source. The first few rooms I walked through reeked of dust and waste. Broken furniture and shards of glass covered the floor, and I had to tread carefully to avoid stumbling. But finally, in the next room, I found what I was looking for.

"Gerhard!" voices came from all sides of the room. They sounded happy, excited even, to have a visitor. I smiled, glancing around the crowded room. There were nearly two dozen men in the small space. Some stood around the table, others sat on chairs and stools, a few even sat on the floor, and still others were sleeping or working on menial tasks. Otto walked up beside me and pounded me on the back, beaming.

"Glad you made it, old friend. . . we were beginning to think you weren't coming."

I smiled back at him, looking to Gerhard's memories to form my response, "You should know better than that Otto. I may not be able to stay long, however. . . I'm expected at 10."

Otto had been one of Gerhard's friends nearly as far back as any of his memories would go. They had grown up near each other, had remained close into adulthood, and after the death of Gerhard's father Otto's family had cared greatly for he and his mother, often helping them out in times of financial hardship.

THE | SPLIT

Several weeks ago, Otto had contacted Gerhard via a letter left at his home. In it, he'd detailed how him and several of his men had left their unit before it headed to Seelow Heights. These deserters had met with others like them in the city to form a group devoted to the protection of the German people. Though their task was daunting, they had narrowed their focus to a crucial objective; in the event of the city being stormed by Allied or Soviet forces, they would provide much needed relief at the hospitals and remaining train depots as armed guards. Gerhard had thought this an excellent idea, and worked with the former soldiers, supplying them with equipment and intel.

"When the hour comes, will you join us Gerhard?" Otto asked, trying to seem nonchalant, an effort that failed; the conversation around us died out as the men around the table looked at me to see what my answer would be. As much as Gerhard sympathized with his friend and his efforts, he'd found it difficult to fully leave his responsibilities behind and join them; the sense of obligation and brotherhood among the Kommandos ran deep, even an unjust cause would be hard to abandon. I could sense it deep within Gerhard's core, he was a soldier, and he would always put his duty above all else.

"If I am able, yes." I replied, to the general encouragement of everyone in the room.

"Well good. I look forward to seeing you, old friend." Otto pulled out a silver pocket watch and opened it to check the time. "You must go, Gerhard. . . it is 9:45." he showed me the white clock face. I saw he was right, and turned to leave the room, grateful for the absence of the heavy bag on my shoulders. "Be careful!" Otto called after me. "Bring Gisela to the depot, I would hate to see her left behind."

As I walked down the stairs away from his voice, my thoughts shifted to this "Gisela", and a flood of memories rushed into my brain.

T H E | S P L I T

XXXV

LGPB://mn34/con/terra/DZ, 7091

(Translated)

Poughkeepsie, New York, 2031

They had finally done it.

For years, we had been planning for ACE's inevitable end, but we had never thought it would be like this. The money for which we had nearly thrown away our lives killing Maddox Hill had been sent to the company – the company we had served for nearly a decade – and we hadn't seen a dime of it. We'd been thrown away like we were nothing.

So this was no longer just business; it was personal. As of now all three of us were free agents, and we only cared about one thing – the money. Our plan was to leave the United States, as soon as we could to track down the man who had stolen it from us. We had flown into New York just yesterday, but planned to leave today once we gathered the necessary equipment.

The sky through the tall windows was darker than it should've been for so early in the evening, as Meela came in and threw another handful of clothes on the couch, next to the two black bags she had already stuffed full.

Echoing through the hall to my right were the sounds of Corbin banging around in the basement below. Like most things he did, he had put off packing until the last minute, and I could hear him swearing loudly as he tried to break down his work station.

"Babe," Meela touched my arm. I looked down to see her holding another load of clothes, "We need to hurry, our ship leaves in three hours."

T H E | S P L I T

I nodded and went over to the front door where we had been propping our rifles against the wall, after moving them up from the racks in the basement. Grabbing as many as I could fit in my arms, I walked back into the living room and put them on top of the clothes in one of the bags.

"Burl..." Meela stopped dead in her tracks, looking up at the ceiling, "... do you hear that?"

I paused and listened. "No... what are you talking about?"

"It sounds like, a... helicopter."

I strained my ears, but still couldn't hear what she was talking about. "I don't hear it. Let's just get this stuff in the truck and worry about it then, alright?"

"Okay."

But as I moved another stack of rifles onto a second bag of clothes, and went back for the box of magazines sitting near the last pile of guns, a dull sound suddenly began pulsating in my ears, seeming to shake the whole house. It got louder, and closer, as I walked back to the living room – now a loud chopping undercut the lower sound.

"BURL!" Meela's scream rang out.

I only heard it for an instant before it was drowned out in the chaos. A pair of men burst through the glass windows overlooking the river out back, dressed in all black gear that matched the color of the rope they were clipped onto above; and the unmistakable sound of a helicopter's blades now roared through the shattered window as the dangling men drew their weapons.

Dropping the box and flattening myself against the wall as a storm of bullets tore through the living room, I reached underneath a decorative table and pulled out the pistol stashed in a hidden holster; there were

THE | SPLIT

guns just like it all over the house. I hoped that Corbin and Meela had remembered where they were.

The firing stopped as the men who had broken through the window rappelled all the way down into the living room, and I leapt out from cover, catching the first two by surprise. Shooting from the hallway, I killed both in five shots, but above them I could see the legs of two more slowly descending the rope. Weighing my options, I decided to move forward into the living room; just as one of the men coming down from the chopper fired back, narrowly missing and shattering a vase on the table beside me.

As the next man's feet touched the wooden floor, I shot at him six times, catching him twice in the chest and once in the stomach, sending him staggering. He fell backwards onto the deck behind him, but the next man had nearly descended when I turned towards him. My first shot hit him in the shoulder, but the next pull of the trigger awarded me a loud click. The magazine was empty.

Ducking behind the couch for cover as the man's retaliatory burst of fire tore through the top half of the couch, sending cotton stuffing flying, I threw the empty gun off to the side and looked around in desperation, seeing that the fireplace was nearby. I'd have to roll out from cover. He began to walk towards me, and a fresh round of bullets tore at the floor around me. But the sound of a magazine release being pressed was something I had been trained to listen for and, as the soldier paused to reload, I grabbed one of the pokers near the fire and barreled towards him.

When he popped the new magazine into place and raised the gun-sights, he only got off a single shot before I jammed the poker's tip through his throat, then his weapon slipped out of his hands as he collapsed onto a nearby table.

T H E | S P L I T

Out of the corner of my eye I saw yet another man being lowered down, and grabbed the gun from the man I had just stabbed, firing at his exposed legs and stomach. The rappeler's hand touched the carabiner's release, and then he slid down the entire rope and off, landing on the deck outside in a crumpled heap.

I threw the sub-machine gun off to the side as the whine of the helicopter's rotors picked up, and rushed to tear open one of the bags of clothes, pulling out a Remington ACR assault rifle. The chopper was Chinook transport, and I knew it was capable of holding much more than just five soldiers, but when I walked over to the window I saw it moving back over the house and out of range. I fired at it's body anyway; the bullet bounced uselessly off of the steel hull.

"Burl!" I turned to see Meela emerge from our bedroom. "I found the keys. . . we need to get Corbin, and-"

A sudden, deafening explosion came from our front entrance.

Raising my rifle, I cleared my corner and stepped into the hallway to guard the blown-in door, just as a small silver canister rolled past me on the floor and two others like it next flew through the large opening. Meela was opening a bag of clothes to pull out a rifle of our own, and looked up at me in surprise as I charged towards her.

"MEELA, FLASHBANG!" Knocking her behind the cover of a sofa, I threw myself flat on the ground, dropping my rifle to cover my ears with my fingers.

But even through my closed eyes, the flash from the grenade turned everything white and, for a few short seconds as I lie on the ground trying to catch my bearings, a ringing sound covered everything else and my world seemed to spin in place. Still under cover beside me, Meela struggled to all fours, slapping herself on the side of the head and swearing as she tried to shake off the effects of the grenade.

T H E | S P L I T

Though my own vision was slow to return, and I still struggled with my recovering sense of balance as I rose to my knees, I saw in front of me a trio of black-armored soldiers, rifles at the ready as they searched for us, and knew that the element of surprise was on my side; I cut them all down with bursts from the ACR.

Voices near the front door called out my now-revealed location, and a pair of soldiers moved up our other flank through a side hall by the kitchen. I fired gratuitously, the sounds of my destruction carrying through the house as the bullets went through the men, and then through the cabinets of metal and glass cookware behind them.

Out of ammo, I set down the gun and called out; "Meela! Watch both sides!"

She was ready, and fired to our left as I ducked under cover and pulled another assault rifle from the bag. "Where the hell is Corbin?!"

"I don't know," I replied. "But do you still have the keys?"

"Yeah, they're in my pocket!"

"Good, keep them close."

Silently, I motioned for her to take one side of the house as I walked through the other. Grabbing another stashed pistol from on the side of the wardrobe entrance to the hidden basement below, I stuffed it into my waistband before turning the corner. The false panel back was closed, but I wasn't sure if that had been Corbin's doing or one of the intruders.

"We got one over here!" a man called out from around the corner. "Cut her off!"

I stepped out of cover to see over a dozen men looking towards Meela's side of the house, with more coming in behind them. A group of soldiers, hastening to obey the command, shuffled towards me, yet their eyes were still turned to the side where Meela was exchanging fire with their comrades. So, from just feet away, I unloaded my entire magazine into the approaching soldiers and the men behind them, and five men collapsed onto the ground before the others behind them returned fire.

Then, a searing pain shot through my right arm, forcing me to drop my rifle. Looking down, I was shocked to see my forearm and hand on the ground below, with a piece of bone jutting out. What was left of my arm was a gory stump, just below the elbow, from which blood streamed onto the floor in a steady trickle.

As I collapsed inside the of open wardrobe, my left hand fumbling at my waistband, more bullets whizzed past me and tore into the furniture's wooden sides. My head was pounding, and every few seconds my hearing would fade completely, but I pulled out the pistol and tried to focus on the space in front of me.

In between bouts of deafness, I could hear the men as they walked towards the wardrobe, calling out orders back and forth. I tightened my grip on the handgun, hoping I would not go into shock from the pain and blood loss, then suddenly felt myself slipping backwards as the hidden panel of the wardrobe opened. I fell against something solid and the shoulder of my mutilated arm touched against something metallic and cold.

"Burl! Get outta my way!" Corbin called from right behind me. "I need to get through, and. . . oh, shit!" He leaned me against the side of the staircase as I sunk to the ground, then pulled out a small cylinder from his back pocket. "Here," he said, tossing it down to me. "Take this and get that thing cauterized. We can't have you bleeding out on us."

In his other hand he held our salvation. The 5mm, full-frame behemoth was fully loaded, a chain of bullets trailing behind and down the stairs from the bottom of the large box magazine.

THE | SPLIT

And now, gripping the mini-gun by both handles, Corbin hoisted it up to his waist; just as a group of enemies stepped up to the entrance of the wardrobe, assault rifles raised. Before they could even fire, before they even knew what hit them, Corbin squeezed the other trigger on the handle and the already spinning barrels tore into the men.

He stepped into the hall, screaming barbarically, and now turned his weapon on the men by the front door. Casings showered down onto me, each one hot and pricking at my skin like a bug bite, but flicking them off, I took the cap from the small cylinder and looked down at a needle, inspecting the green and black writing on the side which said, "SYNTH", in bold letters, above smaller words that listed medical specifics. This product was not available for commercial purchase, we were lucky to have the small amount that we had.

After I jammed the needle's tip into the bloodied skin above my stump elbow, my eyes shot open, and I first felt the advertised effect course through my body. Then my heart began to beat rapidly and I twitched involuntarily, before losing all feeling in my body, starting in my right arm and radiating outward. Finally came the massive rush of energy, and I pushed myself up, struggling to gain my footing despite the lack of feeling in my legs and watching them so as not to fall as I moved up the staircase.

Stepping out of the wardrobe, I saw that Corbin lay crouched under cover near the remains of the front entrance, every few seconds popping out to fire at an unseen assailant in the front yard. Meela was in the kitchen, the keys in her hand as she hustled about slipping multiple bags onto her shoulder. I walked back into the living room, eyes still wide, the world seeming to have slowed down around me. One of the bodies on the ground moved as I neared it, reaching for his pistol sluggishly.

T H E | S P L I T

I shot him in the head before he touched it, then moved to the front of the fireplace to pull a flat-sided iron off of the rack and slide it into the fire.

"Oh no, baby!" Meela gasped as she moved past me. "Y-your arm!"

"Yes," I said distractedly, the rush from the injection making me look past her and grind my teeth. "You don't want to see this. . . go help Corbin."

She hesitated for a moment, but murmured her agreement and disappeared around the corner. I waited for a short minute for the flat-sided poker to grow hot, and when the whole top half was glowing red, pulled it out and set it down on the stone.

Fighting my urge to flinch, eyes closed, I pressed my stump against the hot metal, feeling a tingling run through my arm for a brief second. Looking down, I could see my skin bubbling as smoke ran off the top of the poker, and when it was done the end was no longer bleeding, having been replaced by a purple and black stump.

The rushing feeling intensified as the SYNTH went into overtime, but it kept me from passing out even though my head was spinning as I was returning to the front hallway through the kitchen, where I could see Corbin and Meela both still exchanging fire with men outside.

He looked over at me to ask; "Burl, you ready to go?" and I nodded.

XXXVI

LGPB://mn34/con/terra/QE, 3219

(Translated)

Berlin; 1945

Raised to the rank of Sergeant, Gerhard had been transferred to the *SS Sonderkommandos*, and there had discovered the truth of Hitler's "Final Solution", after reading reports of what was going on in these supposed 'Internment Camps'. Disillusioned and sickened by the actions of his government, he had turned to the bottle, spending his nights in bars and beer halls, always going out alone, never with his fellow Kommandos.

It was in one of these bars that he had met this Gisela. He remembered it perfectly; thought about it nearly every day. When he'd first seen her across the counter, his breath had caught in his lungs and his heart began beating rapidly. She was the most beautiful creature he had ever seen, and he couldn't take his eyes off of her. Her friend had noticed him and whispered to her, giggling. She'd raised her head to see who her friend was talking about, and had looked over at him after a few seconds.

When they'd locked eyes for the first time, she had smiled, then turned red, looking away and giggling nervously. Gerhard had finished his drink and found himself walking over to her. She was deep in huddled conversation with her friend as he came up behind her.

His hand shaking slightly, he'd tapped her on the shoulder and, when she'd turned around to look up at him, had instantly fallen for her. They'd talked for a few minutes, then he'd pulled up a stool beside her and hours had passed as they conversed about everything and nothing.

THE | SPLIT

Gerhard had hung onto her every word, fascinated, and when it was time for the bar to close had asked if he could see her again. She'd told him where she stayed, saying that she would be free on the coming Friday. He'd walked home floating on a cloud, his feet hardly seeming to touch the ground. Their next meeting seemed to go even better than the first. They'd walked through the city, arm in arm, laughing and talking, kept warm in the cold winter air by the drinks they had at the bar earlier.

They had begun to meet at his apartment, to talk of things they couldn't in public, and as the months passed he'd gone on to seeing her nearly every day. He thought Gisela was brilliant. She had been raised by a poor family in south Berlin, but despite her humble upbringing she worked hard, and studied the writings of great German philosophers, as well as the latest in scientific study. She also shared his dislike for the policies of the National Socialist party. She encouraged his thinking as well, telling him he should become a politician once the war was over. Gerhard had felt invigorated to be able to talk to someone about the things he had kept silent about for such a long time, and countless hours had passed with them discussing the future of their country, and the ideas needing implementing to make it happen.

Just several months later they were married, it was a rather Spartan affair; most of Germany's resources were tied up in the war effort. Despite this however, it had been the happiest day of Gerhard's life, and he still remembered the joy his mother had upon seeing the ceremony. They'd moved into his apartment together, and Gisela had quickly set to work making it a true home. Then in October of 1944, she had told him that she was pregnant, and Gerhard had been ecstatic at the news. He had spent his nights since, kissing his wife's small pregnant belly and talking to his future child.

THE | SPLIT

As I now walked out of the run down house and into the alley outside, my brain was silent and still. The sun had now fully risen, and its warm rays reached between the buildings, heating up the streets. Gerhard's thoughts remained with his wife and unborn child. He had tried to hide them from me at first, but I'd encouraged his tender and emotional thinking by showing him images and memories of my short time with Meela.

In any event, we both had plenty to think about on our own, and I found no reason to engage in idle conversation. Having left the more industrial side of Berlin, I now was in an affluent neighborhood. Nice houses with neatly trimmed lawns lined both sides of the street. Children still played outside, and the wealthier of the city's denizens bustled about like they didn't have a care in the world. Surely they had heard the shelling? Surely they had been following the news from the front lines? Such a carefree attitude seemed like insanity.

I knew I was to meet up with Gerhard's commander, a man he wasn't particularly fond of. The building our unit had been running operations from lie center of this part of town; a five story tower over one of the city's busiest intersections. The fire escape had been re-purposed as our private entrance to our section on the top floor, and I walked up the steel frame one careful step at a time.

Soon I was outside of the room, opening the door to see several men gathered around a table. They wore the same uniform I did, and looked up as they heard me enter. The man at the head of the table nodded to me in acknowledgment and began to talk to the collective group. "There is news of success to our North. General Steiner's men have halted a Russian advance, preventing our encirclement. Despite this, there are many reports of the deserters breaking off from the IX Army and IV Panzer divisions, thus there will be no reinforcements to our North, and

T H E | S P L I T

command is transferring all Wermacht forces to our south. . . up onto the north line."

He continued to talk, but I was lost. Over the next several minutes I looked through Gerhard's most current memories to get a sense for what was going on.

The date was April 25th, 1945, and we were in the final stages of the war. Russian forces, achieving great victories at German strong points to the East, had torn through central Germany. To combat this, Hitler and his generals had ordered a defensive line built around the city, and had conscripted thousands of young boys and old men to bolster his depleted troops within the city.

Several days ago, Russian forces had advanced within artillery range, and were shelling the city around the clock, and the line of defenders around the outskirts had been exchanging fire with Soviet troops for the last day and a half. We had been ordered by General Heinrici to remain behind the lines with the rest of the Kommandos, the units of which had been broken into small groups and placed strategically through the city center in well fortified positions, to help halt the Russian advance.

I tuned back into the conversation with a better understanding, listening intently to see what I had missed.

". . . and when the Russian front breaks through the defensive line. We will be the first line of defense, and have been ordered to cover the tactical retreat of General Schörner and his men to the city center."

Both Gerhard and I had our doubts about this, but the men around the table nodded in agreement.

He, knowing I was from a time well into his future, turned his thoughts toward mine with uncertainty. He asked about the outcome of this battle, and what he thought we should do, his mind swimming with fear about the fate of his wife and unborn child.

T H E | S P L I T

I hesitated before answering, able to sense the dread in the back of his mind; he already knew my answer.

Reluctantly I told him what I knew, showing him images and memories from my time studying World War II in my youth. A deep sadness filled Gerhard as he saw the war-wrecked ruins of the city he loved; he was afraid for his unit, afraid for his people, and most of all afraid for his wife and child. But I watched as his sadness turned to anger as he thought about his unit's orders in light of this new information, then he decided to speak up, sending me the words he wished to relay.

"We are expected to defend *this* position?" I asked incredulously.

"That's what I said, Sergeant Gerhard. . . do you have a problem with this?"

"Yes, I do. . . it's *suicide.*" I stated plainly.

The men glanced around at each other nervously, it was almost unheard of for a member of the SS to be insubordinate. Even more so due to our dire circumstances. The leader, who I learned through Gerhard's memories was named Lieutenant Fritz, looked caught off guard from my outburst. "These are our orders-" he started.

"Fuck our orders!" I shouted, drawing gasps from the other men around the table. "The war is **over.** Berlin is surrounded. . . with no reinforcements coming from Seelow or Forst. That just leaves us; a piecemeal force, cobbled together from what's left."

For the first time since I entered the room, the soldiers' faces slipped from behind their masks of stoic passivity to reveal the tension and fear underneath. Even Lieutenant Fritz looked afraid for a second, before doing his best to regain his composure and trying to interrupt, but I continued, drowning out his response by speaking even louder.

T H E | S P L I T

Gerhard's words were passionate, and I felt his emotions rush through me, dictating my tone. "We sit here waiting, as our city is torn to pieces. Our brothers who were ordered to come assist us have deserted. They ordered the Hitler Youth to take up arms, and we did nothing. They brought what remains of the old Wehrmacht soldiers out of retirement, and we did nothing. We cry out for reinforcements and they send us *boys*, and old men. . . all willing to give up their lives for a perverse sense of valor. Men in their 50's. . . 60's! Men who deserve to live what's left of their lives free from battle. Even now, Hitler and his generals hide from the storm, cowering in fear inside the safety of their Führerbunker. Those of us still fortunate enough to have families should go to them. Berlin will be torn apart, and any man, woman, or child left behind will be shown no mercy."

The men began to mumble in agreement, and Lieutenant Fritz, feeling his authority slip away, spoke out indignantly, "You would desert the Fatherland in our of need?! These are words of a coward."

I turned to him, barely able to contain my rage, "*I* would never desert this beautiful country! Yet Hitler. . . and all of his generals. . . have made a war torn mess of our present, I will not stand by idly while they destroy our future too! My wife, my child, THAT is my Fatherland. THAT is what I fight for." I turned to a crate in the corner, to grab what I knew was my pack and rifle, and started out of the room.

"Sergeant Gerhard. . . " the Lieutenant's voice rang out behind me, in a stern tone, ". . . if you leave this room, you will be counted as a deserter. I will be forced to execute you without trial."

I spun around, hand near the pistol on my belt as I glared at him. "I would like to see you try. No man. . . Russian or German. . . will keep me from my family today." We made eye contact, until Fritz dropped his gaze and looked off to the side sheepishly.

THE | SPLIT

Not waiting for a reply, I turned and walked out of the room, Gerhard's raw emotional desire to see his wife bleeding into my own thoughts and feelings as I marched down the hallway and the four flights of emergency stairs at a fast pace. When I made it to the street, I followed Gerhard's memory of the city to get us home.

Passing a rail station after several blocks of walking, I noted that the signs were in German, but that I seemed to instinctively know what they said. *"Anhalter Station"* was what the sign above the large brick building read. It was little more than ruin. Mortar fire had torn through most of the walls, revealing the station's disheveled interior, and there were no trains within the building or outside of it; in the last few months trains coming into the city appeared less and less frequently, as the allies and Russians had destroyed most of the German lines. Rail travel from Berlin was practically nonexistent.

As we made our way through the streets, Gerhard continued to think about Gisela. His passion seemed to have blended with my own, and his memories played through my head, blurring the lines between our independent trains of thought. Soon his own image of Gisela began shimmering and changing, and for a second, I saw Meela's face staring up at me before shifting back. It began occurring with such frequency that eventually every memory of Gisela now wore the face of the girl I myself loved.

Now outside, I could hear the sounds of mortar fire coming from my south and east, and every half minute or so I would catch a glimpse of an artillery shell flying over the buildings, into the center of the city. Soldiers of all ages rushed through the streets around me, then I heard a group of boys say the eastern line had been breached and that soon the South would fall as well. Horrified, I quickened my pace, now nearly sprinting as I made my way East.

T H E | S P L I T

At an intersection I stopped and turned down a smaller, two-lane side street. The shelling sounded closer now, and I strained my ears, feeling a slight sense of relief that I couldn't yet hear any sounds of battle. The defensive lines were a few miles from my apartment; I was close now, hopefully I could make it there before the Soviets did.

Turning another corner, I could hear the faint swirling of water ahead and, as I made it down the street, the sound grew louder and I could see the sparkling surface of the Spree River; on its bank, just a short walk away, was my apartment building. I broke into a full sprint, ascended the short flight of concrete stairs in front, and went inside the door. My breath nearly depleted, I felt fatigue starting to set in as I pressed on up the staircase to my right. One flight. Two flights. Three flights. Opening the door, I turned onto my floor and just a few feet away was my front door.

I had made it. I paused to catch my breath, then knocked loudly on the wood.

T H E | S P L I T

XXXVII

Bought from private Collector, 2077

-A. Fila

Berlin; 1945

It took several seconds for Gisela to open the door, but when I saw her, my heart started pounding. She was as beautiful as the day Gerhard had met her, maybe even more, as she stood there with her hair in curlers, wearing a light blue silk maternity gown and a worried expression on her face.

"Gerhard? What is wrong? Is everything okay? I-"

Before she could finish her sentence I pulled her close and kissed her. She was caught off guard, but as our lips moved together she soon melted into my arms. I could feel her heartbeat, and the heat from her tiny pregnant belly as I pulled her in even closer. Even when we'd stopped kissing I held on to her tightly for a few more seconds, knowing this might be the last time I would get the chance.

"That was nice," she smiled, her eyes sparkling with happiness. "But. . . what are you doing here? I thought your unit was stationed in Wilmersdorf?"

"They are," I replied. "I left to come get you. We must leave, Gisela. The city is falling."

She looked confused. "But, I heard only now on the radio that the city would be getting more soldiers from the North. . . and that the Russians were still miles away. Minister Goebbels said the battle shouldn't reach us for days and-"

THE | SPLIT

"Goebbels lies," I interrupted, trying to keep a gentle and patient tone. "He knows that if the people knew the truth, there would be panic and chaos. Just since I last left yesterday morning the situation has deteriorated. There are no reinforcements coming. All of the men to our North have deserted us and have headed west, I imagine they are going to the Americans to surrender, out of fear of what the Russians will do to them. We number less than 100,000 in the city, and the Soviet army that surrounds us is reported to have as many as a million. Our men are mostly old men and boys, Gisela. . . if the Russians have really broken our lines, Berlin will not last beyond sundown."

Her eyes widened as she heard the grave news, and when I was done speaking she turned to look out of the window, thinking. I gave her a few seconds to process what I had told her. Looking around the apartment, I felt a nostalgic sort of sadness as Gerhard showed me memories of his life here through the years. I had just stepped foot inside, but already it felt like I had been here my whole life. There had been parties and meals filled with laughter, drinks with friends, and deep conversations about the meaning of life lasting late into the night. Gisela turned to me, her face resilient and strong; Gerhard had always loved her for that. Living through this war had been hell, but she had done it with the poise and grace of a queen.

"Gerhard. . . what are we going to do?"

"We are going to get you out of the city."

Her face grew concerned at this. "And what of you, my love? Will you not be coming with me?"

I paused; I didn't want to lie to her, but I knew what she needed to hear. "If I can, darling. . . if I can."

"Where can we even go? If the city is surrounded, and there is no way out by rail, what escape do we have?"

THE | SPLIT

"There is one station still operating," I replied, glad I had overheard this the day before. "Lehrter Station still has trains running. . . medical trains to carry the wounded and children out to the East. The allies have prohibited the Russians from bombing them, so it is our safest bet."

"Lehrter Station?" she replied doubtfully. "That's in the middle of the city, just north of all the shelling."

"I know. We will have to take the long way around."

She thought about this for a minute, but nodded. Then, as she opened her mouth to speak, the blaring noise of sirens cut her off. We both looked up. I could hear them coming from multiple areas in the city, which could mean only one thing; the Russians had breached the outer city limits, and were on their way to the center.

"Let me grab our emergency bag!" she said, walking towards the kitchen.

While I waited. I checked my gear, and as I inspected each individual item Gerhard showed me his memories with them – and how they were supposed to be used. On my right hip, I carried a Luger P-08.

It was a bizarre looking pistol, with a slanted handle and a skinny barrel. The magazine released from a button near the trigger, and carried eight rounds in each box. Beside my sidearm, I had three more magazines, and a serrated combat knife on my left hip. The heavy bag was also filled with many personal items, like a picture of Gisela and books I had been reading when I found the time, as well as a mostly full canteen, a small shovel, and two M-24 stick grenades.

Gerhard showed me how to use these several times, explaining slowly to make sure I understood. The grenades were known to have short fuses – as production quality had waned towards the end of the war – and could be quite dangerous.

THE | SPLIT

Closing the pack now, I felt something solid in a top pocket over the flap, and opened it to find five rifle clips, all loaded and ready to go. Gerhard explained to me that the standard was three, and that he had swiped the other two when the munitions officer wasn't looking. I slung the pack over my shoulders and grabbed my rifle off the counter.

It looked like something out of time; a modern-looking assault rifle in a war I knew to be mainly fought with wooden, low capacity, semiautomatics. He sensed my amazement, and showed me his memory of obtaining the gun. It was an StG 44, the product of years of engineering and tinkering, heralded during its demonstration as the 'Savior of the Fatherland'.

Perhaps it might have been, had it been introduced earlier. Gas operated and fully automatic, the StG had been the first of its kind. It provided copious amounts of firepower designed to dominate the simpler rifles of the Allies and Russians. Gerhard liked the gun a lot, and I could sense he felt more confident with the weapon at his side.

"Gerhard, love, are you coming?"

I turned to see Gisela standing near the door, her jacket on and bag over her shoulder, and smiled, following her out of the door. But as we walked through the building and down the stairs, I began to hear the unmistakable cracking of rifle fire, and paused before we got to the ground floor, prompting Gisela behind me to do the same; we walked through the lobby and out the front door more cautiously.

I stepped out into a war zone. No longer muffled inside of my apartment, the sounds of passing projectiles and screaming surrounded us, bouncing off of the buildings and echoing across the river. A hundred meters to my left was a mass of German troops, crossing the bridge towards our side of the river at full speed.

T H E | S P L I T

    Panicked screams of "Panzer!" and "Retreat!" rang out from the crowd as they pushed back towards the center of the city. Grabbing Gisela by the arm gently, I chased after them for a short ways, before turning down the narrow street I had used to arrive. It was long, but well shaded, and we stuck to the side to avoid being seen by enemy soldiers either in front or behind. Not even a minute later I heard screams in Russian from the direction we came.

    Pulling Gisela behind the cover of some nearby newspaper machines, I peered out carefully as the voices grew closer, to see what was coming our way. A disorganized column of Russian soldiers was crossing between the two buildings at the end of the thru-way, pursuing the fleeing group of soldiers we had seen on the bridge down the main road.

    I tried to count them as they passed, using a grouping technique I had learned in Kommando training. 20...40...60... then a massive group came into view, too many to count, and I gave up. Minutes passed as the Russians kept coming; thousands of them.

    At the end of the procession an officer pointed down the side street where we were hiding, and sent a few dozen men down our way. I tightened my grip on the rifle, shifting my weight to the balls of my feet, ready to go at any time. But instead of continuing in our direction, the soldiers stopped at the first few houses and kicked in their doors.

    I could hear gunfire from inside the buildings, and a moment later the soldiers reappeared, dragging out civilians with them. A younger woman, who was being pulled by her hair, screamed hysterically before a fat soldier smashed the butt of his rifle into her face to shut her up.

    Hastily, they separated their male captives from the women and lined them up, then a volley of staggered rifle fire rang through the narrow street as the men were executed. Then, a woman tried to run away but was caught, and they threw her against the wall and tore off her clothes;

THE | SPLIT

the other soldiers began to do the same to their female prisoners. I turned my head. I knew what was going to happen, and felt sick that I was powerless to stop it.

With the Russians' backs to us, we took off down the street and, after making a sharp left at the intersection we were near the city's center, apparent by the decimated buildings and cars. The ground in the area was rough and hard to traverse quickly, small impact craters dotted the roadways and sidewalks; a testament to the staggering amount of shelling that had taken place. I turned to Gisela to make sure she was alright before we continued. She was sweating and looked tired, but the determined look on her face let me know to press on.

We could hear sounds of combat coming from behind us on multiple roadways, then a group of Hitler Youth in full retreat crossed our path. I glanced around the corner nervously to spot their pursuers; they were several hundred meters back, so I grabbed Gisela by the hand and ran towards a group of buildings ahead of us.

A large sign near the front entrance of one of these buildings read: "**Unter Den Linden**", and I knew we were only a couple of kilometers away. When we made it inside, I closed the door behind us and slid the heavy wooden bar lying nearby into place to seal it shut. We then walked together through the hallway of the large, mostly abandoned building. It felt creepy to see a place like this so empty, just months ago this whole building had been bustling with shops and businesses of all type, now it was a piteous sight, with furniture that had been knocked over and fliers for sales that would never happen littered the ground.

Motioning towards a staircase nearby, I started up it, leading the way, but turned around halfway up to see Gisela still on the first step, clutching her stomach and breathing heavily. Walking back down I scooped her up into my arms; she didn't weigh much, even with the baby, but it took me a bit longer to reach the top of the staircase. Still, I didn't set her down at the top, instead walking into a large room nearby where I laid her down on a leather sofa. She looked up at me affectionately, wordlessly beckoning me to her with the movement of her fingers, and when I leaned down she grabbed my neck, giving me a short kiss before she released me, smiling.

I looked around the room as she caught her breath. There were glasses and bottles on a table nearby, and I realized this place had been a lounge of some sort. Other things around me confirmed my hunch. Leather couches were gathered around low tables, and a phonograph played softly in the corner.

The music was nice, a quaint reminder of what Berlin had been like just days ago, and I listened to it, humming along, as I watched what was going on outside the window. The Russians were converging outside in the city center, and the dug-in defenders were overwhelmed. But they fought on, manning the machine gun nests and returning rifle fire as the soviets approached from several streets at once.

It looked like they would soon overrun the plaza. Our generals would call a tactical retreat to defend the capital district, and the Russians would need Panzer support to proceed, likely diverting to other parts of the city until they received it. Until this inevitable break in the lines, we would be unable to proceed.

Gisela was sitting up and undoing her curlers when I turned around; I had hardly noticed they were still in.

"What?" She laughed nervously as I watched her.

"Nothing," I said, smiling.

She set the curlers on the table and patted the couch next to her for me to sit down, asking firmly, "Tell me, what is happening outside?"

THE | SPLIT

"Nothing you would wish to hear. . . we are safe for now. We must wait for the plaza to clear, and then we shall make a run for it – the station is only a little ways from here. With what was made clear to me by command, it is unlikely that the Russians will interfere with anything marked as a medical transport. . . in fear of retaliation from the allies. . . so I would say that our chances are good my love."

"Gerhard. . . you do always know what to tell me, don't you?" she laughed, but I saw a tear roll down her face.

I pulled her into a one-armed embrace. The song changed on the player just then, and I paused and looked up. The soft melody seemed to warm my entire body as I instantly recognized it from Gerhard's many memories; *Ich weiß, es wird einmal ein Wunder gescheh'n*; "I Know Someday a Miracle will Happen". It had been the first song we had danced to, one night at the bar.

"Darling, our song!" Gisela exclaimed with more tears rolling down her cheek now.

I pulled her to her feet just as Zarah Leander's strong voice came softly into the verse, and she laughed as I put an arm around her waist and drew her to the center of the room. We twirled around the open space to the music, our eyes locked in bliss, and in that moment all that was around us melted away. There was no war, no death, no danger. It was just me, her, and that beautiful song. As the tempo began to pick up, I spun her around faster, then in a rush grabbed her by the waist and picked her up.

She giggled, wrapping her arms around my neck as I held her in front of me – but suddenly, her face turned serious, though her eyes still gleamed lovingly. "I love you, Gerhard von Schleicher. . . even now, there is no other place I would rather be than by your side."

T H E | S P L I T

When she leaned in to kiss me and I met her lips, overwhelming and near-primal feelings I couldn't describe mingled with the feelings of affection which swam through my mind as, through my nearly closed eyes, I watched her turn into Meela...

Then a pain split through my head, and I was lost in the moment.

Note - Arthur Fila, November 23rd 2092

I was fortunate enough to find two groupings of entries that appear to be in order back to back. The author's account of Nazi Germany falls in line with most early century viewpoints on the matter. Yet the following pages are strange. It seems that after this kiss, the narrative changes and he begins to refer to himself as Gerhard only. There is never any explanation for this sudden shift, nor does it happen in any other entries I have found so far.

Upon doing some simple research I was able to find this Gerhard in military records from the time period. There isn't much to go on, but there isn't a doubt in my mind that he existed, and therefore it is likely these words are true. His wife, Gisela, was a different matter. I found a large amount of documentation on her, and was able to piece together her life after the events in Berlin.

She did escape the embattled city, and was treated in a hospital in France. There, she gave birth to their son, yet there is no record of his existence until six months later, when immigration documents show she traveled to the United States and got a birth certificate for the boy. He was named Gerhard, after his father. By all sources, it seems like Gerhard SR. died in Berlin that day; he is listed among the German casualties.

Gisela never remarried, instead pouring her life into a small store she used to support Gerhard. This small store eventually became a chain of supermarkets in the 70's, and the little family became quite wealthy. After Gisela's passing in 1984, her grandson took over the business. His grandson still runs it to this day. I have reached out to contact him with this story but have yet to hear anything back.

Arthur Fila, 2083

THE | SPLIT

XXXVIII

Found in abandoned Subway tunnels, 2080

-A. Fila

Berlin; 1945

I am Gerhard.

The voices in my head tell me otherwise, but I can not listen. . . when they call out I ignore what they have to say. These thoughts. . . these strange. . . other, memories. . . they do not matter now. All I must do is get Gisela to safety, even if it takes my death.

Her lips still locked with mine, I could feel her tremble slightly as I gripped her tighter, holding her above the ground. I felt no strain from my muscles, with death all around us the only thing I could cling to was life, and the love I had for this tiny life whom I had never seen, growing inside my beloved Gisela.

I set her down carefully and walked back over to the window to look out at the plaza. The columns of Russian soldiers were leaving, sporadically, taking off down various streets to the North, and less than half remained. In a few minutes, we would have an opening to the train station.

Gisela was again sitting on the couch, and I walked over and sat down beside her. She cozied up to me, laying her head on my shoulder and sighing with content. We sat there in silence as minutes passed, enjoying each other's company, putting off thoughts of the destruction raging all around us, and I had never enjoyed my time more, had never held onto a moment as tightly as this one.

THE | SPLIT

But after what seemed a blissful eternity, my inner soldier stirred and brought me to my feet. The plaza was completely clear, but who knew for how long?

"Come along, Gisela, it is time to leave. Are you okay to walk?"

"Yes, I think so," she replied nervously. "Lead the way, dear."

We walked out of the room and through the hallway to the staircase at a cautious pace. I could hear artillery in the distance, but there were no sounds of any Panzers or enemy troops, and when after descending the stairs to the entrance of the building I peered out through the cracked doorway into the plaza outside, there were no men in the clearing.

I led Gisela out into the open, a few hundred meters away I could see a large government building, which I knew led to an alley that would take us to the station. As we quickly walked through the plaza we had to step over the bodies left behind in the carnage, hundreds of them; Russians and Germans alike. It was nearly impossible to see the pavement under the gore-strewn scene. Every few meters we would pass a soldier still alive, who called out to us in agony, or cried out for water and help from a medic. It was hard to ignore, but we pressed on. From behind I felt Gisela grab my shoulder for reassurance as she quickened her pace.

Suddenly, a demonic-sounding roar stopped us in our tracks. It echoed off of the buildings for a few seconds before fading, sending a chill through my bones.

"Gerhard. . . " Gisela sounded terrified. "What was *that*?"

"I. . . don't know," I admitted. I had never heard anything like it. "We must continue, we're nearly to safety." She nodded and we broke into a slow jog.

THE | SPLIT

The corpses began to thin out as we made it to the other side, and the steps up to the large building in front of us were cleared entirely. We climbed them and went through the double doors inside. A soldier in a Wermacht uniform passed us, holding his bloodied stump of an arm and muttering to himself, but paid us no mind.

The place still looked as I had last seen it, but the hallways were nearly empty as we continued down the hall. After a few more seconds I began to hear a whispered conversation, coming from a door ahead to our left, and as we moved by it I paused, turning to look inside of the room; two older women sat on a couch. One lay on the other's shoulder as she tried to console her. They were so engrossed in their conversation, they didn't even look up to see me and Gisela standing there.

"I j-just don't know w-what to d-do. Josef said he would meet me here. . . it's been hours past the time he said."

"Hush, Eva," the other woman replied. "Do not entertain such thoughts. I'm sure he is on his way even now."

"H-he always was such a p-proud man, always wanting to serve Germany. I told him he was too old. . . I said to ignore Goebbels's broadcast, and come hide with me. 'Nonsense', he said. . . there was no convincing him otherwise."

The woman broke down into tears. I tapped Gisela and motioned for us to keep walking. There would be many stories like the old lady's by the end of the day. Whole families of sons and fathers had died in the war, it seemed a cruel joke that its last battle would take away grandfathers and boys as well.

We were nearing the back door when I heard the clattering of metal hitting the hard floor and turned around to look for the source of the noise, but I could see nothing.

T H E | S P L I T

Frowning, I led Gisela down a nearby hall to our right, towards the back door that led to the alley behind, and could hear footsteps as I got closer, followed by the slamming of a door a few meters up.

Could the Russians already be in this building?

I thought about it, doing my best to think like a field commander and not as just another scared soldier. The building was tall and well reinforced, the levels above would make an excellent spot for snipers to take position. So there could be several soldiers in the room ahead. I couldn't just move past them, in fear of being snuck up on from behind.

Gisela was standing several feet behind me, clutching her hands nervously. Reaching the door, I took a deep breath and, as softly as I could, turned the knob. With the door cracked open, I pulled my StG to my shoulder and looked through the iron sights, ready to shoot, then kicked it open with a loud bang, making sure to clear both of my sides like I had been taught before entering the room.

There were no soldiers, in fact the place seemed to be empty. But as I turned to back out of the door, a soft whimpering caught my attention, and I spun around to see a head peeking over a leather chair. It was a boy. Dirt smeared his face, and he couldn't have been much older than ten.

He looked up at me with fearful eyes, and I lowered my rifle as he stood up, then could see he was holding a small knife. I motioned for him to drop it, he stared at me for a few seconds, but dropped the knife. Then he burst into tears. A paternal instinct I didn't know I had took over my body, and I found myself hugging him.

He hugged me back tightly, still sobbing for a few seconds before he let go and wiped away his tears. "Mr. Soldier, am I. . . going to die?" he wore a serious expression now, trying to control his sobs with normal breaths.

T H E | S P L I T

"No, son," I replied, looking him in the eye. "I promise you will be safe. You must do one thing for me, yes. . . soldier?"

He brightened at being called soldier. "What?"

"Go to the VERY top of the building and find a place to hide. . . do not leave for two days." His eyes widened, but he nodded and looked at me to continue. "Here," I opened my bag and handed him some of the food and my extra canteen, "This should get you by. . . you must drink the water slowly, you understand that son?" He nodded again and ran out of the room.

I had just called him son again. Was that a sign? My thoughts shifted to Gisela and the baby. Leaving the room, I saw her leaning against the wall – she seemed to be growing more beautiful every time I saw her.

Was that too a sign?

I had to shake my head to clear my thinking as my mind started connecting all of these signs. Focus.

I led Gisela out through the hallway and to the back door, rifle at my side, but had to crouch as soon as I stepped outside; there were voices at the end of the thru-way. The men were loud, yelling in Russian as they shot off their rifles. There looked to be about 20 of them, their backs turned to us, standing down at the end of the alley. I stepped back inside and waited, closing the door behind me. Had they seen me yet? I guessed that it didn't matter; either way, my response would be the same. Setting my backpack on the ground, I opened it and pulled out a stick grenade, then turned to Gisela behind me.

"Gisela my love, there are men in our path. I'm going out there to take care of them, hopefully with the element of surprise on my side. If you do not hear my voice within a minute, run to the top floor and find that little boy. Here, take my backpack, and wait for me."

T H E | S P L I T

She gasped and looked at me, surprised, then her expression saddened and she hugged me. I hugged her back with one arm, leaving the stick grenade behind my back. Gisela stepped back from the door to sit on a crate, and I made my way outside. They were still all standing there, backs turned.

I shut the door behind me and primed the grenade. When I threw it center the group, it immediately exploded, and more than a dozen men were dead instantly, their bodies scattered in mangled pieces on the alley floor.

The few survivors turned around, and I raised my gun as a few hastened to do the same, getting off two rounds before I had blown through them all with the StG, the fierce spray tearing into the cluster of men so quickly most of them hadn't even processed my appearance. I felt a deep sense of gratitude for the gun, as I often had at the range. Reloading the weapon with a magazine from my pocket, I now slowly walked out to the alleyway with it again up and ready, then after a few dozen meters turned to call out to Gisela in a loud but muffled voice.

She scurried out, giving me my backpack as soon as she caught up. Keeping her hand on my shoulder as walked up the alleyway, we reached the end after a minute or two and were now at the crossroads of a large street. Looking both ways, I could see men on both sides in the distance but none within range. We had reached the last building we needed to go through before reaching the station, and I was grateful for my training – and the planning for the city's defense. No one knew the streets and alleyways of Berlin better than the SS, and no one in the SS knew them better than the Kommandos.

But as we started to move across the wide street towards the next building, we heard the loud howling again. Gisela shrieked and moved behind me, clenching the back of my uniform in trembling fear.

Then I turned and saw it.

Dashing towards us, in long powerful strides, was a creature of nightmares. It was a large, muscular humanoid, which looked about two and a half meters tall and had a disproportionately large head. But it was the eyes that sent a shiver down my spine; large and elongated, they were big, white orbs with tiny pupils, and took up most of the thing's face, giving it a look of terrifying insanity. It was wearing a Russian army uniform, and had a rifle on his back, but did not draw it. Instead it chose to sprint towards me, massive ape-like arms swinging.

And it was moving *fast* – as fast as I had seen most cars move through the city. I started for the other side of the street, keeping an eye on the creature as it neared.

"Gerhard, what the hell is that thing?!"

"I don't know!" I shouted. "Stay with me and keep moving!"

My mind suddenly seemed to slow; the other presences in my brain were shouting at me, forcing my attention, and one voice rang out over the others; (the future American) Burl.

*"Gerhard! It's a **hunter**! Get the hell out of there! Get her to safety and-"*

The voice cut out, as my mind went wild with what he had said. A hunter? I crouched and aimed my rifle, firing when he got within range, seeing the short burst hit his chest. But he did not slow, and was much closer now; in just seconds he had moved 20 meters nearer. I laid my finger against the trigger.

Bullets streamed out of the gun only milliseconds apart, hitting his chest and trailing upward. I counted 14 before stopping as he stumbled and fell over. But he was still moving towards me, slowly. Then he got up from his crawl and ran at me headlong.

THE | SPLIT

I only had 6 bullets left in my magazine, and shot the rest at his head. He collapsed face first, but my feeling of relief was cut short when I saw his arms still moving, pulling his body forward as his legs started to rise. Pulling my last magazine out of the backpack, I quickly swapped it with the old one and turned to Gisela, pointing across the way.

"Run into the building, go!"

She took off across the way and I whirled back around to the creature. He was almost back on his feet. I again opened fire on him, but tried to leave myself at least a few shots. The creature keeled over again, and I hurried after Gisela, hearing his roar bellow out behind me as I made it through the front door and closed it quickly. Turning, I saw my wife standing there with the wooden door bar and snatched it to put it into place; seconds later the creature slammed against the now reinforced entry.

Moving quickly, I pulled Gisela down the hall, but turned around to look back at her with concern in my eyes when she doubled over gasping for air. She looked up at me with a forced smile, gasping, but her eyes still wore the same look of terror they had donned upon seeing the demonic hunter. I scooped her into my arms and continued down the hallway, holding her near my chest.

Part of the building had collapsed in the middle of the hallway, and I was searching to find a staircase to make my up and around. When a frustrated roar rang out behind me, and then the pounding on the front door ceased, I wondered if he was still behind us; was he gone, or looking for another way in?

But I had no intention of slowing down to find out, putting distance between us was my only priority.

At the top of the stairs, I set Gisela down and grabbed her hand as I jogged down the hallway. The building brought back memories every

THE | SPLIT

dozen meters or so. I had spent a lot of time here, on guard duty during my tenure with the Kommandos. I also came a lot in my free time to get various documents and licenses; this was the only place in Berlin you could obtain important papers from the government.

The day before our wedding, Gisela and I had waited for hours in the sitting area for our chance to get a marriage license. After we had both signed the form, the clerk gave us a copy of *Mein Kampf* and sent us on our way. Seeing the place now was even stranger than seeing the empty building of shops back near the plaza.

During the daylight hours this building was bustling with secretaries and clerks who would move through the halls at a brisk pace, hurrying to and from their lunch breaks. The frustrated voices of both men and women alike could be heard from the large counter in the wide open area; no one liked waiting, and people liked waiting for the wrong documents even less.

Gisela and I had passed the time watching these angry patrons unload the troubles of their day on the poor clerks. In our newlywed bliss, the troubles of the world had not been able to touch us, any negativity or bitterness seemed petty and foolish. We were infinite, there seemed to be nothing in life we couldn't have.

Oh, how the war had changed things. I tried to hold on to the memory of that feeling, but the reminder of our grim reality brought me back to the present. There were no marriage licenses or business of any kind here today. The only people we saw were groups of frightened survivors, huddled in corners and hiding under cover. Gone was the security of the Fatherland and the pride of it's people; the remnants of the thousand year Reich were here – a dying city abandoned by the very leaders who had promised the entire world for loyalty to them.

T H E | S P L I T

We were almost halfway across the second floor hall, and I slowed our pace to allow Gisela to catch her breath, my mind fully alert with a fear tinted-anticipation. We were so close to the station, but also not far from that monster.

The boarded up window to my right shook violently, causing me to jump, and as I turned towards it suddenly the wood split and the Hunter burst through the frame.

"Gisela, run!" I screamed, raising my StG to my shoulder.

I didn't have to tell her twice; she took off down the hallway.

T H E | S P L I T

XXXIX

LGPB://mn34/con/terra/ZD, 4006
(Translated)

Berlin; 1945

Turning my body sideways to cover her escape, I squeezed the trigger of my rifle, releasing a hail of bullets, the noise reverberating off the walls loudly and deafening me.

The first few hit the creature's shoulder, but the rest hit the wall as he shot his long arm out and knocked the rifle aside. Pushing off him I stepped back in order to make space to aim again with my StG, like I'd been taught; there weren't many rounds left in the magazine, and I knew I had to make the last few shots count.

To my surprise however, instead of drawing his own rifle the creature lurched forward and, before I could react, grabbed my rifle with both hands. I looked up at his face as I tried to pull away, the tiny pupils danced around in abnormally large eyes, sending fear through my heart. The creature laughed as he seemed to sense this; a deep rumbling that sounded powerful and cruel.

Then with an incredibly strong, sharp jerk the creature tore my StG from my grasp as though I were a child clutching a toy, and flung it to the other side of the room. When I raised my leg and kicked him in the thigh, trying to create space and pull out my sidearm, he didn't move at all, instead grabbing the arm reaching for my pistol to keep me from pulling away.

I looked down as I tried to tear him off me because its grip felt cold on my bare skin, then my vision left me and I felt a foreign presence force its way into my thoughts.

T H E | S P L I T

Brushing against it, I was shown impressions and images of scenes too horrible to mention, and the Hunter then tore through my memories savagely. The space around my thinking tightened as thoughts from the creature wrapped around my own, leaving me powerless to fight it.

The other beings, inside my head, were panicked at the intrusion. I felt their fear as they huddled together, communicating with thoughts I could not see. But just as the creature neared my consciousness, the one of my head-mates called the General leapt to the fore of my thoughts and pushed back against the invader. My mind instantly cleared and my eyesight returned in a flash.

Seeking a way to escape, I made the best of the time gained by trying to pry the creature's hand off my arm, which was larger than any I had seen before. Strange, bulging, black veins covered its parchment-like skin as it wrapped around my elbow completely, with almost no effort, clamping down and squeezing my arm tightly. Then I suddenly heard a loud series of cracks, as the bones beneath broke. Pain clouded my thoughts, and I cried out in agony as my limp arm dropped from his grasp.

But I still turned to my side, knocking him back by using my hip with as much strength as I could muster. The Hunter took a step back, to avoid falling backwards, and unslung the rifle. As the butt was raised to his shoulder I reached across my body to pull the pistol out of my belt with my good hand, settling for my knife when my fumbling fingers couldn't grab it, and stepped forward.

The Hunter had his eye to the sights now, and I saw his long finger inching towards the trigger like it was in slow motion. Desperately I threw up my broken left arm, sending pain shooting through my limb as my broken bones collided with the barrel, just as the shot rang through

T H E | S P L I T

the room. I felt the wind from the bullet move past my left side but, catching his counter blow with my shoulder, I plunged my knife through his eye and dragged the blade down to the bottom, near its pupil.

The Hunter grabbed his punctured eye with a deafening shriek, making me want to cover my ears from the shrill noise; my eardrums pounded. But I lowered my body and put my good shoulder to his waist, driving him backwards and out of the window he had came through. He fell hard, yet slowly stirred. I watched as he was pulling the knife from his eye, then turned and sprinted down the hallway, trying to ignore the pain from my shattered arm, calling out, "Gisela!" and looking through the doorways of rooms as I passed. She wasn't in any of them, so I kept running, turning left at the end of the hall – and nearly ran over my wife in my haste.

"Gerhard!" she cried out, as she caught me in her trembling arms.

I did not reply. We were right by the exit to the back alley, and there was no time to waste. I pushed the door open, struggling with just my right hand. Gisela saw my limp arm and grew wide-eyed, asking me what happened. I could see the alley was clear from our spot on the second floor fire escape; assuring her it was nothing, I firmly told her that we needed to keep moving.

She descended the ladder first and I followed her, moving slowly with my good arm so that I did not slip. When I made it down I pulled out my pistol and led her between the brick buildings towards the street ahead, the station was just in front of us.

I could see some old Wermacht soldiers guarding the entrance, hands on their rifles, with many of the citizen soldiers I had met with that morning standing in between them. I scanned their faces looking for anyone I knew, frowning when I didn't see anyone, but motioned for

T H E | S P L I T

Gisela to head through and into the station. Just then, a strong arm grasped me on the shoulder.

"Gerhard!" I turned to see Otto.

"Otto my friend! I am pleased to see you here."

"The pleasure is mine," he replied, inclining his head. He turned to Gisela, "'Sela, my dear. . . it is good to see you, as well. How is my little soldier coming along?" With this he crouched and put his hand lightly on Gisela's stomach, speaking to the unborn child for several seconds as me and Gisela exchanged smiles; Otto had been nearly as excited at the news of our pregnancy as we had been ourselves.

And I wished we had time to continue this happy reunion, but circumstances had forced us into reevaluating our priorities.

"Gisela. . . " I called to my wife, getting her attention, ". . . go inside the station. I must speak to Otto alone."

She nodded and made her way up the short line of stairs, in between the pillars, and inside of the large station door. I looked around at the group keeping guard. Most of the men appeared older than I would've liked, with the exception of Otto and his small group.

Otto walked over to me, a questioning expression on his face. "What is wrong, my friend? You need to get inside the station and get your wife to safe-"

"I will," I cut him off. "Otto. . . something happened on our way here that I need to tell you about." His face grew serious and he nodded for me to continue. "There was this. . . creature. . . it attacked us on the road. I have never seen anything like it before. It fights in a Soviet uniform, but it is not human. It has been chasing us. . . twice now I have had to fight it off. It is on its way here now, I'm sure. Otto. . . if you see it, be careful. I have shot the thing more times than I could count, and even put my knife through its eye. . . yet still it moves. Promise me you'll be careful."

"Monster in a Soviet uniform, yes." Otto replied. "I shall be careful, old friend. . . you must not worry." His tone sounded lighthearted and playful, like he did not fully believe me.

"Otto, I am serious."

He stared at me, but then nodded his head to indicate he believed me. "Just get inside, Gerhard, I will take it from here."

I clasped him on the shoulder, "Thank you, Otto," then turned up the stairs and went inside the station. Inside, the ticket booths were empty, and a sign saying "All Lines Closed" could be seen from across the room, but the cavernous lobby echoed with sound, as bandaged soldiers lay on benches and sat in chairs all around us with Medics hustling between them, trying to attend to everyone's injuries.

A few families clutching little ones were headed towards a side hallway, we followed them, and as we moved down the corridor I saw wooden crates and supplies lining both sides of the hall; ammo boxes and bags of rations, supplies for soldiers in a war that was already over.

The way twisted and turned, deeper into the station, but soon we could both hear the rumbling of a train's engine echoing off the walls and quickened our pace. The station's platform was crowded as we entered through the hallway above it. I glanced over the guardrail at the throng of people standing beside the cars, there were hundreds waiting, pressing forward, looking close to trampling the guards at each compartment door.

"We'll never make it aboard!" Gisela lamented, exasperated hopelessness in her voice.

"Yes, we will," I replied resolutely, my tone having an edge I had

T H E | S P L I T

never heard in it before as I led her down the stairs behind the crowd of screaming people, all packed in tight, all fighting their way ahead. My eyes scanned the group for an opening, finding one few seconds later; the easiest way would be through an opening towards the second to last car. We walked to our left, behind the people waiting, then I turned to my wife.

"Gisela." She looked up at me, curious. "I will push my way through. . . grab hold of my belt, and do not let go. If I feel us separate, I will turn around and come get you. Okay love?"

She swallowed nervously, but nodded, and I began to weave my way through the crowd. The first few rows of people were easy to pass, their eyes glanced longingly at the cars in front of them, and they seemed to hardly notice us moving by. My shattered arm shouted out in pain as it brushed against them, but I gritted my teeth and soldiered on.

The middle of the group was more densely packed, people would have to move out of the way for us to go through, so I tapped a man on the shoulder and asked politely if we could squeeze past him. He looked at me like I was crazy, screaming "Fuck off!", before turning back around. Something snapped inside of me, raising my pistol from my side, I whirled him around by his shoulder. "What the hell do you think-"

He fell silent when he saw my gun, held tightly against my chest, and without a word stepped back and out of the way, allowing us to slip deeper into the crowd. As I looked around at the people waiting, I studied their faces. Their expressions would have chilled my blood mere hours ago, as I had never before seen such desperation and fear, but things had changed. Gone was Gerhard the soldier, Gerhard the professional, Gerhard the patriot.

In less than a day all of that had unraveled. These men and women whom I once viewed as countrymen and the future of my beloved

THE | SPLIT

nation, were nothing more than obstacles now. Everything I had been taught, everything I had been told, everything I believed in, none of it mattered anymore. Germany was dying, and I could not save her. I could only save what was mine, the tiny piece of this big wide world that was more important to me than anything else in it. If the train was full or nearing full, I would just have to talk Gisela's way on board.

After flashing my gun a few more times and pushing anyone in my way aside, we had made it to the front of the crowd. A woman in front of me was screaming at the guard blocking the entrance, and I grabbed the back of her jacket and flung her behind me, then lowered my pistol, taking a few deep breaths. Gisela tugged at my belt, and I turned around to lead her in front of me. She held her bag loosely in front of her, the bottom lightly touching her pregnant belly, and was breathing hard.

As I stepped towards the platform, the guard responded to my movements by turning his head, and rifle, towards my direction. Slipping the handgun into my pocket, I put my good arm in the air in a gesture of cooperation. "It is okay. . . I am SS." I said, trying to sound disarming as his narrowed eyes inspected my uniform, lingering on my broken and limp left arm.

He was a short man, wearing the uniform of a military policeman. His face looked dirty and tired, and he had a large boil on the side of his neck that was hard not to look at. From his clean looking jacket to his clumsy movements, everything about him said he was a recent recruit.

"I do not care if you are Minister Goebbels himself," he replied after examining me. "Only those with passes are allowed to board."

I looked through the window into the car. Most seats were taken, but there was still a whole aisle worth of standing room. It wouldn't be ideal, but anything to get Gisela and the baby out of the city was worth my efforts.

T H E | S P L I T

"There must be something you can do to help us," I tried to sound convincing. "My wife. . . she is pregnant. . . I need to get her out of Berlin."

He gestured with his rifle out into the crowd. "Look around you. . . dozens of these women are pregnant. Why is your family better than theirs?" The train whistled, warning its imminent departure; the man glanced at it before continuing, "Now. . . please step away from the platform. The train is about to leave the station."

In an instant I was on him, my bad hand pinning him by the neck against the side of the train, the other shoving the gun into his mouth. He looked up at me, wide-eyed, muttering incoherently around the cold steel barrel, then looked to his side for help.

I followed his eyes. Another guard several meters to our left stood watching, but he dared not aim his rifle at me, lest the people he was standing in front of charged *him*.

I nodded my head to motion Gisela onto the train, and then turned back to the guard, cocking the hammer. "My wife is getting aboard this train. . . and you are going to leave her be. . . you understand, yes?" He nodded furiously and, satisfied with his answer, I threw him into the crowd.

Looking back at the train I saw Gisela stood on the first step, just above eye level. She now looked down at me, her voice dropping as she realized; "You are not coming, are you?"

I paused, before shaking my head sadly. "That thing back there. . . I have to stop it Gisela. I believe I am the only one with a chance. Who knows how many people it will kill if it is allowed to run free."

She nodded slightly, but tears shone in her eyes. "Gerhard. . . you will come to find me after this, right?"

T H E | S P L I T

"God himself could not keep us apart," I smiled at her.

"*Oh, Gerhard*!" she exclaimed, sobbing as she threw her arms around me and squeezed me like she would never let go.

I hugged her back, trying to memorize every detail of the moment. As she continued to sob into my chest, I reached down to grab her chin lightly, turning her face towards mine and looking her in the eyes. She stared back at me, trembling, a single tear making its way down her left cheek. I wiped it away, and closed my eyes to kiss her, visualizing our child and the man he would become as our lips locked in a desperate sort of bliss, regretting I would not be there to see it happen, or hold Gisela as we watched with pride.

Mostly, I thought of Gisela. I thought of the good times, all of the memories with her I had been blessed with, the few short happy years I wouldn't trade for anything. I thought of the way she bit her lip when she was nervous. How she had started to lightly snore when she became pregnant, and how I had teased her for it. I thought of the first night I had met her, and about how my life was never the same after. A whole lifetime flashed before my eyes in a single kiss, and I realized that even if I had the choice, I wouldn't change a single thing about it.

The train started to move forward and I pulled away as she looked at me longingly, but walked beside her for a few seconds, holding her hand. "I love you, Gisela."

"I love you too, Gerhard. I am so proud of the man you have become. I will wait for you. . . come back to me, soon."

I smiled and nodded, and her hand slipped from mine as the train pulled away. Standing there on the platform, I stared at the train moving out of the station. . . looking at my wife for the last time as the train grew smaller and smaller as it trailed off into the distance, away from the city.

THE | SPLIT

The crowd around me talked among themselves frantically, all looking for another way out of the city now that the train had left the station. Knowing that the scene would soon be chaos, I made my quickly to the staircase that led out to the exit.

T H E | S P L I T

XL

Bought in auction, 2082

-A. Fila

Berlin; 1945

A familiar growl echoed from the halls above.

'Otto. . . ' I thought sadly of my old friend, and the other brave men who had guarded the entrance outside. Had any of them escaped from the terrible creature?

All of the people fell to a hushed silence as the growling grew louder. I backed away from the staircase and pulled out my pistol, with great strain reaching into my pack to pull out another magazine. Placing the new one between my legs, I fumbled for a few seconds before getting the weapon reloaded with my right hand. The creature had completely ruined my left arm, and I was still in agony as it hung there uselessly, paining me every time it was swung in any direction even by the slightest fraction. And now it was coming down here. And it was angry.

Seconds later, the top of its enormous head appeared above the guardrail, and it walked into view, searching the crowd for me. The people screamed when they saw it, and some behind me started to run towards the tracks.

This time it did not charge me with flailing arms. Instead, it carried a Degtyaryov machine gun, and opened fire, shooting the entire 60 round pan into the dense crowd below, tearing through multiple people with each shot and leaving a sickening path of gore behind. I crawled behind a nearby bench for cover, listening as I heard the large creature walking down the steps, waiting to hear it reload.

THE | SPLIT

When I didn't hear anything, I popped my head out in confusion, and my body grew tense with involuntary fear as I saw that the creature had come closer. It also had dropped the machine gun, and was now using another weapon – or more accurately, WEARING another weapon. I had no idea where it could've gotten it from, but the Hunter had a *flammenwerfer.*

I ducked back behind cover but could still see the streak of flame moving past me as fire poured out of the tip and into a group of scattering people. It was almost 10 meters long, and scorched through the panicked crowd with impunity. Miserable shrieks echoed throughout the platform as poor souls burned alive.

I began to scoot backwards, angling towards the edge of the platform and off, down onto the track, just as the creature turned the corner, looking my way. Succumbing to a combination of fear and tactical instinct, I lay flat on my back like a corpse as the jet of flame came over me, sweeping right. My skin burned, I felt it sear parts of my arms and chest down to the muscle, and for an instant I could hear screaming; the people beside me shrieking as they burned. Then there was pained silence.

When the heat suddenly vanished, I struggled to sit up. The hunter was turning his flame the other way, down the tracks, his weapon inaudible as I waited for my hearing to return. Placing my arms down I tried moving backwards, only to be greeted with a sharper pain. Looking down, I saw that my hands were blackened and charred from the fire. The skin left untouched was swollen and red, and hurt on contact. Why couldn't I hear?

A large mass of similarly burned people formed around me, all trying to get away from the Hunter. Pausing, I reached my 'good' charred hand up to my ear; it was completely gone.

T H E | S P L I T

A rough stump sat in a field of raw, bleeding skin, where my hair had once been. I felt the other one; they were both gone. Oddly however, despite my aching hands and loss of hearing I was mostly unharmed, and was able to jump onto the tracks headed in the opposite direction, though my grip on my gun was starting to loosen as I stumbled forward.

When I looked over my shoulder at the creature, I saw another line of flames coming right towards us. Turning, I lowered my head, tucking my gun into my chest as the heat washed over me. My legs grew weak and tight as the searing flame covered me from head to heel, scorching me to my spine, leaving pain spreading through all corners of my body. No longer able to stand, but trying to control my fall, I collapsed; and now laying on the ground I was facing the Hunter, as the creature turned from side to side, running his *flammenwerfer* continuously.

My head was propped up against something, but I could not feel what; my entire body was numb. And yet, I was still able to move; I flexed various muscles, trying to ignore the pain, so I could see what parts of me still worked. From ankle to my pelvis I could do little more than twitch. My shattered left arm was as useless as it had ever been, and I could not bend at the waist. But by some miracle, my right arm had retained most of its motion, and I still held the now-piping hot gun in my hand. Would it even fire?

The Hunter roared in fury, lighting the people ahead of me, and in an instant my increasingly sluggish brain came up with a plan. Raising my gun, I waited for him to turn the other way, then fired all of my rounds at his back. Several shots later – as hoped – a pressurized explosion rushed past me as the tank caught fire, covering the creature in bright yellow and red flame.

It cried out loudly and sank to the ground, an inferno encasing his entire body, its light growing brighter with each second.

THE | SPLIT

Coughing, relieved it was over, I closed my eyes for a short moment as it lay on the ground motionless and burning. But a hideously deformed version of the creature's roar jarred my eyes back open.

It was starting to get up!

As it began moving towards me I raised my gun and pulled the trigger. Click. The magazine was empty.

This was it. It was over. The Hunter was nearly to me; it was coming faster now, just meters away. I tried to relax and accept my fate.

Then a dazzling flash of multicolored light appeared in front of me, and a man in a strange suit burst into view.

'Am I seeing things?'

He turned to see the creature and raised his right arm, revealing a mortar-like appendage where a hand should have been. It was fired at the Hunter, and bright flashes of light created even brighter explosions as the Hunter seemed to pop outwardly, sending chunks of gore and its strange, black blood, all over the tracks.

Then the man paused upon seeing me, and bent down. His armor was black, and seemed mechanical. Scales. . . of a type I had never seen before. They were moving around on the surface, changing the plating at will. His helmet was rounded, yet strangely angular in places, and bright blue lights burned where his eyes would be.

I tried to look at his gun, but found my vision limited as blood crept into the corners of my eyes; I was dying. The man looked like he wanted to help. He touched me in places with a strange instrument and gestured wildly.

'He has been talking,' I realized.

I wondered what he was saying. . .

T H E | S P L I T

XLI

(The narrative returns to only Burlington here. - A. Fila)

Mexico; 2031

"Corbin, please tell me you have the transfer ready." Meela sounded annoyed. Silence came from the other end of the line as she waited for a response. "CORBIN!"

"Yes, yes... I'm here," Corbin said over the sound of his fast typing fingers. "Ow, by the way... you don't have to yell, that's RIGHT in my ear."

Meela ignored him. "Transfer. Status. What is it?"

"I'm connected," he said confidently. "You just give me the word."

"Good," Meela sighed. "Be ready, and STAY ON THE LINE. I'm going back into the bar... and won't be able to respond. If you need anything, let me know now."

"I don't need anything," Corbin answered. "Burl, you need anything?"

"We're all good over here," I replied.

"Copy that. Corbin pay, attention... and Burl, babe... let me know when you're going in. I need to have the signal this time."

I laughed to myself quietly as the line went silent. In the last few years Meela had easily become the best out of the three of us. She was methodically efficient and thought tactically, and her brain's natural mechanical ability seemed to translate over well when it came to understanding nearly any operation's inner workings. She had planned this all on her own; me and Corbin had just followed her orders, amazed as she addressed each problem one by one.

"Boss, we good?" The voice came from my left, and I turned to see

THE | SPLIT

Ramon, clutching his AK-47 closely as he stared up at me with narrowed eyes, sweat dripping down from his forehead and off the side of his face.

"Yes Ramon, we're fine." I stood up and addressed the rest of the truck, "We're about five minutes out. Everyone check your magazines and ready up. Say your prayers if you have to."

The men sitting on both benches let out an uneasy laugh that echoed through the back of the truck faintly as we made our way down the bumpy road. Before escaping through the cloth covering at the end, I looked at each of their faces.

Alvaro. Diego. Simon. Luis. Jesus. Ricardo, and nearly a half dozen more, just in this truck. It had been such a short time and yet, I already felt that these men were my brothers. It was a strange feeling, but one I suspected to be entirely normal.

My whole career it had been just me and Meela, with Corbin coming along later. Meela was my partner, my other half, and it felt strange to do anything without her. She had been the only person I had fought beside, the only one I *knew*. Going into combat with other soldiers was a different feeling entirely. For the first time, I had been working with an actual team. It had taken some adjustment.

The men inside the truck, and in the truck behind us, were just some of the contacts we had made during our time with our old employer. Their former organization had been the subject of one of the last official contracts ACE had ever sent us on.

As the United States and INTERPOL began to pursue the company, the number of corporate and state sponsored contracts had plummeted. ACE was reduced to taking work from various gang and underworld factions, like the hit on Boss Kagoya, and the contract on Ramon and his men in Peru, from a Brazilian militia.

THE | SPLIT

They had been one of the newest and most aggressive cocaine traffickers in the Andes, and of course their rise to prominence had come with its share of enemies. Unfortunately for them, most of these enemies made up the ranks of the Peruvian, Colombian, and Brazilian intelligence services – who were the first to finally have had enough. Unable to strike across borders, they had outsourced the job to one of their many militias; who outsourced the job to ACE, and for nearly a month we'd worked on infiltrating their organization, posing as German mercenaries.

But as time passed, and we grew to be more accepted by Ramon and the younger members, we had taken a liking to the group, sensing in them a kindred spirit. A lifestyle of violence had been thrust upon them, and though me and Meela had chosen it, our willingness to do whatever was necessary matched their own.

One night over several bottles of rum we had discussed as a group how, to us, success wasn't a ladder with rungs to climb, or some metaphorical plant that needed to be watched and tended to. Success was a pile of struggling bodies, all trying to pull their way to the top. Life was a zero sum game, and the only way to make it was to step on other people.

After talking with Meela, we had approached Ramon and several others later on in the night and, taking a chance, revealed to them our true identities and how we had been sent by ACE. Before they could respond, Meela had assured them that if we could find them this easily, it would be even easier for an actual government.

They had reluctantly agreed, and asked what they should do. That night we made a partnership. They would go on to purge their organization's leadership, then lay low off of whatever money they could make with the jobs they could find. We would wire them three million

THE | SPLIT

in cash, and in return, they would agree to come work for us in the event of ACE collapsing.

We hadn't been sure if they would honor the arrangement, but they came to us within a week of arriving in Guatemala, after fleeing Poughkeepsie, and since then they had stayed on the payroll, guarding us loyally as we planned our next move. Our cash reserves were nearly halfway depleted, but if the mission went well today that would soon turn around.

As the men talked among themselves quietly, I stood up and banged on the partition separating the back from the cab.

"Yes?" The voice of the driver came through muffled.

"How close are we to our destination?"

He hesitated before replying, "Two minutes, I would think."

I sat back down, and released the magazine on my AK-47, making sure it was topped off before I put it back in, then patted my vest to make sure I was ready. Magazines, grenades, my 1911, and my large folding knife, everything was there. The Soviet-era rifle wasn't my ideal choice for such an operation, but with our limited resources, it was the best we could do. ACE had taken everything and left their agents out to dry. Today I intended to take everything back, and repay their kindness with interest.

Tom Bennett was a man who didn't have to worry about much. As the former leader of Allied Corporate Exchange, he had access to the top security in the world and could travel anywhere as he pleased. Meela and I had expected to never hear from him again. When the company went under, it seemed logical that anyone involved would leave the operation far behind, and start a new life elsewhere. Following the close call in Poughkeepsie, the small number of other agents we knew in ACE had gone silent. It was unlikely many others made it out.

T H E | S P L I T

Bennett surprised us all however, when he turned himself over to the CIA. Then all assets within American jurisdiction were ordered captured or killed, and after the widely reported take-down of the company's small office in Brooklyn, the handful of agents stupid enough to be taken alive were featured prominently on international news. In exchange for information on all of ACE's past contracts within the United States, Tom had been granted immunity. Not wanting to stick around after being debriefed, Bennett moved to Mexico with a dozen of his most loyal soldiers.

There he enjoyed a life of luxury, as members of governments from all over the world came to him to get information on operations run within their countries. He couldn't be left alive. Although ACE had come to an end, me and Meela were just starting to hit our stride, and our new life couldn't start until we had closed the door on our old one. Anything that kept us from our fresh start – or the money we were owed – would be purged.

I clasped my hands together as we drew closer to Bennett's compound, recoiling slightly as I touched the cold steel of my prosthetic hand. Though fighting in a squad was an adjustment, it was nothing compared to a completely new hand.

We had left New York with nearly four million in cash. One and a half million had gone to Ramon and the other members of the crew, twenty five men in total. Another million had gone to buying a space to work from and the equipment and weapons we would need. The last bit we had spent was on my prosthetic, costing just over 1.1 million, all off the book.

We'd hired a specialist from Sweden, who after much convincing flew to Guatemala. The prosthetic he had picked was the top of the line, with more receptors than any other model, and offered near complete mobility. But it had only four fingers, a fact he apologized for, saying that future prosthesis would help me even further and that mine could be removed for a replacement with just a simple surgery.

After a three hour operation, he had been even more successful than he hoped in grafting thousands of my nerve endings into the device and making a successful connection. I flexed it from the back of my palm, watching the metal fingers twitch. It lacked the refined movement for intricate processes like writing, but it's raw power could crush a small rock easily, something I was eager to see in combat.

It felt fitting for some reason. The man I had become was nothing like I had ever imagined in my early twenties. Efficiency was now key, and I had begun to look at the world objectively. The only thing that mattered was function; and this new hand only made me deadlier.

Meela and I had made several meaningful connections during our time in the field, and earned more than our fair share of favors. Soon, it would be time to call those favors in. Admittedly, our continued existence had brought a feeling of invulnerability, especially after we found out that the team that had been sent to eliminate us in Poughkeepsie was one of the CIA's most elite units, but building a network on our own wouldn't be easy.

Still it was crucial to our survival, and South America was a good place to start. It felt like it was still the Wild West down here, and in such a climate, people with a skill set like me and Meela thrived.

Shortly after the operation in Tunis, Corbin had tracked down one of the scientists, Alexis Montoya, who had headed the gene management project from the time I was in the Army. Following her stint with the military, Alexis had taken a job with GlenKline as a genetic consultant, and had been instrumental in creating the next generation of SYNTH, which had been canceled after FDA trials.

THE | SPLIT

She'd tried to slip away by moving to Montana, and had nearly fainted upon seeing me and Meela on her doorstep. Just our being there was enough to scare her into divulging all of her latest work, and after a few not so subtle threats, she'd turned over all of her research, samples and scientific logs to us.

Right before we left, Meela had strangled her and hid the body in the basement. Killing non-combatants wasn't really something we enjoyed, but leaving behind loose ends was something we enjoyed even less. With the data now safely in our custody, we planned to find someone as quickly as we could that had the skill to start producing a new batch of SYNTH.

The truck hit another bump, making the slight headache I'd had all day even worse. I looked around the back of the truck. The men were all staring straight ahead, hands clenched around their rifles as they thought about the task ahead of them. They were all skilled soldiers, and the operation was well planned, but even with all of that, things could still go awry. Most of them had families, and though we had assured each of them that their families would be compensated in the event of their deaths, it was hard to trust another man with the future of your kids.

I felt a tapping on the wall from the cab.

"The gate is right ahead."

I put my mouth to the wall so I could be heard, "Thank you, Rico," then turned to the men, "Alright. . . here it goes. . . brace for impact."

T H E | S P L I T

XLII

Recovered from Bloc Vault C1
-T. Acerz, 2131

Mexico; 2031

The courtyard was a sea of corpses. The call from the circling birds above mingled with the wails of the wounded men below, creating a hideous chorus of nature. The clay walls and pillars surrounding the inner grassy area were smeared with blood and chunks of viscera, a grisly reminder of the events that had just taken place. One man, in a dark suit, was moving among the bodies, crawling towards an assault rifle several meters away.

I watched as Meela calmly walked towards him, her high heels leaving deep imprints in the sand between the yellow grass. When he was just inches away from the gun, she stepped on his forearm, shot him in the head with a pistol, and walked on, pulling back the slide to look at the chamber then releasing the magazine to replace it with a fresh one from her purse.

Meela looked absolutely stunning. She wore a dark purple dress, cut just above the thigh, that lit up faintly with sequins throughout. Her jewelry was elegant but not flashy, a pair of simple hoop earrings and a thin platinum bracelet.

She wasn't wearing her wedding ring, nor should she have been; for this operation we had needed a man inside, and it turned out that the best man for the job was a woman, so she had been undercover inside of Bennett's stable of high dollar prostitutes. To avoid detection, Meela dyed her hair dark, and had worn a prosthetic nose that she had since removed.

THE | SPLIT

She'd been sitting at the bar when the two trucks burst through the gate, and as guards swarmed the first truck, had opened fire from behind it, creating a diversion that allowed us to get outside safely. From there, not being dressed or properly armed for a firefight, she had played a minimal role, remaining under the cover of the bar and selecting her shots carefully.

Another man, beside me, suddenly opened his eyes and gasped for air. Despite the blood covering his mouth and chin, I recognized him as Roy, a man I had known for several years. He was one of Bennett's personal guards, made up of his most loyal agents, who had followed him to Mexico, presumably in the hopes of finding more lucrative work now that Bennett had eliminated most of their competition through his immunity deal.

Of the ones I had seen so far today, I hadn't liked any of them, and Roy was no exception. A former marine who had served in Iraq, Roy was well suited for the violent life of a corporate assassin, and seemed to relish the brutal nature of his job, describing the gore in vivid detail on the rare occasion we would run into him. His simple but brutish nature had also made him a perfect choice for Bennett's personal security post-ACE. All of the men had been similarly trained and were experienced after varied amounts of years on the job.

I suspected that Bennett had between ten men and a dozen, of which only six were out here in the courtyard, all wearing dark suits, and armed with sub-machine guns. But Bennett had prepared for a hit squad, and we had brought an army.

Roy's eyes widened as I neared, "B-B-Burlington?"

"What's up, buddy. . . " I crouched beside him.

"You did t-t-this?" As he spoke, blood dribbled out of the corners of mouth.

T H E | S P L I T

"Well, not just me," I gestured to Luis and Ramon standing nearby talking, "I brought some friends I made. . . after you sold us up the river."

Roy looked down at the wound on his chest; the blood had seeped through his white shirt and was now soaking into the fibers of his suit.

"It. . . it wasn't personal, Burl."

"It never is, Roy."

"Y-you. . . " he stammered, looking for the words. "You know. . . I would never hurt you and Meela. D-d-don't let me die like this."

"It sure felt like you were trying to hurt me when the goddamned CIA kicked in my back windows."

"T-that was Bennett!" Roy protested.

I looked him in the eyes for several seconds, before patting him on the head affectionately, "Sure it was buddy," then took out my pistol from a side pocket and shot him through the temple. Blood splattered onto the side of my face, and I wiped it off on the hem of his suit before standing up and walking back to lean against the wall.

My headset crackled to life. "Burl, do you read me?"

"Copy, what's up Corbin?"

"The transfer is ready, we're just waiting for the input. How are things looking on your end?"

I looked back into the courtyard. There were only four of my soldiers outside, plus me and Meela. The rest had gone inside the house, searching for Bennett and the last of his guards. Judging from the intermittent gunshots and screaming, I would say it was going rather well. "We should be ready here in just a minute," I replied. "Go ahead and prepare the transfer."

"Copy that."

THE | SPLIT

Meela and I had both made it very clear during our planning stages that we wanted Bennett captured alive. I had lost two of my men, Alvarez and Tomas, in the courtyard earlier, and I didn't want any more deaths on my hands than had to be. On top of being hard to replace, and the costs of paying off their families, these men now meant more to me than anyone else outside of Meela and Corbin.

As I continued to think about going in to help find Bennett myself, the large wooden double doors nearby burst open and out came a small group of my men, carrying Bennett by both of his arms. His legs dangled behind him, scuffing his once shiny black shoes with every step his captors took, and his left eye was purple, nearly swollen shut. Long cuts dripped blood onto his suit jacket.

Tom Bennett's trademark feature had always been his hair. It was well groomed and regularly combed, and looked reminiscent of the hairstyles worn in "Mad Men" and other pieces done in the 60's – no doubt the look he was going for.

He would often brag to new employees that his hair was so thick that his barber charged him extra. Now, his hair was more of a mane, sticking up in different places, and ripped out in clumps. The men carrying Tom turned to me, and I motioned towards a rusted chair nearby. They nodded and threw him down in it forcefully. He looked around the courtyard, trying his best to retain a poker face.

Upon seeing his arrival, Meela walked up beside me, quickly kissing me on the cheek before turning to face Bennett.

"Tom Bennett. . . " I smiled as I stepped towards him. "For a man in the field you're in, you should have been MUCH harder to find."

"Burlington," he scoffed, looking at me through the eye that wasn't swollen. "I'll be damned. YOU did this?"

"Were you expecting someone else?"

T H E | S P L I T

He laughed. "I have more enemies than you'll ever know, boy."

"And yet. . . " I grabbed his sleeve, "I'm the one who found you."

"Yes, you found me son. Now why don't you and your whore wife just kill me and get it over with."

Before I could react, Ramon lunged forward. Tom threw up his arms in defense but was too late, Ramon's fist slammed against the front of his face. The blow broke his nose with a loud pop and nearly knocked him out of his chair, but as Ramon cocked his fist back to hit him again, I caught his hand.

"Not yet," I said softly, looking him in the eye. He nodded and stepped back, crossing his arms, but continued glaring at Tom. I started pacing in front of our captive. "Do you know the difference between me and you, Tom?"

He smiled back menacingly. "I have connections all over the globe. and a net worth ten times yours?"

I laughed. "You have people you USE all over the world, Tom. The difference between us. . . is that you're a simple man. All you know is using force to get your way, and how to best serve your own interests. I'll admit, you made it far on just those two things, but you missed something. People, Tom. . . When you treat people the way you do, they feel indebted to you. But no more. "

I clapped the nearest soldier on the shoulder. "You recognize any of these faces? I don't reckon you would, but you signed off on a contract to kill all of them, and you sent me and Meela to do it. As you can see now, we didn't. With how shady ACE had been acting the last couple of years, me and Meela figured we needed friends in other places. And unlike you, I treat the people I deal with fairly. So I formed a partnership with these fine gentlemen. . . a partnership that has led us to this very moment."

T H E | S P L I T

"So what?" he scoffed. "You got yourselves a group of spic soldiers, congratulations."

"We got more than that," Meela stepped forward, turning away from Tom to talk into her ear piece. "Corbin, is the transfer complete?"

"It just finished," Corbin replied. "I'm looking at it now. It's just. . . it's beautiful guys. It's beautiful."

Meela pulled out her phone and began typing onto the screen, talking to Tom without looking up. "You see Tom, I never liked you. Everything Burl said about you is true. You're a pawn, who has always tried to be a player. Every deal you have, every arrangement you've made, every connection you cling to, depends on one thing. . . " she leaned in, just inches away from his face as she added, ". . . money," and now held up her phone in front of him. "You see this? This is the deposit that was just put into me and Burl's account in Zurich. Do you see the total?"

Tom's eyes widened, and a vein on his forehead began to swell as his hands clenched the armrests on his chair.

"That's right, Tom," Meela laughed, stepping back. "105 million. . . taken straight from your accounts. That's one hell of a payday. You've acted stoic through this whole thing, because you knew that your money would keep your friends and family safe and secure when you died. It was the one thing that brought you peace of mind, the one thing you worked your entire life for. It's gone now, Tom. . . your life was wasted in the pursuit of the last thing taken from you before death. Karma's a bitch, Mr. Bennett. . . enjoy yours." She turned to walk away.

"YOU **BITCH**!" he called out to her, enraged. "*THIS ISN'T OVER! PEOPLE WILL COME FOR YOU NOW!*"

I turned to follow her, and felt Ramon tap on my shoulder, "What do we do with him, Boss?"

THE | SPLIT

"That's up to you," I replied. "We lost two good men today, and that man back there is the one responsible. I've only known them... Tomas and Alvarez... a short while, and yet I still deeply mourn their loss. I can't imagine how you must feel. Make the man responsible for their deaths feel the pain in your hearts. Get creative with it."

Ramon smiled and nodded. I turned back around to follow Meela towards the front of the complex. Bennett was still screaming. "*YOU ASSHOLES! NOT EVEN ALL THE MONEY IN THE WORLD CAN SAVE YOU NOW! I'LL SEE YOU IN – **ARGH**!*" Then I heard the sound of fists connecting with flesh, and smiled as Tom's screams worsened.

Later that evening, we traveled back to the hacienda on a remote hill, where we were staying. A celebration had erupted, and the air was filled with the sound of laughter and the scent of Tequila. The party lasted late into the night, with local girls coming in from the village nearby. Several times I was asked about the money, and each time I brushed the question off, waiting for a better time.

That hour finally arrived when the last of the girls had left. The men sat around the tables, chatting animatedly, most fueled by coffee, and some by cocaine. "Excuse me," I stepped up in front to gather everyone's decision.

All talking stopped, and 23 pairs of eyes met mine. I took a deep breath before continuing; the plan for mine and Meela's immediate future rested solely on what I was about to say.

"I know all of you are wondering about the money." The men nodded their heads and murmured in agreement. "I have come up with a plan that I think we can all agree on. A plan that not only rewards you for our job today, but will ensure our future in the days to come." I spoke slowly and carefully, not wanting to mispronounce any words in the men's native tongue.

THE | SPLIT

"We obtained 105 million today... and plan to split it like this. Two million will go to each of you, that's 46 million. Meela, Corbin, and I will take 30 million as the planners of this operation... a finder's fee."

"Here, here!" Corbin called out from the back, raising an early empty bottle of Tequila.

The men began to whisper to each other, their voices getting louder as their soft conversations grew heated, and finally Ramon stood up. "What is to happen to the other 29 million?"

I nodded and waited for the room to settle. "When I met you all, you were a formidable operation. Perhaps you could've grown even stronger if not for our arrangement. I intend to honor your sacrifice. Four million of what's left will go to outfitting a new crew, bigger and stronger than ever before. Ten million will go towards buying properties and rebuilding your networks."

The men started to nod, and Miguel stood up, "We can never make it with the way things are now. The cartels on the border are too strong. They hijack shipments, and kill whom they please."

"Yes," I agreed. "But they have always done this... just because there are obstacles, that doesn't mean we should give up. You saw what we did today. You saw what you and us can accomplish together, what our connections can bring you. The last fifteen million will go towards recruitment. The cartels ARE too strong, but not if the oppressed peoples of Central and South America stand together. All of you, all 23 of you, are strong and capable, good leaders and men of vision."

"So you want us to work for you?" Miguel responded, the men muttering their agreement.

"No," I replied simply. "In this new organization the profits will be split differently. Sixty percent will go to all of you, while twenty percent will go to the three of us to use for networking and other equipment.

THE | SPLIT

The last twenty percent will go to the men you work with. A well paid soldier is likely to do a better job."

Ramon stood back up as the men started nodding, "I think we could all agree that we like the sound of that, but what's the plan?"

"You were right when you said you had an enemy," I answered. "The cartels are brutal and have many soldiers, but we have the connections and training to make up for it. If you bring me an army, all of the cartels will fall before you, and the whole industry will be yours."

The men erupted in a cheer, and I looked over to see Meela smiling.

T H E | S P L I T

XLIII

Found in abandoned Subway tunnels

A. Fila, 2080

Undetermined

I felt Gerhard slip away as I was deep in conversation with John, and the train station disappeared right after the brave Nazi had taken his last pained breath and succumbed to his injuries. We had been discussing the appearance of the mysterious stranger who had just shown up to finish off the Hunter. He seemed to have teleported into the station. When I asked John about this, he seemed as puzzled as I was. Even in his time, decades into my own future, mankind had yet to figure out a way to appear and reappear the way the mysterious stranger had. Could he have been someone from even further in the future?

His armor was a point of curiosity as well; John said the material looked to be made of nano-composites, but that he had never seen anything as advanced, as with the way this man's gear seemed to shimmer and shift. And, there was a possibility he might not have even been human at all.

My emotional side was starting to slowly return to me as I traveled through the dark plane with no body. The latter half of my time in Berlin had been. . . disorienting. Gerhard had not only taken back possession of his own body, he had used my own mind to do it.

The sheer force of his passion for his wife in that moment near the plaza seemed to have commandeered my emotional spectrum, and parts of my critical thinking, leaving me as little more than a mental

THE | SPLIT

imprint within my own thoughts, comparable in size and influence to John and Sun. John had called this a mere anomaly, similar to my past experiences, and Sun agreed.

But I had a different theory; they had not *felt* the feelings Gerhard felt for his wife and future child. I argued that the stress of the battle, compounded by the hijacking of his own mind, had forced Gerhard's hand and, as I was nothing more than a stranger to him – a stranger that did not prioritize or think of things in the same way – such intense emotions had spawned a primal sense of survival, and his bond with his mate had put Gerhard back in the driver's seat. John considered this unlikely, but possible.

Truth be told, the whole thing had worked out in my favor. In my time as an observer, I was able to almost completely recover from the effects of the extreme torture the Being had subjected me to and which had been so difficult to move past.

John and Sun had talked me through it, convincing me that my movements in my travels could be compared to their daily experience as digitally altered consciousnesses. My reality through the Being was subjective to its own desires, thus any emotion that was inspired, or fear that was summoned, must be nothing more than the Being manipulating its own, created, space. All pain inflicted was only as I real as I perceived it to be.

"Burl," John got my attention. *"Are you ready to attempt this once again?"*

I hesitated a moment before replying, feeling my thoughts move through the dark space – which wasn't a dark space at all, as John had told me, that being only how I perceived it to be with the absence of my senses. In the past, the only experiences I'd had of being left alone in my thoughts with no connection to my body were while I was sleeping, so naturally my mind had compared the sensation to the darkness of my own shut eyelids.

John had theories on a lot of things going on through my journey. During his time in the passenger seat his thoughts had run wild, trying to make sense of the situation, so his ideas seemed plausible, as he was drawing from his own wealth of scientific knowledge and logic to make connections.

He had speculated that this motion, this space, was merely us being sent through the dimension of time itself to an alternate timeline, or isolated series of events in our own universe, insisting that it would validate the Multiverse Theory; a complex series of ideas that he had struggled to explain to me and Sun. Direction was mostly meaningless, but if his thinking was correct, there would be pockets of reality, separate from our own, just outside of our stream of motion.

"I'm ready," I replied; still preparing my mind for whatever was coming next as John, Sun and I formed the link and spread out from each other like we had done before.

We settled into the direction corresponding to the small stream of thought connecting us, John gave the word, and I pushed out away from the current of motion, spinning us end over end. Soon I felt us slip out of the stream and into a still space, but John kept us moving, and then without warning we tore through an invisible barrier, into a world I had never been in before.

Unlike my experience leaving Cyrus, this time I was not given a body; our thoughts continued to tumble alone through a bright blue sky, overlooking a massive city. But I recognized where we were, or at least I thought I did. Things were different from my last time there but, seeing some familiar buildings I knew we were soaring above New York. The skyline was larger and taller than I had ever seen it, and massive, steel-

THE | SPLIT

gray airships hovered around the densely packed island; some floating, others attached to buildings by large cables. Upon closer examination I was surprised to see the Nazi swastika on the tail fin of one. Others I saw were similarly marked, and as we passed the Empire State Building I spotted a massive golden eagle affixed to the bottom of the tower's spire, the same eagle I had seen in documentaries – the symbol of the Third Reich.

John signaled for us to turn in the other direction, so we stopped mid air and began spinning the other way, climbing higher and higher into the sky, until things went black. I felt us enter back into the current of motion we had just pulled away from.

"What the hell was that, and why could I see it without a body?" I asked.

"I don't know," John admitted. "From the looks of it, that was a world where the timeline had split, and Germany won the Second World War. As for us being able to see it without working eyes, I have no idea. My hypothesis on that seemed to be incorrect, and it just goes to prove how little we actually know."

"Time is running out," Sun interjected. "We must move in the other direction, we may not get this chance again."

We both agreed with him and began whirling the opposite way, end over end, until we made it out of the current and into the stillness. Pushing through, we entered a world just as we had seconds before – but my thoughts cried out in alarm when I saw what was below me.

This wasn't a 'world'. We had stumbled into a long, flat plain, which stretched as far as I could see in either direction. The ground was covered with moving figures with spouts of bright blue flame, and bodies of creatures I had never seen before littered about.

They were shadowed by much larger forms; demonic looking shapes of creatures that looked like the Being from the Green Hallway. The whole world appeared to be a battle between these poor life forms and these towering figures.

No, this wasn't a battle, it was a massacre. I watched as an alien that looked vaguely like a rhino was lifted by one of the creatures and torn in half – then the rhino-shaped creature reappeared only a moment later, a few meters away, just to be set upon by another tormentor. Every time a creature was slaughtered, it would be brought back only to be slaughtered again.

My eye caught on a small cluster of humans. They fought together in a tight circle, hounded by a group of humanoid Hunters similar to the one I had just fought, their faces masked with a level of fear I had never seen before. They screamed as they were brutally dismembered by their attackers, only to come back and fight the same battle over again.

"John, we need to get out of here," I didn't know how much more of this I could watch. Even a few brief seconds was enough to form a scarring image of this terrible place.

They agreed and we began turning to leave, tumbling upwards, climbing higher and higher into the dark sky. I felt a sharp sense of relief when we were back in the familiar darkness, moving once again through the current, even if back to the Being and his hallway.

"John..." Sun said faintly, *"I do not wish to return to that place, ever again."* I could sense John was in agreement.

We all slowly dropped the string connecting our minds, and each kept to our own thoughts as we tried to process what we had just seen. The Being's own species had been there. What could that mean? Had we just been in hell? Or was it something much worse that I had yet to comprehend?

THE | SPLIT

Our experiment had brought nothing but more questions, and I became clouded with doubt that we would never discover the truth.

But then, a light bulb came on in my mind, distracting me from the thoughts of the hell we had just been through.

"Sun, I need to talk to you about something."

"Very well," he replied. "But it will need to wait, we are nearly there."

He was right; in the distance I could see a bright light bursting from the hole in the darkness, that grew larger as we approached. I was soon pushed from the steam and into my body.

I was back in my own skin, but I wasn't in the spot I usually returned to. Instead I stood near the frame of a wide open entrance. Looking behind to see the green screens of the hallway, my eyes followed the platform past my feet to see what was in front of me; I stood at the opening to the throne room. The Being stood above his chair at the end of the way, and I could already feel his presence starting to surround my brain. I tried to pull away, desperate to get a message to Sun before I succumbed to its power.

"Sun!"

"Yes?"

"I don't have much time, listen to me very carefully. I don't want the Being to know my plan and will have to keep it out of mind." I judged from his silence that he was waiting for me to continue. *"Do you remember when the Hunter tried to invade Gerhard's mind, and you stopped it by engaging his thoughts with your own?"*

"Yes. . . what-"

I interrupted him, words forming as fast as I could put them together, the Being would be in my head soon. *"On my signal, I'll need you to do the same thing. It sensed your presence before, but seemed to dismiss* it. We have the element of surprise on our side. Can you do it?"

Sun paused before responding, thinking of the risks and advantages his actions could bring, before responding: *"I can do this task, yes."*

"Good. Thank you, Sun." Stepping into the room, I did my best to keep my mind completely clear as, after a few more steps, the Being broke through and began pouring through my memories and thoughts from my time in Berlin. It seemed angry.

Sun encouraged me to take advantage of this, to provoke it into more anger and capitalize on its mistakes. But could a life form so advanced even make mistakes? I started to doubt his strategy as the Being roughly moved through my scattered memories, but even with my doubts followed through, talking aloud as I tried not to flinch from the pain inside my head.

"Your Hunter was weak and incapable," I sneered, my words sounding braver than I really felt. "But what could I expect from a species that sits on their ass all day and watches stronger beings fight?" This made it pull from my thoughts; it was trying to present a calm front, but below the surface I could feel its frustration building.

"We will see how you feel about my creatures the next time you encounter them. As to my kind, you know nothing about our intention, or power. Your limited mind does not possess the scope to comprehend such knowledge. Mankind. . . and Terra itself. . . are **nothing** compared to the story of my kind. You are beneath us, mere creations. . . you will know your place at our feet."

"Your creations, huh? Was that why a limited human was able to slay your creature with so little effort? I assume you didn't send him. . . so that must mean. . . There's a weakness in your power. But, that couldn't. . . "

That had done it.

T H E | S P L I T

The Being cut me off mid-sentence to lift me into the air. There was no denying its anger now, waves of it seemed to crash through the whole room. An alien blend of fury and hatred, filled with a cruel disdain for other creatures spanning back beyond antiquity. It redoubled its assault on my mind, and I winced as tendrils of probing thought shot through my brain like claws, tearing their way haphazardly through my thoughts, searching.

I heard its voice in my head, so loud it covered all other thinking, **"What was that thing that saved you?!"** as it picked apart my most recent thoughts on my enigmatic savior. But if it didn't know what had saved me, I certainly didn't. The presence realized this, but continued to press me on the matter, with a sort of fervid, wishful thinking.

"WHO WAS THAT?!" It was screaming now, the voice inside my head began to somehow pound on my eardrums outside.

"I don't know!" I shouted back.

It tore through my mind even faster now. Memories, from early childhood to thoughts about my AA meetings all collided together, and the damage was starting to affect my core personality. I could feel mental traits, essential to who I felt I was, being twisted and ripped apart.

As it kept questioning me and screaming I, for some odd reason, began to find it really funny. The feeling started near the area he was probing, quickly spreading through the rest of my body, and before I realized it I was laughing out loud. Big gusts of hysterical laughter, which rang through the cavernous hall.

Confusion mixed with the Being's anger, as it paused at my sudden outburst, shocked. Then it went at my memories with even more force, grinding away at my basic instinctual knowledge. I could feel my legs weakening, my muscles' natural instinct to stand starting to slip away.

THE | SPLIT

My eyelids were drooping, and I began to feel myself losing consciousness. In desperation I turned to Sun.

"*Sun, now!*"

Sun's thoughts left the corner of my my mind and met the Being head-on in the center of my memories. Clarity came rushing back to me as the presence turned to deal with its surprise antagonist, and my strength slowly began coming back – though not quickly enough; another assault like that one, and I would be nothing more than a hollow shell.

Sun was struggling to keep the Being at bay, his thoughts now being picked apart like mine had just been, and a wave of courage coursed through my brain as I approached their epic clash, seeking a way around the Being's guard. When I found it I charged forward, entering the presence's own mind.

My thoughts instantly scattered.

Slowly I tried to re-center myself, but found it hard in the hostile climate of the foreign mind; clearly I was not meant to be here. A force I couldn't see or detect was blowing apart my mind, into pieces, and it took nearly all of my willpower to keep myself together.

T H E | S P L I T

XLIV

LGPB://mn34/con/terra/AR, 0125
(Translated)

Undetermined

My surroundings were unlike anything I had ever seen before. Indeed, I was having problems seeing *anything* consistently. Every other instant the colors seemed to change, figures and shapes that had once been there would disappear entirely, to be replaced with new ones in different places.

Panic engulfed my thoughts as I realized I couldn't trust my vision, and I looked up into the sky out of desperation. Above me, the scene remained the same, regardless of what happened below. Dark green clouds stretched as far as I could see, shifting in places but never revealing what sat above.

Just below the cloud line were massive orbs, seemingly made from a strange looking rock, hovering in place above the ground below. From my vantage point I could see three of these circular formations, each at least a couple hundred kilometers in diameter. The surface did not change as the clouds around it did.

I looked down to see my own form shifting as well, as my body hovered a few centimeters off the ground; changing from that of a baby, to an adult, and then into a child. Finding this movement disorienting, I forced myself to look away, but the wind-like force continued to pull me in different directions. It was unlike any motion I had felt before, moving *through* my body instead of around, like I wasn't even there. It seemed my mind couldn't translate the data from the world around me, inside the Being's mind all the laws of physics were different.

T H E | S P L I T

My rapidly changing body was affected just like my thoughts, and I had to move slowly to keep from being torn apart. I needed to go back, anywhere instead of here.

A bright shape of white light appeared in front of me, standing apart from the other shifting colors in the strange world. I hurried towards it, moving as fast as my changing body could. After making it to the door-shaped opening, I stepped through it and into a white void; even my body disappeared around me. That place I had just left was a memory, or something that resembled it, and now I was in the Being's own thoughts – which was not much better, the same strange force continued to pull my thoughts from different directions, threatening to pry them free of my consciousness.

My mind was slowly putting the pieces together and, unlike the dark constraints of my own the space here was bright and as white as the door I had just stepped through. But its mind was expansive and confusing, and its thoughts spread into pulsing shapes of a type I had never seen before, and seemed to travel faster than I could perceive them. After what seemed like hours in the bright expanse however, I was able to approach an entangled cluster of them.

Unlike the others, these did not separate and teleport away as I neared, so I urged myself forward to access them before they could. Cautiously stretching a tendril of my own thoughts toward the knotted mass ahead, I did my best to keep my mind ready for whatever was about to happen.

No amount of preparation could have eased my horror for what I found. Upon making the connection I felt my consciousness stretching towards channels beyond my reason. The logic and thought patterns within the nightmarish plane began to twist my mind into nonsense, all images, all impressions, slipped from my grasp as soon as I had seen

T H E | S P L I T

them, and I soon gave up on trying to understand these thoughts. I was beginning to panic as I felt my sanity being pulled out from under me. The whole scope of events that I *could* recognize, played at the same time alongside those I could not; each figure, each story, each detail blending together into a larger perspective I couldn't comprehend.

The sequencing of my own consciousness seemed altered, and all of my memories, emotions, and questions passed in the same instant. Time had no power here, and without the spacing of time to order and prioritize my thoughts, I would succumb to my own thinking; my ego to be forever spread among thoughts that weren't mine. My concept of self would soon no longer be.

Accepting my fate, I released control.

Then I felt a different presence latch on to me, seeming to pull at each part of my mind by an infinite number of strings. It yanked me out of the thoughts I had just entered, and for a timeless instant, I was gone; each part of my ego separated, my stream of consciousness halted entirely. An account of this occurrence would be impossible. Not for any personal or hard to explain reason, but simply because in this separation, *I* no longer existed.

In the time it took to put my consciousness back together, I had traveled somewhere different entirely. Had it just been seconds? Millennia? Or maybe there had been no experience of time at all. When I regained my perspective, I was in the familiar darkness of my own thinking, without a body, and without feeling. But the order to my thoughts had returned, and I was able to regain my mental stream of motion.

Then without warning I was given vision; A world similar to the one I had first entered when I came into the Entity's mind emerged around me, and I felt a strange tingling near my neck.

THE | SPLIT

Looking down, I saw that I was nothing more than a floating head. But the tingling slowly moved as my body was formed, from the top down. After several seconds the process was complete and I stood there, without covering, alert with anticipation, looking around. The scenery was the same, but there were no shifting figures, no force was pulling at my thoughts and, looking down, I was relieved to see my body's shape did not change.

Now, out of the corner of my right eye I saw movement, and turned to see a small group of upright figures several meters away. I walked towards them carefully, pausing when they looked up to see me, but continuing when they didn't respond. As I got close enough to see what was in front of me, my mind felt fuzzy with surprise and excitement. Gathered in a small half circle, just meters ahead, stood the unmistakable forms of the Being's own people.

They shared many of the same features I was familiar with, blank faces on wide cobra-like heads that descended down onto thin gray bodies. Each of them stood at roughly the same height, but were dwarfs compared to the Being from the Green Halls, and their attire seemed more primitive than their larger cousin's; simple robes of cloth-like materials instead of the dark bio-mechanical suit I had become accustomed to. When I stopped in front of them they did not reach towards my thoughts, instead staring back at me with eyeless faces. Hours seemed to pass as I waited, awed, wondering what would happen next.

Then, feeling a gentle touch on my thoughts I reached towards it, making contact with this new visitor as it entered my mind slowly. It briefly examined my latest thoughts, but remained in one place, waiting for me to approach it. I made the connection, but also remained at a distance – firmly inside my own mind.

T H E | S P L I T

It sat there, observing me. I decided to break the silence. *"Who are you... and where am I?"* It took several seconds before responding. Its mind seemed hard at work, trying to decipher what I had said.

"You are in a safe place now. We pulled you from the place of your struggle, and have created this space for you to be protected."

'My struggle?' I didn't know what it was saying; it hasn't answered my question, only inspired more. *"Well, thank you,"* I replied. *"But... who **are** you?"*

It paused again at my words, and I again could sense confusion at my question.

"We are who we always were."

That didn't clear anything up. Maybe I was asking the wrong question. I racked my brain for a way to bridge this gap in our thinking.

"This world that you live in is so... different... than the one I come from. Here, all the events seem to run together, at the same... time. Do you know that word... 'time'?"

Recognition dawned on the genteel presence. *"My kind does not use words. The way we communicate is the way we speak now. The Mind has no one set way to do things... when two different thoughts... or, groups of thoughts... come into contact, they will find a way to communicate."*

I thought on its words as it paused, but before I replied it continued, *"This concept of time... I can see it even now, in your memories and thinking. Without it you were lost in this place, doomed to be a spectator in a world you could not understand. In this clearing we have created this force of time... more accurately... a force similar, from the descriptions in your memories."*

"You created time, just for me?" I asked incredulously.

THE | SPLIT

"Not, quite," it responded patiently. *"All we have done is take your perception of this 'time'... and place it within the structural parameters of this memory."*

"So this is a memory?" I looked around at the world, gesturing.

"It is what you would call a memory, yes. Within each mind of our species lies that mind's whole existential experience, in it's entirety. Your mind seems to just remember pieces, sequentially... whereas the record of our lives is playing all at once in perfect detail."

"So, you're not real?"

The presence seemed amused at this. *"Do I not seem real? Can we not touch minds? Can we not share ideas and observations, as we are doing right now?"*

I hesitated before responding, knowing it was right, but what I was being told hurt my head to try and follow. I was still inside the creature's mind. But, within a memory... talking to what seemed like entirely separate consciousnesses.

How could this be? What didn't I know?

My visitor felt my confusion and did his best to clarify, *"It should come as no surprise to you. Our species are indeed very different. While your memories are little more than images, with predestined inhabitants, our recorded accounts are alive... constantly shifting with our own observations and participants, all covering multiple events at once. This moment you are in right now, even among my species would be considered exceptional. This scene was born out of paradox... and hidden deep inside the mind of our host. All of us you see here, we are from the time before. After the great rift in our species, those of us who opposed our people's journey have remained here, stripped of our physical world and imprisoned within this copy."*

T H E | S P L I T

"Copy?" I asked. What few parts I seemed to understand from his speech, had fascinated me.

"Precisely," it responded. "After coming to this place, we knew that this was a forgery. Our society and culture has been stripped away. . . now we devote ourselves wholly to our task."

"What's this task?"

"To put it in simple terms, we are here to determine what our species has done since the schism. These outside forces, foreign in our home, can be felt. . . even deep within a hidden thought. Thus we knew of your 'time' even outside your arrival, and of our descendants' meddling with it."

"You know? Well, can you help me?"

The presence felt a tinge of sadness as I asked this. "Unfortunately, no. Our power here is limited, reaching only to parts inside our host's mind. It seems that through unspeakable sacrifice, our kind has reached levels of power that were only discussed as theoretical by our greatest minds back home."

"Where is home?" I asked, hoping to get a straight answer for once.

"It is impossible to determine. Our kind has gone far and done much since we were last outside of this place. The mere nature of our existence within a thought has kept us from discovering much."

I felt crushed. This had been the closest I had come to an answer, and yet still the truth eluded me. If I could not find the knowledge I sought within the Entity's own mind, would I be able to find it all?

The smaller being answered my question, as if my own introspection had been intended just for it.

"There is no knowledge for you here that you did not already possess, however our paths seem entwined. For such a primitive mind, your

T H E | S P L I T

'time' is more complex than I could begin to explain to you. Come, this event is over for you, you must move on."

The being in the middle gestured, and another bright portal opened in front of me, pulling me through to the blackness of my own infinite thoughts.

XLV

Gift from South American Consulate, 2099
T. Acerz, 2131

Quito, Ecuador; 2034

"I can't keep risking the lives of my crew on your promises! No, forget about the men, think about how expensive it is every time we lose a shipment!"

Though the light was dim both outside and in the parlor, the equatorial levels of humidity warmed my skin and I could feel a trickle of sweat forming on my forehead. Ramon's house was large but sparsely and poorly decorated, and from personal experience I knew that this wing of the house was the only place in it that showed any signs of its owner's wealth.

"Santiago, Santiago. . . " Ramon smiled at the frantic man to calm his nerves, ". . . it will be handled soon, I promise."

I had already reached the point in these conversations where I would tune out. Though I was now completely fluent, not being a native speaker at times made it all too much to follow when someone was speaking quickly or with emphasis. Santiago was loyal and capable, but I had heard these complaints too many times, and I had already explained to him that we were working to fix his problem.

It wasn't my call anyway; I had kept my word two years ago in Mexico. I ran no part of the business, and my input only carried weight because of mutual respect.

The crew we had stormed Bennett's compound with were back on the scene, and they were bigger than ever. *'El Veintitrés'* was the fastest growing cocaine operation in the entire world.

THE | SPLIT

Santiago narrowed his eyes suspiciously. "When?"

"Very soon," Ramon assured him. "My brothers up North are planning something very big. We will take everything West of Puerto Penasco, and then the entire peninsula itself!"

I looked over at Ramon, unable to help smiling. Though there were some standouts in the original 23, Ramon was exceptional. In just two years I had watched him rise from being a desperate mercenary to the de facto leader of a major international organization. The other 22 might have an equal share of power and wealth, but he had the vision.

Years ago, before ever becoming a criminal, Ramon was in the Peruvian Naval Special Forces. When he had gotten his share of the money from Bennett's account, he went back to his old comrades, many of them discharged and unemployed, and offered them salaries and starting bonuses to join the cause, promising that they would get a bonus when they signed other people on.

Though I had warned against this idea, calling it a sort of pyramid scheme, it created a tipping point. Thousands of out of work soldiers flocked to our camp, and Ramon convinced the other 22 to split the men equally. A hierarchy had naturally formed, with cells or teams working for captains, who worked for an individual member of the ruling body, the 23.

With the soldiers' training, my team's equipment, and Ramon's tactics, *El Veintitrés* had carved up the coca fields of Peru, Colombia, and Ecuador within six months, and now controlled seventy percent of the world's supply of cocaine – in a time where demand was at an all time high. A process to purify and enhance the effects of cocaine had been discovered. Injecting a mixture of accelerant chemicals into the cutting – then known jokingly as 'fracking' – had brought cocaine's relevancy back to its peak.

T H E | S P L I T

El Veintitrés would not sell their product as cheaply as their predecessors, and the infuriated cartels had cut off the entire American border as a way to get the product to market. In response, Ramon had put together a team to develop a fleet of highly mobile and cost effective, long-range narco subs. Santiago had been on the first one of these shipments underwater, and since then had become in charge of the whole operation, answering only to the founders themselves.

We'd made the money back for the first group of subs in a week and a half of shipments, and now had over twenty. For almost a year, we had done it right under the cartels' noses, going to secret harbors in the strip of land between the Baja Peninsula and mainland Mexico. Recently however, they had gotten wind of our operation, and had been hijacking our deliveries.

Santiago laughed derisively, ashing his cigar on his pants in a fit, "All of the peninsula huh? Every Buchon, from Nogales to Matamoros, will come gunning for us."

"I'm counting on it," Ramon said without missing a beat, "And so are the eleven brothers and five thousand soldiers that just got into the bay."

"You are joking."

Ramon turned to me, "Am I joking, Burl?"

I locked eyes with Santiago and shook my head, "Nope."

"There, you see?" Ramon clapped me on the shoulder. "Straight from the golden boy himself."

"How?" Santiago seemed genuinely confused.

"That doesn't matter right now," Ramon stood up and held out his arms to embrace the other man. "We have other things to talk about. . . without you, old friend. I will see you soon."

THE | SPLIT

Reluctantly, Santiago weakly returned the hug as the door cracked open. "Where am I supposed to go in the meantime?"

"I don't know," Corbin blurted out as he walked into the room. "Do they have a support group for gay little submarine captains, who complain about stuff all the time?"

Santiago's nostrils flared in anger, "You better watch your mouth and who you're calling gay."

"Well. . . " Corbin sat down on a chair against the far wall and laid his glass of scotch on the table, "I am an *actual* homosexual. . . and you, my friend, are WAY gayer than I am. When are you not complaining?"

 "That's it, Gringo!"

Santiago stepped towards Corbin, but was stopped by Ramon. "Santiago, enough. Get out of here."

Santiago took one last look at Corbin and left the room. "Corbin, come on man. . . go easy on my guys, all right?"

"Fine. . . fine," Corbin said, dismissively. "I just really don't like that guy."

When I was sure Santiago had left the room, I addressed the two men; "Corbin, Ramon. . . we really need to talk about the elephant in the room here."

"I agree," Ramon nodded. "That damn powder is turning your brains to mush."

"Our brains?" Corbin snorted with laughter, "I recall a certain cocaine kingpin taking large amounts of that exact same powder."

"Not as much as you two do," Ramon shot back.

"Maybe not," Corbin shrugged. "But the two of us don't snort it."

In the two years since acquiring Dr. Montoya's research, we had done a significant amount of experimenting on our own. The form of SYNTH that her team had been crafting was highly specialized, and had required recruiting several top chemists from prominent South American universities for us to start producing it on our own. The effects did not disappoint however. Within weeks of starting to regularly take the drug, Corbin, me, and Meela had all shown substantial progress.

On top of tricking the brain into wiring more neural connections, the SYNTH improved each of our IQs and levels of mental acuity. Our ability to learn new things was drastically accelerated; Corbin was working tirelessly on new types of code, Meela was constantly creating new devices, and improving old equipment, and I was able to learn any language I deemed relevant. During the year of taking the supplement, I had become fluent in Mandarin, Portuguese, Hindi, Urdu, and Russian.

Ramon muttered something under his breath. Taking a cigar out of his pocket and lighting it, he took a long puff before looking me in the eye. "I know that all three of you have been enjoying the effects-"

"You have too," Corbin interrupted. "You forget that I go by the docks all the time. I've seen your little project sub."

"Yes," Ramon admitted. "It is something I enjoy, but the side effects. . ." An uncomfortable silence settled through the room. Corbin and I both knew what he was referring to, but had no desire to comment on it any further.

Ramon continued, "Yes, it is hard to talk about. . . but that doesn't mean we should not do so."

"What specifically are you referring to?" Corbin asked, trying to seem casual.

"I am speaking of the events that took place in the village, Corbin. What me and Burl did. . ."

THE | SPLIT

I looked away, unable to meet either of their eyes.

Ramon was right to mention the village; no matter how much I didn't want to hear it. In the last few months, our progress in improving the chemical had stagnated, and we had tried adding other compounds to the mixture so we could observe the effects. The new formula had been completely different than its predecessors, and what followed was nothing short of a scene from a horror film.

Unlike the previous batches, this dose did not clear and improve our minds. Instead, shortly after taking it, Ramon and I both began to feel a sort of aggressive euphoria. It engulfed us with an irrational sense of blood-lust, and to satisfy our urges, Ramon and I had gone to the compound of one of our competitors, nearly fifty miles away.

Though they were at first excited to go into battle with their leaders, Ramon's men had sat back in disgust as me and Ramon stormed the small collection of buildings alone.

Our rival's operation had been built in a small village, where they used the local population as human shields. Normally this would have given us both pause, but in our erratic state, the lives of the innocent were of no consequence. Ramon and I killed indiscriminately during our fugue-like spell of violence, storming the compound and killing both enemy and civilian alike.

Our men had reported us taking great pleasure in the sight of blood, painting our arms and faces with the liquid, and even venturing into perverse acts of battlefield cannibalism.

After returning to Quito we both awoke the next morning with no recollection of the night before, and when told by Ramon's soldiers what had happened, neither of us could believe it. Though we were both men of violence, hearing of our own slaughter on such a scale was disconcerting and worrying.

THE | SPLIT

Soon afterward, we met with Corbin, who'd promised to look into the new batch of SYNTH we had taken – though it had been a week since the massacre in the village, and still he had not come to us with the information about the strain we had experimented with.

"What you did is in the past," Corbin said simply. "You know as well as I that you don't stop something this important because of momentary setbacks."

Ramon was astonished.

"Momentary setbacks?!" he exclaimed. "Burl and I ATE people... you would call that a momentary setback?"

"Relative to this, yes," Corbin said, brushing off Ramon's criticism. "This drug could change everything. It's changed us for the better."

Ramon scoffed, "It hasn't changed **me** for the better."

"Well, yeah," Corbin rolled his eyes. "Like I said, it's intended for intravenous use, and you've been taking it like cocaine. You even got Burl to snort it with you that night in the village. That's probably what went wrong, you're supposed to use a needle. Oh, speaking of..." he reached into his pocket and pulled out three small syringes, each one capped on the end. "Here you go Burl, and one for me, and one for Meela... where is she?" He looked around the room. "MEELA!"

A second later she popped her head in the door frame, "Yes Corbin? You don't need to yell, I was right down the hall."

"But I like yelling..." Corbin smiled. "Here, come take your dose."

"Not today."

Ramon clapped his hands. "Good for you, Meela!"

"No," Corbin shot Ramon a pointed glance. "Not good for her. The withdrawal effects could have a serious impact on your body. Can I ask why you don't want to take it?"

THE | SPLIT

"Well," Meela came into the room, typing on a thin screen which she slipped back into her pocket. "I wanted to just tell my husband about this at first, but if you must know. . ."

She lay a hand on my shoulder and gently moved my head up to look at her. "Burl and I. . . are pregnant."

"What?!" Corbin yelled.

"Congratulations!" Ramon cheered happily.

As they continued to talk about the exciting news, the world went silent around me. I could hear the muffled sounds of my friends talking, but nothing more. I could only stare into Meela's eyes, unable to believe what I had just heard, as she smiled and she took my hand in hers. A cold rush of feeling ran down my spine, causing me to shiver.

I was going to be a father. . .

XLVI

Previous location unknown

Bought in Venice, 2077

- A. Fila

Undetermined

I felt John, his thoughts within mine like I had never left, but Sun was missing. And something was off; the way we were moving was sporadic, turning and then cutting back in the other direction.

"John!" I had to focus my words, our bumbling course made it hard for me to keep my thoughts together. *"What happened to Sun?"*

"I don't know," he replied, concerned. *"We were separated from you for an instant, and then I was torn from Sun, and me and you were here."*

I showed him my collection of memories from inside the Being's mind. *"There's a lot for you to catch up on, but it will have to wait. I don't think this is a normal time-stream, who knows where our path is going to take us."*

Suddenly, we shifted and dipped into a bizarre world with a green sky. The landscape appeared barren, and without movement of any kind, but just above the ground hovered millions of tiny red orbs. From high in the sky they appeared no larger than bowling balls, bobbing up and down slightly, but other than that did not move.

As soon as we arrived, we were whisked upward and back into the darkness, cutting through the plane at haphazard angles.

"Burl," John reached out to me, *"This isn't like our other trips. Even when we left Cyrus, we were still moving in only one direction."*

THE | SPLIT

"What's your point?" I asked absently, focusing on keeping my thoughts together on our unorthodox path. I could feel his thoughts working quickly.

"*My point,*" he replied, "*is that it seems the source of our present journey appears to be different. . . we lack the, precise movement of a planned transition. I don't know what happened when you went into the Being's thoughts but, between then and now, it seems we weren't sent out by the Being itself, like we had been every other time.*"

I was beginning to see his point. Several times during his speech we had popped into other worlds, none of them human. It had been hard to focus on John's words instead of looking down at the fascinating worlds and creatures below.

"Okay, I'm following. But how does the source of our travel, relate to our current position? Here. . . this is relevant." I picked out the memory of me leaving the Being's mind through the portal out of the batch I had shown him earlier.

He watched it with great curiosity, replaying the event several times before responding.

"*Well, if these other, smaller, beings sent us on this trip, it's possible that they lacked the control to send us towards a direct target. Do you feel the space around you? There is no current of motion, no time stream like in the past.*"

"So then, where are we headed?" I inquired, hoping he had a plan rather than just observations and questions.

"*I would say that, until proven otherwise, we must assume we are headed nowhere. We have accessed the same slip in time that the larger Being used, but lack the intended destination.*"

"Then you're saying we're trapped."

T H E | S P L I T

"Not necessarily. With no intended location or period of time, we can assume that we are free to travel as we please. Our most prudent course of action would be to find a portion of earth, and/or group of humans to inhabit until we can find out more."

This made sense. As much as I enjoyed my sense of freedom from the Being, I had no desire to remain in the darkness of time forever. We had passed dozens of worlds since we started on our path, but none of them had been Earth. Picking another human was important, after my time in the Being's head I was wary of trying to put my mind in a species that wasn't my own.

"I agree." John was pleased that I agreed, but I still felt nervous and unsure of his ideas. *"I suppose we keep trying places until we come across one that's suitable."*

"It's our only option," he replied. *"But even if we find what we're looking for, there are still issues. With Sun's disappearance, it will be harder to move on our own like we did previously."*

"So we just try with two people."

"Yes, but none of it will matter unless we find a suitable body for us to inhabit. While we're searching, we can practice."

The chaotic movement through the darkness had made it even more difficult than usual, so the link between us broke several times before our first attempt. We moved closer together to correct the problem, and after another several failed attempts were able to bridge our thoughts and form a connection.

But our improvement was slow at first; every time we would move through a world's atmosphere we would become unattached. Hundreds of planets passed by before we could consistently stay together once out of the dark void, then having mastered that, the problem became how we would move ourselves once within the atmosphere of these planets;

THE | SPLIT

with just two sets of thoughts our level of control had been reduced severely. Every movement by one of us would have to be perfectly mirrored by the other, or we would break apart, so our progress became a tedious process of slight adjustment, and trial-by-error.

Several times during this period we shot off in the wrong direction, getting dangerously close to the ground in some and going straight up through the blackness and with others directly into another world. During one of these close encounters, I brought up the question of what would happen if we did crash into the ground. John pondered for a while and then replied that he did not know. He assumed, just like I did, that our lack of a physical form would keep us from all means of traditional harm, but in truth, neither of us knew.

We passed Earth once by mistake. The atmosphere had been littered with skyscrapers reaching miles into the sky. Around these steel monoliths, darted an uncountable number of flying vehicles, weaving through the Megapolis at breakneck speeds. In our combined excitement we had not properly communicated which direction we were moving, and ended up splitting apart and being pulled back out into the darkness.

The hundreds became thousands as we continued our search, and over the course of our journey we saw much. On planets of all forms and sizes, we encountered creatures of unimaginable shape and scale, ranging from primitive tribal societies to space-faring empires commanding ships the size of entire worlds.

The universe was *teeming* with life, and I was dying from curiosity – without the knowledge to understand it. Did all of these places have inhabitants trapped by the Being? The green screen-tiled walls in the long hallways had depicted many various life forms. Were all of them having their histories manipulated like Earth?

T H E | S P L I T

I brought this up to John and found him to be having similar thoughts, so we briefly discussed it, but had to drop the issue abruptly; the world we had just entered had a dark blue ocean. Without land it would be impossible to confirm it as Earth, and there was none in sight so, careful to stay in control, we moved down slowly towards the water.

All we needed was one sign, one distinct marker to show us that this was where we wanted to be.

CAAAAAW

A bird was approaching, but there had been many flying forms of life on the planets we had passed through so, although this one looked more promising we had to be sure.

I signaled to John and we pursued it as it cried out again, and then turned the other way, forcing us to adjust our course. At last I saw it as it turned; black tipped wings, and a white body that led to a pair of beady eyes and a bright orange beak.

It was a seagull; we had made it home.

THE | SPLIT

XLVII

Recovered from Bloc Vault C1
T. Acerz, 2131

Mediterranean; 1801

We were on Earth, but there was nothing around; no land, no ships, no people, nothing but ocean for kilometers across. Traveling slowly so as to not drift apart, me and John wandered the barren stretch of water, zigzagging across the sea for a long period of time. We then agreed that it would be wiser to head in a single direction and, once we'd made up our mind on which way that was, set off in a straight line. The gulls grew in number just moments later; a sign that we were close to land, John told me. So we hopefully followed the birds, but were disappointed as they turned off our course and we shot past them. But John suddenly alerted me to a dark speck on the horizon.

My thoughts leapt with excitement as I saw it too. This was not wreckage like the pile we had mistaken for a ship earlier, it was too big. I saw the gleam of the masthead, then my vision soon shifted to that of the massive white sails, stretched taut in the wind.

It WAS a ship.

A wooden warship, from the look of it; fully crewed and ready for battle. The deck was a blur of activity as men set about on their tasks, some adjusting the rigging, others scrubbing the decks. As our pace quickened and we got closer, I could feel both of our minds rife with anticipation at what was ahead.

Then without warning John and I lost control, falling prey to a powerful force which drew us closer to the ship. I panicked, trying to fight it, but it was no use. John and I couldn't re-form our bond, even

THE | SPLIT

after several attempts, and the mysterious force only grew stronger every instant we were under its influence, drawing us towards the ship at an alarming rate, and faster as the pull on us grew more powerful.

Right as it looked like we were about to hit the side of it, we were pulled through a circular port hole and inside of the hull into a small, cramped room where a man was lying on a hammock, amidst stacks of crates and barrels.

At dizzying speed, I was across it and entering into his body. The first thing I felt was a throbbing pain. My head pounded, making it hard to think straight, and the cloth of the hammock pressed against my back uncomfortably. I flexed my legs and found them hard to move; this body felt sluggish and heavy. My face felt moist, near my mouth, and I reached up to feel spittle drooling out of the corners.

The host mind seemed to barely even acknowledge my presence, keeping himself and his memories cordoned off from my probing thoughts. But I could hear men talking outside my room, and I tried to listen though the strain of my efforts made my head hurt even worse.

Eventually I stopped trying, then out of nowhere I burped; my throat and mouth stung, and I could smell alcohol on my breath.

"Great," I said to John. *"I'm either hungover, or inside the head of a dying man with a drinking problem."*

John laughed at this. *"Either way, there's not much you can do. Just close your eyes and wait it out."*

I shut my already narrowed eyes and tried to do as he said, but my head was still pounding and it took effort to control my breathing. Nor was the movement of the ship doing me any favors. Each pitch and turn of the wooden frame caused my stomach to lurch forward, making me feel like I was about to vomit. I tried to clear my mind and settle into sleep, but the body was affecting even my most distinctly separate

THE | SPLIT

thought processes. I was mentally suffering for this body's actions, and I was suffering badly.

Just then man knocked at the door outside. "Johnson? Are you in there? Wake up, lazy chap, you're wasting good daylight!" The voice was upbeat and quick, joyful even, the tone different than those I had heard muffled through the ship's walls. Then the door opened and I heard the man walk in. "There you are, Johnson! You. . . " he trailed off for a second. "You aren't Johnson. . . you. . . you. . . *my god*! I have another visitor, it's been ages!"

I tried to open my eyes but they were heavy from my attempt at sleep and only opened by a sliver. Through a blur of eyelashes I could see a man. He was large, appeared to have a mustache, and what looked like...glasses?

The man laughed loudly, a pleasant noise that filled the room. "Oh. Well. . . I do think it would be fair to first mention that Johnson and I had a fair bit to drink last night. I'm sure you're paying the toll for his bad decisions. I'm sorry about that. . . But enough with the small talk, we have things to discuss!" A strong hand shook me. My facial muscles strained as I forced my eyes open, looking up.

It was the smiling face of Theodore Roosevelt.

EPILOGUE

Auction to Benefit the Atlanta Historical Society

June 25th, 2098
Lot No. 13287

A collection of pages studied by philanthropist and author, Arthur Fila. In his later years several historians, and Fila himself, claimed that these pages appeared throughout history in a supernatural fashion, but this has yet to be confirmed by independent study.

Description: Approximately 104 physical pages of what appears to be standard post-millennium copier paper bearing black letters, likely made by a primitive inkjet printer. The printing contains pieces of a story told by a young narrator, about an experience that takes place throughout history.

Starting Bid: $1,700,000 USD
Last Bid: $35,250,000 USD

Recipient: Anonymous party, said to be working closely with the newly formed Collective's Council.

Coming Soon

The open air bazaar was a fascinating sight. Men and women all bustled throughout the crowded area, some carrying plastic bags, others carrying rugs over their shoulders or leading newly purchased livestock through the dense crowd. There were men with weapons everywhere – a few women as well. Several of the booths sold them, the display racks behind the salesmen stacked high with assault rifles and pistols of various make and caliber. There was nothing you couldn't buy here, I had even seen stands where people were being auctioned off.

I turned around to see our ride driving off into the distance, honking at pedestrians and weaving through the narrow alleyway. Meela suddenly took my hand and I looked down to see her smiling at me warmly. I smiled back, and made my way into the bazaar, my eyes peeled for the men we had come here to meet.

It had been nearly a decade since Meela and I had been in the field. Our time with *El Veintetres* had made us rich beyond our wildest dreams. The gang had finished their war against the cartels a few months prior, during a bloody two day purge of corrupt politicians and cartel leadership. Ramon and his partners had reached levels of power previously thought impossible, and with their sponsorship and our connections, it was time to open back up for business.

We passed a pair of camels being led by a short old man in a purple robe. After nearly bumping into him, I apologized quietly and continued onward. After a few minutes of walking, I saw who we were looking for. Above the tents, men in dark clothing looked down from a rooftop. They wore sunglasses and held rifles at their waist as they surveyed the crowd below.

Pulling Meela gently, I quickened my pace towards the base of the building they were guarding, mentally preparing myself for the meeting ahead. In our time as *El Veintetres'* benefactor, we had been anything but idle.

Meela and I had envisioned a completely new business model in the world of private military operations, and this would be our first chance to attempt it. The PKPN, or the Pakistani Reform Party, had been struggling to make its mark on the Pakistani political landscape since its inception five years ago. Despite its massive number of members, the parties' moderate stance and desire to see their country transform into more of a Western democracy was deemed radical by some, and subjected them to intense and sometimes violent persecution at the hands of the theocratic government in power.

We had reached out to them several months ago, offering our services as "revolutionaries for hire". Though the man who had answered our request had been skeptical, he had nonetheless set up the meeting.

Meela and I made our way through a pair of stalls, and soon stood in front of the rundown adobe building. Several men dressed and equipped like the ones guarding the rooftop stared at us warily as we approached.

When we made it to the door, a man in front held up his hand to stop us. "Who are you? What is your business here?"

Meela smiled disarmingly, "We have a meeting with Adnan Zaman."

The men turned to each other, and after a short conversation in Urdu, a man towards the back went inside the building.

"Wait here." One of the other men said before raising his rifle back to his waist and continuing to survey the crowd.

About The Author

Born and raised in Oklahoma, Chandler Ogle has long been an avid consumer of all types of media containing history or sci-fi. Thus, in his writing, he has sought to blend the two into a new type of story. While on a lazy day you can find Chandler cracking open a cold one with the boys, and discussing ideas with some of his friends, who include stand-up comedians, artists, and other writers, he is as often hard at work writing more for his new fictional Multiverse, from which he dreams of creating video media as well.

He and his partner, Meredith, recently celebrated the birth of their beautiful daughter, whose name is Amelia. Professionally, Chandler works in IT support, and plans to soon start his own security contracting firm.

Made in the USA
Columbia, SC
09 August 2017